Amanda Stevens is an a[...] fifty novels, including th[...] *Graveyard Queen*. Her b[...] eerie and atmospheric, and 'a new take on the classic ghost story.' Born and raised in the rural South, she now resides in Houston, Texas, where she enjoys binge-watching, bike riding and the occasional margarita.

New York Times and *USA TODAY* bestselling author **Bonnie Vanak** is passionate about romance novels and telling stories. A former newspaper reporter, she worked as a journalist for a large international charity for several years, travelling to countries such as Haiti to report on poor living conditions. Bonnie lives in Florida with her husband, Frank, and is a member of Romance Writers of America. She loves to hear from readers. She can be reached through her website, bonnievanak.com

Also by Amanda Stevens

Without a Trace
A Desperate Search
Someone Is Watching
Criminal Behaviour
Incriminating Evidence
Killer Investigation
Pine Lake
Whispering Springs
Bishop's Rock (ebook novella)
The Restorer

Also by Bonnie Vanak

Rescue from Darkness
His Forgotten Colton Fiancée
Navy SEAL Seduction
Shielded by the Cowboy SEAL
Navy SEAL Protector

Discover more at millsandboon.co.uk

LITTLE GIRL GONE

AMANDA STEVENS

COLTON 911: UNDER SUSPICION

BONNIE VANAK

MILLS & BOON

First Published in Great Britain 2021
by Mills & Boon, an imprint of HarperCollins*Publishers* Ltd
1 London Bridge Street, London, SE1 9GF

www.harpercollins.co.uk

HarperCollins*Publishers*
1st Floor, Watermarque Building,
Ringsend Road, Dublin 4, Ireland

Little Girl Gone © 2021 Marilyn Medlock Amann
Colton 911: Under Suspicion © 2021 Harlequin Books S.A.

Special thanks and acknowledgement are given to Bonnie Vanak for her contribution to the Colton 911: Chicago series.

ISBN: 978-0-263-28366-2

1221

MIX
Paper from
responsible sources
FSC™ C007454

This book is produced from independently certified FSC™ paper to ensure responsible forest management.

For more information visit: www.harpercollins.co.uk/green

Printed and Bound in Spain using 100% Renewable electricity at CPI Black Print, Barcelona

LITTLE GIRL GONE

AMANDA STEVENS

Chapter One

The faded blue sedan had seen better days. So had the driver, a raw-boned, dauntless woman named Reggie Lamb. Her eyes squinted as she scanned the arriving passengers at Tallahassee International Airport. The sun and her past had carved deep crevices in her leathered complexion and the once blond curls had turned to wiry gray ringlets. She was only forty-nine, but looked at least a decade older.

Watching from afar, Thea Lamb chided herself for the unkind assessment. She wasn't there to find fault with her mother. Another child had gone missing in Black Creek, Florida, and Thea had come down from DC to offer whatever assistance might be needed.

Black Creek.

The very name of her hometown seemed synonymous with the brooding landscape along sections of the Florida-Georgia border, an area far more Deep South than any other part of the Sunshine state. Backwoods was a more apt description in Thea's book. Acres and acres of thick, verdant forest shrouding an underground labyrinth of caverns and springs. A place where screams went unheard and bones could stay hidden forever.

The phantom perfume of moss and mud seeped into

Thea's senses until she drew a sharp breath and let the very real odor of exhaust flush away the smell of her nightmares.

Twenty-eight years ago, the first child to go missing had been her twin sister, Maya. She'd been taken from the bedroom where Thea lay sleeping. Even now, dark images floated at the back of her mind when she thought of that night. She had to remind herself that she was a grown woman, a federal agent no longer susceptible to the night terrors of her youth or to the whispers that had once permeated her hometown. But some fears never really went away. Some doubts never truly died.

She'd come down here with the best of intentions, but the past had hovered like a storm cloud ever since she'd boarded her flight. She couldn't help worrying that nothing good would come from a reunion with her mother. The years of estrangement stretched like ten miles of bad road as Thea slung her backpack over one shoulder and wheeled her carry-on out to the curb.

The sedan rattled to a stop and Reggie jumped out to help with the luggage. She was dressed in the typical Floridian uniform of shorts, tank top and flip-flops. Despite her scrawny frame, she hoisted the bulging carry-on into the trunk as if it weighed no more than a handbag. Then she checked the airport traffic before shifting her wary blue gaze to Thea.

"I'm glad you came." She made no move to embrace her daughter and Thea was glad for that.

Heat rose from the pavement, activating perspiration along her backbone as she tried to sound normal. "How are you holding up, Reggie?"

The rasp in her mother's voice deepened. "So it's Reggie now, is it?"

"It has been since I was ten years old. Or had you forgotten?"

"I always preferred Mama."

"It never seemed to suit you," Thea said without thinking.

Something flitted across Reggie's suntanned face. Pain? Regret?

Her mouth tightened, emphasizing the harsh lines. "I guess I can't blame you for feeling that way. I did the best I could, but that's not much of an excuse, is it?"

Something fluttered in the pit of Thea's stomach. Pain? Regret?

This was so much more difficult than she'd anticipated. Her feelings for Reggie were darkly complex, a messy patchwork of anger and resentment stitched together with lingering doubts. Regardless of what else lay between them, Reggie was still her mother, the woman who'd worked double shifts at the local diner to put food on the table and keep a roof over their heads. The woman who'd doctored Thea's skinned knees and sent bullies sniveling home to their mamas when their cruelty had made her cry.

She took a deep breath. "I didn't come here to dredge up the past."

"No help for that, given what's happened," Reggie stated flatly. "Another child has disappeared from my home. Considering my history, you can imagine what the cops are thinking and the neighbors are saying. Half of them already have me on my way to prison."

Thea didn't have to imagine anything. She'd only been four when her sister was taken, but she'd lived in the shadow of Maya's abduction until she'd left home for college at seventeen. She wished she could say she'd learned to ignore the malicious gossip but, truth be told, she'd never been as strong-willed as Reggie. The taunts had always gotten under her skin. *Your mama murdered your twin sister. How do you sleep in the same house with that monster? Ever wonder if you were the one she meant to kill?*

"Is it as bad as it was before?" Thea asked.

"Bad enough." Reggie rubbed the inside of her elbow.

"I didn't stay at the house last night, but I ran by there this morning to get some fresh clothes before I went to work—"

"Wait a minute," Thea cut in. "You worked this morning?"

"Why wouldn't I? The town's flooded with state troopers and volunteers, and the diner's shorthanded. Somebody's got to pitch in and help feed them."

"Yes, of course. I just thought under the circumstances…never mind. So you went by the house…?"

Reggie's expression remained stoic but her eyes glittered angrily. "Somebody had spray-painted *murderer* across the side of my porch."

"I'm sorry."

"It is what it is. I tried to scrub it off, but you can still see the outline. Figured you should know what you're walking into."

She nodded, avoiding her mother's gaze. Reggie was still tough as nails on the outside, but Thea had never thought of her as vulnerable until now. With an effort, she swallowed past an unexpected knot in her throat. "I'm still not clear on how Taryn Buchanan and her daughter came to be staying with you in the first place."

"It's a long story. I'll explain everything on the way home, but right now we need to get moving. We're holding up the line."

As if to punctuate her point, a shiny black pickup with tinted windows inched forward impatiently.

Reggie glared at the driver before turning back to Thea. "Get in."

Thea dropped the backpack in the trunk, but kept the cross-body bag containing her SIG-Sauer 9 mm and FBI credentials over her shoulder. She climbed into the passenger seat while Reggie went around and got in behind the wheel. The interior of the car wasn't in much better shape than the outside. The upholstery was worn through in places, and there was a hole in the dash where the radio had been removed. But the motor caught smoothly when Reggie turned the key in the ignition. That wasn't surprising. She'd always been a whiz with engines. Had to be, since there'd never been any money for mechanics.

She was good with engines, but not so much air conditioners, Thea thought as she twisted up her long hair and pinned it in the back. She couldn't remember a time when any of Reggie's old beaters had had working AC. She peeled off her jacket and placed it on the bench seat with her bag.

Reggie gave her a sidelong glance before easing away from the curb. "You always dress like that? Like you're going to a funeral? Girl, you'll melt in this heat."

Thea tried not to bristle at the critique. "I dress for the job, not the weather. People tend to be more cooperative if they're even slightly intimidated by a professional appearance."

"But you're not on the job," Reggie pointed out. "You said you were taking some personal days. So who are you trying to intimidate?"

"No one. I'm here to offer moral support and any other help that may be needed."

Reggie braked suddenly to allow the pickup to whip around her. Muttering under her breath, she double-checked the rearview mirror as she merged with the line of cars exiting the terminal.

"Somebody's in a hurry," Thea said.

"Looks to be," Reggie agreed. "People drive like idiots these days."

"I'm surprised you didn't flip him off. I admire your restraint."

Reggie flashed her a look. "I don't do that sort of thing anymore. I don't do a lot of things I use to. You'd know that if you ever came to see me."

Thea tamped down her irritation. "I'm here now, aren't I?"

"Yes, and I'm grateful for that. God knows I need all the moral support I can get. But let's not kid ourselves as to the real reason you came, *Althea*."

No one had called her that in years. Thea frowned as she dug out her sunglasses. "I'll bite," she said as she slipped on the Wayfarers. "Why am I here?"

"Be honest," Reggie said. "You think Kylie's disappearance is somehow connected to Maya's, don't you?"

"Maya was taken nearly thirty years ago. The likelihood of a connection after all this time is slim."

"Both girls disappeared from my home through the same bedroom window. You're telling me that's a coincidence?"

"No, not a coincidence," Thea said. "It's possible Kylie Buchanan's kidnapper mimicked Maya's abduction to disguise his or her true motive."

Reggie chewed her lip in contemplation, her gaze trained on the road. Traffic was bumper-to-bumper leaving the airport. "The FBI profiler said something similar. She and the other Feds swooped in fast this time. A bunch of SUVs arrived in town just a couple hours after the local cops called for assistance."

"That's good. The sooner CARD hits the ground running, the greater the chances of a positive resolution," Thea said, referring to the FBI's elite Child Abduction Rapid Deployment team. "There's nothing anyone can say that will offer much comfort to Taryn Buchanan at the moment, but you should both know the people out there looking for her little girl are the best of the best. Every agent on that team has years of experience and expertise working crimes against children cases. They have a nearly ninety percent success rate in identifying and apprehending child abductors."

"What about their success rate in bringing children

home safely?" Fear crept into Reggie's voice. "It's been well over twenty-four hours since Kylie went missing. We both know what that means."

"Try not to get hung up on the timeline," Thea advised. "Every case is different." But she knew better than most that nonparental abductions rarely turned out well, especially when the child was a tender age. "Who's the agent in charge?"

"I have his information somewhere." Reggie patted her shorts pocket and withdrew a business card. "Here. A guy named Stillwell."

Thea's heart thudded as she glanced at the card. Special Agent Jacob Stillwell. *Jake.* She'd known their paths would likely cross when she'd made the decision to come down here. He headed the southeast CARD team that worked out of the Jacksonville field office. Stood to reason he'd be sent to Black Creek. Thea told herself she could handle a face-to-face. Whatever they'd once shared had been over for a long time. Jake Stillwell was just a guy she used to know. A colleague with benefits who'd packed his bags and left town with barely a backward glance.

At least, that was the way Thea had regarded his departure at the time. In retrospect, everything about their relationship had been so much more complicated than either had wanted to concede. They'd gone into it with their eyes wide open—or so they'd told themselves. The job would always come first. No guilt. No resentment. No having to justify long hours or making hard choices. When it ended, it ended.

What a crock. After four years, the cavalier way he'd told her about his transfer still stung, but it would be a cold day in hell before Thea ever admitted it aloud.

She placed the card facedown on the seat and turned to stare out the side window.

"Do you know him?" Reggie asked.

Thea answered in a careful monotone. "Agent Stillwell has an excellent reputation."

"That's not what I mean. Do you know him personally?"

"Why does it matter?"

"I'm just curious. He seems to know you. He asked about you…how you're doing, that sort of thing. I couldn't tell him much seeing as how I don't know the first thing about your life in DC. I don't even know what it is you do all day."

"Mostly, I stare at a computer screen." Thea's fingers curled around the edge of the seat. "As for Agent Stillwell, I'm sure he was just trying to be polite."

"Maybe. But there was something about the way he said your name." Reggie shrugged. "Then again, maybe I imagined his interest."

Thea wasn't about to get into the details of her personal life with her mother. She and Reggie had come to an agreement years ago about staying out of one another's private affairs. But she feared her silence would reveal far more about her feelings than she intended. Reggie was nobody's fool. If Thea didn't give her something, she might end up making an embarrassing assumption in front of Jake. "We worked together a few years back. We were partners for a time."

"What happened?"

Thea adjusted her sunglasses as she gave her mother a frustrated glance. "Nothing happened. He was promoted and transferred to the Jacksonville field office. I stayed in DC."

"Ah," Reggie murmured. "Now I get it."

"What do you get?" Thea demanded.

Her mother shot her a meaningful glance. "I'm guessing his promotion rubbed you the wrong way. You were always crazy competitive, even as a kid. With your classmates, with your sister. Even with me."

Thea swung around. "That's not true. I worked hard to get your attention, but never at Maya's expense."

Reggie looked stricken. Then a mask dropped as her shoulders stiffened. "I'm sorry. I shouldn't have said what I did. You and Maya were always so close. I couldn't punish one of you without the other lighting into me. You were each other's fiercest defender."

Thea winced. "Some defender I turned out to be."

"You were four years old. What happened to Maya wasn't your fault. It wasn't anyone's fault except for the person who took her, though plenty of folks around here still blame me. They think I was the kind of mother who would murder her own child and bury her body in the woods." She gave Thea a long scrutiny. "Maybe you think that, too. Maybe that's why you don't come down here anymore."

JAKE STILLWELL CLIMBED out of the SUV and stood for a moment, letting his gaze roam over the rows of dated brick ranches. The façade color varied, but the houses all had the same carports and concrete porches with scrolled metal posts. None had been updated, but some had been better maintained than others.

The quiet neighborhood was located less than a quarter mile from the center of Black Creek, technically within the town limits, but the mature trees and outbuildings gave the area a rural ambience. A thick canopy of oak leaves hung over the sidewalks, casting deep shadows onto the street.

Under normal circumstances, Jake would have welcomed a respite from the relentless heat, but when he took in the shrouded yards and encroaching woods, all he saw were hiding places. All he could think was how easily someone could move through the neighborhood without being seen.

"Hey! Can I help you with something?"

Jake turned to see the neighbor from across the street ambling down his gravel driveway with a bluetick at his side. The man looked to be nearing sixty, tall and lanky, with grayish-blond hair thinning at the top. He wore a pair of stained cargo shorts and a dingy white T-shirt with a sailfish on the front. The coonhound looked elderly and lethargic, his hunting days long behind him.

"If you're looking for Reggie, she's not home," he informed Jake. "I saw her over there earlier, but that was hours ago. You might try the diner."

"I'm not here to see Reggie."

The man paused at the end of the drive to take a long swig from the insulated mug he carried. His relaxed manner belied the suspicious glint in his eyes. He lowered the tumbler and wiped his mouth with the back of his hand. "Then what's your business here, if you don't mind my asking?"

Good question. Jake wouldn't be able to explain his compulsion even if he were inclined to try. He had come back to Reggie Lamb's house because he'd had to. As simple and as complicated as that. "I'm Agent Stillwell with the FBI."

"FBI, huh?" The man leaned an arm against his rickety mailbox. "I figured you were a cop of some kind, but I wouldn't be much of a neighbor if I didn't ask to see some ID."

Jake took out his credentials and held them up so the man could see the gold badge from across the street.

He squinted in Jake's direction, then crossed the street, flip-flops slapping against the pavement. He called to his companion, who moseyed after him. Jake waited beside his SUV for the languid pair to approach. The man scrutinized Jake's photograph and then reached down to give the dog a reassuring scratch behind a floppy ear. The hound took that as his cue to find a shady spot to stretch out, chin on paws, and wait patiently.

"Sorry for being such a pain in the rear," the man said in a friendlier tone. "Can't be too careful after everything that's happened."

"I agree. It's good that you look out for your neighbors." Jake put away his credentials, his gaze still on the stranger. "I didn't catch your name."

"Lyle Crowder. That's my place over yonder, but you probably already figured that out." He glanced over his shoulder, cocking his head with a frown. "Do you hear that?"

"Hear what?"

He turned back to Jake. "Exactly my point. Yesterday, the police were all over the neighborhood, knocking on doors, searching garages and storage sheds, and today it's like a ghost town around here. Even the helicopter I saw circling earlier is gone." His shoulders hunched as if a cold wind blew down his neck. "Did you find the little girl? Is that why you're here? You came to tell Reggie and her mother in person?"

"Kylie Buchanan hasn't been found," Jake said. "As I understand it, no one is staying here at the moment. The lack of activity in the neighborhood is due to the fact we've expanded the search into other areas. We're trying to cover as much territory as we can in a short amount of time."

Lyle nodded, his eyes dark and knowing. "Lots of woods around here. Lots of lakes and creeks."

"The terrain is challenging," Jake agreed.

"I've been thinking about that old cave on Douglas McNally's property. It's not far from here. A couple of miles through them woods." He nodded toward the back of Reggie's property. "If someone needed to hide out for a few days, that would be a good place. There are tunnels and caverns most people don't even know about. No one from around here will go down there anymore. A couple of teenagers lost their way and drowned in an underwater passage years back. Mr. McNally fenced off the entrance and posted a bunch of signs, but it wouldn't be hard to climb over the fence and throw a body down in the pit."

"You've been down there?" Jake asked.

"Back in my younger days when you didn't have to sign a waiver. Some of the passageways are belly crawls and my knees aren't what they used to be. But I could still cover some ground if I take old Blue down there with me." The dog's ears twitched at the sound of his name.

"We'd prefer you not go out on your own, especially into dangerous terrain," Jake said. "We like to keep track of all the volunteers so that no one gets lost and we don't end up covering the same ground twice."

Plus, the criminal background checks required of each volunteer could potentially lead to the kidnapper's identity if he or she decided to join in the search.

Lyle nodded. "Makes sense, I guess."

"You can sign up at the command center we've established at the police station. In the meantime, would you mind answering a few questions while I'm here?"

He seemed agreeable. "I've got no place I need to be anytime soon. But you should know I've already talked to the police. A couple of officers stopped by my place after I got home yesterday. I told them everything I know, which isn't much."

"That's okay. Sometimes something can come back to you a day or two later."

Lyle leaned against the side of the SUV and folded his arms. "Fire away then."

"Were you home Sunday night through early Monday morning?"

He shook his head regretfully. "I wish I had been home.

I might have seen something. But I was in Pensacola on a fishing trip with my brother."

"When did you leave on this trip?"

"Saturday morning right around sunrise. I wanted to beat the beach crowd. Drove over to Crestview, picked up my brother, and then we cruised on down to the Gulf. We were on the water all weekend. Didn't hear about the kidnapping until I got home around four or five in the afternoon. That's when the cops came by."

"You didn't get an Amber Alert on your phone Monday morning?"

Lyle rubbed the back of his neck. "Don't think so. I'm sure I would have noticed since the missing kid was local. But we were out on the water early. I probably had my phone turned off. I like peace and quiet when I fish."

"So you were away from your house from early Saturday morning until late yesterday afternoon?"

"That's right. My brother has Mondays off. We had to get back so he could go to work today. He's not retired like I am."

"You didn't see anything out of the ordinary before you left on Saturday? No strangers in the neighborhood or any unfamiliar cars on the street? Maybe someone paying a little too much attention to Reggie's house?"

"I think I would have noticed if someone had been watching Reggie's house."

"They would have been discreet," Jake said. "Maybe you saw the same car drive by her house a few times. Or maybe you noticed workers or repair vans nearby."

"Like I said, I would have noticed anything out of the ordinary." He opened the lid of the tumbler and tossed out the ice. "I keep a sharp eye out when I'm home."

Jake glanced across the street. "You have a good view of Reggie's property from your front windows. Did you ever see Kylie Buchanan playing in the yard alone?"

A brow lifted. "Alone, no. Why?"

"It could have provided someone the opportunity to approach her, maybe under the pretext of being a neighbor out looking for a lost pet. It's a known ploy," Jake said, his gaze narrowing slightly. "A way to gain her trust."

Lyle shrugged. "Anytime I saw the girl outside, her mother was always hovering nearby. She seemed to watch that kid like a hawk. I didn't know who either of them was until all this happened. I didn't even know Reggie had someone living over there. She has a grown daughter. I thought maybe Thea had had a kid since the last time I'd seen her, and they were down here visiting."

"You didn't recognize Taryn Buchanan? She and her husband, Russ, have lived in Black Creek for the past five years. They have a house in Crescent Hill."

"That area of town is a little rich for my blood. I don't get over that way much." He paused as if something had occurred to him. "How does someone with a house in Crescent Hill end up in this neighborhood living with Reggie Lamb?"

"We're still trying to sort out the details," Jake said. "Do you live alone, Mr. Crowder?"

"If you don't count my coonhound. He's about the only family I have left besides my brother. We get along fine on our own, don't we, Blue?"

The dog's tail flapped lazily.

"How long have you lived across the street?" Jake asked.

"I've owned the property for over thirty years, but I wasn't around for a lot of that time. I worked as an offshore welder before I retired. Spent more time on a platform than I did at home. 'Floating cities,' we called them. I'd sometimes be away for two or three months at a time."

"Were you home when Maya Lamb went missing?"

Lyle Crowder's easygoing demeanor vanished. A wall

seemed to go up as he straightened, pretending to move into deeper shade.

"That was a long time ago."

Jake nodded. "Twenty-eight years, to be exact, but you don't forget something like that, especially when it occurs across the street from your home."

An odd note crept into the man's voice; a curious combination of defiance and uncertainty. "Why are you asking about Maya Lamb? You don't think the same person took the Buchanan girl, do you? After all this time?"

"We don't leave any stone unturned when a child goes missing," Jake said.

Lyle's brow furrowed. "Yeah, okay. I remember now. I'd started a new job that summer working on a rig out of New Orleans. I didn't get home much that whole year."

Two little girls had gone missing from the house across the street and Lyle Crowder had conveniently been away each time. For someone who liked to keep an eye out, he seemed to have a knack for making himself scarce when crimes were committed.

"We all heard about the disappearance," he said. "You couldn't turn on the TV or open a paper all summer long without seeing that little girl's picture. There was a lot of speculation about what had happened to her. Like she might have been dead before she went missing, if you know what I mean. But after a while, people lost interest and moved on."

"How well did you know Reggie back then?"

A frown flitted as he studied the front of her house, his expression so intense he might have been peering into one of her windows. Or into her past. "When you live in a small town, you know everybody to a certain degree. Reggie was a lot younger than me, so we didn't socialize much. I guess you could say we were friendly acquaintances. But anyone in Black Creek will tell you she was pretty wild back then."

"What do you mean by 'wild'?"

"Booze and men, men and booze. She kind of went off the deep end after her baby daddy wrapped his car around a light pole one night. Not that he was ever going to marry her anyway. His mother didn't approve. Wrong side of the tracks and all that. After he was killed, June Chapman hardly had anything to do with those little girls. Never offered financial support or anything, and her old man left her loaded. That's pretty cold if you ask me, shunning her own grandkids."

He was getting a little too gossipy, but Jake didn't try to rein him in. He liked to think that his silence would encourage Crowder to let down his guard. But, if he were honest with himself, he'd have to admit he found these peeks into Thea's past riveting. She'd been gone from his life for four years and yet she remained the most enigmatic woman he'd ever known. In all their time together, he'd never been able to figure her out and maybe that was why, in all their time apart, he'd never been able to forget her.

"Reggie must have been young when she had her twins," he said.

"Not much more than a kid herself," Lyle agreed. "You'd think two babies would have slowed her down, but not Reggie. Every Saturday night, she'd have a bunch of people over here to party. Maybe it was her way of thumbing her nose at June Chapman and all the other old biddies in town that looked down on her. She and her friends would crank up the music and hang out in the yard. Somebody would tap a keg or light up a joint. It got pretty rowdy at times. I don't know how those little girls managed to sleep through all the ruckus."

"Did you ever attend any of these parties?"

"Nah. Even if I'd been around, that crowd would have considered me a geezer."

Was that a note of resentment in his voice? A lingering umbrage?

Lyle Crowder's gaze met Jake's then shifted away. "Reggie wasn't much of a mother in a lot of respects, but I'll say this for her. She was always a hard worker. Made sure her kids had clean clothes and plenty to eat. When her landlord died, she managed to scrape together a down payment and somehow convinced his boy to sell her this place. No telling how many double shifts she had to work just to make the mortgage payments. Regardless of her failings, you have to admire her for that."

Jake's eyes roamed the yard. For a moment, he had a vision of two little girls playing on the old tire swing hanging from one of the oak trees. If he listened hard enough, he could almost hear the echo of their forgotten laughter. Then one of the girls vanished and the other erected impenetrable defenses. "Did you see anyone besides Reggie here this morning?"

"If you're asking whether or not I saw who painted that on her wall? No, but it's not the first time some creep tagged her house. You know how it is in a place like this. People have small minds and long memories. Some folks around here still think Reggie was responsible for her daughter's disappearance."

"What do you think?"

He stared broodingly at the faded letters at the side of the porch. "You don't want to believe someone you've known your whole life, let alone someone who lives across the street, could do such a terrible thing to her own child. I mean, Reggie had her faults, and plenty of them, but from what I saw, she loved her kids. If something happened to that little girl before she went missing, it must have been an accident. Reggie was young and impulsive.

Maybe she panicked and got rid of the body instead of calling the police."

"Is that what you think happened?"

Lyle shrugged. "It's plausible, isn't it? Although, to tell you the truth, Reggie never struck me as the panicky type. Personally, I've always wondered about that old boy she used to go with."

"Do you remember his name?"

Lyle's mouth curled in contempt. "Derrick Sway. Had such a bad temper, he'd fly off the handle for no apparent reason. Some of that dope will make you real unstable."

"What makes you think he had something to do with Maya's disappearance?" Jake asked.

"Just a gut feeling I've always had. If Sway was somehow responsible for what happened to Maya, I wouldn't put it past him to threaten her sister just to keep Reggie quiet."

"Sounds like you knew Derrick Sway pretty well."

"Everyone in town knew him by reputation. He'd steal anything he could get his hands on. Peddled meth, too, when it was just getting started around here. I never understood how someone with Reggie's looks and smarts could take up with a lowlife like him."

"Do you know if he was at the party the night Maya went missing?"

"That's what I heard, but I can't swear to it since I wasn't here. The cops must have talked to him after it happened. It's probably all in a file somewhere."

"How long did he and Reggie stay together after Maya went missing?"

"Not long. She wised up and kicked his sorry hide to the curb. Maybe she suspected something, I don't know. Rumor had it, he tried to come back a time or two and she chased him off with a shotgun."

"Sounds like there was bad blood between them," Jake said.

Lyle gave a vague nod but his gaze remained wary and shrewd. "Sway spent the next few years in and out of county lockup for one petty crime after another. But the last time he got busted was for armed robbery. That got him a dime over in Lake City. You know about that place, right?"

"The Columbia Correctional Institute is considered one of the most violent prisons in the state of Florida," Jake said.

"You think? You heard about what happened a while back. One of the prisoners strangled his cellmate, mutilated the body and then wore the guy's ears around his neck to breakfast. I'd call that violent, all right. You don't survive a decade on the inside of a place like that without resorting to your baser instincts. Put it this way—now that Derrick Sway's a free man, I wouldn't want to meet up with him in a dark alley. Or on the street in broad daylight, for that matter."

"When did he get out?" Jake asked.

"I don't know. Been a while, I guess. Last I heard, he was living over in Yulee with his mother. Probably freeloading off her social security."

Jake studied Lyle's expression. He seemed genuinely distressed by Derrick Sway's release. "You haven't seen him around Black Creek?"

"Black Creek, no. But about a month or so back, a buddy of mine was fishing on Lake Seminole. He said a man came out of the woods looking all wide-eyed and crazy. Had these crude tattoos on his neck and arms. Dark stuff like skulls and horns and snakes. Prison gang tats, mostly likely. My friend, Carl, swore the man looked just like Derrick Sway."

"What happened?"

"Nothing. The guy never said a word, just came to the edge of the water and stood there staring at Carl. He thought for a moment that the dude was going to wade out after him. Maybe knock him in the head and steal his boat. Then he just turned and walked back into the woods. Gave Carl the creeps. He hightailed it out of there and never went back to that spot. I didn't give it much thought until you started asking all these questions about Maya's disappearance."

"Do you know the exact location of this sighting?" Jake asked.

"No, but Carl owns a store just south of town. C & C's Tire Service. You can go by there and ask him yourself. Tell him I sent you."

"Thank you, Mr. Crowder. You've been a big help."

"You bet." He thrust a hand in his pocket and jangled some change. "There is one other thing. I don't know if I should even bring it up. Maybe it means something, maybe it doesn't."

"I'm listening."

The jangling stopped and his expression turned grim. "After Sway got arrested, there was talk around town that Reggie was the one who turned him in. If he's carried a grudge against her all these years, God help her. If he had anything to do with that little Buchanan girl's disappearance, God have mercy."

Chapter Two

Lyle Crowder called to his dog and the pair sauntered back across the street, leaving Jake alone in the heat to ponder their conversation. As he waited for the man to disappear into his house, a strange feeling of being watched came over him. That wasn't unusual for Jake. He'd always had a heightened sensitivity to his surroundings that went beyond his training. He'd never put a name to his perception and had no interest in digging deep enough to figure it out. Suffice it to say, he'd learned early on in foster care to trust his instincts. That keen situational awareness had saved him more times than he cared to remember.

Slowly, he trailed his gaze along the row of aging houses as the hair at the back of his neck lifted. Could be nothing more than another nosy neighbor staring out a window. People were curious when something like this happened. They watched from the safety of their homes, telling themselves that something so terrible could never happen to their family. But sometimes the kidnapper also watched.

For all Jake knew, Kylie Buchanan's abductor could still be in the neighborhood, monitoring police activity from behind closed blinds, reveling in the chaos he'd created and smug in the certainty that he'd outsmarted the authorities.

Rubbing the back of his neck, Jake searched for the twitch of a curtain or the subtle shift of a shadow. Then his eyes moved to Crowder's house. Despite the man's chattiness, Jake sensed Reggie's neighbor hadn't been entirely forthcoming. Reading between the lines, he wondered if Lyle Crowder had had romantic feelings for Reggie in the past. His opinion of her had seemed to vacillate between condemnation and respect, and Jake had detected a flicker of something unpleasant when he spoke about being left out of her parties. Unrequited feelings could sometimes fester into resentment, but thirty years was a long time to carry a grudge or a torch. One thing Jake knew for certain: Lyle Crowder had done everything in his power to focus the FBI's attention on Derrick Sway.

Moving out of view of the street, Jake pulled his phone and called the local police chief to verify that Crowder's brother had corroborated their weekend fishing trip. He then related Lyle's concern about Derrick Sway and requested that an officer be sent to the mother's home to check on Sway's whereabouts. Statistically speaking, Sway was a long shot. Stranger abductions were more rare than most people realized, and Sway had no apparent connection to the Buchanans. He did, however, have a past with Reggie Lamb and, at this point, no lead could be ignored. No one could be ruled out, and that included Reggie herself.

Jake had spoken with her twice since his arrival in town. The first time here at her home. The second time at the command center when she'd come in with Taryn Buchanan. His initial impression was of a hard-boiled woman who spoke her mind regardless of the consequences. Jake had liked her at once and had to remind himself that she was the common denominator in two child abductions. He couldn't afford to cut her any slack because she happened to be Thea's mother.

Still, he'd been at this for a long time and he knew how to read people. He didn't think Reggie was responsible for

Kylie Buchanan's disappearance, but he couldn't shake the notion that she was hiding something, too.

So here he was.

Instinct was one thing, but Jake didn't believe in premonitions, second sights or any of that nonsense. He'd never put faith in psychics. Yet something inexplicable had drawn him back to Reggie Lamb's house.

Slipping on his sunglasses, he moved from the shade and dragged his gaze along the edge of the woods. He imagined the kidnapper creeping silently through the trees on the night of the abduction, then hunkering in the shadows until the lights in Reggie's house had gone out. Cloud coverage would have obscured the moon. Even if someone had been passing by at that hour, whoever took four-year-old Kylie Buchanan would have gone undetected as he eased across the yard and peered through the glass before sliding up the window.

The peal of Jake's ringtone shattered the heavy silence. He took the call and ended it quickly. Guided by the prickles at the base of his neck, he let himself in through the gate in the chain-link fence then moved across the backyard to where the woods edged up against Reggie's property line.

A latticework potting shed had been erected behind a detached single-car garage. Both structures looked freshly painted in the same color as the trim on the house. Jake could hear birds trilling in the oak trees and the steady *click-click-click* of an ornamental windmill rotating in the breeze. The yard was like a peaceful oasis, fragrant and sleepy, and yet he felt the heaviness of a strange oppression as he unlatched the back gate and stepped through.

He followed a footpath into the trees. He didn't know what he expected to find. The local police had used K-9 tracking to search the area early Monday morning, and a small army of law enforcement personnel and civilian volunteers walking at arm's length of one another had combed the woods later that same day. Every square inch had been covered. Nothing of importance would have been missed. Jake told himself his time would be better spent at the command center assisting the local PD, yet he couldn't bring himself to turn back. He couldn't assuage the compulsion that drove him deeper into the woods.

A few hundred yards from the house, he halted abruptly, searching the shadowy underbrush and then swinging his scrutiny up into the treetops. A sound had come to him.

Maybe it was that subtle intrusion that had been guiding him through the woods all along rather than any premonition. Maybe, in the back of his mind, he'd conflated the hollow clatter he heard now with the distant tick of the windmill so that his subconscious had dismissed the sound.

He tipped his head, searching for the source. Almost hidden by leaves, two primitive stick figures swung from a tree branch about five feet above his head. Twig arms and legs had been attached to the bodies with coils of raffia. Red fabric hearts had been glued to the torsos and tufts of blond hair to the heads.

Jake watched, mesmerized as the dolls clacked together in the breeze, creating an eerie, hollow melody that reminded him of a bamboo wind chime.

THEA RECLINED HER head against the back of the seat and tried to relax as Reggie exited the freeway onto the state highway that would take them straight into Black Creek. But the closer they drew to their destination, the more anxious she became.

She kept the window open, pulling the damp, verdant smell of the countryside deep into her lungs. The scent stirred something powerful inside her. The memories that stole out of her subconscious were as thick and pervasive as the kudzu that snaked up abandoned utility poles and curled around old phone lines. There was something almost mystical about that lush perfume, something evocative and sinister about the shadowy landscape.

She gave her mother a sidelong glance. Did she feel it, too?

Seemingly oblivious, Reggie gripped the wheel and stared straight ahead. They'd both fallen silent miles ago. Thea didn't try to initiate further conversation. She welcomed a few minutes of quiet introspection to analyze her feelings. It was so disconcerting, this homecoming. She hadn't been in the same room with her mother in years, let alone in the close confines of a vehicle. Now here they were with all the old doubts and resentments crowding into the same narrow space.

How long had it been since she'd been back anyway? Four years? Five? Surely not six? Where had all that time gone?

The odd thing was, she and Reggie had never had a real falling out. The distancing had been gradual. Phone calls had tapered off, visits had never come to fruition. It was just plain easier being apart. Easier to ignore the ghost that had always haunted the space between them.

Maya's abduction had defined their relationship in so many ways, yet even the mention of her name had at times been taboo. Thea had learned early on to keep any questions about her sister's disappearance to herself if she didn't want Reggie to shut down. Those long silences had taken a toll.

You freeze a kid out enough times and she'll put up her own defenses. She'll find all kinds of ways to act out and then she'll leave home as soon as she's able, rarely to return until another child goes missing.

Thea didn't want to dwell on all those old doubts. She didn't want to resurrect her obsession over her twin sister's abduction, but how could she not when another child had gone missing from the same room? When little Kylie Buchanan might still be out there somewhere, tormented and terrified and crying for her mother as Maya had undoubtedly done before she died?

She took a long, tremulous breath and allowed her mind to drift back in time.

On the night of Maya's disappearance, Reggie had put them to bed early. Twilight had just fallen, but already music and laughter drifted in from the front porch where some of her friends had gathered. Thea didn't like it when her mother had people over. She and Maya were always sent to bed early and Thea had a hard time sleeping through all that noise. Bored and fretful, she'd lie awake for hours while Maya slept peacefully in the next bed.

Their room had been exceptionally hot and sticky that night. The AC unit in the front part of the house did nothing to cool the bedrooms. Thea lay on top of the covers, hot and miserable as she tossed and turned. Sometime later, Reggie came into the room to raise the window that looked out on the backyard.

"Read me a story, Mama."

"Not tonight, baby. Your sister's already asleep and I don't want to wake her up. Besides, Mama has friends over."

"I don't like them." Thea pouted. "They smell bad."

"That's just cigarette smoke. The breeze will blow it away. Now settle down and go to sleep. It'll be morning before you know it."

Thea pretended to do as she was told. She nestled under the covers and watched her mother through half-closed eyes as she stood at the open window staring out into the night. After a moment, Reggie came over to the bed and kissed Thea's cheek, then tiptoed from the room and pulled the door closed behind her.

At the sound of the clicking door, her sister sat up in bed and whimpered. "I'm scared, Sissy."

"Why?" Thea asked her.

"I heard something."

Thea listened to the night. "It's just a coonhound out in the woods. See? Mama opened the window."

"It's not a coonhound." Kicking off the covers, Maya slid to the floor and padded the short distance between their beds. Clutching her favorite doll, she crawled beneath the cotton sheets and snuggled close. "Somebody's out there, Sissy."

"Nobody's out there. Stop being a fraidy-cat and go back to sleep." Thea patted her sister's shoulder until Maya finally rolled over and drifted off. Thea remained wide awake. Despite the breeze, she was still too hot with her sister's clammy little body pressed up against hers. The open window allowed in dozens of night sounds. Not just the eerie baying of a neighbor's dog, but also the closer serenades of crickets and bullfrogs and the occasional hoot of an owl. Sounds that stirred Thea's blood and tingled her scalp.

She slipped out of bed and dragged a chair to the window so that she could stand and stare out the way her mother had done. For the longest time, she watched shadows dance across the yard as tree limbs thrashed in the breeze. When she grew drowsy, she climbed into Maya's empty bed and pulled the covers to her chin, and when she finally fell asleep, she dreamed the outside shadows had crept into their room and stood whispering between their beds.

The next thing she knew, it was morning and her mother's best friend, Gail, was shaking her awake. "Where's your sister? Thea, wake up! Where's Maya?"

They searched the house and all up and down the street.

The police came and later the FBI. Search parties were formed and dogs were brought in.

A week after Maya went missing, a wooden box had been found in the woods containing her doll and a blood-stained blanket that matched her DNA. The police reasoned but couldn't prove that Maya had been buried in the box and her body later dug up and moved to a more remote location.

They'd dragged Reggie back in for questioning, along with her boyfriend, Derrick Sway. Eventually, they'd both been released, but suspicions lingered in Black Creek. Those dark whispers had dogged Thea all through school, at times poking at the doubts that dwelled at the fringes of her memory.

She'd managed to put her misgivings aside when she left her hometown for college. Those four years had been the most peaceful time of her young life. But then, as a federal agent, she'd been able to access Maya's file. In Reggie's official statement, she'd neglected to mention her second trip into the bedroom to raise the window. Maybe the oversight had been an honest mistake. In the shock and horror of her daughter's disappearance, she could have easily forgotten the sequence of events. It was a small thing, really. Hardly worth thinking about in the scheme of things.

Yet Thea knew only too well that what went unspoken was often far more important than the information revealed in any interview or statement.

And that seemingly insignificant omission had started to niggle at her again.

"WHY ARE YOU staring at me?" Reggie demanded.

Her voice jolted Thea from her deep reverie and she physically started. "What? I'm sorry. I was lost in thought. I didn't realize I was staring."

Reggie gave her a quizzical look. "What were you thinking about so hard?"

Thea answered without hesitation. "The abduction. You were going to tell me how Taryn and Kylie Buchanan came to be living with you."

Her mother turned her eyes back to the road. "Like I said, it's a long story. I hardly know where to start."

"How did you meet?" Thea prompted.

"They started attending my church a few weeks ago. We have a new preacher and a lot of folks have been coming to check him out. The kids adore him. I think even you would approve of Brother Eldon. He's already done a lot for the community and he's been a godsend to Taryn."

That got Thea's attention. "How so?"

"He's counseled her all through the separation with her husband. Been there for her every step of the way. I don't know if she could have handled the stress without him. He got her a job at the church so that she could keep Kylie with her all day, and he even helped her find a little apartment in town. She and Taryn were supposed to move in at the end of the week. Since the police are treating my house as a crime scene, the landlord let her stay there last night. Brother Eldon has barely left her side since Kylie went missing."

"Are they romantically involved?" Thea asked bluntly.

The question seemed to rub Reggie the wrong way. "Now why would you ask a thing like that? Don't turn a good deed into something dirty."

Thea put up a hand. "Sorry. No need to get defensive. I'm not accusing or judging, just trying to get the full picture. But we're getting ahead of ourselves anyway. Let's go back. You met Taryn and Kylie at church…"

Reggie nodded. "They started coming on Wednesday nights, which I thought a little odd. We typically have a short service on that night followed by church business.

We hardly ever have visitors. Nonmembers almost always come for Sunday morning service."

"Why did she come on Wednesday nights?"

"She told me later her husband frequently stayed overnight in Tallahassee on Wednesday nights. Anyway, Taryn would sit at the very back, clutching little Kylie's hand and glancing over her shoulder as if she were afraid someone would burst through the door and snatch the child away from her." Reggie paused as reality sank in. "I could tell she needed a friend, so I made a point of speaking to her after every service."

"What happened then?"

"She and Kylie came into the diner one day. She asked if we could talk. I took my break and we walked across the street to the park where we could speak in private. She was shy at first, and maybe a little embarrassed about her situation. Then everything just came pouring out of her. She told me that she'd only been nineteen when she and Russ Buchanan first got together. Her mother had died when she was a kid and her father had passed at the end of her senior year. She used the little dab of money left after his burial to move to Tallahassee where she could find steady work. Russ was older, handsome and charming, and already a successful lawyer. He saw her in the lobby of his office building one day and swept her off her feet. They were married two months later."

"Let me guess," Thea said. "Things didn't work out as she'd hoped."

"Same old story," Reggie said with a heavy sigh. "Butter wouldn't melt in his mouth until he had her under his spell. She was exactly the type of vulnerable young woman men like him prey on. He moved her into a house he bought in Black Creek, away from everyone she knew in Tallahassee. He started asking her to dress a certain way, wear her hair a certain way, cook his meals and clean his house a certain way. Then he stopped asking.

"By the time Taryn realized the kind of man she'd married, she was pregnant and had nowhere else to go. Everything was in Russ's name, of course. The house, the cars, the bank accounts. He gave her an allowance, but she had to justify every penny she spent. When he stayed overnight in Tallahassee, he'd check the mileage on her car when he got home. Things only got worse after the baby came. He threatened to take Kylie away from her if she ever tried to leave him."

"Was he physically abusive?"

"I'm sure he was, though she claims he only grabbed her arm and pushed her around a bit."

"Only?" Thea looked at her mother. "You think she downplayed the level of violence?"

Reggie's expression tightened. "That's my suspicion. She was clearly terrified of him. I told her things would only get worse if she stayed. She needed to go home, pack her bags and get Kylie out of that situation before something truly bad happened. I offered them a place to stay for as long as they needed it."

"You weren't afraid a man like that would try to retaliate against you?" Thea asked.

Her mother lifted a hand from the steering wheel. "What was he going to do to me that hadn't already been done?"

Thea felt a little tremor go through her. "Go on."

"A few nights later, Taryn and Kylie showed up on my doorstep with their suitcases," Reggie said. "I put Kylie in your old room and Taryn slept on the couch. I don't know how Russ found out where they were so quickly. Maybe he had someone watching her or maybe he planted some kind of tracker on her car. When I saw him pull up the next morning, I called the cops and then met him on the front porch. He pushed me aside and kicked open the door.

He grabbed Taryn and tried to drag her outside with poor little Kylie screaming bloody murder in the corner. It was a horrible scene. Thank God a patrol car was nearby. I don't know what would have happened if the cops hadn't come when they had."

"Did they take him into custody?"

"No. You know how that goes. A guy like Russ Buchanan has pull even in a place like Black Creek. One of his golfing buddies is a state senator. The cops finally managed to calm him down and got him to leave. Chief Bowden advised Taryn to take out a restraining order, but she was afraid that would only trigger his anger. Things quieted down for a bit. Russ didn't give her any more trouble. He even called ahead the one time he wanted to see Kylie. Taryn was hopeful for a peaceful divorce. And then Kylie went missing. Now Russ blames her for everything."

"Of course he does. Tell me everything you can remember about the day Kylie disappeared."

Reggie nodded. "I had to work. Normally, I have Sundays off, but one of the other girls called in sick and I agreed to take her shift. By the time I got home that evening, I was bone-tired. Taryn was getting ready to go to the evening service and I told her Kylie could stay home with me. Both of them had been through so much, I thought Taryn might enjoy some time to herself. But she said Brother Eldon had a surprise for Kylie that night."

"What kind of surprise?"

"He and some of the other members of the congregation had erected new playground equipment behind the church and he promised Kylie she could be the first one down the slide. After they left, I took a bath and went straight to bed. I was so tired, I didn't even hear them come home. The next thing I knew, Taryn was standing over my bed screaming that Kylie was gone. I got up and ran into the bedroom. When I saw the open window—" She stopped short and drew a sharp breath. "I knew what had happened. I knew it was just like before."

Thea's pulse thudded as her mind went back to that night. "Was the window open when Taryn put Kylie to bed?"

"That window is kept closed and locked at all times."

"Are you certain Taryn didn't go in sometime later and open it to let in some fresh air?" Thea turned to stare at her mother as she waited for her response.

"There's no reason why she would have. I had central AC installed in the house years ago. The bedrooms stay plenty cool."

"Had the lock been jimmied?" Thea asked.

"The police said there was no sign of a forced entry anywhere in the house."

"Who has a key besides you?"

"No one. Taryn has been using the spare I keep in a flowerpot on my front porch."

"Would she put it back after each use?"

Reggie glanced at her. "The police checked. It was still there on Monday morning. Why?"

"If someone was watching your house, they would have seen her take the key out of the flowerpot and return it. They could have waited until you were both out of the house, let themselves in and unlocked the bedroom window."

Reggie returned her attention to the road. "Someone like Russ Buchanan, you mean."

"Considering his previous threats and behavior, I'm sure the police are giving him a hard look."

Her mother scoffed at the suggestion. "For all the good it will do. I told you he has pull. If he took Kylie, they'll never be able to pin it on him."

"What makes you so sure?"

A bitter edge crept into Reggie's voice. "Because bad men do bad things and get away with it all the time."

"Not all the time," Thea said. "The prisons are full of bad men who did bad things and got caught."

"Not men like Russ Buchanan."

They both fell silent after that. Thea shifted her attention to the outside mirror where she could watch the road behind them. A black pickup had been following them ever since they'd exited the freeway. She hadn't given much thought to it earlier, but now she realized that the vehicle had been maintaining the same distance between them.

"Check out the vehicle behind us," she said.

Reggie glanced in the rearview mirror. "The black pickup? What about it?"

"I'm wondering if it's the same vehicle that cut you off at the airport."

Reggie took another perusal. "I doubt it. Trucks are a dime a dozen in this part of the state. Be a pretty big coincidence if that truck was headed in our direction."

Thea kept her gaze on the mirror. "Normally, I would agree, but the driver has been keeping pace with us for several miles. Just seems odd to me."

"Why? We're both doing the speed limit."

"Give it a little gas," Thea said. "I want to see if he falls behind."

"Are you going to pay my speeding ticket?" Reggie demanded.

"I said a little gas. No need to floor it."

Reggie mumbled something under her breath as she pressed down on the pedal.

After a moment, the truck faded.

"See there? Nothing to worry about. Your job is making you paranoid."

"I prefer to think of it as cautious." Thea turned to

glance over her shoulder. "Do you happen to know if Russ Buchanan owns a black truck?"

"He's not the pickup truck type. He drove a silver Mercedes when he came to the house." She flashed Thea an uneasy glance. "What are you getting at? You think Russ is having us tailed? Why would he do that?"

"Could be an intimidation thing. You took in his wife and child. It's possible he blames you for Taryn leaving him." Or maybe Russ Buchanan had heard the rumors about Reggie and suspected her of harming his daughter.

No sooner had the thought occurred to Thea than the vehicle appeared once more in the outside mirror. It was coming up fast behind them.

"Reggie—"

"I see him. What do you want me to do?"

"Nothing. Maintain your current speed. If he tries to pass, let him."

Reggie frowned. "What if he tries to ram us?"

"That would be pretty brazen in broad daylight."

"Brazen or not, he's coming up behind us hell-bent for leather." Reggie gripped the wheel as she flicked another glance in the rearview mirror.

Thea turned to track the pickup through the back window. The vehicle was close enough now she could see that the grille and front bumper were splattered with mud, partially concealing the license plate number. She hadn't noticed any mud on the truck at the airport, but then, she'd been distracted by the awkward reunion with her mother. Still, an obscured license plate would have surely caught her attention.

"I keep a .38 in the glove box," Reggie said.

Thea turned at that. "I hope you're not suggesting I open fire."

Her mother met her gaze. "I'm just saying, it's there if we need it."

Thea leaned back against the seat and checked the vehicle in the outside mirror. The driver continued to gain
ground. Reggie reflexively sped up.

"Don't try to outrun him," Thea warned. "Let him go
around."

The driver edged up as close to Reggie's bumper as he
dared without making contact. Then he whipped the truck
into the left lane and drew up beside her. For a moment,
they were dead even on the two-lane highway. Thea tried
to get a look at the driver, but he wore a cap and sunglasses
and kept his head turned so that she could make out little
more than his silhouette.

"Ease up on the gas," she told Reggie.

Before the pickup could pass, another vehicle came
barreling around a curve in front of them. Reggie hit the
brakes to allow the truck room to merge into the right lane,
but the driver swerved too early, sideswiping Reggie's car
and sending them careening onto the shoulder. The rear
end fishtailed as the tires whirled in loose gravel.

Reggie fought to maneuver the car back onto pavement,
but the momentum of the spin plunged them down the embankment toward a line of trees. Everything seemed to
happen in the blink of an eye. Thea caught a glimpse of her
mother's tense face a split second before they hit a rock and
the car went airborne. She tried to brace herself, leaning
deep into the seat and folding her arms over her chest. She
would later remember a strange feeling of weightlessness.
Then the car bounced off the ground and rolled.

When the world finally stopped spinning, she was still
buckled into her seat in the upside-down vehicle.

Dazed, she sat quietly for a moment, trying to recali-
brate her nervous system as the airbags deflated. Then she
ran her hands over her head to check for blood and broken
glass. *You're okay. You're okay.*

She glanced at Reggie and her heart almost stopped. Her

mother was slumped sideways, motionless. Thea touched her shoulder. "Reggie? You okay?"

No answer.

Don't panic.

As if in slow motion, Thea reached over and shut off the engine while simultaneously searching for the cross-body bag containing her phone. Bracing one hand on the ceiling and her feet against the floor, she snapped off her seat belt and crawled through the open window. By the time she managed to stagger to her feet, a man was running down the embankment toward her. She checked the side of the road and saw a dark blue SUV. The black pickup was nowhere in sight.

"Hey!" he called out. "Everybody okay?"

Thea fumbled in her bag for her phone. "My mother's unconscious inside the vehicle."

"I called 9-1-1 as soon as I saw the collision. An ambulance is on the way," he said.

Thea hurried around the car and dropped to the ground beside the window, keeping the newcomer in her line of sight while trying to take stock of Reggie's injuries. She had a deep cut on her upper arm that bled profusely. Thea reached for her mother's wrist to check for a pulse.

"I work for the fire department," the man told her as he hunkered down beside her and glanced through the window. "We shouldn't try to move her until the EMTs get here. Spinal chord injuries are always a danger in this type of accident."

"Her pulse is thready," Thea said. "Her skin feels clammy."

"She may be in shock from blood loss." The man whipped off his shirt and pressed the folded fabric to Reggie's arm. "Can you keep up the pressure? I've got a first aid kit and a blanket in my truck."

Thea nodded and took over. She glanced up as the man stood. "What happened to the vehicle that hit us?"

"Kept going and never looked back." He gazed down at her. "You sure you're okay?"

"Yes, but please hurry."

After he left, Thea adjusted her position so she had better access through the window. She talked to her mother as she applied pressure to the wound. "You're going to be fine. Help is on the way."

Blood soaked through the stranger's shirt onto Thea's hands. "The ambulance will be here any minute now. Just stay with me, okay?"

She tried to bite back her panic, but Reggie was so pale, and her lips were turning blue. *Oh, please don't die. Please, please, please don't die.* "You hear me, Mama? Don't you die on me."

Chapter Three

After an anxious dash through the maze of hospital corridors, Jake finally found Thea in the surgical waiting room. She stood staring out a window with her back to the entrance. He called her name softly as he approached. He didn't want to catch her off guard, but she jumped and whirled as if startled by unexpected gunfire.

Her blue eyes went wide when she saw him, and something flashed a split second before she glanced away. Jake didn't want to put a name to the emotion for fear he'd imagined the tiny flare. But he could have sworn her initial response to his presence had been relief. Perhaps even happiness. He was going with that.

She controlled her visible reaction as she gave him a puzzled frown. "Jake! What are you doing here?"

"Chief Bowden told me what happened. I wanted to see for myself that you're okay." His heart dropped in spite of himself as he took in the cuts and bruises on her face and the bloodstained white blouse. *Talk about trying to hide your visible reaction.* "Damn, Thea."

"It looks worse than it is." She brushed back a loose strand of dark blond hair from her forehead. "I'm fine. Most of the blood isn't mine."

"How's your mother?"

"She regained consciousness in the ambulance, so that's

a good sign. She has cuts and bruises, and the CT scan showed some internal bleeding. They took her into surgery a little while ago."

"I'm surprised they didn't transport her to Tallahassee," Jake said.

"Black Creek General was closer, and she'd already lost a lot of blood. This is a good hospital." Her expression turned apprehensive as she glanced at the clock on the wall. "But it seems to be taking forever. You know how it is when you're waiting. Time crawls."

Jake nodded. "Why don't I go see if I can find out anything?"

"No, that's okay. They'll let me know when there's an update. I would like to go wash my face, though. Do you mind waiting in case someone comes to find me?"

"Take your time."

As Jake watched her disappear down the hallway, he found himself reflecting on how long it had been since he'd last seen her. Four years and some change, but in a way it seemed as if no time had passed at all. She was still a swimmer judging by her lithe figure and sinewy muscle tone. Still practical in her manner of dress and demeanor, yet even in bloodstained clothing, Thea Lamb had an allure that went well beyond the physical. Tough as nails when she needed to be and unflinching in the face of danger, but Jake had seen her break down inconsolably at the sight of an injured kitten. She mostly kept that side of her personality hidden. It was there, though, beneath the battle-hardened surface, and he could only imagine what a decade of working crimes against children had done to her. To him, too, for that matter. Their defenses were strong for a reason.

He gave her a benign smile when she came back into the room, though all he could think about was how much he wanted to wrap his arms around her. Now was not the time or place, of course. Too many years had gone by and Thea had never been demonstrative even when the smallest of gestures would have kept him in DC for as long as she wanted him there.

Water under the bridge. "You've had someone look at your injuries, right? That cut above your eye looks pretty deep."

"What?" She put a hand to her face. "Yes. They removed glass fragments in the ER and gave me a tetanus shot. No stitches required. Reggie's side of the vehicle got the worst of it."

"Can you tell me what happened?"

"I can, but I already gave a statement to one of the officers at the scene. It should be in his report."

"I'd like to hear it from you."

She looked as if she might refuse his request then she shrugged. "A vehicle trying to pass swerved into our car to avoid oncoming traffic. He knocked us onto the shoulder, we spun out in loose gravel and Reggie lost control."

"Can you describe the vehicle and driver? Or better yet, did you get a plate number?"

"I really didn't get a good look at the driver. He wore a baseball cap and sunglasses, and he kept his head turned toward the road, so I only glimpsed his profile. He was white and I had the impression he was middle-aged or older—in his fifties maybe—and heavyset. Heavyset as in brawny. Muscular. The vehicle was a late-model black pickup truck with chrome wheels. I didn't get the make, and the grille and bumper area was splattered with mud, so the plate was partly hidden."

"Deliberately hidden would you say?"

She hesitated. "Possibly. The rest of the truck looked fairly clean. I remember noticing the shiny paint. I'd been watching the vehicle in the outside mirror for a while before the accident. I thought it strange that the driver kept the same distance between us mile after mile. There were hardly any other cars on the road and Reggie was driving the speed limit. Most people go a few miles over, especially in a vehicle like that. I asked her to speed up to see if he would do the same. He dropped out of sight for a minute and then he came up behind us quickly. That's when he tried to pass."

"How long do you think he'd been following you?" Jake asked.

"At least since we left the freeway."

"Did the driver have any distinguishing marks? Piercings or tattoos? Scars? Anything like that?"

"None that I noticed. As I said, I only had a glance." She gave him a long scrutiny. "Why all these questions, Jake? Do you know something I don't?"

He said uneasily, "Emotions are running high in this town. There was an incident at Reggie's house."

"The vandalism?" Thea nodded. "She told me. Do you have a suspect? Is that why you're asking about scars and tattoos?"

"We don't have a suspect. Apparently it was painted late last night or early this morning under cover of darkness."

"And you're thinking the two incidents are somehow related?"

"I'm not thinking anything at the moment," Jake said. "I'm just trying to put the information together."

Her blue eyes looked troubled and faintly disapproving. "Okay. But why are you involved at all? The local police have jurisdiction over the vandalism and the Florida Highway Patrol over the accident. Why not let them do their jobs? Your sole focus should be on finding Kylie Buchanan."

Her censure touched a nerve. "She is my sole focus," Jake said quietly. "I assure you, everything that can be done is being done to find that little girl."

Thea looked contrite. "I'm sorry. That didn't come out the way I intended. I'm not questioning your integrity or your priorities. No one is better at this job than you are. I just meant…" She glanced down at her hands and shrugged. "I guess I'm wondering why you're really here. You could have easily called to check up on me."

"I could have," he agreed. "And you're right, I do have an ulterior motive."

"Which is…?"

He hesitated, choosing his words carefully. "Your perspective on this case is unique. Considering your history and Reggie's connection, it shouldn't be surprising that I'd seek you out." *In spite of* our *history.*

"When you put it that way…" She looked tense and her voice sounded strained. "How can I help?"

He motioned to a pair of uncomfortable-looking chairs. "Let's sit."

She gave a weary nod and sat facing the entrance. Her gaze went back to the clock as Jake took the seat beside her.

"You want some coffee?" he asked.

"I'm fine."

"You've been through a lot. Would you rather I come back later?"

"No, but before we start, can you at least catch me up? Reggie filled me in on her end, but I don't know what's going on regarding the overall search. I assume there's no real news or you wouldn't be here asking for my perspective."

"You know the procedure." Jake ran fingers through his hair as he shifted impatiently. "We're still conducting canvasses and we've set up vehicle checkpoints on all the main roads. For the past day and a half, we've had choppers and drones in the air, but the area is heavily wooded with dozens of creeks, lakes and sloughs. It would take weeks to search them all."

"Lots of places for someone to disappear," Thea said worriedly. "Do you think there's a chance she's still alive? The timeline isn't working in her favor."

"She's alive unless and until we recover a body," he said with grim resolve.

Their gazes locked.

"Three percent," Thea murmured.

He nodded. "Three percent."

Neither of them said anything for a long moment but Jake knew the statistics were rolling around in her head just as they were his.

In seventy-four percent of stranger abductions, the victims were found dead within three hours after being reported missing. After twenty-four hours, the number rose to eighty percent and leaped to a staggering ninety-seven percent after a week. Kylie Buchanan had already been missing for thirty-two hours. They were rapidly approaching the point where everyone involved in the search began to cling to the three percent of victims found alive days after they'd been taken.

"Forget about numbers," Thea said. "What does your gut tell you? You always have a feel for how these things will go."

"Not this time."

"Why is that?"

He hesitated, unable to verbalize the disturbing vibes he was getting from some of the people connected to Kylie Buchanan any more than he could explain his visit to Reggie's house earlier that day and the inexplicable pull that had lured him into the woods. "It's an unusual case," was all he said.

Thea looked as if she wanted to press him further, but the surgeon came into the room and Jake heard her catch her breath as she instinctively reached for his hand. The contact shocked him to his core. Earlier he'd wanted nothing so much as to wrap a comforting arm around her shoulders, but now his first instinct was to pull away. His defenses were strong, too. Then he squeezed her fingers in reassurance as they both rose to meet the doctor.

THE SURGEON INTRODUCED himself as he came forward. "I'm Dr. Vaughn. You're Miss Lamb's daughter?"

"Yes, I'm Thea." She realized she was still clinging to Jake's hand. Embarrassed, she let him go and folded her arms over her chest. "How is she?"

"Your mother's a strong woman. She came through surgery like a champ. She's stable and her vitals look good. We'll keep a close eye on the concussion for the next twenty-four to forty-eight hours, but if all goes well, you should be able to take her home by the end of the week."

"When can I see her?"

"She'll be in recovery for a while yet. You can see her as soon as she's moved upstairs."

"Thank you, Dr. Vaughn."

He shook her hand, nodded to Jake and then left the room.

"Good news." Jake gave her a warm smile. "I know you're relieved."

"I am." Thea kept her arms folded at her chest as if she could protect herself from his smile. It had always done things to her, that smile. The way his lips turned up slightly at the corners. The way a single dimple appeared now and then in his right cheek. "I'll feel even better when I can see her," she said.

"It won't be long. In the meantime, are you sure I can't buy you a cup of coffee? The cafeteria is just down the hall from the lobby. You look like you could use a boost."

Thea started to decline, but the adrenaline from the crash had long since worn off and she was starting to deflate. A jolt of caffeine would keep her going for another few hours.

She glanced down at her bloodstained blouse. "I don't know how welcome I'll be in the cafeteria, but I don't have anything with me to change into."

Jake shrugged. "You're in a hospital. If they can't handle a little blood, they're in the wrong line of work."

Thankfully, the cafeteria was nearly empty. Thea found a table in a discrete corner while Jake bought the coffee. He fitted the disposable cups with lids and carried them over.

"You still take it black?"

"Yes." She took a tentative sip and cringed.

"Tastes a little like tar smells," he said as he took the seat across from her. "But it's hot and strong."

"It'll do." Thea cradled the cup in her hands. "What about leads?"

He glanced up from pouring a healthy dose of creamer into his coffee. "What?"

"You were telling me about the investigation before the doctor came in. You must have narrowed down your suspect list by now."

"Not as much as we'd hoped." He stirred his coffee and replaced the lid on his cup. "We're still in the process of tracking down and interviewing anyone who had contact with Kylie or her mother in the days leading up to the abduction. Friends, neighbors, acquaintances. We're still hoping someone may have seen or heard something. We've also identified and located all the known sex offenders in the area, but that angle hasn't been helpful so far." He looked frustrated and worried. "The truth is, we just don't have much to go on. No fingerprints or trace evidence left at the crime scene. No eyewitness accounts. It's like she vanished into thin air."

"No child ever vanishes into thin air," Thea said.

Another look passed between them. Another flash of understanding.

Thea had forgotten about the unspoken communication she and Jake had once shared, those brief, tender moments of solidarity. They'd spent so much of their time convincing themselves and each other they had no need of a meaningful relationship that they'd failed to appreciate the depth and rarity of their camaraderie. Over the years, Thea had tried not to dwell on how much she missed Jake's friendship, but the loss hit her now as forcefully as the car crash. She took another sip of bad coffee while she tried to regain her composure.

She glanced across the table. Jake stared back at her, his brown eyes so dark and intense her heart thumped. *So much for composure.*

She pretended to adjust the lid on her cup so she could break eye contact. "What about Russ Buchanan? According to Reggie, he physically abused his wife and threatened to take Kylie away from her if she tried to leave him. Reggie said he made a terrible scene when he found out Taryn and Kylie were staying with her."

"We've talked to Buchanan at his home and at the police station. He's arrogant and smug, and seems to think he's untouchable, but he's been cooperative for the most part and his story never changes. Both he and his assistant swear they were together in his Tallahassee apartment on the night of and the morning after Kylie's disappearance. They dined out at a local restaurant on Sunday night and several people saw them arrive at the office together early Monday morning."

"Sounds like they made sure they were seen together. It wouldn't be the first time an employee having an affair with her boss gave him an alibi." Thea watched two nurses come into the cafeteria. They didn't pay the slightest attention to her shirt. They did, however, notice Jake. She could hardly blame them. He was a good-looking man, tall, fit and in the prime of his life at thirty-four. "Even if the assistant is telling the truth, it doesn't necessarily put Buchanan in the clear. A man with his resources wouldn't get his own hands dirty. He has motive and apparently the means to create the opportunity."

"We've got eyes on him," Jake assured her.

"And Taryn?"

She watched in fascination as something inexplicable flashed across Jake's face.

"Now that's interesting." She folded her arms on the table as she searched his expression.

"What is?"

"Your reaction when I asked about Taryn."

He took a moment to answer. "She's hard to read. More difficult in some ways than her husband. Something is going on with her. The fear is palpable, and I'd swear genuine. She's obviously terrified for her child."

"But?"

He gave her a brooding frown. "I can't help wondering about the real source of her fear."

"Meaning?"

He leaned in, lowering his voice as his dark eyes met Thea's. "She took Kylie to church on Sunday night. More than a dozen people say they saw them together on the playground and later inside the sanctuary. But a witness who left early and drove back after the service to retrieve a forgotten umbrella claims she saw Taryn exit the building, get in her car and drive away without Kylie."

"What does Taryn say?"

"She went back inside to collect some paperwork from the office. Kylie was asleep in the back seat and she didn't want to wake her. She says the child was alone in the car for no more than a couple of minutes."

"You don't believe her?"

"One of Reggie's neighbors said that Taryn was always hovering nearby anytime Kylie played in the front yard. She wouldn't let the child out of her sight." Jake paused as he absently swirled his coffee. "Leaving her daughter alone in the car at night, even for a couple of minutes, doesn't exactly jibe with this neighbor's observation."

"And Reggie was asleep when they got home that night. She said she didn't hear them come in." Now it was Thea who leaned forward. "What are you saying, Jake? Do you think Taryn had something to do with her daughter's disappearance?"

A mask dropped over his expression. "All I can say is that we're exploring every possibility."

"Don't do that," she grumbled.

"Do what?"

"Shut me out. You're the one who wanted my perspective, remember?"

He hesitated then nodded. "Fair enough. I'd like to hear what you think of what I just told you."

Thea shrugged. "I haven't talked to Taryn Buchanan. I've never even met her, so all I can do is speculate. But something occurred to me while you were describing her behavior. It won't make a lot of sense at first, but hear me out."

"I'm listening."

"Do you remember Operation Innocent Images?"

"Yes, of course. It was an undercover operation, launched back in the nineties, that identified and tracked predators through chat rooms and electronic bulletin boards. The expanded program eventually brought down entire networks of online pedophiles and the producers and distributors of child pornography. It became the Innocent Images National Initiative when it was absorbed into the Violent Crimes Against Children unit.

"One of the agents I've been working with in Cold

Cases came from Operation Innocent Images. That's how long she's been tracking missing children. She has a theory that an underground railroad for at-risk kids of a tender age has been active in various parts of the country for at least thirty years. The people involved operate exclusively from the shadows. They step in when the system fails."

"How does it work?"

"I'll give you one example. Someone from the organization approaches a woman in a similar situation to Taryn Buchanan's. The contact can be made directly or through an intermediary. The woman has already exhausted every legal means available to protect herself and her child. She's desperate and has no place to turn to for help. The police and courts have either been powerless to help her or are too slow to react.

"The underground operative presents a plan of last resort and if the mother agrees, her child goes missing. Vanishes into thin air," Thea said with a note of irony. "He or she is moved through a series of safe houses until the dust settles and the mother and child can eventually be reunited with new identities. It's much more complicated than I've made it sound, but you get the gist."

"Who are the operatives?" Jake asked.

"Social workers, police officers, FBI and Homeland Security agents. People in trusted positions with wide-ranging resources. Professionals who've seen firsthand what goes on inside the system, and have figured out a way to work around it when a child is in imminent danger. If both parents have failed the child, a friend or family member is sometimes contacted to make the arrangements. The child is then kept hidden until a permanent home can be found and a new identity established."

"Does money change hands?"

"Sometimes. Which means no matter how noble the intent, an operation of this nature is ripe for exploitation."

"And vulnerable to the infiltration of child traffickers, I would think."

"The fastest growing criminal enterprise in the world," she said with a grim nod. "The sheer number of trafficked children worldwide is mind-blowing, Jake."

"You think this group accounts for some of your cold cases?"

"We think it's a very real possibility," Thea said. "Let's suppose for a moment that someone approached Taryn with a way to remove her and Kylie from Russ Buchanan's reach forever. It could explain why, despite her genuine fear, you've picked up on something from her that doesn't ring true. It could also explain why you have a witness that saw her leave church on Sunday night without Kylie."

He seemed to ponder the possibility. "A plan like that would be risky in any number of ways. The person making the approach would have to be someone Taryn trusted implicitly. Someone with intimate knowledge of her situation. I take it you have someone like that in mind?"

"The preacher at her church is new to the area and has evidently been quite helpful. According to Reggie, he and Taryn have grown very close very quickly. He helped her find an apartment and even arranged a job for her at the church so that she could keep Kylie with her during the day. Also, according to Reggie, he hasn't left Taryn's side since Kylie went missing."

"His name is Eldon Mossey," Jake said. "We've looked into him. He doesn't have a criminal record."

"I wouldn't expect him to. Although he could be using an alias."

"All the database searches came back clean, including CODIS. But the phone number he provided for his former church in Butler, Georgia, has been disconnected."

Thea sat back. "There's a red flag."

"Could be. The Atlanta division is sending an agent

from their Macon office to see what he can turn up." Jake studied her for a moment.

She frowned at the scrutiny. "What?"

"We both know of someone else in town that Taryn trusted."

"You mean Reggie." Thea tucked a strand of hair behind her ears. "I figured you'd get around to her sooner or later."

"Given her personal experience with your sister's abduction, it's not hard to imagine how protective she'd feel toward a child she perceived to be in danger."

Thea's defense was automatic. "She doesn't fit the profile. She wouldn't have the know-how or resources to pull off something like that. And, besides, I can't see her subjecting even a creep like Russ Buchanan to the hell she went through when Maya disappeared."

"She might if she thought she was saving Kylie's life."

Even as Thea formulated another argument, Reggie's words echoed at the back of her mind. *Bad men do bad things and get away with it all the time.*

She glanced up. "What is it you want me to do, Jake?"

"Nothing overt. Keep your eyes and ears open."

"Spy on my mother, you mean." Thea took a breath, suddenly so weary she could hardly hold up her head. His request distressed her in a way she couldn't explain. It prodded at all her old doubts. Dragged too many memories out into the open. Why had she ever thought coming back here a good idea?

The answer to that question was simple. This wasn't about her. This was about a missing child. In the world she and Jake had chosen for themselves, nothing else could ever be allowed to matter.

"I'll do what I can, but Reggie's injuries are serious. I have to be careful," she said.

"Of course. I would never ask you to do anything to impede her recovery."

She brought her eyes back to his. Their earlier camaraderie had vanished. The walls were up again and, everything considered, maybe that was a good thing. "Why do I get the feeling you've something else on your mind?" Her voice sounded stilted and slightly accusatory.

He returned her scrutiny for a moment then wordlessly took out his phone and slid it across the table.

Thea tore her gaze from his and picked up the phone. Goose bumps prickled as she studied the primitive figures then enlarged the image to bring the grotesque faces into focus.

"Have you ever come across anything like that?" Jake asked with a strange note of dread in his voice.

"Looks like some kind of talisman or totem," she said. "Not like any voodoo doll I've ever seen. Maybe Santeria, but I'd guess more Appalachian in origin. Or the Sea Islands, maybe. Seems like something that might be used in folk magic." She swiped and enlarged, bringing various parts of the figures into focus. "Where did this photo come from?"

"I took it. I found them hanging from a tree limb behind Reggie's house. Someone must have put them there after the initial canvass."

Thea couldn't tear her attention from the screen. "Where are they now? I'd like to see them in person."

"I've sent them to the lab for analysis."

She swiped again. "Do you think that's real human hair?"

"We'll know soon enough. I asked for priority."

She said slowly, "Maya had blond hair."

"So does Kylie Buchanan."

"And you found them behind Reggie's house? Where exactly?"

"Three or four hundred yards into the woods and directly over the path. I don't see how they could have been missed during any of the searches."

"Do you think they were put there as a way to connect the two missing girls?"

"That would seem the logical conclusion."

Thea studied the image a moment longer before handing back his phone. "Can you send that photo to me? I'd like to run it by someone. She's had some experience with occult-related abductions."

"Your number is the same?" When she nodded, he texted the image and then pocketed his phone. "You'll get back to me if you find out anything?"

"Of course." She pushed away from the table and stood. "I'm willing to help in any way I can, but right now I need to go and check on Reggie."

Jake stood, too. They walked out into the corridor and paused to say their goodbyes. He seemed hesitant to leave her alone. Sliding his hands in his pockets, he gazed down at her. "It's been a long time."

It was crazy how emotional she felt all of a sudden. "Yes, it has."

"I'm glad you're here, Thea." He turned and walked away, and this time she was glad he didn't look back. She brushed her hand against the wetness on her lashes and went to find her mother.

Chapter Four

Thea sat with Reggie for the rest of the afternoon and into the early evening. Still under the effects of anesthesia, her mother drifted in and out of sleep, rousing briefly to eat a few bites of Jell-O before falling back under. After the dinner tray had been collected and the doctor had come by, Thea gathered up her things and left.

One of the patrol officers at the crash site had rescued her backpack and carry-on from the trunk of her mother's car before it had been towed. As a courtesy, he'd promised to see that the bags were delivered to the Magnolia Hotel in downtown Black Creek where she had a reservation. Thea had murmured her gratitude as she'd climbed into the ambulance and then promptly forgotten about the luggage, though she'd kept the cross-body bag with her gun and ID close to her side. She hadn't given the rest of her things another thought until this very moment when the prospect of a hot shower and change of clothing had become irresistible.

She considered calling for a cab or car service, but the hotel was only a few blocks away and, despite the stiffness that dogged her every movement, she decided some fresh air would do her good.

Traffic was brisk in and out of the hospital parking lot, but the noise on the streets had already started to fade. It was that time of evening when daylight lingered and twi-light hovered, and Thea's senses heightened. She could smell the jasmine that spilled over walls and fences, and the faint, dusty fragrance of the oleanders that lined the esplanade.

She left the main thoroughfare and turned down Market Street. Black Creek was modestly famous for its multitude of flea markets and antique shops that lined several blocks. Many of the stores had been in business since Thea was a little girl, but a few start-ups were sprinkled in among the originals. The passage of time struck her anew as nostal-gia drifted in on the breeze and dread deepened with the shadows. She thought of Maya and little Kylie Buchanan and all the other missing children that had passed through her life since she'd left Black Creek. She thought of Reggie and the wedge that had been irrevocably driven between them after her sister's disappearance.

She tried not to think about Jake at all, but how could she not when she'd responded so viscerally to the sight of him? When, in a moment of fear, she'd reached instinc-tively for his hand to bolster her courage?

Her reaction had taken her by surprise, but how on earth had she not seen it coming?

It's over, she reminded herself. *It's been over for a long time. Don't even think about the possibility of going back there.*

They were too alike, she and Jake, and that had become an insurmountable obstacle. They each had things in their pasts they didn't want to talk about. Dark things that had turned both of them into scarred, wary loners.

The Magnolia Hotel was straight ahead. Shrugging off the melancholy, Thea crossed the intersection and entered the lobby. The desk clerk informed her that her bags had already been delivered to her room on the third floor. One of the perks of living in a small town, Thea decided as she thanked him, collected the key card and went straight up, barely taking the time to appreciate the artwork and antiques that decorated the careworn lobby.

The pair of queen-size beds in her room looked so inviting and Thea felt so worn out that she was tempted to shed her stained clothes and crawl under the covers right then and there. Instead, she went into the bathroom and turned on the tap. While the water heated, she stripped.

Plugging the drain, she climbed into the tub and lay back, letting the hot water soak away some of the aches and pains from the crash. She drifted off and when she startled awake, she had the strangest feeling that she was no longer alone.

She lay completely still in the tepid water, her senses attuned to the gloom outside the bathroom. She hadn't turned on any lamps in the bedroom and twilight had segued into night while she'd been soaking. Tilting her head, she tried not to splash as she peered out into the tiny hallway.

Nothing seemed amiss, but something was most definitely amiss. She could tell by the feathery warning at the back of her neck and another at the base of her spine. Her cross-body bag was on one of the beds where she had left it when she first walked in. She glanced around, taking stock of anything useful in the bathroom, and then eased up out of the water.

As she stepped over the side of the tub and reached for a towel, her heel came down on something sharp enough to pierce the skin. She muffled an exclamation as she sat on the edge of the tub and pulled a shard of glass from her foot. She thought at first it was a fragment from Reggie's shattered windshield that had clung to her hair or clothing. But rather than a chunky piece of safety glass, the sliver was thin and razor-sharp. Someone had broken a glass on the tiled floor, most likely.

Blood oozed from the tiny puncture. Thea grabbed a

tissue and pressed it to the wound as she kept her attention focused on the bathroom door. Where there was one piece of glass, there were likely others, but she couldn't worry about that at the moment. She got up from the tub slowly and shrugged into her robe then hobbled out into the corridor.

A faint breeze drifted through the bedroom, raising goose bumps on her damp skin. She suddenly felt woozy and disoriented, which was odd. She'd never been squeamish at the sight of blood and the cut wasn't deep enough to put her in shock.

She tried to steady herself as she took a quick perusal of the room before removing her gun from the bag. Clutching the weapon in both hands, she scanned all the corners. The window that looked out onto the fire escape was open. Had it been open when she'd entered the room? She didn't think so, but she couldn't be sure. Exhaustion had dulled her senses. Just in case, she kept an eye on the opening as she backed into the corridor and checked the closet.

Satisfied she was alone, she returned the firearm to her bag and limped over to close the window. Her every move seemed slow-moving, heavy, and the room seemed to spin around her.

A car passed below and as the engine noise faded, Thea detected a melodic sound that seemed to reverberate across her nerve endings. The hollow clacking was strangely enticing and dangerously hypnotic. She slid the window all the way up and climbed out onto the metal landing, swaying precariously as she grabbed for a handhold.

Suspended from the fourth-floor landing, a pair of twig figures like the ones in Jake's photo hung down over her head. Their movement as they danced together in the breeze mesmerized her. Still slow motion, she put up a hand to touch them, except they dangled just beyond her reach. The shadows were deep on the landing. She could just make out tufts of blond hair and red fabric hearts. Or was she imagining them? Were the figures really there?

Everything seemed trippy, surreal. The streetlights below became elongated and so brilliant Thea had to glance away. The metal landing tilted beneath her and she dropped to her knees with a gasp. Threading her fingers through the grid, she clung for dear life even as she realized she must be stuck in a dream. None of this could be real.

Had she been drugged? But…how? When?

No sooner had the thought occurred to Thea than she became captivated once again by the sound of the twig figures. She sat cross-legged on the landing and tilted her head. The hollow carvings danced happily together and the music they made was as sweet and lyrical as summer rain.

At some point, she heard footsteps on the metal rungs below her, but she was too beguiled by the figures to turn her head. She had the strongest sense that someone watched her from the shadows, reveling in her entrancement.

Something changed then. The twig figures bumped together in the breeze, creaking and clacking as they rotated. Now she could see their faces, those grotesque black holes for eyes and the hideous gaping mouths.

Heart pounding, she tore her eyes from the frenzied figures and concentrated on the open window. She needed to get inside to her phone. Jake would come. He might already be nearby.

Rising again to her hands and knees, she wove her fingers through the metal grid to propel herself up the slanted landing. It seemed impossibly steep all of a sudden. She didn't dare look down. Above her, the figures swayed even more frantically as they tried to recapture her attention. They were now clearly malevolent with their grasping twig arms and pulsing red hearts.

In some part of Thea's consciousness, she realized she was deep into a drug-induced hallucination, but the danger seemed so real. She tried to shut everything out as she pulled herself inch by inch toward that open window then somehow over the sill and into the safety of her bedroom. She lay sprawled on the floor, terrified and shivering as she summoned the energy to reach for the phone. *Too far.*

The last thing she remembered was the melodic clack of the twig figures stirring in the breeze and a shadowy face with dark eyes and a gaping mouth peering in at her through the window.

THEA OPENED HER eyes slowly, blinked a few times and then threw her arm over her face to deflect the sunlight that streamed in through the window. She lay on top of the covers in her bathrobe, with no memory whatsoever of having gone to bed the evening before.

She squeezed her eyes closed as vague images danced at the edges of her consciousness. She remembered boarding the plane and landing in Tallahassee. She remembered Reggie picking her up at the airport and the car crash on the way home.

The car crash.

Ah. That explained the soreness in her joints and the deep ache in her every muscle. Probably also explained the throb behind her eyelids and the unpleasant roil in her stomach. She struggled to recall subsequent events. The hospital. Jake. Her long walk from the hospital to the hotel.

The Magnolia Hotel.

That's where she was. It was all coming back to her now.

She lifted herself onto her elbows and gazed around the room. Her backpack and carry-on were on the other bed, along with her cross-body bag. Fighting a wave of nausea, she swung her legs over the bed and sat with her head in her hands before reaching for the bag to make sure everything was still there. Firearm, credentials, phone. All there. All good.

Whatever the cause for her disorientation, she seemed mostly okay. Her right heel was tender when she tried to put weight on it, but the pain only blended with her other aches. She sat on the edge of the bed and examined the bottom of her foot. The skin was red around a small puncture wound and stained with dried blood.

Hobbling into the bathroom, she brushed her teeth and rinsed the bad taste from her mouth. As she reached for a fresh towel, her gaze dropped to the tiny smears of blood on the tiled floor. Okay, something else was coming back to her now. A vague recollection of pricking her foot on a piece of glass embedded in the fibers of the bath mat. She checked for other fragments and then rolled up the mat and placed it under the vanity along with the damp towel she'd used the evening before. Limping out to the bedroom, she left a note for housekeeping about the broken glass and grabbed a pair of flip-flops from her carry-on to wear in the bathroom just in case.

After a hot shower, she felt much better. Not as disoriented and queasy, though her memory was still sketchy. She put a Band-Aid over the puncture wound, dressed comfortably in jeans and sneakers and went to find coffee. A line had formed outside the hotel restaurant downstairs. The influx of volunteers and law enforcement personnel had no doubt stressed the capacity of the tiny dining room. Thea didn't feel like waiting for a table so she left the hotel, placing a quick call to the hospital to check on Reggie as she crossed the street to walk in the shade.

The antique shop on the corner was called the Indigo Dollhouse. Thea remembered it well from her childhood, in particular the signature blue Victorian dollhouse the owner had kept on display in the large bay window. The shop had once held a particular allure for Thea because it had been forbidden. Reggie had never allowed her to go inside to admire the antique dolls for fear she'd break something they couldn't afford to pay for. *This is June's kind of place, not ours*, she would say with that faint look of contempt she always got when she spoke of Thea's grandmother.

On impulse, Thea went over to the window. The dark blue dollhouse with its turrets and towers and gingerbread trim was still on display. Still beautiful and grand, though perhaps not quite as grand or as large as Thea remembered. A woman dusting inside the shop noticed her through the window and waved. Thea waved back and started to move on, but the woman came hurrying out of the shop and called her name.

"Thea? Thea Lamb?"

The shopkeeper looked familiar, but her name remained elusive. Thea's silence was awkward and a little embarrassing, but the woman didn't seem to notice.

"I thought that was you!" she exclaimed. "My goodness, I never expected to see you outside my window. How many years has it been?" She prattled on while Thea desperately tried to recall her name. She looked to be Thea's age, early thirties with highlighted brown hair braided down her back and wide hazel eyes. She paused after a moment and gave a little chuckle. "Oh dear. You don't remember me, do you?"

The name came to Thea in the nick of time. "Grace. Grace Wilkerson."

The woman beamed as she held up her left hand, allowing the gold band to catch the light. "It's Bowden now."

"Bowden." Thea's brow wrinkled in concentration. "Why do I know that name?"

"My husband is the chief of police," she said proudly. "You've probably heard his name around town. Nash Bowden."

"Yes, I'm sure Reggie has mentioned him."

The woman's smile vanished. She touched Thea's arm in concern. To Thea's credit, she managed not to back away. "How is your mom? I heard what happened."

"Do you mean the wreck or the kidnapping?" Thea asked brusquely.

"Both." Grace dropped her hand as she gave a little shudder. "After everything she went through all those years ago and now to have a child taken from her home in exactly the same way as her own. I mean, what are the chances? I just can't imagine what she must be going through. What you both are going through with all the memories."

"It's a difficult time for everyone," Thea said. "But especially for Kylie Buchanan's family."

"Yes, of course. I didn't mean to discount their pain. My heart goes out to them. But I can't help remembering the way it was around here after Maya went missing. The awful things people said about Reggie. As if losing a child wasn't bad enough." Her eyes glittered with compassion. "I also remember how it was for you in school. Kids can be so cruel. I only wish I'd been more supportive."

"You ate with me in the cafeteria and you came to my house to play with me. That's more than a lot of kids were allowed to do," Thea said.

"I should have stood up for you," Grace insisted. "If the situation had been reversed, you would have gone to battle for me."

"Who knows what I would have done? It's all ancient history at this point."

She nodded sadly. "There's no going back, is there?"

"No." Thea glanced away. Why was she thinking about Jake all of a sudden and wondering what her life might have been like if the promotion had never come through and he'd remained in DC? Would they still be together? Doubtful. And why did it even matter? Grace Bowden was right. There was no going back. Ever.

Grace sighed as if intuiting Thea's twinge of regret. "Tell me about Reggie. How is she physically? A car wreck on top of everything else. That poor woman. Can she ever catch a break?"

"She'll be okay. I'm on my way to see her now," Thea said.

Grace frowned in concern. "Please tell me you aren't walking all the way to the hospital in this heat. Forgive me for saying so, but you look as if you might keel over at any moment."

"I'm fine," Thea said. "I just need to find some coffee."

"There's a new coffee bar on Decatur where the old comic book store used to be. I hear it's quite good, but that's several blocks out of your way." Grace touched Thea's arm again. "I just made a fresh pot. Come inside and have a cup with me."

"I couldn't possibly impose."

"It's no imposition. Please. I would love the company." She seemed naturally effusive; a caregiver personality who gained energy from her physical and emotional connections with others. If one believed in personality types. In Thea's experience, people were complicated and so much more than just one thing.

"I really should get to the hospital," she said.

"But you wanted coffee first," Grace reminded her. "Come inside. It'll give us a chance to catch up. It's just lucky I spotted you through the window. I'm usually not even here on Wednesdays. I only open the shop on weekends these days. Otherwise, it's by appointment only for collectors." The bells over the door chimed as she beckoned persistently.

"Is doll collecting still a thing?" Thea stepped over the threshold and let the cool air wash over her. She caught herself and added quickly, "I hope that didn't sound rude. I've always been fascinated by this shop."

"It's a valid question," Grace said. "Interest ebbs and flows, as with any collectible. The hard-core magpies will always be around. I do most of my business online through eBay, Etsy and a few other sites. I'm only open today because I have a dealer coming in to look at one of my pre-Civil War dolls."

"Wow, that's old." Thea glanced around curiously, taking in the old-fashioned display cases, half of them empty. The floorboards creaked as she moved inside and a fine layer of dust hung in the air despite Grace's earlier efforts. *So this is the Indigo Dollhouse.*

"Dolls have been around since at least the ancient Romans," Grace explained. "The oldest in my collection dates back to the seventeenth century. She's priceless, though everything does have a price," she added with a wry smile.

"Whatever happened to the lady that used to own the shop?" Thea asked. "Wasn't she a relative of yours?"

"Yes, my great-aunt. She died a while back."

"I'm sorry."

Grace acknowledged Thea's sympathy with a brief nod. "She was sick for a long time. Nash said she was ready to go. He was probably right, but I still miss her."

"I'm sure you do."

She seemed to lose her train of thought for a moment, then shook off the shadows and gave Thea a bright smile. "So what do you think? Does the shop look the way you remember it?"

"Oh, I've never been inside until now," Thea said. "Reggie would never allow it. She was afraid I'd break something."

"Well, that's too bad. Aunt Lillian always loved when children came in. She used to keep some dolls and a little tea set in the back room to keep them occupied while their mothers browsed the more expensive items. I'm surprised

you never came in with your grandmother. She was one of
Aunt Lillian's most ardent customers."

"My grandmother?"

"Mrs. Chapman." Grace bit her lip. "I hope I didn't
touch a nerve. I remember now that you were never very
close."

"You didn't touch a nerve. I'd forgotten she collected
dolls. I was rarely at her house." In truth, Thea knew very
little about June Chapman. Maybe that was another reason
the Indigo Dollhouse had enthralled her. Gazing through
the big bay window was like glimpsing a small corner
of her grandmother's strange world. Thea suspected that
might account in part for Reggie's disdain. *I swear she
sometimes acts as if those things are real. That can't be
healthy, living alone in that big old house with no company
but the cleaning lady and those creepy old dolls.*

"Make yourself at home," Grace said warmly. "Look
at whatever you like. I'll go pour the coffee."

Thea moved around the shop, gazing inside the display
cases as another memory tugged. She'd been eight or nine
the first time she'd ever visited her grandmother's home on
Crescent Hill. At least, that was the first and last time she
could remember. The house hadn't been a place for children with its polished wood floors and pristine white sofas.
She couldn't recall now why Reggie had left her there. She
must have been desperate if she'd called June for help.

Her grandmother had made her play on the sunporch
all day and she'd kept a cool, wary eye on Thea from the
open French doors. At some point, the doorbell rang and
she'd disappeared into the foyer to answer it. The shadowy interior had beckoned to Thea. Too curious for her
own good, she'd crept inside and padded down the hallway
until she came to an open doorway. Inside was a collection of the most beautiful porcelain dolls she could ever
imagine. Most of them were protected inside glass cabi-

nets, but a few had been artfully arranged around the room in intriguing vignettes.

Thea had already outgrown her own dolls by then. She was more into her bike and the secondhand rollerblades Reggie had found at a yard sale, but that forbidden collection had drawn her inside the room as surely as a moth to flame. She'd gone straight to a doll in a rocking chair. The blond curls and blue eyes had reminded her of Maya. Thea had trailed her fingers along the satin gown in reverence, the picked-at scab on the side of her hand long forgotten until a bead of blood left a rusty smudge on the delicate lace collar. Her grandmother had been speechless with rage when she found Thea trying to scrub away the stain at the bathroom sink. She'd grabbed her arm and dragged her back out to the sunporch.

Do you have any idea what you've done? That doll was priceless. You've ruined her beyond repair.

I'm sorry, Grandma—

Never call me that. Do you hear me? I am not your grandmother and you are nothing more to me than a horrible mistake. An abomination spawned by my son's weakness and that awful woman's conniving. He'd still be alive if not for her.

Thea hadn't known the meaning of "abomination." She'd gone home and looked it up. *A scandal, eyesore and disgrace.*

She'd never told Reggie about the doll incident, but as far as she knew, neither of them had set foot inside her grandmother's house after that day.

"How do you take your coffee?" Grace called out.

"Black is fine," Thea said as she tried to shake off the memory, but the lingering images left her unsettled.

"Come on back when you're ready." Grace glanced up when Thea appeared in the doorway. "I made blueberry muffins for my client. I always go overboard when I bake, so there're plenty. I thought you looked as if you could use a little something more than coffee." She motioned for Thea to sit.

Thea pulled out one of the painted chairs and sat. The kitchenette also showed the wear and tear of decades. The appliances were old and the ceiling stained from a persistent leak. A child-sized table and chairs with a miniature tea set and two raggedy dolls had been relegated to a dark corner. The sad little tableau depressed Thea for some reason.

"You really shouldn't have gone to so much trouble," she said as she picked up her cup and sipped.

Grace watched her with an anxious smile. "How is it?"

"Excellent. Hot and strong. Just the way I like it."

Her smile brightened. "Nash used to say he would have married me for my coffee alone."

"It's very good." Thea took another sip. "How long have you two been together?"

"We met during my senior year at Florida State. He was a police officer in Tallahassee. He ticketed me for speeding one day and then had the nerve to ask me to dinner that night. It was actually quite romantic." She smiled dreamily. "We were married six months later."

"What made you decide to come back to Black Creek?"

"My aunt got sick. I needed to come home and take care of her." She glanced across the table at Thea. "I don't know how much you remember about my family situation, but neither of my parents was all that reliable. They'd sometimes drop me off at my aunt's house and leave me there for days. God only knows what would have become of me without her. So I had to come back when she needed me."

"Of course," Thea murmured.

"Nash commuted for a while, but then he was offered the chief of police position here and we decided to relocate permanently. Despite what happened to your sister, Black

Creek seemed like a good place to raise a family back then. Now I sometimes wonder if we'd been better off in Tallahassee. It's ironic, I suppose, that my husband came here because of me and now I stay because of him." Longing flickered across her features before she dispatched the melancholy with another quick smile.

You're hiding something, Thea thought. Aloud she said, "Relationships can be complicated."

"Yes, but enough about my boring life. Tell me about DC."

"How do you know I live in DC?" Thea asked.

A brow lifted. "Have you forgotten what it's like to live in a town this small? Everyone in Black Creek knows you work for the FBI. Isn't that why you're here? To help search for Kylie Buchanan?"

"Not officially. I came to be with Reggie. But, naturally, I'll help in any way I can."

"It's just so hard to believe something like this could happen again in our community. And the police don't seem to have any leads." She gazed at Thea expectantly over the rim of her cup.

"Your husband would know more about the case than I do," she said.

"Nash isn't one to bring his work home. I'm always the last to know anything."

"I'm sure you know as much as I do," Thea murmured in appeasement and wondered when she could politely excuse herself. She was starting to feel a bit claustrophobic in the tight space. Or maybe it was the hard edges behind Grace Bowden's too quick smile and the slightly bitter aftertaste of her coffee that made Thea suddenly apprehensive.

"Kylie and Taryn came in here once," Grace said.

Thea's mind had wandered, but now she snapped herself back to attention. "When was this?"

"A few weeks ago. I'd seen them around town now and then, but that was the first time they'd come into the shop. Kylie was like a beautiful little doll, so quiet and shy, you'd hardly even know she was there. I remember that Taryn seemed distracted. She kept glancing out the window. Her nervous behavior made me wonder about all the rumors I'd heard."

"What rumors?"

"That her husband was controlling and abusive. It was obvious she and Kylie were afraid of their shadows. I just wanted to wrap my arms around that sweet little girl and never let go."

"I can understand the impulse," Thea said. "How long were they here?"

Grace shrugged. "No more than ten minutes. After they left, they went down the street to the back entrance of the park. Kylie played on the swings while Taryn watched from the shade. After a while, a man came and sat beside her. I don't know why, but I had the impression they didn't want to be seen together."

Thea tried to picture the back entrance of the park in relation to the doll shop. Someone standing at the bay window would have to position herself just right to see all the way down the street and through the wrought-iron gate. Even then, she wasn't certain how much could be witnessed from that distance.

"You didn't recognize the man?" Thea asked.

"Oh, I did. He was Brother Eldon."

Eldon Mossey had been counseling Taryn since she'd left her husband, according to Thea's mother. Had the alleged clandestine meeting taken place before or after Taryn and Kylie had moved in with Reggie?

"You referred to him as Brother Eldon. I take it you go to his church?"

"Whenever I can. It's not always possible since I sometimes have appointments on Sunday."

"Did you ever see Kylie and Taryn at church?"

"A few times. Brother Eldon is quite the dynamic speaker. His sermons are so engrossing, I don't pay a lot of attention to the people around me."

Thea set aside her cup as she studied the woman's expression. "Did you attend service on the Sunday night before Taryn went missing?"

The question seemed to disturb Grace. She closed her eyes briefly and nodded. "Yes. I saw Taryn playing on the new playground equipment before the service. I remember thinking how happy she looked compared to the shy, scared little girl I'd seen in my shop. Who could have known then what would happen to that sweet child in a matter of hours?"

"Did you stay for the whole service or did you leave early?"

Grace gave her a puzzled look. "Why would you ask that?"

"I just wondered if you'd seen Taryn and Kylie after the service."

"I don't think so. Not that I recall."

"Can you remember the exact day they came into the shop?"

"Why? Do you think it's important?"

"Probably not, but you never know."

Grace nodded. "I'll have to check my calendar and see if anything comes back to me. I'll do whatever I can to help."

"You didn't mention their visit to your husband?" Thea asked. "I'm surprised he didn't already have you check the date."

Her brow furrowed in concentration. "I don't know that I even thought about it until now."

"Have you ever met Russ Buchanan?" Thea asked,

dropping any pretense that this was just a cordial reunion with an old school friend.

"Once, about a year ago. He came in looking for a birthday gift for Kylie. He was quite charming. A little too charming, if you know what I mean, but the rumors may have prejudiced my opinion." She got up and removed their plates. "Can I get you anything else?"

Thea took the hint and rose, too. "No, thanks. The coffee is excellent, but I need to be on my way."

Grace glanced over her shoulder as she stacked the plates in the sink. "It was good to catch up. I hope you'll stop by again if you get the chance."

"I'll try. Please do get back to me after you've checked your calendar." When Grace turned from the sink, Thea said, "You don't need to show me out."

Alone in the shop, she walked over to the bay window and glanced out. She could just make out the wrought-iron entrance to the back of the park, but no matter the angle, she couldn't glimpse inside the gate. Had Grace Bowden followed Taryn and Kylie to the park that day? Was that how she'd witnessed the clandestine meeting with Eldon Mossey? Maybe that was why she hadn't mentioned the incident to her husband. Her actions might be awkward to explain.

Thea started for the door, but an odd sound drew her around sharply. The melodic clacking was distant and elusive, like the tug of another old memory. She glanced around the faded shop as if the antique dolls in their dusty cases could somehow tell her what she needed to know.

Turning, she retraced her steps to the back room. Grace stood at the open door, staring out into a shady courtyard.

"What's that sound?" Thea asked.

The woman must have been deep in thought because she started and whirled, her hand flying to her heart.

"I'm sorry. I didn't mean to startle you," Thea said. "I'm curious about that sound."

Grace looked perplexed. "What sound? The dripping faucet? It's annoying, isn't it? I really need to call a plumber and get that thing fixed."

"No, not the faucet. That hollow, lyrical sound."

"Oh, you must mean my aunt's wind chime."

Thea stopped to listen. "That doesn't sound like any wind chime I've ever heard."

"No, it's wooden, but not like the cheap bamboo ones you see in discount stores. It was hand-carved by a local artisan. My aunt hung it in her white fringe tree for luck. Each chime has a distinct note. That's why the sound is so unusual." Grace stepped into the courtyard. "Sometimes, if the wind blows just right, it sounds like rain."

Like rain.

Something nudged at Thea's subconscious. A memory or an image that couldn't quite break free.

She followed the woman outside. The courtyard was cool and fragrant, a peaceful refuge from the noise of the busy street, yet Thea's disquiet deepened.

"Is this the sound you mean?" Grace went to stand beneath an ornamental tree, rippling her fingers through the wooden chimes that hung in varying lengths from one of the branches.

The hollow tubes were intricately carved with flowers and vines. No gaping mouths and eyes. Still, the hair prickled at the back of Thea's neck as she lifted her gaze. The Magnolia Hotel was just across the street. She could see the upper stories above the courtyard wall. It wasn't hard to pick out her room at the corner of the third floor and the window that opened onto the metal fire escape.

Was it possible she'd heard the wind chimes in her sleep last night? Had the hollow sound triggered bizarre dreams about the twig figures from Jake's photograph?

She turned to find Grace Bowden starring at her.

"Is something wrong?" Thea asked.

The woman smiled enigmatically as she rippled her fingers through the chimes. "I just love this sound."

Chapter Five

Jake was seated behind a table in the room Chief Bowden had designated for the FBI when he spotted Thea through the glass partition. She'd just come into the station and had stopped to show her badge and credentials to the uniformed officer at the front counter. The squad room was nearly empty. Most of the department was either on patrol, attached to a search party or assigned to one of the traffic stops. Jake saw her glance around curiously before the officer pointed her toward the back. She walked with a slight limp as she made her way through the maze of desks and cubicles. He got up and waited for her at the door.

"Thanks for coming," he greeted her.

She answered with a brief nod. "Of course. You said in your text you needed to see me as soon as possible." She took in his space with a glance. "Where's the rest of your team?"

"We had to set up a new command center at the courthouse. We ran out of space here. Most of the agents are either there or in the field. I haven't made the transition yet."

"You always did work best alone."

"Not anymore. I like to think I've become a team player."

"I suppose you have to be when you're in charge." Her gaze met his. Was that another note of censure he heard? A flicker of disappointment he detected in her eyes? Surely she didn't begrudge him his promotion and relocation. Because that would mean she still cared.

"I've learned to make the necessary adjustments," he said.

"Haven't we all?" She seemed to dismiss their past with a shrug. "So, what's up? I noticed a strange vibe when I came in just now. The officer at the front desk seemed on edge. You have news?"

"Nothing concrete and nothing good," he said then quickly added, "We haven't found Kylie."

"But there's been a break in the case?"

"Have a seat." He went around and took his place behind the laptop, closing the screen. "You want some coffee?"

She pulled out a chair and sat. "I just had coffee with the police chief's wife."

"I didn't know he was married," Jake said.

"I'm not surprised. You don't like small talk any more than I do."

"Then I'm going to surprise you by asking how you are."

She gave him a reluctant smile. "That's not really small talk, considering what happened yesterday."

"No, I guess it's not." He trailed his eyes over her features. Her skin looked pale in the artificial lighting and as fragile as parchment beneath the cuts and bruises. "Seriously, are you okay? You don't look so good."

His blunt assessment didn't seem to faze her. "I had a rough night. I think I dreamed about those weird twig things you showed me yesterday. And I kept hearing an odd sound all night. That sound is probably what triggered the nightmares."

"What kind of sound?"

"Hard to explain. Hollow and melodic is the best way I can describe it, but I know that won't make a lot of sense."

"It makes more sense than you know," Jake said. "That's the sound I heard in the woods yesterday before I discovered the figures hanging from a tree branch."

She stared at him. "That's a disturbing coincidence."

"Yes, it is."

"But I think I can explain the sound I heard," she quickly added. "There's a set of wooden wind chimes in the courtyard across the street from the hotel. My room looks down on it. The sound must have drifted up to me in my sleep."

"Do you know who owns the courtyard?"

"Yes. Grace Bowden. I saw the chimes myself before I came here. They look nothing like the figures you found."

Probably nothing to worry about, Jake decided, but he made a note to check out the chimes for himself. "It still seems a little coincidental that you would hear that particular sound in your sleep."

"Maybe. But it was a strange night all the way around," she said. "This morning I woke up queasy and disoriented. It took me a moment to even remember where I was." She paused. "If I didn't know better, I'd think I was drugged."

His voice sharpened in alarm. "Drugged? Where did you go last night?"

"Nowhere. I was with Reggie all afternoon until early evening. I left the hospital around eight and walked straight to the hotel, went up to my room, took a bath and then…" Her brow furrowed as she thought back. "Everything gets hazy after that. But memory loss isn't unusual under the circumstances. Car wrecks are stressful. People sometimes feel shock for days. I'm no exception."

"Shock could certainly explain the nightmares and the confusion," he agreed. "But it wouldn't hurt to see a doctor and get checked out."

"I was examined in the ER yesterday. I'll be fine in a day or two. I wouldn't have said anything, but I know how perceptive you can be. It was only a matter of time before you picked up on something. Then you would have weaseled it out of me one way or another."

He smiled. "If only it were that easy. I'm just glad you're okay. And Reggie? How's she doing?"

"She sounded surprisingly strong when I spoke to her earlier. She said she had a restful night."

"That's good to hear." He gave her another long scrutiny before dropping his regard.

"Jake." She leaned forward. "Are you going to tell me what's going on or not?"

"The police found the truck we think was involved in the hit-and-run. It was abandoned on a dirt road a few miles from the crash site. The vehicle had been torched, so no fingerprints or DNA, but we were able to recover the VIN number. The truck was reported stolen from a campsite near Lake Seminole a few days ago. It's possible the driver panicked after he hit you. He knew the highway patrol would be looking for the vehicle, so that's why he burned it."

"That doesn't explain why he followed us from the interstate and maintained the same distance until Reggie sped up," Thea said.

Jake picked up a pen and toyed with the cap. "Can you think of anyone who might harbor a grudge against Reggie?"

She didn't seem particularly surprised by the question. "As you noted yesterday, emotions run high in this town, especially when it comes to my mother."

"I'm not talking about gossip or even suspicions. I mean someone who has an actual vendetta."

His grim tone seemed to give her pause. "No one comes to mind. She and my paternal grandmother have never gotten along, but June is getting on up there in years. Back in the day, she could harbor a petty grudge for decades, but acting on a vendetta at her age? Just to be clear, that is what you're getting at, right? That someone deliberately ran us off the road to get even with Reggie? You must also think the driver is somehow connected to Kylie's disappearance. Why else involve yourself in a hit-and-run investigation?"

"It's a possibility on both counts," he said. "For the record, I don't see your grandmother being involved in either incident."

"Then who?"

"Do you remember a man named Derrick Sway?"

The name seemed to jolt her. She returned his scrutiny, her eyes narrowed and slightly accusing. "What does Derrick Sway have to do with Kylie Buchanan's abduction?"

"Just answer the question, please. Do you remember Derrick Sway or don't you?"

"Of course, I remember him. He was Reggie's boyfriend at the time of Maya's disappearance. The police hauled him in for questioning any number of times, from what I later read, but they never found anything to connect him to the kidnapping."

"What can you tell me about his relationship with Reggie?"

"I was only four years old at the time. You're asking a lot."

"I realize that."

She tucked back her hair, taking a moment to think about her response. "I don't know how helpful I can be. I have vivid memories about the night Maya disappeared, but I'd be surprised if even half of what I remember is real. It's possible—probable, even—that I've used everything I read and heard over the years to embellish a few vague images and impressions. For a time, I devoured everything I could get my hands on about the abduction."

"That's understandable," Jake said. "You never wanted to talk about it when we were together."

When we were together.

Their gazes clung for a moment before Thea glanced away. Did she remember, as he did, all those lazy Sunday mornings in bed, with their phones silenced and their coffee cooling on the nightstands? Something glimmered in her eyes that told him she did remember. But maybe that was only wishful thinking. His way of embellishing a delusion.

"It's still hard for me to talk about," she said. "Maya and I weren't identical twins but we looked a lot alike and we had a very strong bond. 'Two peas in a pod,' Reggie used to say. On the night she went missing, Maya climbed into my bed because she heard a dog baying in the woods and it scared her. I was hot so after she went to sleep, I moved over to her bed."

"You never told me that." Jake got up and walked around the table, leaning against the edge as he folded his arms and looked down at her.

"If I'd stayed in my own bed, maybe I would have been taken instead of Maya. Twenty-eight years later, I still wonder about that."

"Thea…"

Don't, her eyes seemed to plead. *Don't look at me that way.* As if he had the power *not* to look at her that way.

She cleared her throat. "Anyway, you were asking about Derrick Sway's relationship with my mother. They used to argue, sometimes loudly, but I never saw him lay a hand on her."

"How did he treat you and Maya?"

"He mostly ignored us. If he'd ever gotten physical, Reggie would have kicked him out. She had a lot of faults, but she wasn't shy about defending herself or her kids."

"Maybe she didn't know."

"If he'd done anything bad to us, I would remember," Thea insisted.

"That's not necessarily true," Jake said gently. "You know as well as I do that children often block traumatic memories."

"And yet I'm able to recall that howling dog as clearly as if it were yesterday."

"Isn't it possible—"

"No. Maya and I were inseparable back then. I would have known if he'd hurt her."

Jake didn't try to push the issue any further. "Did you know that Sway was in prison for ten years?"

"Reggie mentioned it once."

"Do you remember what she said about it?"

"Just that he finally got what was coming to him."

"That's a pretty powerful statement. What do you think she meant by that?" he asked in that same gentle tone.

"He was a thief and a drug dealer. I imagine that's what she meant."

"Did she suspect he had something to do with Maya's disappearance?"

"She never let on if she did."

"But they parted on bad terms."

"Relationships end for all kinds of reasons. Maybe she finally saw him for who he really was." Thea seemed to grow weary of the conversation. Or maybe she didn't like him poking around in her past. She was a private person who'd experienced tragedy at a young age. He hated stirring up all her old memories, but she'd be the first to agree that nothing could be off limits when a child's life was at stake.

She got up and walked over to the glass partition, studying the deserted squad room before turning to face him. "Reggie changed after Maya's disappearance. She stopped drinking and smoking, and started experimenting with religion."

"'Experimenting'? That's an odd way of putting it."

"Not if you knew Reggie."

"Do you know if she and Sway kept in touch?"

"I doubt it. When Reggie was done, she was done."

Like mother, like daughter, Jake thought.

Thea sighed. "This is getting very tedious. Why all the questions about Reggie and Derrick Sway? I think I deserve an explanation. It's obvious you regard him as a suspect, but why? You must have something more than an abandoned truck and a gut feeling to go on."

"He was released from prison several months ago. The last known address we have for him is his mother's home in Yulee. A police officer went by there yesterday afternoon, but Sway was nowhere to be found. His mother claims she hasn't seen him in weeks."

"That doesn't answer my question. Is he a suspect or isn't he?"

"Right now, he's certainly a person of interest."

"Why?" she demanded. "Stop beating around the bush and tell me what you have on him."

"There was a possible sighting of him a few weeks ago at Lake Seminole."

"Where the truck was stolen," Thea said. "What else?"

Now Jake was the one who considered his answer carefully. "Sway may be under the impression that Reggie was the one who turned him in to the police. If so, he could blame her for his incarceration."

Thea came back over to the table. "That's a very big if, isn't it? How would abducting Kylie Buchanan give him payback? Unless he thinks he can make Reggie relive Maya's disappearance. Or somehow frame her for the kidnapping."

"There may be an even darker motive," Jake said. "A neighbor said he mistook Taryn for you when he first noticed her and Kylie living at Reggie's house. He assumed Kylie was your daughter."

That seemed to take her aback.

"It's an understandable mistake from a distance," Jake said. "Especially if he hasn't seen you in years. You and Taryn have a similar build and coloring. Both blond. Both trim and fit. If Sway made the same assumption about Taryn and Kylie as the neighbor, he could have taken Kylie because he thought she was your daughter. Reggie's granddaughter."

Thea let out a breath. "My God. That's a chilling thought."

"It is."

She bit her lip as she contemplated the implications. "It still seems like a reach to me."

"I thought so, too, until the officer went to talk to his mother. He said the woman seemed scared to death of Sway. He was always trouble, according to her, but she hardly recognized him when he got out of prison. He was into some very disturbing things, apparently."

"Like 'making hideous twig dolls and hanging them in a tree behind my mother's house' kind of disturbing?"

"Mrs. Sway wouldn't elaborate, only that after he moved in, strangers started showing up at the house at all hours. She didn't know what they were up to, but she called them evil."

"Could she identify any of these people?"

"Unfortunately, no. She said they always stayed outside in the dark or came in through the back door, like they didn't want to be seen. If she questioned Derrick about what he was up to, he'd burn something in his bedroom to make her think he was setting the house on fire."

"That's sadistic."

"*Sadistic* would be a good word to describe his behavior, according to his mother."

"Where is he now?"

"She swears she doesn't know. She said he got a phone call a few weeks ago and took off in the middle of the night. She hasn't seen or heard from him since. But she did allow the officer inside to look through his room." Jake reached across the table for an evidence bag. "Most of his things had been cleared out, but the officer found this slid behind the baseboard in the closet."

Thea's face went even paler as she stared at the photograph in the bag. "This was found in his possession?"

"In his room, yes. Do you recognize it?" Jake asked.

She closed her eyes. "It's a snapshot of Maya standing on our front porch. It was taken on our fourth birthday, just a couple of months before she went missing. Reggie used to keep that photograph on the refrigerator where she could see it every morning when she had her coffee. Then one day she boxed up all the photographs and put them away in her closet. Maybe that was the day both of us gave up on Maya ever coming home."

"How long ago did you last see this photograph?"

He saw her take a deep breath as she thought back. "I don't know. I was still a kid. Maybe ten or eleven when she put everything away."

Maya had been taken when she was four years old. That was a long time to wait for a sister to come home. "The photo has been torn in two."

"So I noticed."

"The raw edge looks like it's been singed." Jake paused. "Were you in the other half of the photograph?"

"Yes." She couldn't seem to tear her eyes from her sister's image. "You can tell from the position of Maya's arm that we were holding hands. We always did when Mama took our picture."

Jake had never heard her call her mother anything but Reggie. She had a soft, faraway look in her eyes, as if she'd slipped back in time. He wanted to reach over and take her hand, to tell her everything would be okay, but the present-day Thea knew better. "How do you think Sway came to be in possession of this photograph?"

"I have no idea. There's no way Reggie would have ever given it to him. He must have come into her house and stolen it at some point or else there were two similar photographs and he took one when he left."

"Why would he do that? You said he showed no particular interest in you and Maya. He ignored you. Why tear you out of the photograph? Why keep an image of your sister all these years?"

"It makes me sick to my stomach to even contemplate." She handed him back the bag. "You think he took her, don't you? Maya, I mean."

"You said yourself the police never found anything to connect him to her disappearance. Even so, I don't think we can discount the possibility."

She was visibly shaken but trying desperately to cling to her composure. "What can I do to help?"

"You've already done your part. You've answered all my questions. Now the best thing for you to do is to go be with your mother at the hospital."

"Just like that. No further need of my services."

Jake gave her a soft smile. "You know that's not what I mean. We've got people actively searching for Derrick Sway. Every law enforcement body in the state is on alert. I'll let you know as soon as I hear anything. You have my word."

"I guess that will have to be enough."

He placed the evidence bag on the table and turned back to her. "I know I don't have to tell you this, but please be careful. Even Sway's own mother is terrified of him."

"The torn photograph seems to indicate he has no interest in me," she said.

"Or maybe it indicates the exact opposite. If he abducted Kylie out of mistaken identity, he's probably been following the news and is aware of who she is by now. If he's out for revenge against Reggie, his desire for payback won't have been satisfied. In fact, he may be even more determined. Reggie should be safe enough in the hospital. Sway won't show his face in public. He'd be too easily recognized. But you need to watch your back."

"I'm not concerned for my own safety," Thea said. "What if your theory is true? What happens to Kylie if Sway took her by mistake?"

Jake said nothing for a moment. He didn't have to.

"All we can do is stay focused and keep looking."

"Why do I get the feeling you're holding something back?"

He ran a hand across his eyes. "It's nothing tangible. Even with this new lead, I can't help thinking we're missing something hidden in plain sight. Something darker than any of us has imagined." He gave her a worried look. "I can't explain it, but I can feel it."

Chapter Six

Thea felt drained after her conversation with Jake, which wasn't surprising. She'd prepared herself for an emotional roller-coaster ride when she'd made the decision to come to Black Creek. The similarities in Maya's and Kylie's abductions were bound to stir old memories. She'd spent a lifetime building up her defenses, but the news about Derrick Sway combined with the lingering shock from the car crash had left her temporarily vulnerable. Physically, she was nowhere near a hundred percent, so when Jake had offered her a ride to the hospital, she'd gratefully accepted. Why push herself beyond her limit just to prove she could get there on her own steam?

She waited for him outside in the shade of the building, relieved to have a moment alone to regroup. She wanted to believe he'd been forthcoming about Derrick Sway and what they'd found at his mother's house, but something was always held back from the public. Since she had no official standing in the investigation, she couldn't expect to be read in on every new development, but how could she protect herself—let alone Reggie—if she wasn't given the whole picture?

A day ago, she might have dismissed his mistaken identity theory out of hand, but something strange had happened to her last night. She could explain away the nightmares and disorientation, but what about the doubts that niggled at the back of her mind? What about those vague images that drifted at the fringes of her memory?

What if Derrick Sway had been creeping around on the fire escape last night?

What if he'd slipped through the window while she'd been soaking in the bathtub or sleeping in her bed?

Thea shivered despite the heat. That torn photograph was the first lead they'd had in her sister's case in twenty-eight years, not to mention the first concrete link to Sway. Little wonder she felt blindsided by Jake's revelation. The notion that Maya's abductor had still been around all these years, that he might even have kept a picture of her with him in prison, sickened Thea to her very core.

What had he done with the other half of that photograph? Had Thea's image been tossed in the trash years ago or did Sway have another purpose for her in mind?

For a dizzying moment, she thought she might have to vomit in the grass. She sucked in air and tried to focus. The faintness subsided, but her fears only grew stronger. Jake was right. Something very dark pulsed beneath the surface of this town. Two children had gone missing from her mother's home. Maya was lost forever, but Kylie Buchanan still had a fighting chance.

Three percent, Thea thought fiercely.

No way could she sit idly by at the hospital while another child was in danger, perhaps from the same monster that had taken her sister. Reggie was safe for now. She didn't need a daughter she barely knew hovering over her. Thea's time would be better spent out searching for Kylie Buchanan. Jake was the best at what he did, but Thea wasn't without experience and insight. She knew the town and she knew the people. She knew things he didn't. *Go back to the beginning. Go back to the place where Kylie and Maya were taken.*

The roar of a car engine drew her attention to the street. She thought at first Jake had brought his vehicle around to pick her up, but instead a silver Mercedes wheeled to the curb in front of the police station. A tall man in his late thirties got out and strode toward the front steps, pausing on the bottom stair when he caught sight of Thea in the shade. A look of bemusement swept over his features. He stepped back down on the sidewalk.

"Excuse me, miss. Are you okay?"

"Yes, I'm fine, thank you." She glanced at the street. "I'm waiting for my ride."

He hesitated. "I know this may sound trite, but have we met?"

"I don't think so," Thea said, although she'd quickly deduced who he was from the make and color of his car. Even on such a hot day, Russ Buchanan was sharply dressed in a gray suit and crisp white shirt. He was tall, trim, and Thea supposed he was handsome if one could ignore his imperious demeanor.

"Wait a minute. I know who you are," he said in a low drawl. "I can see the resemblance now. You're Reggie Lamb's daughter."

"Thea," she said with a nod.

"The FBI agent. I heard you were in town. I'm Russ Buchanan." He moved off the sidewalk and approached her in the shade. Thea couldn't help noticing that every lock of his dark wavy hair lay perfectly in place and that even with a few feet between them she could catch a whiff now and then of something understated and expensive.

She gave him a subtle assessment as she offered her sympathy. "I'm very sorry for what you're going through, Mr. Buchanan. My family has been where you are. If there's anything I can do—"

He cut her off. "Do you mean that?" His tone was genial, but the eyes that locked onto hers were cold and empty. Or was she letting the accounts of his abuse color her first impression of him?

Thea tried to tamp down her prejudgment. "Yes, of course I mean it."

He set his jaw as the cordiality drained from his voice and he took a step toward her. "Then you tell that hag of a mother of yours to stay the hell away from my wife."

And there it was. The underlying threat of violence. The impervious disregard for anyone else's feelings or welfare. So much for giving him the benefit of the doubt.

Thea stared into those soulless eyes without flinching. "Surely that's a decision your wife can make for herself."

"The last time she made a decision for herself, my daughter ended up missing. Taryn is now learning the hard way that actions have consequences."

Thea's gaze narrowed slightly. What did he mean by that? Aloud, she said, "I understand the need to blame someone—"

"Oh, I know exactly who to blame," he assured her. "Let me put it to you this way. If anything happens to my little girl, Reggie Lamb will wish she'd gone to prison twenty-eight years ago when she murdered her own kid."

Thea kept her expression neutral as anger and dread battled inside her. The worst thing she could do was let a sociopath like Russ Buchanan believe he'd gotten under her skin. He obviously intended to provoke a confrontation, maybe create an unpleasant scene in front of the police station that he could somehow use against Reggie.

"Are you threatening my mother, Mr. Buchanan?"

"I'm simply letting you know that I'm on to her. And for the record, I'm on to you, too. I know why you're here. If you think you can use your influence to steer the investigation away from Reggie, I would strongly suggest you reconsider."

"What are you talking about?"

He gave her an odd smirk before glancing up the steps to the police station. "I knew as soon as I heard you were in town it would only be a matter of time before you tried to insinuate yourself into the investigation. That's why I'm here, actually. To warn Chief Bowden to block you from anything related to my daughter's case."

"The more people working to find your daughter, the better, I would think."

"Yes, you would think that. After all, it would be so much easier to destroy incriminating evidence if you were assigned to Kylie's case."

"I won't be assigned to Kylie's case," she told him. "But even if I were, I'd never destroy or compromise evidence regardless of who it incriminates."

"You say that now, but what happens if you suddenly find yourself standing between your own mother and prison?"

"You seem so certain of her guilt," Thea said. "Why is that, I wonder?"

"Her history speaks for itself."

"No. It's not that." She searched his face, letting a pensive note seep into her voice. "If I didn't know better, I'd think you're trying to deflect."

Another sneer flashed, along with a subtle gleam in his eyes that warned her she couldn't touch him. He was in full control.

We'll see about that.

"Reggie took your wife and child into her home when they had no place else to go. I think that's the real reason for your animosity," Thea said. "You resent her for giving Taryn and Kylie a way out."

His dark gaze flickered for the first time. He didn't like being reminded of his failure to keep his family in line. Thea couldn't get a read on his true feelings for Kylie, but he made no attempt to disguise his utter disdain for the child's mother.

"Taryn is a sick woman," he said. "For as long as I've known her, she's been prone to depression and delusions, especially when she's off her medication. Your mother took advantage of her fragile mental state. She manipulated Taryn into believing that I was a danger to my own wife and child. Ironic—isn't it?—considering Reggie's past."

"She was never charged or convicted of anything," Thea reminded him.

"A box was dug up in the woods behind her house containing her daughter's DNA. That's right," he said as if interpreting Thea's surprise. "I know all about that box. I had Reggie Lamb thoroughly investigated the minute I found out Taryn had moved our daughter into her home. No matter how long ago it happened, people in this town remain unconvinced of your mother's innocence. Some of them believe she murdered your sister and buried her hastily in the woods. Then she went back later and moved the body. Maybe she threw her in a lake or dug a deeper hole somewhere more remote."

Thea suppressed another shiver. "That's quite a vivid picture you've painted."

He'd gone straight for the jugular, but now he softened his voice and demeanor as easily as a chameleon superficially changing its color. "I can only imagine how it must have been for you. Your twin sister, the person you were closest to in the whole world, abandoned to a cold, hidden grave by your own mother."

He was good. Thea would give him that. Even with her experience and insight, she felt the pull of his devious accusations.

He canted his head. "I feel for you. I truly do. I can't imagine what it must have been like growing up in the house with that woman, feeling her lips against your cheek before you went to sleep. Hearing her footsteps in the middle of the night, knowing what you knew."

You creepy bastard.

He put out a hand in supplication. "Please understand. I have nothing against you personally, Agent Lamb. I wish you no ill will. In fact, I was very sorry to hear about your accident. Roads have become hazardous places these days. People become enraged over the slightest infraction."

"Sometimes for nothing more than a perceived infraction," Thea said. She waited a beat. "Do you own a black pickup, Mr. Buchanan?"

"What would I do with a pickup truck? Although I suppose they're useful for hauling things."

"You're a defense attorney, correct? A successful one, from what I hear. That gives you access to an extensive roster of criminal clients, some of whom might be persuaded to do any number of dirty deeds for the right price. I wonder if one of them owns a pickup. Or would be willing to steal one for you."

He shook his head sadly. "Such a wild imagination. It must be a burden in your line of work. If you're not careful, you might start to see and hear all sorts of strange things."

Like hollow dolls with twig limbs and gaping holes for mouths and eyes? "Do you know an ex-con named Derrick Sway?"

"No, why? Is he someone important?" Was that a slight twitch at the corner of his mouth? The barest telltale flicker deep down in his cold, calculating eyes?

"If I were to dig into Derrick Sway's background, I wouldn't find your name on any of his court filings?"

"You bitch." He purposely let his mask slip, giving her another glimpse of the violence that simmered beneath the surface of his carefully refined façade. "You have no idea who you're dealing with."

"On the contrary," Thea said. "I know exactly who you are."

"Then you should be smart enough to keep your nose out of my business." He reached out as if to grab her arm, but the look on Thea's face stopped him cold.

"Or what?" she demanded. "You'll have someone run me off the road?"

He dropped his hand to his side and smiled. "You said it yourself. I have a whole cadre of criminal clients at my disposal. You'd be surprised at how creative and enthusiastic—not to mention, grateful—some of them can be."

"THAT DIDN'T APPEAR to be a friendly conversation," Jake observed when Thea climbed into his SUV.

"Anything but," she confirmed as she watched the silver Mercedes peel away from the curb and swerve into traffic, narrowly missing an oncoming vehicle. Evidently, he'd changed his mind about talking to the police chief, at least for now.

Jake swore under his breath. "Good way to get somebody killed. You must have really touched a nerve if he's driving like that in front of the police department."

Thea made a disgusted face. "He's under the impression the police can't or won't touch him. He's actually pretty open about it. I wouldn't be surprised if he has a friend or two on the inside protecting him. They're probably also feeding him information about the investigation. He certainly knew I was in town."

"I wouldn't read too much into that," Jake said. "Word gets around in a place like this. Half the town probably knows you're here by now." He glanced in the rearview mirror before merging with traffic.

"What's your take on Chief Bowden?"

He gave her a surprised look. "Seriously? You think the police chief is in Buchanan's pocket?"

"I'm just asking what you think of him."

Jake focused on the road. "He's a good cop. Dedicated and by the book. Mostly."

"Mostly?"

He gave her another look. "Come on. We both know no one is perfect. Liberties are sometimes taken when a child's life is in danger."

"Did you know he used to be with the Tallahassee Police Department? According to his wife, they moved down here so that she could take care of her ailing aunt. I got the impression from Grace that she would like to move back to the city, but she stays here because of her husband. I guess that makes me wonder about him."

"Why? Because he likes living and working in a small town? There's something to be said for getting out of the rat race." He stopped at a traffic light. Up ahead, the silver Mercedes sped through another intersection and disappeared.

"You wouldn't last a month in a backwater place like this," Thea scoffed. "Neither would I, for that matter."

"I can tell you this about Nash Bowden. He did everything right when he received the call about a missing child. He alerted the field office immediately so that CARD could be activated. Not a moment's hesitation over territory. He's also the one who initiated the door-to-door canvass and K-9 tracking. His quick response saved us hours of valuable time once we were on the scene."

"You like him," Thea said.

"I respect what I've seen of his work. I'd be very surprised if he could be bought off by anybody, let alone a man like Russ Buchanan."

Thea settled back against the seat as the light changed and they moved down the street. "I trust your judgment. It's just... I got a strange vibe from his wife this morning.

Like she was hiding something. Like maybe things aren't so great in the Bowden marriage."

"How is that relevant?"

Thea shrugged. "Maybe it's not, but sometimes people do things out of character when money becomes a problem. Grace runs an antique doll shop she inherited from her aunt. You should see the place. It looks as if it hasn't been updated in fifty years and the display cases are half empty. She says she does most of her business online, so maybe that accounts for the lack of inventory in the shop. But how much of a living can someone make selling dolls?"

"Depends on how rare and valuable they are, I guess." He turned to give her a quick scrutiny. "What are you thinking? That the chief takes money under the table to pad their bank account? Or are you suggesting the Bowdens are somehow involved in Kylie Buchanan's abduction?"

"It sounds ridiculous when you say it out loud," she conceded. "It's possible I imagined the weirdness with Grace. She caught me off guard and God knows I'm not at my best at the moment. Still…"

"What is it?"

"Maybe you're not the only one who has a premonition," she said.

He frowned at the road. "I never called it that."

"Relax. It was a lame joke. But like you, I can't help feeling that we're missing something." When he didn't respond, she said his name softly. "Jake. You do know I was kidding, right?"

He gave her a lingering glance. "Yeah. Bad memories."

About what? Thea wondered. Bad memories from their time together or from his early years in foster care? He never talked much about those days. Neither of them had been willing to open up about their pasts, but she'd gleaned enough to know he'd had a tough childhood. Abused and abandoned by the time he was seven. No wonder he fought so hard for the children who went missing.

She thought about the scars on his back and the deeper wounds inside his soul. For all her faults, Reggie had never mistreated her children. She'd hardly ever raised her voice to them. Thea couldn't imagine what it must have been like to lay awake at night trying to intuit his tormentor's next move. Honing his senses to detect the slightest sound or motion and then scrambling under the bed or into the closet to escape a drunkard's inexplicable wrath.

Jake's brooding scowl tore at Thea's resolve. She resisted the urge to reach across the console and take his hand. Neither of them had ever believed in any kind of psychic phenomenon, but at times his instincts seemed uncanny. She would never try to label his insight any more than she would attempt to explain the feel of a child's hand against her cheek in the dead of night. The overwhelming certainty at times that Maya was near could be nothing more than wishful thinking, a sensation akin to the phantom ache of a missing limb.

"Are you okay?"

Jake's voice cut into her reverie. She sighed. "Bad memories like you said."

"You've had a rocky homecoming."

"Yes. Although it's hard to remember a time when I considered this place home."

He gave her a quick perusal. "You never told me why Russ Buchanan got so riled up earlier."

"I guess I pushed the wrong buttons. He had a definite agenda when he approached me. He insists Reggie is responsible for his daughter's disappearance, and he thinks if I'm involved in the investigation, I'll hide or destroy evidence that could incriminate her."

"We both know that's not true."

His certainty gratified her, but Thea couldn't quite turn

off the little voice in her head that reminded her of the discrepancy she'd uncovered in Reggie's statement. She hadn't told anyone what she'd found, even Jake. Why make a mountain out of a molehill about an open window? But no matter how hard she tried to convince herself Reggie's omission was just an oversight or an innocent mistake, Thea had never quite put those doubts to rest.

She studied Jake's profile before turning to stare out at the passing shops. "I think Buchanan is the one who had us run off the road yesterday. He didn't outright admit it, of course. He's too smart for that. He said just enough to try to get under my skin."

"Did he succeed?"

"He's a narcissistic sociopath who beats his wife. What do you think?"

"You need to be careful with Buchanan," Jake warned. "Whether he has the local law in his pocket or not, he's the kind of guy who'd take satisfaction in causing as much trouble as he can for you and your mother."

"I didn't seek him out. He's the one who came to me. He said he wanted a word with the chief, but I wonder if someone tipped him off that I was at the station. In any case, I'm not afraid of a creep like Buchanan. Reggie certainly isn't," she added with a note of pride.

"Like mother, like daughter," Jake muttered.

"What?"

"Nothing. What else did he say?"

"I think he may know Derrick Sway. I'm pretty sure I detected a slight reaction when I mentioned Sway's name."

"Pretty sure?"

"I may not possess your keen powers of observation, but I have a strong suspicion there's a connection. I think Sway may be a former client."

"Ten years ago when Sway went to prison, Buchanan would have barely been out of law school," Jake pointed out.

"Which would have made him hungry for even a low-life client like Derrick Sway. It's also possible he came in later to handle an appeal or some other type of legal proceeding. I know it's a long shot, but so is your mistaken identity theory."

"I'll have it checked out," Jake promised. He shifted the blinker to merge into the right lane.

Thea sat up. "Wait. I've changed my mind about going to the hospital."

"Isn't your mother expecting you?"

"I'll give her a call and tell her I've been delayed. She'll understand."

His gaze turned suspicious. "What are you up to?"

"Nothing. I just want to spend some time in the house where I grew up."

"Why?"

"Because I want to see where Kylie was taken."

"Kylie or Maya?"

She swung around to face him. "Does it matter? If your theory is true, the same monster took both girls."

"It's too early to draw that conclusion," Jake cautioned.

"Maybe. But I know you're thinking it, too."

Ever since he'd shown her the torn photograph, Thea had felt compelled to return to her old house, to revisit the room she'd once shared with her twin sister. To spend time in the place where she'd felt closest to Maya. If she closed her eyes, she could almost feel the breeze from that open window...she could almost hear her sister's tremulous voice in the dark. *I'm scared, Sissy.*

"You don't have to stay," she said a few minutes later when Jake turned down Reggie's street.

He gave her a skeptical look. "You expect me to drop you off and leave you without any transportation?"

"Why not? I know my way around the area." But despite her familiarity with the surroundings, Thea was starting to get a surreal vibe from the neighborhood. She'd forgotten how old the houses were in this part of town, how the mature trees blocked all but slivers of sunlight in places. The lots were bigger on Reggie's side of the street. Rather than backing up to another row of houses, the yards ran right up against several acres of untouched woodland.

If you walked all the way through the trees, you came out near an opening in the rocks that led into one of the few known caves located outside the state park system. The locals had dubbed the entrance the Devil's Pit, a gross exaggeration since the initial descent was no more than fifteen or twenty feet. Most of the cave was dry, but an underground river ran beneath the structure, bubbling up into pools in some of the caverns. Thea had never gone down into even the first room. She wasn't claustrophobic, but the place frightened her. Years ago, two teenagers had become disoriented trying to find a way out; they'd drowned inside an underwater passageway. Now the whole landscape around the cave seemed heavy and oppressive. Or maybe she'd watched too many horror movies growing up.

"Has anyone searched the cave?" she asked.

"The local police sent a search party in with a guide early on. From what I understand, even some of the dry passageways are hard to navigate. They searched as far as they could go, but they didn't find anything."

"The locals didn't find those twig figures in the trees, either," Thea reminded him.

"I'll talk to Chief Bowden. Can't hurt to take another look." He pulled up in the driveway and cut the engine.

"You really don't have to stay," Thea said. "I know you're needed elsewhere."

He watched her for a moment as if trying to detect an ulterior motive. "You're not planning on going down in the cave alone, I hope."

She gave a slight shudder. "I wouldn't do that. I meant what I said. I want to spend some time in the house. I'll be fine. I'll call a cab when I'm ready to leave." Her attention strayed to the faint lettering at the side of porch. *Murderer.*

Memories assailed her as she moved her focus over the vandalized siding and up the porch steps to the place where the photograph of her and Maya had been taken. Their birthday dresses had been identical except for the color. Maya's pink and Thea's yellow.

She glanced at Jake. He stared almost trancelike out the windshield toward the backyard and the woods beyond. His utter stillness unnerved her.

"What is it?"

He gave a casual nod at the house. "You go on inside and do what you need to do. While I'm here, I may as well take a walk back through the woods." He opened the door and got out.

Thea climbed out after him and came around the vehicle to confront him. "Why do I get the feeling you're the one who's up to something? You know I don't like it when you get all cryptic. What's going on in that head of yours?"

"Nothing. I won't be long."

Thea let out a frustrated breath. "I forgot how maddening it is when you get like this."

He turned with a frown. "I'm not being cryptic. If someone has been creeping around your mother's place, they may have left another clue."

"Are you sure that's all it is? You didn't see or hear something I should know about?"

"I didn't see or hear anything. I'm being straight with you. I'm here, so why not take another look?"

She tried another tact. "Maybe we shouldn't separate."

"I'll be fine."

He started to turn away but she caught his arm. "Call or text if you need me. You know I'll have your back, right?"

He nodded. "That's the one thing I've never had to worry about."

Chapter Seven

The woods were too quiet. Jake half expected to hear that strange hollow melody as he headed deeper into the trees, but nothing so much as a birdcall came to him. It was almost as if someone else moving through the woods ahead of him had scared all the wildlife away.

He wasn't anticipating trouble, but if he'd learned anything during his time as a federal agent, it was always best to prepare for the worst. His weapon was holstered, and he had his phone and a flashlight with him in case he decided to walk all the way to the cave. He had no intention of descending alone, but he could at least search the terrain around the entrance and shine his light inside the pit. If he saw anything suspicious, he'd call for backup. For now, he wasn't about to pull his team away from their current assignments to assist on a hunch that could end up a wild-goose chase.

He kept to the path, walking slowly but steadily as he searched tree branches and all through the underbrush, still uncertain of his objective. He hadn't seen or heard anything out of the ordinary. He'd had no bursts of insight, no strong compulsion to enter the woods like he'd experienced the day before. Just a persistent needle at the back of his neck that told him to keep walking. Keep looking. *Children don't disappear into thin air.*

Pausing on the path, he glanced over his shoulder. Sunlight glimmering down through the canopy created a strange surreal effect on the trail. For a moment, he could have sworn someone stood in the shadows, just beyond reach of the dappled light. His imagination, of course. His dazzled vision had conjured an image of Kylie's faceless abductor as he'd traveled through the woods that night, carrying the child in his arms. He'd probably subdued her back at the house with bindings and duct tape or even drugs. She was a light burden. He would have walked at an easy pace, unafraid of detection. The woods would have been dark enough to give him plenty of cover.

The vision was so vivid that Jake felt compelled to step off the path and allow the imagined kidnapper to pass. Then he moved quickly along the trail until the landscape began to shift from deep forest into a craggy hillock. He'd walked a good two miles from Reggie's house and now found himself in the middle of nowhere. No sign of life except for a distant tumbledown farmhouse that had been eaten by kudzu.

He followed a ten-foot metal fence until he came to a padlocked gate. Posted signs discouraged exploration of the cave without an experienced guide and waivers from the property owner. However, as Lyle Crowder had mentioned the day before, there was nothing preventing anyone from climbing over the fence and descending at their own risk.

Jake tested the metal links for an electrical current before he climbed over. Landing softly on the other side, he took a moment to scout his surroundings before scrambling up the rugged terrain to the cave entrance—a narrow hole between two boulders that dropped straight down into the earth. Crouching at the edge, he angled his flashlight beam inside the natural cylinder. About fifteen to twenty feet down, the passageway appeared to open up into a larger cavern.

He lowered himself to the ground and hung over the opening, shining the flashlight beam along the limestone walls as far down as he could see. Time and erosion had carved plenty of hand-and footholds in the soft rock. Descent would be easy. No need for a rope and harness.

Even so, he still had no intention of going down into the cave alone. Hadn't he cautioned both Thea and Lyle Crowder against that very thing? Besides, it seemed like a waste of time. People far more familiar with the underground structure than he was had already searched the passageways.

So why did he linger? Why did he suddenly hear Thea's voice reminding him that he'd found the twig figures in the woods *after* the police and volunteers had conducted a thorough canvass?

No sooner had the image of those strange totems materialized in his head than a sound came to him straight up out of the earth. He could have sworn he heard the odd clacking of the twig bodies as they bumped together in the breeze. He listened intently, trying to determine if the noise might have come from the woods rather than from deep inside the cave. The hollow melody drifted up to him again, followed by a different sound—a faint, unidentifiable mewling.

A chill skated down Jake's backbone. He let himself imagine for a moment the end of the kidnapper's journey. He would have come out of the woods near the fence just as Jake had. Scaling the chain links with his precious burden would have been a challenge unless he was exceptionally strong or had cut the fence earlier. Jake hadn't seen any holes, but the damage could have been hidden by scrub brush. Then what? Had he climbed into the cave with Kylie and hidden her body in a tunnel or simply tossed her over the edge? Left for dead in a pitch-black environment, could the child have crawled deep inside one of the dry passageways to hide? Was that how the search party had missed her?

More than likely the kidnapper hadn't come this way at all. Maybe the sound Jake heard was nothing more than a draft of air whistling through one of the tunnels.

But what if it wasn't? What if Kylie was down there somewhere? Still alive and whimpering in pain and fear as she ran out of time and air? What if she crawled into one of the passageways filled with water? Jake knew he would never have a moment's peace until he made certain.

He called his second-in-command and told him where he was and what he intended to do. The agent responded in alarm. "Sounds like a risky move, boss. Shouldn't you wait for backup? Be even better if we can find a local guide to go down with us."

"We may not have that kind of time," Jake said. "I saw a diagram of the cave in Chief Bowden's office. I can pull up a similar image on my phone before I go in. As long as I stick to the main passageways, I should be fine. Gear up and get here as soon as you can."

Jake thought about calling Thea, but she'd come running and he didn't want to take the chance she'd crawl down into the pit to look for him. He wasn't the overly protective type when it came to a trained agent, but Thea had admitted earlier that she wasn't physically or mentally herself since the accident. Under the best of circumstances, a cave environment could be disorienting. It was too easy to wander along a passageway and become lost and confused by the strange topography. He'd let her know his position as soon as his backup arrived.

Tucking away the flashlight, he bent and scooped up some loose pebbles from the dirt to make a little pile beside the entrance. Then he squeezed through the crevice and lowered himself inside.

So this is the Devil's Pit, he thought as he felt for handholds and footings in the limestone. He enjoyed wall climbing at his gym, so the relatively short descent wasn't much of a challenge, nor did he expect to have any trouble getting out. The biggest obstacles were the narrowness of the opening and the absence of light once he'd descended a few feet. The close confines made him a little uneasy at first, but then he was through the narrow shaft in a matter of seconds and, after maneuvering over the rocky debris at the bottom, he could stand upright. He took out the flashlight and swept the beam over the cavern.

He'd done some cave diving in his college days, strictly amateur and always with an experienced guide. Dry caves were a whole different ecosystem. He turned off the flashlight and stood in the dark for several minutes, letting his eyes adjust as he tried to tune into the keening he'd heard from above. When nothing came to him, he wondered again if he'd let his imagination get the better of him. What if he hadn't? What if Kylie was down there somewhere?

"Kylie! Kylie Buchanan! If you can hear my voice, call out to me, okay? Don't be afraid. I'm here to take you home."

His voice echoed back to him. Jake waited until the resonance died away before he called to her again. "Kylie, can you hear me?"

Nothing.

After his eyes and equilibrium had adjusted to the blackness, he turned on the flashlight and shone it once again around the large cavern. A narrow opening in the wall opposite the entrance presumably led back into a second cavern. From what he remembered of the diagram, this particular cave system was a string-of-pearls formation—a series of tight tunnels opening into larger caverns one after the other for a couple of miles or so with dozens of belly-crawl passageways that led to nowhere. A headlamp would have made exploring those dead-end spaces easier, but he'd have to make do with his flashlight. At least it was waterproof if he ran into submerged areas in the passageways.

As he had aboveground, he marked the shaft where he'd climbed down with a pile of pebbles before he set out. He judged the temperature to be a mild seventy degrees or so, a welcome respite from the relentless heat on the surface. Crossing the floor, he aimed his light down the first passageway. Someone had left a candle and matches at the entrance, but he didn't use them. He left another pile of stones beside the candle and entered the first tunnel. Crawling over the loose rocks in the narrow space would have been tricky but not impossible for a four-year-old child. The image drove Jake forward.

He emerged from the passageway into another room. He could hear water dripping nearby, and the air became dank and musty. The speleothems were more pronounced in this cavern. The eerie limestone formations glistened in the beam of his light. Curious, he took out his phone. No signal.

According to the diagram, an underground river ran beneath the cave floor. From here on in, he might well come upon passageways at least partially filled with water. The prospect was unnerving, but he wasn't about to turn back. He left his stone bread crumbs at the entrance and moved into the next passage. Several feet in, he had to drop to his hands and knees and then to his elbows and belly. The stone was wet and muddy beneath him, but at least he found no standing water.

The third and largest cavern yet was riddled with tunnels. Jake wanted to believe the search party had been through every square inch of those channels, but the territory was rugged with lots of dead ends and, in those first critical hours, even professionals could get careless in the initial frenzy.

He felt the onset of a very bad feeling. There were too many places to hide a small body down here. Too many narrow tunnels and tubes a child might have squeezed into and become lost and disoriented.

"Hello?" His voice echoed back to him, as hollow as the clacking figures. "Kylie, can you hear me?"

He waited for the sound of his voice to die away again before he called out, "Don't be afraid. I'm a police officer. I'm here to take you to your mommy."

He could have sworn he heard a shuffling sound from one of the tunnels. Squatting in front of the entrance, he shone the light into the narrow channel. "Kylie?"

Something flew out at him. The sudden movement startled him and he lost his balance, sprawling backward on the floor as he threw up an arm to cover his head. The light had disturbed a colony of bats. Jake waited for the migration to pass and then, gagging at the smell, crawled far enough into the tunnel to see all the way to the dead end. Nothing.

Either he'd imagined the shuffling sound or he'd heard the bats stirring. Being belowground could play tricks on the senses. Not to mention the havoc certain fungi and bacteria could wreak on one's perception. He paused to clear his head. Was he crazy for coming down here alone? Yes, but he'd had no choice. Nor was backtracking to the entrance and crawling up out of the pit to wait for reinforcements an option. That would take too much time when he was very much afraid every second counted. His team knew where he was and he'd left a trail. Nothing for him to do now but keep going.

Methodically, he made his way around the third cavern, checking the dead-end tunnels that he could fit into and angling his light into the others. When he finished, he stacked stones in front of the next passageway before he entered.

He exited into another chamber where the underground river bubbled up into a large pool surrounded by slick limestone walls. He didn't immediately see another tunnel although, according to the diagram, the cave went on for at least another mile or so. Maybe the passageway into the next opening was underwater. Given the challenging terrain, he didn't see how Kylie could have made it this far by herself.

Crouching on a slippery ledge above the pool, he shone the flashlight beam over the water where something bobbled on the surface.

THEA USED THE spare key hidden in the flowerpot to unlock the front door. It had been years since she'd been inside her mother's house. She stepped across the threshold and paused to take stock of the changes. The couch and paint color were different. The armchair in front of the TV had been slipcovered, but she recognized the bulky shape. Everything else was the same, careworn but clean and tidy, with very little clutter except for a stack of home improvement magazines on the coffee table.

Her mother had only been away for two nights, but the air seemed stale, as if the place had been closed up for a very long time. Thea wrinkled her nose at the fusty odor as a shiver skimmed across her nerve endings. Something was wrong in here. She couldn't put her finger on it. Told herself it was probably nothing more than her imagination. Yet she could almost feel the air settle around her as if someone had moved out of the room just ahead of her.

Unsnapping her cross-body bag, she slipped her hand inside and gripped her weapon. "Hello? Anybody here?"

It occurred to her that Taryn Buchanan might have

come by to pick up something she'd left behind or even to spend time in the room where her little girl had been taken. Thea didn't draw her weapon. Instead, she left the bag unsnapped and resting against her hip as she moved across the room.

Unease trailed her down the hallway, past Reggie's bedroom and the hall bathroom to the second door on the right. Thea's hand hovered over the knob before she pushed the door open and entered. She'd grown up in this bedroom. Had spent her childhood, adolescence and teenage years alone inside these four walls after Maya had been taken. But when she looked back, everything that came after her sister's disappearance seemed hazy and surreal, as if she'd sleepwalked through her life until she'd been old enough to move out of this room, out of this house. Even then, the past had followed her. She'd just become more adept at eluding the ghosts.

The musty odor was more prevalent inside this room and the temperature was uncomfortably warm. Thea wondered if Reggie had adjusted the thermostat or turned off the AC altogether before she'd left the house. That would be like her. Frugal out of necessity and habit.

One of the twin beds had been removed a long time ago. The other had been pushed up against the wall facing the window. After her sister had first gone missing, Reggie had moved Thea into her bedroom and she'd slept in here on Maya's bed. But Thea hadn't been able to stay away. She'd get up in the middle of the night and return to her own bed, where she would lie awake for hours staring into the darkness, waiting for Maya to come home. Finally, Reggie had moved back to her room, but she would leave both doors open to the hallway all night. Sometimes Thea would hear her pacing through the house. Sometimes Reggie would come into the room and check the lock on the window. Thea always pretended to sleep. To this day, she didn't know why. Or maybe she did. Maybe she just didn't want to think too hard about her reason.

Shaking off the memories, she walked around the room. A few remnants of her teenage years remained, along with evidence of Kylie Buchanan's brief stay. A coloring book on the desk and a small suitcase in the closet. Some neatly folded clothes on the dresser. Not much here to entertain a four-year-old child.

Maybe Taryn had already moved the rest of their things into the apartment, or maybe she'd been in such a hurry to leave Russ Buchanan's house that she'd fled to Reggie's with only the basic necessities. Thea thought about her conversation with Jake regarding Taryn's possible role in her daughter's kidnapping. Had she set up the abduction to get the child away from an abusive father?

Having met Buchanan face-to-face, Thea could well imagine Taryn's desperation. A man like that would stop at little to keep his family under his thumb. But would he go so far as to kidnap his own daughter as punishment for his wife's betrayal?

On and on her thoughts raced as she walked over to the window and glanced out. In broad daylight with the sun shining down on all the flowerbeds, the backyard looked lovely and peaceful. By nightfall, however, the atmosphere changed. The woods were very dark even under a full moon. Thea used to see all manner of shadows at the edge of those trees. She would stare into the night certain someone lurked behind the fence, waiting until Reggie's bedroom light went out before creeping across the yard to Thea's window.

For years, nightmares had tormented her sleep until she'd eventually outgrown her fear of the woods. They still came back now and then when she was tired or sick or had suffered an emotional trauma. She still occasionally dreamed about those whispering shadows standing over her bed.

Was someone out there now? Thea knew she was letting the past and her imagination prod her uneasiness, but she could have sworn she saw someone at the corner of the latticework potting shed. Maybe Jake was searching the outbuildings before he set out for the woods. She opened the window and leaned out. "Jake?"

No answer. No sound of any kind except for a faint *click-click-click* as the windmill rotated in the breeze.

Returning to the hallway, she backtracked to Reggie's door. Her bedroom was smaller than Thea's. Funny, she'd never noticed that before. The windows looked out on the side yard and street. If anyone pulled up in the driveway in the middle of the night, the headlights would arc across the ceiling and wake Reggie.

The furnishings were spare and simple: bed, nightstand and dresser, a matching set. Nothing fancy or frilly, but serviceable and every piece paid for, no doubt. That had always been important to Reggie, and a good lesson for her daughter. Thea owed nothing to anyone.

She went over to the closet and riffled through her mother's belongings until she located the box she was looking for pushed back in a corner. She doubted she would find the other half of the torn photograph among Reggie's keepsakes, but it was worth taking a look.

The task of going through her mother's old picture box was both painful and tedious. Thea was struck anew at the scarcity of individual photographs of her and Maya. They were always together. Smiling. Holding hands. *Two peas in a pod.* After the abduction, there were hardly any snapshots of Thea at all. It was as if their whole world had stopped on that night. Sometimes it had seemed to Thea as if Reggie could barely stand to look at her after Maya went missing.

She'd gone through about half of the photographs when her head jerked up and she listened intently to the quiet house. The sound of ruffling paper came to her from the hallway. She'd left the window open to air out the other room. Maybe a breeze had caught the pages of Kylie's coloring book.

Thea rose and slipped across the room to the hallway door. The ruffling came from her right, toward the front of the house. She followed the sound back down the hallway and into the kitchen. The house had grown so warm that the air conditioner had finally kicked on. A draft from one of the vents had caught the edge of a child's drawing pinned to the refrigerator. Kylie's artwork, Thea thought with a pang. But then she saw the painstakingly scrawled names above the crudely drawn figures and her heart thudded. *Me. Sissy.*

Not Kylie's artwork. Maya's.

Two stick figures with red hearts colored onto their torsos and yellow hair sprouting from their circular heads.

The drawing was so reminiscent of the totems Jake had found in the woods that Thea didn't see how it could be a coincidence. Why had she not seen it before? Someone had deliberately turned Maya's innocent rendering of her and her beloved Sissy into something dark and grotesque. It was as if Maya's abductor had come back after all these years to taunt her family, using little Kylie Buchanan as a pawn in some sick, perverted game.

Derrick Sway would have known about that drawing. Reggie had always displayed their artwork on the refrigerator. He would have seen it every time he'd made a trip into the kitchen for a beer. Had he kept that drawing with him in prison, along with the torn photograph of Maya? Had he returned it to Reggie's refrigerator after he'd taken Kylie Buchanan?

Thea removed the magnet and clutched her sister's artwork as she sat down heavily at the kitchen table. The drawing hadn't been there all along. The police would surely have taken note of it during a search of the house. Someone had come into Reggie's home after the kidnapping and pinned the artwork to the refrigerator, where Thea was certain to find it.

She and Jake had been so wrong about motive. The twig totems were never meant to connect Kylie Buchanan's abduction to Maya's. The nearly identical carvings with their hideous grinning faces and hollowed-out eyes had been left in the woods behind Reggie's house as an offering—or a warning—to Maya's twin.

THE DOLL BOBBLED gently on the surface of the black water, seemingly caught in two opposing currents that propelled her in a gentle circle around the pool. When she floated into Jake's light, the glass eyes glinted eerily so that, for a moment, he had the wildest notion she was alive.

It's a doll, not a child.

Left deep inside a cave.

Hunkering on the rocky ledge above the pool, he grabbed for an outstretched arm, but the currents carried her out of his reach. He trailed his light after her, recognizing the golden hair and pink dress from the description Taryn Buchanan had provided to the police. She'd claimed the only thing missing from Kylie's room after the abduction was the child's favorite doll. Jake thought about another doll that had been dug up in a wooden box containing Maya Lamb's DNA. Two abandoned dolls found in underground places. Two children taken through the same bedroom window twenty-eight years apart. More and more it seemed as if the same predator had taken both girls. Or else someone was working very hard to make him think so.

The doll seemed a good indication that Kylie had been in the cave at some point, but where was she now? Jake shone the light into the pool, dreading what he might see beyond his reflection. Divers would have to go down there. He felt an urgency to search the water himself, but without the right equipment, the effort would be dangerous and futile.

As he watched, the doll began to circle faster in tighter loops toward the center of the pool. An eddy or whirlpool sucked her under, but she surfaced a few moments later, still floating just beyond Jake's reach. He flattened himself on the wet ledge and cupped his hand through the cold water, trying to pull the doll toward him. Released from the eddy, she floated lazily around the pool, the circles widening until she bumped up against the rock wall.

So intent was Jake on his task that he hadn't a clue someone had entered the cavern behind him until a shadow wavered briefly on the glinting water. Lying facedown on the slippery ledge—one hand clutching the flashlight, the other submerged in the pool—he found himself caught unaware in a vulnerable position. So much for his uncanny instincts. The irony of his predicament registered a split second before the back of his skull exploded in pain. Dazed, he rolled and reached for his weapon as he put up a hand to deflect the second blow. A hard kick in his side and the next thing he knew, he was underwater.

Something grazed his cheek. The doll or something living? Trying to fight off the shock of pain and icy water, he relaxed his muscles so that his body could float upward. Too late, he realized he was caught in the whirlpool that had sucked the doll under moments earlier. His weight had carried him deeper. Several feet below the surface, the undercurrents were much stronger. Jake had heard of sinkholes at the bottom of rivers that created maelstroms so powerful even expert swimmers could become trapped and pulled to their death.

Confronted with an unknown force dragging him down,

possibly into an abyss, he did what most people would do
in his place—he panicked and lashed out with his arms
and legs. He knew the frenzied effort would quickly expend his energy, eventually forcing him to inhale water
and drown. He *knew* this. Yet for a few precious seconds,
he fought frantically against the swirling waters until his
brain finally processed the situation in a rational manner.
Stay calm and hold your breath.

Eventually the currents would change their flow and
direction and he would pop back to the surface the way
the doll had done earlier. *Just ride it out.* But the whirlpool
spun him around in ever-tightening circles and he soon
grew dizzy and terrifyingly disoriented. It was one thing
to tell himself to remain calm, doing so while completely
blinded underwater was something else altogether. Time
and again, he had to fight the urge to try to break free.
Expend energy. Inhale water. Drown.

The circles finally began to widen and slow. Jake's instinct was to swim sideways out of the weakened current.
Far below him, however, his flashlight was still caught in
the dying eddy, creating an eerie illumination as the waterproof housing spun in the water. Common sense told him
to let it go. He couldn't take the chance on getting caught
in an even stronger whirlpool if he went deeper, one that
could either bash him into the rock wall or suck him into
an underwater crater where he would be hopelessly lost
with or without the flashlight.

He supposed it was human nature to gravitate toward
light. Still dizzy and disoriented, he found himself following that swirling illumination until his lungs screamed for
relief and he realized he was fighting an unwinnable battle.
He couldn't reach the flashlight. It was sinking too fast
and he was quickly running out of air and energy. Abandoning the light, he changed course and swam in the opposite direction.

What if the light wasn't sinking? What if the buoyancy of the rubber housing carried the light upward and, rather than swimming toward the surface, Jake was going deeper into the vortex?

For a heart-stopping moment, he had no idea which way was up or down. Without light from the surface, he had nothing to guide him, not even the bubbles from his expelled air. He tried once again to relax his body so that he could rise to the surface, but maybe he was descending instead.

This is why you don't go into a cave alone.

Okay, think. The flashlight was waterproof and designed to float. Logic told him that once free of the undercurrents, the unit would rise to the surface. *Follow the light.*

Decision made, he reversed course yet again and swam toward the radiance. He couldn't have been under water for much more than a minute, and yet it seemed he'd been down forever. When his head finally broke the surface, he gulped air on a gasp and swam in total darkness until his body scraped up against the rock wall. He found a slippery handhold and clung for dear life as he waited for the residual dizziness to pass.

He looked around for the flashlight. The bulb must have gone out or maybe the light had floated into an underwater passageway. His phone was gone, too, but at least he still had his weapon. Gripping the slick wall, he tuned into the silence. His assailant could be anywhere in the pitch-blackness.

After a few moments, he could feel the undercurrents tugging him away from the wall. The force came in concentric waves, each stronger than the last. He searched for more handholds in the rock. Using the last of his energy, he hoisted himself out of the water and onto the ledge, uncertain that he was even in the same cavern. Maybe the currents had carried him beneath the wall into another chamber. Without a flashlight or phone, he would be hard-pressed to find his way out.

Don't panic.

That was quickly becoming his mantra, he realized. Help was on the way. His team knew he was down here. They'd search every nook and cranny until they found him. But what if they couldn't find him?

Don't panic.

He felt along the ledge to determine the width. Enough room to navigate if he was careful. He rose slowly, hands above his head to make sure he could stand upright. Then he shuffled away from the edge of the pool until his shoulder grazed the limestone wall. Earlier, he'd piled pebbles in front of the passageway from which he'd emerged into the cavern. All he had to do was make his way around the wall until he found the stones. *If* they were still there and *if* he was in the same cavern. He wouldn't let himself dwell on either possibility.

He crept forward on the ledge until he felt a draft on his wet skin. If he hadn't been soaked to the bone, he might never have noticed that whisper of fresh air. Now he turned slowly until the breeze skimmed his wet face. He walked toward the waft, guided by little more than instinct, determination and a faint melodic clacking that chilled him more deeply than the bottomless pool.

Chapter Eight

Thea stepped through the gate behind Reggie's house and paused to scan the tree line. Jake had been gone for an awfully long time. She wasn't so much alarmed as she was impatient. He was a trained federal agent with keen instincts. He could more than hold his own in almost any situation. But Maya's drawing was a significant discovery and Thea was anxious to discuss the implications. At least, that's what she told herself.

She flicked an uneasy glance over her shoulder, unable to shake the niggling worry that someone had been in the house just ahead of her. Her sister's artwork hadn't appeared out of thin air. Someone had deliberately left it on the refrigerator for her or Reggie to find. But why? If Derrick Sway had taken Kylie Buchanan out of mistaken identity or retribution, why would he come back here in broad daylight? Was he that confident he could elude detection, or did a craving that superseded caution drive him? The same dark need that compelled murderers to return to the scene of the crime and kidnappers to join in the search for their victims.

Turning back to the woods, Thea started to call out Jake's name, but the utter silence of her surroundings stilled her. Earlier she could have sworn she'd spotted someone at the corner of the potting shed, but she'd chalked the sighting up to imagination or shadows. Now she whirled again, this time searching all across her mother's backyard and probing the hiding places between the outbuildings. Then tilting her head, she skimmed the treetops. The mild breeze drifting through the leaves seemed to whisper of danger. Of something so dark and insidious that it shouldn't be spoken aloud.

Fishing her phone from her bag, she called Jake's cell, left a voice mail and then sent a brief text.

Where are you?

No response. She waited a moment and sent another.

Jake? You okay? Text me back.

Maybe the trees were blocking the signal, she decided, but apprehension slid like an icy finger down her backbone. She returned the phone to her bag and removed her weapon, slipping it into the back of her jeans for easier access. She wished she'd worn her holster, but nothing she could do about that now.

Taking another scan of the trees, she set out. Mosquitos buzzed around her ears as sweat trickled down her back. It was barely ten o'clock and the heat and humidity had already become stifling. A few hundred yards in, she stopped once more to listen for signs of life. Jake had to be nearby. He was on foot. How far could he go? But if he was that close, he was surely receiving her texts. Why wasn't he answering her? It wasn't like him to simply vanish when he knew she'd be concerned.

The sound of rustling leaves came from somewhere behind her and she spun, her senses on high alert. "Jake?"

No answer, but now she heard the crackle of trodden underbrush as someone advanced quickly down the path in her direction, still concealed by the thick vegetation. Not Jake. He would have responded. This was someone who seemed intent on overtaking her.

A bird took flight from a treetop, startling her. Drawing her weapon, she automatically flexed her knees and extended both arms straight out as she brought the sight to her eyes. She waited for the space of a heartbeat, her attention 100 percent focused before she called out, "Federal agent! Come out now with your hands where I can see them!"

For a man of his age and size, Derrick Sway's furtive movements struck Thea as almost uncanny. One moment the trail was clear, and then in the next instant, he plunged through the low-hanging branches and halted in front of her, a hulking, formidable presence. He'd been so much on her mind since Jake had showed her the torn photograph that, for a crazy moment, Thea thought she might have conjured him from thin air. But no, he was there and all too real. Either he'd followed her from Reggie's house or he'd already been in the woods, heard her on the trail and circled through the trees to come up behind her.

In the ensuing silence of their face-off, Thea took in several details about his appearance and committed them to memory in case she would later need to give a description. Ragged jeans. Sleeveless black T-shirt. Steel-toed work boots even in the scorching heat. Scar across his right cheek. Hair closely cropped, allowing the ink on his scalp to show through.

What struck her the most forcefully about his appearance was how much he'd changed since she'd last seen him. He hadn't just aged. The years of his incarceration had transformed him from brooding hoodlum to sneering psychopath. If Thea remembered correctly, he was only a couple of years older than Reggie, probably just over fifty with the brawny physique of a middle-aged man who lifted weights not for health or conceit, but for the ability to inflict pain on anyone who crossed him.

He had a pistol stuffed in the waistband of his jeans. That he hadn't already drawn on her was a testament to his supreme confidence in his physical abilities. He was ready for her, though. His hands were splayed out from his sides as if he were waiting for her to make the first move.

"Stay where you are," she warned.

His eyes narrowed to slits as he grinned. "You pull that trigger, little girl, you better make damn certain it's a kill shot."

"Not a problem," she said with steely determination. "Remove your weapon and toss it toward me. Do it now!"

He hesitated a fraction of a second before removing the pistol and dropping it to the ground.

"Kick it over here," Thea said. "Then down on your knees, hands behind your head." The adrenaline was pumping so hard through her veins she sucked in air, trying to control her racing heartbeat. She couldn't let him see how badly he'd caught her off guard. She couldn't let him know that the very sight of him had churned her stomach and beaded cold sweat upon her brow.

As the reality of the situation crashed down on her—alone in the woods with the man who may very well have killed her twin sister—Thea wanted nothing so much as to bring her weapon to his temple to force him to tell her why a picture of Maya had been found in his possession twenty-eight years after she'd gone missing. She wanted to slam her fist into his vile, grinning face and make him own up to what he'd done to a four-year-old child.

She could do none of that, of course. Professional conduct aside, he would physically overpower her if he got half a chance. Her only recourse was to hold him there until backup arrived. But she didn't take out her phone to call for help. Not yet. Instead, she eyed him coldly as she fought her baser instincts.

He lowered himself to his knees and laced his fingers behind his head, all the while returning her scrutiny with that blood-chilling grin. What was he up to? Why had he given up his weapon so easily?

Thea kicked the pistol aside, keeping a bead and her distance. "What are you doing out here?"

"Just out for a morning stroll." Mockery dripped around the edges of his voice. "I always did like walking in the woods. Lots of secrets buried beneath some of these trees."

Like her sister's remains?

He tilted his head and closed his eyes as if drawing in a scent only he could detect.

"What secrets?" Thea demanded.

"They wouldn't be secret if I told you, now would they?" He wasn't afraid of being arrested. He certainly wasn't afraid of her. Thea reminded herself she had to be careful he didn't bait her into doing something foolish. "I'm not breaking any laws, so what's your beef with me, officer?"

"Agent. Possession of a firearm by a felon is a felony," she said. "That alone will get you one to three."

"How do you know I'm a felon?"

"All that prison ink is a pretty good indication."

He cocked his head. "Nah, I don't think that's it. You remember me, don't you, Sissy?"

White-hot anger wrenched at her resolve as sweat trickled down the side of her face. She resisted the urge to wipe it away with her shoulder. "Don't call me that."

He knew he'd hit a nerve. She was making this too easy for him. His grin slid into a leer. "Yeah, you remember me, all right. I'm a hard man to forget. Just ask your mama." He ran his tongue slowly over his lips. "That gal was a real wildcat back before she got religion."

The thought of their intimacy physically sickened Thea. She swallowed back her nausea as she filed away more details. Mud on his jeans and the bottoms of his work boots. Fresh scratches on his hands and arms. Some of his tattoos were more than a little disturbing. In addition to the usual prison black and white—dots on his knuckles, spider web at his elbow—he had what appeared to be occult symbolism on his biceps and along the side of his neck disappearing down into his shirt. The imagery reminded Thea of the mysterious twin totems Jake had found in these woods near this very spot. She'd sensed from the first there was something sinister about those depictions. Something meant to instill fear.

"I'll ask you again," she said. "What are you doing out here?"

"And I'll give you the same answer. I'm out for a morning stroll."

She gave him a hard, knowing glare. "You know what I think? I think you came back looking for something you left behind."

His eyes glinted with amusement but something dark and depraved lurked beneath the surface. "Just a simple walk, nothing more."

"With every law enforcement agency in the state looking for you? I don't think so."

"Let them look," he said with an unconcerned shrug. "If you had anything on me, you'd have these woods swarming with cops. Instead, there's no one around for miles but you and me. Know what *I* think? You don't want anyone else joining our little party just yet. You want me all to yourself. You know if you take me in, I'll demand a lawyer. As long as it's just the two of us out here in the middle of nowhere, you might get me to talking. Maybe I'll let something slip." He gave her a nod of admiration. "You like to live dangerously, don't you, girl? I like that."

"Then you'll talk to me?"

"I might if you ask the right questions."

"Why did you have a torn photograph of my sister in your possession?"

He scowled at her. "What photograph?"

Thea wasn't in the mood. "Don't play games. You know damn well the photo I mean. The one found hidden behind the baseboard in a bedroom closet at your mother's house."

He lifted a brow as something indefinable flickered in his eyes. "Ever think someone else might have put it there?"

"No."

"Because a cop has never been known to plant evidence, right?"

"Just answer the question," Thea demanded. "Where did you get that photograph?" *And why did you cut me out of the image and singe the edge?*

"Don't know about any photograph. Final answer."

Thea let his vague response stand for a moment. "Then let's go back to my original question. Why are you lurking around in the woods behind my mother's house?"

"The truth? I saw you from a distance and thought you were Reggie. Honest mistake. It's been a while since I saw her up close and you favor her enough to fool me." His gaze dropped. "It's the way you wear those jeans, I expect."

Thea suppressed a shudder. "Were you in her house just now?"

"Why would I be in her house?"

"That's not an answer."

"Can't make things too easy for you unless I get a little something in return."

Thea's voice hardened as she battled her temper. "This isn't a negotiation."

"Everything's a negotiation. It's just that this time I'm the one in the catbird seat."

"Funny, because last time I checked, I'm the one with the gun," Thea said.

"For now." He dipped his head and looked up at her in a way that sent a shiver straight through her heart.

She subtly adjusted her stance. "You say you mistook me for my mother. Why would you follow her into the woods?"

"That's an easy one. Reggie and me got an old score to settle."

"What score?"

"That's between her and me."

"You've been out of prison for months. Why come here now?" Thea pressed.

"After ten years in that hellhole, I had a lot of scores to settle. Saved the best for last." He shook his head slightly as he looked her up and down once more. "So Reggie Lamb done raised herself a cop. Who would have ever thought?"

"Why does that surprise you?"

"Your mama wasn't exactly the law-and-order type when I knew her. She was up for anything back in the day. Always dragging you damn kids with us all over creation." He squinted up at her. "You remember sleeping in the back seat of my car?"

"No."

"That's probably a good thing for your sake. Might have seen something that was bad for your health."

"Like what?"

He gave her a meaningful look, but didn't answer. "I used to wonder what you girls would look like when you grew up. Reggie was a mighty fine piece of—"

"Watch your mouth," Thea snapped.

He pursed his lips in appreciation. "You're not so hard on the eyes, either, but the other one? Maya? I could tell even then she'd be a real little heartbreaker someday."

Bile rose in Thea's throat. She could feel her hands start

to tremble in rage. *Don't take the bait. Don't let him goad you into letting down* your *guard.* She pulled in air. "Did you take her?"

"Which one?" His drawl still had that mocking edge.

As much as Thea wanted to learn the truth about her sister—and she intended to do exactly that—there was a more pressing issue at hand. "What do you know about Kylie Buchanan's disappearance?"

"Only that she's long gone by now."

"How do you know that?"

"Use your head, girl. It's been…what? Two days since she went missing? Reason should tell you she's already dead or on her way out of the country. Either way, you're wasting your time searching these woods."

"There's only one way you can be that certain," Thea said.

"Nah, I'm just being realistic."

She lowered her voice as she tried to filter out her anger and disgust. *Just keep him talking, see what you can learn.* "Like you said, there's no one around but you and me. You'll notice I haven't arrested or read you your rights. That means anything you say can't be used against you in a criminal case. Tell me the truth. Do you know where she is?"

His expression turned sly. "Which one?"

He was enjoying this too much. He knew he was getting under her skin. "Are you admitting you took my sister?"

"If I say yes, will you let me go?"

She tightened her grip on the firearm. "Confess and find out."

His laugh was a low, ugly rumble. "I'm not confessing to anything, but even if I did, you couldn't lay a hand on me. I could get up and walk away this very instant and you wouldn't dare shoot me. Know why? Because if you really believe I nabbed that little girl, you won't risk killing the one person you think can tell you where she is."

"Try me," Thea dared him. "I'm an excellent shot. I can make you wish you were dead without hitting anything vital."

"Go ahead," he said as he rose slowly to his feet. "Let's see how good you really are."

Thea shot off a round close enough to stop him dead in his tracks. Tree bark exploded near his head. He picked a splinter from his cheek as he sized her up. No longer taunting or leering, he had the look of a man who would enjoy ripping her heart out with his teeth.

He spread his hands at his sides.

"Don't do anything stupid," Thea said. "I don't want to shoot you, but I will if I have to."

He was right, though. How could she risk putting him down when he might be the only link to Kylie's whereabouts? But if she didn't do something quick, the confrontation could rapidly escalate into a kill-or-be-killed situation. She mentally ran through her options, which were few from where she stood.

Then something unexpected happened. A male shout came from somewhere nearby. She thought, at first, it must be Jake. When he called out a second time, she realized she'd never heard the voice before.

"Did you hear what I said?" he bellowed. "We're out here looking for the missing child. Stop shooting before you hit someone!"

Thea responded to the faceless stranger without taking her eyes off Sway. "I'm Agent Thea Lamb with the FBI. Stay where you are and identify yourself."

Silence. Then, "You're Reggie Lamb's daughter?" The underbrush rustled close by. A man rushed out of the trees.

"I said stay where you are!" Thea yelled.

Instead of using the distraction to his advantage, Sway

pivoted toward the stranger. Thea kept her gaze and weapon trained on Sway as she observed the newcomer from her periphery. He'd stopped short a few feet from the path to take stock of the situation. From what she could see, he was of medium height and build with longish brown hair and wire-rimmed glasses. He wore jeans, sneakers and a white T-shirt with some kind of logo on the pocket. Nothing stood out about him except that he seemed to know her mother.

"What's going on here?" he asked, his gaze moving from Sway to Thea and back to Sway.

"Stay back, sir," Thea cautioned. "I'm taking this man into custody."

The stranger adjusted his glasses as he took an awkward step back from the path. "What's he done?"

"Go on about your business and let me handle this," Thea said.

The stranger halted his retreat as his gaze shot again to Derrick Sway. "Wait a minute. I know who you are. I saw your picture at the command center this morning. You're the ex-con everyone's looking for." He swung back around to Thea. "I'm Eldon Mossey. Your mother is a good friend of mine."

He certainly didn't match the image of the charismatic country preacher Thea had visualized in her head. His appearance was the very definition of nondescript. And yet even as her first instinct was to dismiss him as a harmless bystander, she caught a look in Derrick Sway's eyes that made her wonder again why he hadn't attacked when he'd had the opportunity. What was going on here? Did the two of them know each other? Had she interrupted a clandestine meeting in the woods?

As if sensing her suspicions, Eldon said quickly, "Kylie's mother and I came out here to look for her. We couldn't sit around in the police station all day and do nothing. We split up to cover more ground. When I heard the gunshot, I was worried an inexperienced deputy or civilian volunteer might have gotten trigger happy."

A young woman came hurrying out of the woods and halted behind him. She was a few years younger than Mossey—probably in her midtwenties, though her snarled ponytail and gaunt frame made her look much younger on first glance. Her pale blond hair shimmered golden in the spangled light. For some reason, Thea thought of the yellow hair that sprouted from the figures in Maya's drawing and from the wood totems.

Even with her drawn features and the dark circles beneath her eyes, Taryn Buchanan was a very beautiful young woman. Beautiful, fragile and tragic. Catnip to a man like Russ Buchanan and possibly to Eldon Mossey.

Taryn came up beside Eldon, breathless from her sprint through the trees. "I heard a gunshot—" She broke off on a gasp when she saw Derrick Sway, who had hardly moved a muscle. Thea had no doubt he was planning something. He wouldn't wait around passively for her backup to arrive, let alone for her to put him in cuffs. He was biding his time for the right opportunity.

Mossey put out a hand as if to hold Taryn back. "Stay behind me. This is Reggie's daughter. She's taking this man into custody."

"What's going on?" Taryn asked in a shocked voice. "Who is he?"

"We saw his photograph earlier at the command center, remember? His name is Derrick Sway."

Taryn let out a gasp as her hand flew to her throat. Mossey tried to put a protective arm around her shoulders, but she stumbled out of his reach. Her eyes widened as she stared at Sway. Thea saw something in the blue depths that alarmed her.

"Stay calm," she advised, but she feared she was quickly losing control of the situation.

Taryn's keening rose to a shrill howl. "You're a monster! You took my baby! Where is she? What have you done to her? *Tell me where she is!*"

Mossey started toward her. "Taryn, honey—"

"Don't touch me!" She seemed on the verge of hyperventilating as her fingers clenched into tight fists at her sides.

Sway pounced on her vulnerability. "What say you and me take a stroll through the woods? You treat me right and maybe I'll tell you what you want to know," he taunted.

Before Mossey could stop her, Taryn lunged for Sway, playing right into his hands. In the blink of an eye, he had her by the throat, pulling her back against him as he whipped out a knife.

"Put down your piece or I'll slit her throat and gut her like a pig," he warned.

Thea had no doubt he would do exactly that and laugh while doing so. She bent and placed her firearm on the ground.

Taryn had been struggling to free herself from his grip, but now she went limp as her eyes darkened with fear.

"Don't hurt her," Mossey pleaded. "Just let her go and walk away."

"Throw your phones over here," Sway commanded. When they complied, he smashed them with the heel of his boot. "Here's what's about to happen. She's coming with me. If either of you tries to follow, she dies. If I see or hear sirens, she dies." He started backing toward the trees, his arm still around Taryn's throat. When she stumbled, he lifted her off the ground, crushing her windpipe. She clawed at his beefy arm, gasping frantically for air. He eased the pressure but didn't let her go. Within seconds, the trees swallowed them up.

Thea retrieved her gun and started after them. Eldon Mossey caught up with her and grabbed her arm. "What are you doing? He said he'd kill her if we follow."

For the first time since he'd appeared out of the woods, Thea got a good look at her mother's preacher. Maybe it was her imagination or maybe her job had made her overly suspicious, but it seemed to her now that his appearance was *carefully* unremarkable. A benign façade created to court trust and calm doubts. But behind the glasses, his eyes were a flinty bluish gray with a hint of hostility.

She glanced down where he clutched her arm before shaking him off. "Find a phone and call 9-1-1."

"You're still going after him?" he asked incredulously. "You're going to get her killed!"

"Find a phone! Now!"

He retreated with a reluctant nod. "If anything happens to her…"

Thea didn't wait around to hear the rest of his threat. She plunged into the trees, following a trail of snapped twigs and trampled underbrush. She tried to suppress the sound of her pursuit, but she didn't dare let Sway get too far ahead. Sooner or later, he'd have to let Taryn go. She'd only slow him down. The only question was whether Thea could catch up in time to save her.

The trees began to thin as they circled back toward Reggie's neighborhood. Sway must have left a vehicle parked somewhere nearby. Up ahead, she saw something on the ground. Then she recognized Taryn's white shirt and pale blond hair. She wasn't moving. As Thea closed in, she saw blood on the woman's hands where she clutched her throat.

Thea approached with caution, her gaze darting through the trees and underbrush. She knelt beside Taryn and felt for a pulse. Weak but steady. Her eyes fluttered open.

"Did you see where he went?" she rasped. "You have to go after him!"

"Shush. Don't try to talk," Thea said. "You're losing blood, so we need to get you to a hospital." She jerked her T-shirt over her head. She wore a sports bra beneath but modesty was the least of her worries. For the second time in as many days, she pressed a makeshift bandage to a wound to staunch the blood flow. The cut was about three or four inches long, though it didn't look deep enough to have damaged any major arteries or veins. Still, there was a lot of blood.

"Go after him!" Taryn rasped. "Don't let him get away!"

"We'll find him again, I promise. Right now, we need to make sure you're okay."

She clutched at Thea's arm. "I don't care what happens to me. Don't you understand? He knows where she is!" She struggled to sit up, but Thea pressed her down.

"Just lie still—"

"Please!"

Thea hesitated and then, putting herself in Taryn's place, nodded. "Keep pressure on the wound. Like this." She took Taryn's hand and pressed it against the T-shirt. "Don't let up until help comes, okay?"

Then she stood and, with one last glance at Taryn Buchanan, struck out in pursuit.

JAKE HAD BEEN operating in total darkness since surfacing from the pool, but now he noticed a flicker of light up ahead, so thin and faint as to be nothing more than an optical illusion. Or wishful thinking. But he wasn't imagining the draft against his wet skin or that strange hollow melody that came to him now and then like a ghostly warning.

He kept one hand on the damp limestone wall as he moved slowly but steadily toward that sliver of wavering light. He had no idea where it was coming from. Earlier, when he'd first emerged from the tunnel, he hadn't seen any other passageways in the cavern, but maybe he'd missed it somehow. Maybe his attacker had crawled into a tunnel and Jake was seeing the illumination of his flashlight or headlamp.

Could his team already be in the cave? He started to call out, wanted badly to call out, but what if his assailant still lurked nearby? Someone had hit him hard enough to daze him and then kicked him into the pool to drown. Whatever other delusions the blackness might conjure, Jake wasn't imagining the bump on his head or the pain in his ribs. Nor was he imagining the whisper of fresh air that drifted in from some hidden place.

He kept going, his hand feeling along the clefts and recesses in the limestone. The glimmer was coming from a narrow gap in the wall. As Jake shuffled closer, his feet bumped against a pile of crushed rock and debris on the floor. He bent and felt his way over the obstacles.

Except for the draft and that minuscule beacon, he detected nothing unusual about this corner of the cave. If the flickering light had been there before, he surely would have noticed it. But it was possible the faint illumination had become lost in the brighter beam of his flashlight. Also possible that the doll floating in the pool had already captured his attention.

Had he been in the cave long enough for the sun to shift position? If there was an opening to the outside, maybe that was why he could see the light now and not earlier. He didn't think he'd been belowground much more than an hour, two at the most, but the blow to his head could have distorted his perception. His predicament seemed so surreal that he actually wondered if he was still trapped in the vortex, unconscious and dreaming as he swirled into a sinkhole.

The needle stings in his palms from the jagged rock grounded him in reality. His heart quickened as he crawled over the debris and closed in on the quivering light. He put up a hand and the shimmer disappeared. He lowered his hand, letting the pinhole brightness tunnel back through the darkness. He could make out a two-or three-foot indentation in the wall from which a tunnel opened up from the side. This really was an optical illusion, he realized. The passage was invisible unless you crawled up inside the depression. The flickering light came from a crack in the wall at the rear of the cavity.

He could hear a steady drip of water somewhere nearby. Hunkering inside the depression, he peered into the mouth of the tunnel. As soon as he entered the passage, he would once more be exploring in complete blackness. The illumination in the alcove wasn't much, but it was something. Still, a wisp of fresh air on his face made him wonder if there was another way out of the cave through the tunnel.

He considered his options as he crouched in the recess. Check out the hidden passage or sit tight and wait for his team. He knew what he *should* do. But the niggle had returned to the back of his neck, prodding him forward until he realized he didn't have a choice, after all. As long as there was a chance—no matter how slim—that Kylie could be lost somewhere inside the cave, he would keep going regardless.

Cocking his head toward the sound of dripping water, he took a moment to steady his nerves. Then he crawled through the tunnel until he bumped up against a wall. Feeling his way with an outstretched hand, he turned right, maneuvering through a space so tight, he worried he might get stuck between the walls. After a few stomach-clenching moments, the tunnel widened and the darkness seemed to thin. Another right turn back toward the pool cavern and then several more yards on his belly and elbows. Up ahead, he saw another crack in the wall through which a brighter radiance emanated.

Squeezing through into a small cavern, he slowly rose

with his hands overhead. He could stand in a stooped position. Reason told him Kylie could never have found her way back through the maze of tunnels. Nor was it likely that someone had carried her or even dragged her through the tight passages. He was down here wasting precious time. Still, he moved forward, turning once more to the right—and then suddenly the wavering illumination seemed to explode.

The light was so brilliant at first, he thought he must have emerged from the cave into full sunlight. Yet another illusion. The cavern was large, but he was still surrounded by limestone walls. When he lifted his head, he could feel the draft on his face. Somewhere above him, there was an opening to the surface where fresh air and a sliver of sunlight seeped in.

But the flickering light didn't come from the sun. Someone had been in the cavern moments before him and left candles burning in old wine bottles. That person might still be inside, Jake realized as he peered through the dancing shadows. Despite the fresh air from above, the relentless dribble of water down the limestone walls gave the place a dank, mildewy smell.

He appeared to be alone, but he wasn't taking any chances. He drew his weapon as he searched for another way out or even a fissure in the wall where his attacker might lurk. Judging by the faded graffiti on the walls and the rusty beer cans strewed across the floor, the cavern had once been used for clandestine parties. If not for the lighted candles, Jake might have thought the place had gone untouched for decades. But someone had been inside just before him. Someone who knew the hidden grotto's dark secret.

The drip of water seemed to fade away as the pounding in his ears grew louder. He dropped his weapon to his side as he focused on another pile of dirt and rock. On the wall behind the heap, someone had painted a cross. Rather than randomly placed, the wax-covered wine bottles had been arranged around the mound like votive candles at an altar.

At one end of the old grave, a partially exposed skull peeked through the rubble.

Chapter Nine

"I just spoke with Eldon Mossey," Nash Bowden told Thea as they stood on the street in front of Reggie's house. "He's at the hospital with Taryn. Looks like she's going to be okay."

"That's a relief," Thea said. "But still no sign of Derrick Sway?"

Chief Bowden shook his head. "We've got officers sweeping the area and traffic stops on all the major roads. There's always a chance someone will spot him and call in."

"Let's hope so. He's not exactly the type to blend in." Thea combed fingers through her tangled ponytail in frustration. "I can't believe he got away. He didn't have that much of a lead on me. I could have sworn I was right behind him. For someone of his age and size, he moves fast. Makes me wonder if he was able to vanish so quickly because someone helped him."

"When you first got here, did you notice a vehicle parked on the street? Anyone that looked suspicious or out of place hanging around the neighborhood?"

"No, but I haven't lived here in years," she said. "I don't know the neighbors or the cars they drive. A parked vehicle or even someone walking down the street wouldn't have stood out for me. Although I'm certain I would have noticed Derrick Sway."

They were going back over the same information Thea had already provided earlier to one of the responding officers. Both she and Eldon Mossey had given brief statements as the paramedics had loaded Taryn into an ambulance. Then Thea had gone back to Reggie's house to clean up and borrow a shirt. Once Nash Bowden arrived, he'd wanted to hear the details for himself.

He was a tall, serious man with a calm demeanor and brooding eyes. As they stood talking, she couldn't help thinking about Grace Bowden with her too bright smile and flashes of melancholy. Thea still suspected all was not well in the Bowden marriage—a notion that his ringless finger seemed to confirm—but a few minutes into her interview and any lingering questions about his character began to wane. She could see why Jake liked him.

"Don't beat yourself up over the Sway situation," he said. "He got away because you stopped to help Taryn. I would have done the same in your position. If not for your quick action, she might have suffered massive blood loss or worse before the paramedics arrived."

"I appreciate the kind words, Chief, but you're giving me far too much credit. The cut wasn't so deep as to be life-threatening. I'm sure she would have been fine regardless."

He seemed determined to cut her some slack. "You couldn't have known that for sure. The important thing is she's alive."

"Yes, but I can't help wondering why Sway let her go. He could just as easily have killed her."

Bowden shrugged. "He bought himself some time. He knew if he wounded her, you'd stop to assist. If he'd killed her outright, you'd pursue."

"Which is exactly what I did, and I lost him anyway," Thea said. "He could be anywhere by now."

"He won't risk any of the main roads. My guess is he'll go to ground as soon as he's able. For all we know, he may have a hideout somewhere nearby. That could explain why you happened upon him in the woods. Anyone in his position with a lick of common sense would have already fled the area. There must be a reason he's sticking around here."

"He did say he has a score to settle with my mother," Thea said.

"What kind of score?"

"He didn't elaborate, only that he had a lot of scores to settle after ten years in prison. That's about all I got out of him. He didn't seem at all concerned about being caught, which makes me wonder again if he has someone helping him evade the police."

"It's possible. He was born and raised around here. He could still have friends in the area or someone he's coerced into helping him." Bowden paused, his dark gaze moving over the street. His casual attire—jeans, rolled-up sleeves and dusty black boots—belied the tenacious vigilance in his eyes. "Tell me again what he said about Kylie."

"That common sense should tell us she's either dead or halfway out of the country by now—an implication that she might have been trafficked. An associate of mine is keeping a close eye on the deep web sites we routinely monitor in case Kylie's photograph pops up."

He frowned. "What kind of sites?"

"Auction sites," Thea said.

He looked visibly shaken. "She's four years old."

"I've seen photographs of children even younger."

He swore under his breath. "How do you get any sleep at night?"

"I don't sleep well," Thea said. "I do my best to compartmentalize. Sometimes it works, sometimes it doesn't. I'm sure you have to do the same."

"Four years old." He looked sad and angry.

Thea understood only too well. "Sway sounded confident we wouldn't find her, but he never confessed to anything."

"Confession or not, he's our most viable suspect at this point." His features tightened resolutely.

"Maybe, but I got the feeling he enjoyed toying with me. Spouting things to try to set me off."

"You don't like him for the kidnapping?"

"I never said that. No, I agree with you. He's certainly a viable suspect." *And it's my fault he got away. I should have called for backup as soon as I saw him in the woods. I shouldn't have tried to take matters into my own hands.*

Aloud she said, "There's something else that worries me about my run-in with Sway. Agent Stillwell and I drove over here together earlier, but we split up. I wanted to check on something in my mother's house and he left to search the woods. I haven't been able to reach him since. It's probably nothing. I'm sure he's just out of range or something. But after everything that happened with Sway..." She trailed off. "You can understand why I'm concerned."

Bowden gave her a puzzled look. "You don't know?"

A little tingle of fear worked its way up Thea's spine. "Know what?"

"He called in earlier to one of his agents. He heard a suspicious noise coming from the cave."

"What kind of noise?"

"Something that convinced him Kylie might be inside. He went down to check it out."

Thea's heart dropped. "He went in alone? People have died in that cave."

Bowden gave her another strange look. "His team and some of my officers are down there with him now. He's fine but..." An uncomfortable silence followed. For an experienced law enforcement officer, Nash Bowden didn't have a very good poker face.

"What happened?" Thea demanded. "Tell me."

"He found human remains in one of the caverns."

Anyone involved in child abduction cases dreaded hearing such news, and yet Thea realized she'd been steeling herself for the tragic possibility ever since she'd arrived in Black Creek. But he'd said "remains," not a body. Goose bumps prickled at the back of her neck. She took a gulp of air. "Not Kylie?"

He said with quiet emphasis, "I should have been clearer. He found *skeletal* remains."

Thea stared at him silently.

"The body was buried under a pile of rocks and debris in a remote area of the cave," he explained. "Whoever it is has been down there for years, possibly decades."

The implication punched through Thea's shock with the force of a physical blow, squeezing the air from her lungs in a painful rush. "Maya."

"That was my first thought," he admitted. "But we don't know anything for certain. The remains are only partially exposed. Agent Stillwell had the tunnel that runs back to the cavern sealed until a forensic anthropologist from Tallahassee can get here to oversee the excavation."

"When will that be?" Thea asked with a hitch in her voice. She swallowed and tried again. "We can't leave her down there indefinitely. We have to bring her up."

"We will, but the recovery has to be done right. You probably know better than I do that excavating skeletal remains is a delicate process."

"I know. I know. It's just…" She closed her eyes. "We've waited so long."

His gaze was kind. "I understand. I can't imagine what it's been like for you folks. I see Reggie in the diner now and then. Tough woman."

At the mention of her mother, Thea's heart sank even deeper. Reggie would have to be told sooner rather than later.

"I'm headed to the cave now, if you want to come along," Bowden said. "There's always the possibility that something may have been buried with the body that you or your mother will recognize. That could speed up the identification process. Barring that, we can test your DNA against the remains."

"I need to talk to Reggie before she hears about this from someone else," Thea said.

"I thought you might. Just so you know, we're trying to keep a lid on the news for as long as we can. Last thing we need is a bunch of sightseers getting in the way of the recovery efforts."

"I'll be discreet," Thea said. "So will Reggie."

"I didn't mean to imply otherwise. I just wanted to bring you into the loop. Anyway, I'll have one of my officers drive you to the hospital whenever you're ready."

"Thank you. But on second thought, I'd like to go out to the cave first." Thea would never be able to explain it so that it made sense to anyone else, but she felt the need to be close to her twin. Maya had been alone in that cave for nearly thirty years.

"We'll take the road," Bowden said. "It'll be faster than hiking through the woods."

By the time they got to the cave, the owner of the property had been notified and had arrived to unlock the gate. Thea assumed he was the elderly gentleman with white hair and stooped shoulders who watched the activity from the shade. She wondered what had run through his mind when he'd heard the news. Did he think this place was cursed? He'd erected a fence and posted warnings after the drowning deaths of two teenagers, when all the while another body—possibly that of a four-year-old girl—might already have been hidden deep inside the cave.

Two uniformed officers positioned between the boulders were gazing down into the pit. One of them bent to offer a hand as Jake emerged from the opening. When he saw Thea, he gave a little nod of acknowledgment before he turned to say something to the person coming up out of the cave behind him.

Chief Bowden left her to join the officers at the opening. For some reason, Thea hung back. She'd been eager to get here as quickly as possible, but now she felt strangely out of place as she observed the commotion around the cave entrance. She received a few deferential glances from some of the officers who recognized her. Their well-meaning attention took her back to the night Maya had gone missing and to the following terror-filled days when the whole community had turned out to look for her. Had she been this close all along? Had she died alone in a dank, hidden cavern crying out for her mama and Sissy?

"You okay?" Jake touched her elbow and she jumped. "Sorry. I thought you saw me come up."

His hair and clothing were wet and muddy, and there were scrapes on his hands and across both cheeks, most likely from crawling through close spaces.

Thea shuddered. "Jake, is it her?"

His voice was both soft and grim. "I'm sorry I wasn't the one to tell you. I did try to call—"

"It's okay. Just tell me now."

"We don't know. The skull is only partially exposed. Until the grave is excavated, we won't know if the rest of the skeleton is even intact. Predation and the damp environment will have taken a toll."

"How long do you think the excavation will take?" Her voice sharpened in a way she hadn't meant it to. She didn't want to take her nerves and impatience out on Jake.

If he noticed, he didn't let on. He glanced over at the pit. "Under these conditions? Your guess is as good as mine. Getting all the equipment back to that cavern will be tricky.

It's a tight squeeze in places." He rubbed his elbow. "Once everything is in place, the tedious work begins. The area will need to be gridded and the dirt sifted one screen at a time. It's time-consuming for a reason. The bones and artifacts have to be meticulously labeled and cataloged. After so many years, we only have one shot at getting it right."

The implication stunned her, though she wasn't sure why. "Are you saying the cavern is a crime scene and not just a place where the body was dumped?"

"We don't know that, either. But we can't take the chance that a minute piece of evidence or DNA could be lost or overlooked out of carelessness or impatience. Something that might have the power to break the case wide open."

"After twenty-eight years," Thea said.

"After twenty-eight years."

"Justice." She said the word softly, but her voice was gritty with emotion.

He nodded, his jaw set with the same determination. But he said nothing else, giving Thea the opportunity to catch her breath. She'd noticed the abrasions on his face and arms and the wet, muddy clothing straight away, but now she saw something in his eyes that shook her—the look of a person who'd come too close to death. She'd experienced an inkling of that back in the woods with Derrick Sway, but this seemed different.

He must have seen something in *her* eyes because, just like that, a mask dropped, closing her off before she could probe too deeply.

Don't do that, she wanted to tell him. *Don't shut me out. Let me in.*

But he'd already turned his attention back to the pit where a uniformed officer had just emerged. "We'll try to get as much done as we can before Dr. Forrester and her team get here," Jake said in a matter-of-fact voice. "We're setting up a harness and pulley system at the entrance and placing battery-powered lanterns throughout the passageways and caverns. The one thing we have in our favor is that we don't have to worry about losing the light on the surface. Belowground, there is no night or day."

Thea nodded. "When do you think she'll be here?"

"Sometime this afternoon, if all goes well. She agreed to drop everything, but we're still in for a long wait before we'll know anything conclusive. Maybe you should head over to the hospital and talk to your mother. Let her know what's going on."

"Yes, I intend to, but I wanted to come here first." Thea folded her arms around her middle as if she could calm the fluttery sensation in the pit of her stomach. She was hardly a novice to recovery operations, but no experience or training had prepared her for this eventuality. After decades of waiting, she hadn't expected the discovery of her sister's remains to hit her so hard. "I need to go down there, Jake."

He looked worried. "I don't think that's a good idea. It's a hard scrabble through some of those passageways."

"I'm not claustrophobic. I can handle it."

"Under ordinary circumstances, I'd agree. But you were in a serious car accident yesterday. You admitted only this morning that you're not at the top of your game."

"I don't need you to protect me," she snapped.

"When have you ever? Being down there..." He lifted a hand to the back of his neck. "It's weird. It can mess with your head even under the best of circumstances."

Foreboding crept in as she wondered again about that look in his eyes. "I don't care. I need to go down there. I need to be with her. And yes, I'm well aware of how unreasonable that sounds, but I can't help it. It's how I feel."

"We don't even know if it's her," he said. "You should be prepared for that possibility, too."

"I still want to go in. And before you say anything else,

let me point out that you're hardly in a position to lecture me about safety." She gave him a hard stare. "What were you thinking going down in the cave alone?"

He stared right back at her. "I was thinking that if Kylie was in there, frightened and possibly hurt, I'd never forgive myself if something happened to her in the space of time it took to get a crew out here. I was thinking that leaving her alone down there for even another second was too long. You would have done the same."

"That's exactly why I have to go down there. If the remains are Maya's, she's been alone in that cavern for twenty-eight years."

It wasn't even remotely comparable. He'd thought Kylie was still alive. Maya had been gone for a long time. She may have already been dead before her killer had carried her into the pitch-blackness of the cave. There was no rescuing her. No happy ending for her family.

Thea wanted to believe her sister had never experienced pain or loneliness or fear. She couldn't bear to think even now how Maya might have suffered. Year after year, there had been nothing Thea could do but wait and imagine. Now, finally, there was something she could do.

Jake lifted a hand and brushed back her hair. His touch both shocked and moved her, but she didn't want to react. Too many curious eyes were upon them. If she and Reggie had learned anything from all those years of side-glances and open stares, it was how to remain stoic in the face of unwanted attention. It only occurred to her later that her stoicism had shut Jake out, too.

He dropped his hand to his side. "I can tell you feel strongly about this."

"I do."

"Then I'll take you down there myself. We're trying to limit the number of people in the cave at a time, so it may be a little while."

"I can wait. Jake…" She resisted the urge to touch his arm in spite of all those curious eyes. "I need to ask you something and I want you to tell me the truth. Something else happened down there, didn't it? I can see it in your eyes. I'm guessing that's why you're all wet."

"It's damp and muddy in some of the passageways."

She wasn't buying it. "Your clothes are soaked. You may as well tell me what happened. I'll find out sooner or later."

Reluctantly, he took her arm and led her away from the opening where they could speak in private. "We're not releasing a statement about this yet."

"You know you can trust me. What is it?"

"About a mile or so back in the cave, an underground river flows up into a pool in one of the caverns. I found a doll floating on the surface. It matches the description of the doll that was taken with Kylie."

"Oh my God."

He glanced away, studying the activity back at the cave. "We've got divers on the way."

"That's why I can't go in right now," Thea said. "You should have told me. Of course, I'll stay out of the way. Unless there's something I can do to help."

"No, trust me, this is a job for professionals. We just need to give them room to do their thing. I'll go in with you as soon as we're clear."

"That doesn't even matter anymore. Nothing matters now except finding Kylie. She could still be alive. A doll floating on the pool doesn't prove anything. Three percent, Jake."

He nodded wearily. "I'm not giving up, but the cave is a maze. Dozens of passageways and dead ends, and I only made it about halfway through. Combing back through all those tunnels will eat up at least another day. I can't help wondering if that doll was put there as misdirection. A way to tie up our resources and manpower until it's too late."

"Maybe, but how would anyone know you'd go down there and find it?" Thea asked.

"No one could know for certain, but it was a good bet the cave would be searched more thoroughly after the initial canvass."

"What about the sound you heard earlier? Chief Bowden said that's why you went down in the first place."

"I don't know what I heard. Or who I heard." He ran fingers through his wet hair, a physical sign of his frustration. "I very much doubt it was Kylie."

Something in his tone alarmed her. "What do you mean?" Then, "You never said why your clothes are all wet."

"While I was trying to fish the doll out of the pool, someone came from behind and hit me over the head hard enough to daze me. Next thing I know, I'm caught in a whirlpool several feet below the surface. I lost my flashlight, so I was spun around underwater in complete darkness. No up, no down." He paused. "For a while there, I wasn't sure how I'd get out."

Thea watched his expression as he spoke. He still seemed shaken from the experience. She'd never seen him like that. "I knew something bad must have happened."

He summoned a brief smile. "I know what you're thinking. I even thought so myself at the time. So much for my keen instincts. Someone came up behind me and I never sensed a thing."

"That's not what I'm thinking."

"No?"

"I'm thinking you could have died down there and I would never have known what happened to you."

"Thea." He said her name so softly she might have thought the tender missive was nothing more than a breeze sighing through the treetops.

The sun bearing down on them was hot and relentless,

but Thea felt a little shiver go through her. It hit her anew how much she'd missed that tender glint in his eyes as their gazes locked. How much she'd missed his husky whispers in the dark. The glide of his hand along her bare skin, the tease of his lips and tongue against her mouth. The way he had held her afterward, as if he never wanted to let her go. But he had let her go and she'd done nothing to stop him.

She drew a shaky breath. "Don't ever do that to me again."

"Get caught in a whirlpool? I'll do my best."

She scowled at him. "Don't make light. You know what I mean."

"I'm fine, Thea." He seemed on the verge of saying something else, but he held back. Maybe he thought she wanted his restraint. She did, didn't she? They were in a precarious situation. Adrenaline and attraction could be a dangerous combination. Throw in unresolved issues and they were asking for trouble.

She flexed her fingers to try to release the pent-up tension. "You didn't catch a glimpse of your attacker?"

"It's pitch-black down there even with a flashlight. You can only see what's directly in front of you."

"Could it have been Derrick Sway? I had a run-in with him in the woods earlier. I'll tell you about it later, but I don't want to get sidetracked."

"Yes, I heard about that run-in from some of the officers before you arrived." A shadow flickered across his expression. "From the sounds of it, things got tense."

"You could say that. I'm trying to figure out if he had time to attack you in the cave and then swing through the woods and come up behind me on the trail."

"Aside from the timeline, Sway's a big guy. He might have a hard time in some of the narrow passages." Jake paused. "I thought at first the assailant must have followed me into the cave, but I was wrong. He or she was already inside. That's how I stumbled upon the remains. I noticed a flickering light through a crack in the rock wall."

"A flickering light?"

"Yes. Whoever was down there lit candles and left them burning in the cavern."

"How strange," Thea said with a pensive frown. "Why would someone leave lighted candles?"

"I have my suspicions." He seemed hesitant to finish his thought. "Whoever was down there obviously didn't want to be seen in the cave. He hit me over the head and pushed me off the ledge, hoping the whirlpool would suck me under. But even with me out of commission, he had to figure backup was already on the way. He fled without taking the time to crawl back to the cavern and snuff out the candles. I doubt he had any idea the light could be seen through a crack in the wall."

Dread seeped in despite Thea's best efforts. "I don't want to say it out loud… I hate to even think it."

"Go on."

"Do you think he was down there to dispose of another body?"

Jake glanced away. "I'd be lying if I said I hadn't considered that possibility."

"Maybe he intended to bury her in the same cavern where you found the remains, but when he heard you in another part of the cave, he had to improvise. I know I said finding Kylie's doll in the pool doesn't prove anything, but we can't discount the evidence."

"Which is why we have divers on the way." He had one eye closed as he tracked a hawk against the sun. Now he glanced back at Thea.

"You're holding back," she said. "Something else happened that you don't want to tell me."

"It may be nothing."

"Tell me," she insisted. "If Maya's remains are in that cavern, I have a right to know everything you found."

He glanced away before he nodded. "There was something strange about those candles."

"How so?"

He paused to consider his answer. "It seemed to me they were arranged ceremonially around the mound, as if it were an altar or…something. It sounds a little out there, but that's the impression I had."

She stared at him in horror. "Are you saying he came back down into the cave to specifically visit the remains? To *use* them in some kind of ceremony or ritual?"

Jake shrugged, but his expression remained sober. "We're assuming the suspect is male because of the profile. But we don't even know that for certain."

Male or female, what kind of monster would come back after all this time to desecrate the grave of a four-year-old victim? The imagery shook Thea.

"We're dealing with a very sick mind, Jake."

"So it would seem." His expression turned regretful. "Maybe I shouldn't have told you about the candles. It's all conjecture at this point."

"No. Don't keep secrets. The not knowing has always been the hardest part. The things that go through your head…" She paused. "I never imagined *this*."

"Let's wait until after the excavation to draw conclusions. In the meantime, you have my word I'll tell you everything I know as soon as I know it."

"Thank you."

"For what?"

"For your candor. For finding her."

"We don't—"

"I know. But if it is her…do you have any idea what this means to us? All these years, we never knew where she was or what had happened to her. To think she was right here all along. So near I should have heard her calling out to me."

He seemed at a loss. "I don't know what to say."

"It's all right. Neither do I."

Their gazes clung for a moment longer before Jake said, "Do you want to take a walk?"

That surprised her. "A walk? Where to?"

"There's something I need to check out. I'd like you to come with me, but it could be a hike. I noticed you were limping back at the station."

"I'm fine. Just a superficial cut on my heel. I hardly feel it now. But, Jake, don't you want to be here when the divers arrive?"

"This won't take long. If my hunch is correct, I think you'll want to see this," he said mysteriously.

Chapter Ten

Jake spoke to the property owner before he and Thea set out. Douglas McNally could give him only a vague sense of where an opening might be over the hidden cavern. He claimed he'd never known of a second cave entrance and clearly thought searching for one in his rocky field a waste of time. However, Jake had felt fresh air in the tunnel, and he'd glimpsed a sliver of sunlight through the limestone roof. Whoever had attacked him at the pool, and left burning candles around the grave, might well have exited through that opening or another one nearby.

One of Jake's team members had loaned him a phone so that he could stay in touch until he could get a replacement. He glanced at the screen now to first check the time and then the compass. They were still on course as far as he could tell. Strange to think that the cave ran beneath their feet. Stranger still to hike through their pastoral surroundings when only a short while ago he'd been trapped in a subterranean whirlpool, fighting for his life in pitch-blackness. The sunlight and songbirds seemed to mock his close call.

"From the Devil's Pit the cave runs south," Mr. McNally had told him. "Then it slants slightly eastward before you get to the final dead end. Head off in that direction. If there is another entrance, you might get lucky and stumble across it. But I wouldn't get my hopes up. As far as I know, there's only ever been one way in and one way out. I'd tell you again that you're wasting your time, but I can see you're determined. Besides, it's possible rain and erosion have carved out another opening since I last went exploring. Wouldn't surprise me if that old cave has a few more secrets to give up."

Yes, maybe it does, Jake thought. He wanted to believe they were getting close to a break in the case, but even with his experience, he could still be susceptible to wishful thinking. Forty-eight hours and counting since Kylie Buchanan had been reported missing. Spirits had visibly flagged back at the cave while they'd waited for the divers. Jake had sensed despondency and an unnerving sense of calm, as if they were no longer working against the clock. The discovery of Kylie's doll in the pool and the skeletal remains in the cavern were somber reminders of how many abducted children never came back home.

He slanted a glance at Thea as they walked along the rough terrain. She'd been quiet since they'd left the others.

She sensed his gaze and returned his scrutiny. "You're still not going to tell me where we're going?"

"To be honest, I'm not sure. But I'll know it when we get there."

"Always so cryptic." She stopped in the shade of a pine tree to tie her shoe.

He gave her a worried frown. "Are you sure you're up to this? I know you must be in pain. You didn't exactly walk away from that crash without a scratch." He searched her upturned face, noting the cuts and bruises that were more pronounced today than yesterday, and the circles under her eyes that seemed to have darkened since earlier that morning. "Wait for me here if you need to."

"I'm just a little winded." She finished with her laces

and stood. "Guess I've been sitting behind a computer screen for too long."

"Yes, I've been meaning to talk to you about your career choices." He tried to lighten the mood with a joke.

"Some other time." She idly toed a pine cone out of the way. "Actually, I didn't really need a breather. I stopped because we need to talk about what happened in the woods earlier."

She had his undivided attention. "With Sway? I'm all ears."

"You said you heard things got tense. That's an understatement." She gave him a quick summary of the drawing she'd found on Reggie's refrigerator, the subsequent confrontation with Sway, and how the situation had escalated with him on the run and Taryn Buchanan in the hospital.

"But she's going to be okay," Jake said when Thea paused.

"No thanks to me. There's no excuse for my behavior. I should have called in the minute I spotted Sway on the trail. Instead, I lost control of the situation. I'm lucky I didn't get someone killed."

"Why didn't you make that call?" Jake asked.

She cringed. "It sounds stupid now, but in the back of my mind, I thought I could get him to talk because of his previous relationship with Reggie. It was never going to happen. He led me to believe he'd reveal something about Maya, but all he did was play me. What I can't figure out is why he forced the confrontation in the first place. He said he mistook me for Reggie from a distance—you were right about a grudge, by the way—but I think he had another agenda."

"Maybe he was trying to keep you away from the cave."

"That's possible. He had mud on his jeans and boots, and he's certainly capable of violence. We shouldn't underestimate him, Jake. He's strong and he moves quickly and quietly for a man of his size and age. I can imagine him sneaking up behind you in the dark." She paused on a shiver. "He has the usual prison ink, but also occult imagery on his neck and arms. It's not a stretch to think he could have been the one to place the candles around the remains."

"Scary dude," Jake said.

"He is." Thea paused again. "It's odd. When Taryn and Eldon Mossey showed up, Sway could have used the distraction to try to disarm me. He could have easily overpowered me. Instead, he just stood there and waited. Maybe his plan all along was to provoke Taryn into attacking him, but how could he know she'd react so viscerally?"

"She's the mother of a missing child. Not that difficult to predict her behavior."

"I guess. The whole time I had my gun on Sway, I had the feeling that I'd interrupted something. I couldn't help wondering if he'd gone into the woods to meet Eldon Mossey."

"That's jumping to a big conclusion," Jake said. "Especially since Mossey and Taryn were in the woods together. A meeting seems risky unless you think she was there to meet Sway, as well."

"I don't. Not after I witnessed her reaction to him. However Eldon Mossey may be involved, I don't think Taryn had anything to do with Kylie's disappearance."

"Because she attacked Sway?"

"Because she was desperate for me to go after him regardless of what happened to her. The whole thing went down so quickly it's possible I misread their interaction, but I don't think she and Eldon Mossey are as close as Reggie assumed. I got the distinct impression that Taryn didn't want anything to do with him. She kept shrugging his hand away when he tried to touch her."

"Yet she was out in the woods alone with him."

"At this point, she'd probably accept help from the devil himself if he promised to find Kylie. We've been focused on Derrick Sway for obvious reasons, but I think we need to take a harder look at Eldon Mossey. You said yesterday the information you have on him is sketchy. Have you learned anything else?"

"Nothing concrete, but there is one piece of information that may be significant," Jake told her. "His father was also a preacher. He used to lead a prison ministry group out of his church in Butler, Georgia. According to some of the former congregation, the elder Mossey died about ten years ago. Eldon continued the ministry for a while but he moved away a few years after his father passed. The church has since burned down, and no one seems to know where Eldon went or what he was doing until he turned up in Black Creek."

Thea swung around. "Could he have met Sway through this ministry? If they kept in touch, he would have known when Sway got out of prison. In fact, Sway could be the reason Eldon came to Black Creek in the first place."

"I can request Sway's call and visitation recordings from the prison, excluding any communication with his attorney, of course. If the facility still has copies of his jail mail, we can get a court order to look through his incoming and outgoing correspondence. But all that takes time. Meanwhile, I've asked the Macon office to keep digging around in Mossey's hometown. I'll let you know if anything else turns up."

Thea shaded her eyes as a shaft of sunlight slanted across her face. "Why didn't you tell me about this earlier at the police station?"

"It didn't seem particularly relevant until you mentioned a possible meeting in the woods with Sway. Mossey's ministry operated in Georgia. Derrick Sway was incarcerated in Florida. A connection between the two seemed unlikely."

"It's still a long shot," Thea conceded. "It's also possible I imagined the vibe I picked up between them. But I'm not wrong about Eldon Mossey. There's something off about him. He's just a little too ordinary, if you know what I mean."

"I know exactly what you mean. It's like he's purposely cultivated an image that allows him to fade into the woodwork. You'd glimpse him on the street and forget about him."

"Yet both my mother and Grace Bowden seem captivated by him."

Jake said in surprise, "The chief's wife? What does she have to do with Eldon Mossey?"

"Apparently she attends the same church as Reggie. She said Brother Eldon's sermons are so riveting that she sometimes forgets to pay attention to anyone else in attendance."

"That's quite a testimonial."

"Reggie said all the young people in the church adore him."

"This guy," Jake muttered.

"Sounds a little too good to be true, doesn't he?"

"I'm beginning to think so, but we'll need more than gut instinct to get a warrant. At the very least, we can bring him in for another chat."

Thea kicked aside a pine cone in a burst of frustration. "Why did I let Derrick Sway escape? If he took Kylie and we don't find him in time—"

"It won't be your fault."

"It's hard not to think so."

"Let it go," Jake advised. "I've been where you are, and it does no one any good to obsess over what you could have done differently. We need to stay focused."

She glanced at him. "Then give me something to do. Let me help you."

"We'll talk about it later, after you've seen Reggie. Right now, let's keep moving."

They set out again with Jake periodically checking his compass. Cabbage palms dotted the rocky landscape, along with clumps of pine trees and southern red cedars. The temperature climbed steadily until Thea stopped again to fan her face.

"Maybe I really am out of shape."

"The humidity is killer," Jake said. "And you did get pretty banged up yesterday."

"I can't keep using the wreck as an excuse. I need to hit the gym hard when I get back to DC."

Jake gave her a sidelong glance. "Maybe you need a workout partner. You used to kick my ass on the stair mill."

"Beating you was serious motivation." She was only half teasing.

"Ever wonder if I let you win?"

"No. The thought never crossed my mind. And it better not have crossed yours."

How easy it was to slip back into their old banter, Jake thought. He would have liked nothing better than to sit in the shade and spend the rest of the day talking about unimportant things with Thea. But they were serious people with a serious job to do. If they were lucky, a lighter moment might come later.

"Come on," he said, "we're almost there. I can feel it."

No sooner had the prediction left his lips than a breeze swept down through a massive live oak, stirring the Spanish moss that hung almost to the ground. With the breeze came the eerie hollow melody that Jake had heard first in the woods behind Reggie's house and then from inside the cave.

Thea turned toward the sound. "Do you hear that? Reminds me of the wind chime in Grace Bowden's courtyard."

"We're definitely getting close," he said.

She looked slightly alarmed. "Close to what?"

"When I heard the sound earlier, I thought it was coming from inside the cave. Now I think it must have been coming from up here. There has to be an opening in the ground where air and sound seeps down into the tunnels." He moved away from her, searching along the uneven terrain. "Keep an eye out. The entrance could be small and covered over by rocks and scrub brush."

She remained in place, her head still tilted toward the sound. "You heard this all the way down in the cave? That must have been creepy."

"Close your eyes for a moment and you'll get some idea."

"No thanks," she said with an exaggerated shudder.

Jake moved quickly up the slope, searching through the trees and bushes and all along the rocky summit. Even with his eyes peeled, he almost missed the narrow opening, camouflaged as it was by brush and boulders. Only a child or a very small adult could squeeze through the fissure. He doubted whoever had been in the cave had climbed up the limestone wall and exited the cave that way.

High up in one of the trees, a wooden wind chime had been hung to either mark the opening to the cave or the hidden grave below. Or both. The chime was old and weathered. The hollow tubes had been strung together on fishing line. Some of them had rotted and fallen to the ground. Enough remained intact, however, to create a haunting melody when the wind blew through the treetop.

Jake turned to call to Thea, but she was right behind him, her eyes riveted on the ground. "Do you see them?" she asked in a hushed voice.

"See what?"

She dropped to her knees and began to paw frantically through a patch of wild rosemary, releasing a pungent scent reminiscent of camphor. He hunkered beside her, mesmerized by her frenzy. Then he saw them and leaned in to take a closer look.

Hidden beneath the vegetation, two primitive stick figures had been etched into the surface of a flat rock partially buried in the ground near the opening.

BY THE TIME they arrived back at the main entrance, the divers had arrived and were checking their tanks and equipment before they entered the cave. The operation would take hours, and as much as Thea wanted to stay, she couldn't put off her visit with Reggie any longer. Once people started to notice the activity to and from Mr. McNally's property, curiosity seekers would eventually show up at the cave. Word would get out about Jake's discoveries. Reggie shouldn't have to hear about either from anyone but her daughter.

Jake gave her the keys to his SUV and promised to get in touch as soon as he knew anything. Hot and tired, Thea hitched a ride back to Reggie's place with one of the uniformed officers. Thankfully, he wasn't in a chatty mood, so the trip passed quietly, giving her a few minutes to think and catch her breath.

Her mind wandered back to the cave. She couldn't help dwelling on those lighted candles placed around the remains and the stick figures carved into the surface of the rock like a headstone. Two stick figures that mimicked Maya's artwork and were reminiscent of the twin totems Jake had found in the woods. What did those crude renderings symbolize? The answer seemed obvious—two figures, two sisters. But only Maya had been taken. Had the kidnapper meant to take Thea that night, as well? Maybe his plan had been to carry the twins away one at a time, but for some reason his second trip had been thwarted. If Thea hadn't climbed into Maya's empty bed, she might well have been the first to be taken.

Think! What do you remember about that night?

She summoned memories she couldn't be sure were even real. They *seemed* real. So vivid she could feel the breeze from the open window on her face. She could hear muted laughter and music from the front porch, and the eerie sound of a neighbor's dog baying in the woods. Something else. A sound that mingled with the bullfrogs and cicadas.

I'm scared, Sissy.

Why?

I heard something.

It's just a coonhound out in the woods. See? Mama opened the window.

It's not a coonhound.

"Agent Lamb?"

She roused at the sound of her name. She glanced at the officer and then at her surroundings. They were sitting behind Jake's SUV in her mother's driveway. For a few moments there, she'd lost track of time and place.

She gave the officer a sheepish smile. "Sorry. I must have drifted off."

"I thought you were awfully quiet over there. You need anything before I go?"

"No, I'm fine. Thanks for the ride."

"No problem."

She climbed out of the car and watched as he backed out of the driveway. He gave her a little salute as he straightened the wheel and stepped on the gas. After a moment, the sound of the car engine died away, leaving the street empty and quiet. So much had happened since she'd left the hotel earlier that morning to look for coffee. She almost wished she could go back in time and pull the covers over her head.

Lingering at the edge of the driveway, she glanced up and down the street. Was Derrick Sway still in the area? Was he hunkered down somewhere nearby, waiting for his chance to get to Reggie? To get to her?

As preoccupied as she was by what had been found in the cave, now was not the time to lower her guard. She wanted to believe Sway would have the good sense not to accost her twice in one day, but he'd made it clear earlier that he had no fear of being caught. After ten years in one of the most dangerous correctional facilities in the state, she doubted there was anything he did fear.

Had he taken Maya and then returned twenty-eight years later to abduct Kylie? Had he hung the totems in the woods to taunt Reggie? To make her suffer for the ten years he'd spent behind bars?

Thea scanned the backyard through the chain-link fence and peered into the shadowy recesses between the outbuildings. She searched along the side of the house and across the front porch. Up and down the street once more, and into shadowy yards and behind windows.

Are you watching me?

Yes, the wind seemed to whisper.

She tried to rein in her imagination, but a person didn't go through what she'd experienced at a tender age and come out unscathed. No one could hunt monsters by day, even from the safety of a computer screen, and sleep peacefully ever again. She knew what was out there.

Sweeping the street one last time, she turned her back on the row of modest homes and crossed the yard to the porch. The back of her neck prickled as she climbed the steps slowly, but she resisted the urge to glance over her shoulder. No one was there. No one that she could see.

Letting herself in the front door, she pocketed the key

rather than return it to the flowerpot. Someone had apparently been coming and going as they pleased. She wasn't about to make it easy for them.

The house had a different smell this time. The fresh air from the open bedroom window had removed the fusty odor she'd noticed earlier, but now she detected something faintly medicinal. Eucalyptus maybe or camphor. It reminded her a little of the wild rosemary that had covered the etching on the flat stone. Had someone been in here while she'd been exploring with Jake?

Drawing her weapon, she walked across the room and checked the kitchen. Maya's artwork was still on the table where she'd left it. Thea studied her sister's creation for a split second before she whirled and made her way along the hallway.

She wouldn't have been surprised to hear the eerie clacking of a wooden wind chime somewhere nearby. Already she'd come to associate that hollow melody with the disappearances. Whoever had left the totems in the woods had years earlier marked the spot of Maya's grave by etching stick figures onto the surface of a rock and hanging wind chimes from a tree branch. Then her killer had gone back to visit the remains and to light candles in a ritual that only he could understand.

There must be some significance to that sound, Thea thought. A clue hiding in plain sight that had eluded her for twenty-eight years.

She went into her old bedroom and made certain the window was closed and locked. Then she did the same throughout the house. When she let herself out the front door, she noticed a man circling Jake's SUV as he peered through the tinted windows. He was tall and lanky, with the nonchalant demeanor of someone unafraid of getting caught or standing out. Probably a neighbor, Thea decided. A bluetick reclined in the shade a few feet from the driveway.

She called out to the man as she came down the steps. "Can I help you?"

The hound dog opened his eyes and flapped his tail lazily, but he didn't get up.

The man came around to the front of the vehicle and leaned an arm against the hood. "Saw you over here. Thought you might know what happened to the fellow that drives this Suburban."

"What makes you think anything has happened to him?" Thea strode across the yard, mindful of her weapon tucked beneath the tail of her borrowed T-shirt. Now that she had a closer look at the interloper, she recognized Reggie's across-the-street neighbor. The familiarity did nothing to quell her caution. Instead, her nerve endings prickled a warning. Reggie had never made any bones about her dislike of Lyle Crowder. Thea tried to remember why as she closed the distance between them. *It's creepy the way he sits over there on his front porch staring across the street at our house. Probably peeps in our windows while we're asleep at night.*

"I couldn't help noticing that his vehicle has been parked in the driveway all morning. Reggie's not home, so it struck me as odd." He paused to give Thea a closer scrutiny. "She know you're here?"

"I'm her daughter."

He squinted and straightened. "You're Reggie's girl? Damn, I never would have known you. You don't look like I remember."

"It's been a minute," Thea said. "How've you been, Mr. Crowder?"

"No need for the 'mister' part. We've been neighbors since you were yay high." He bent to measure the air a few feet from the ground. "How long you in town for?"

"I haven't decided."

Lyle Crowder had changed, too, Thea noted. He'd grown

older, grayer and a good deal thinner. He seemed friendly enough, but she couldn't dismiss the lingering unease from Reggie's contempt. *If he ever comes over here when I'm not home, you go inside and lock the door. Don't even think about letting him come inside.*

A thrill skittered up Thea's spine but she kept her expression neutral.

"I heard about Reggie's car accident," he said. "She okay?"

"Her injuries are serious, but she'll recover."

"Glad to hear it. My buddy owns the junkyard where they towed her old car. He said it was a real mess. Said she's lucky to be alive."

While he spoke, Thea cataloged his appearance as she had earlier with Derrick Sway. Cargo shorts, paint-stained T-shirt and flip-flops. His hair was damp from sweat or a recent shower. She thought of Jake's close call in the cave and wondered if Lyle Crowder would have had time to hightail it back home and clean up while they'd searched for the second entrance. Crawling through tight passageways would certainly explain the scratches on his arms and shins.

"Any idea when she'll get to come home?"

Thea forced her mind back to the present conversation. "Probably by the end of the week. I'll be sure to tell her you asked about her."

She watched his expression. He nodded as if he didn't have a care in the world, but something ambiguous glinted in the depths of his eyes.

"Have you noticed anyone or anything suspicious in the neighborhood this morning?" Thea asked.

"Heard a gunshot earlier. That's not so unusual around here. Some of the local boys like to shoot beer cans in the woods. But the sirens caught my attention. Cop cars and an ambulance. Do you know if they found the little girl?"

Which one?

"I'm afraid not," Thea said. "You haven't noticed any-one hanging around Reggie's house, have you? Or seen anyone go into or come out of the woods?"

"No, but I was working out back most of the morning, digging up some old blackberry vines and whatnot. Thorns got me good." He examined a long scratch on his forearm. "You say they haven't found her yet, but something must have happened, else why all those sirens?"

"Do you know a man named Derrick Sway?"

The name seemed to give him pause. Then he gestured toward the SUV. "I was just telling the FBI agent about him yesterday."

"Agent Stillwell?"

"That's the one. Was I right? Did Sway have something to do with little Kylie's disappearance?"

"We don't know that yet. He's certainly a person of in-terest," Thea said. "We think he may be hiding out some-where in the area. If you see him in the neighborhood, we'd appreciate a call to the police."

"Don't have to tell me twice. That guy's always been bad news in my book. Smartest thing your mama ever did was giving him the boot."

Thea couldn't disagree.

"Speaking of…" Crowder said, still with that curious glint. "I'd keep an eye on Reggie if I were you. Could be nothing more than rumors, but I hear Sway's got it in for her. You cross a guy like that, he'll get even sooner or later."

"She's well protected in the hospital," Thea assured him.

He nodded and glanced away. "Good to know."

The hound got up and wandered over to rub against Crowder's leg. He reached down and scratched behind the dog's ears. "This here's old Blue. Not much of a hunter these days, but still good company."

As if on cue, the dog plopped down on a shady patch of grass and closed his eyes, oblivious to the squirrel hopping from branch to branch above him.

"Didn't you have a bluetick hound years ago?" Thea asked. "This can't be the same one." Was it Crowder's dog that had been baying in the woods the night Maya had been taken?

"I've had a few over the years," he said. "Always did love a good coonhound."

"I seem to recall you worked away from home a lot. What happened to your dogs when you were gone?"

"I'd drop whichever one I had at the time at my brother's house and pick him up on the way home. That wouldn't work with Blue, though. He won't let me out of his sight."

"Do you ever take him into the woods?"

"Sometimes."

"Have you ever seen anything hanging from the trees?" Thea asked.

He looked startled. "Hanging from the trees? What in the hell are you talking about, girl?"

"I'm talking about dolls of a sort made from hollow pieces of wood with carved faces and twigs for arms and legs. Fabric hearts glued to the torsos and tufts of hair strung from the heads. If there's more than one, they sound a bit like bamboo wind chimes when they bump against each other in the breeze."

He said in a hushed voice, "You found something like that in *these* woods?"

"Yes, behind Reggie's house."

He glanced past her toward the backyard. He didn't strike Thea as the religious type, but she wouldn't have been surprised if he'd crossed himself. "What do you think it means?"

She shrugged. "I was hoping you could tell me."

He ran a hand up and down his arm as if trying to

wipe away chill bumps. "I've never seen anything like that around here, but I witnessed plenty of weirdness when I worked on the rigs. Grown men carrying gris-gris pouches in their pockets and perforated dimes around their necks or ankles. Not that I didn't send up a prayer now and then myself. You need something to believe in when you're trapped out there at night with nothing but ocean for miles. Gets spooky as hell when the sun goes down. What you described sounds like a poppet."

"You've seen one?" Thea asked.

"A guy that worked on my crew found something similar under his pillow once. Crude thing. Looked liked it was made out of old rags and dirty yarn. This dude was crazy superstitious and a regular horndog to boot. We figured someone put it there as a joke, or maybe a jealous husband or boyfriend wanted to give him a scare. We ribbed him about it for days, but then he just up and disappeared one night. No one saw anything and nothing was caught on the security cameras. He was just gone. Never found so much as a trace."

"You think someone threw him off the platform?"

"Either that or something caused him to jump." Crowder stared down at his dog with a frown. "That's my one and only experience with voodoo, hoodoo—whatever you want to call it. But that sound you described? I don't think there's anything too spooky about that. Used to be an old widow woman out on the highway that made wind chimes and sold them on the side of the road. At first people bought them just to help her out, and then it became popular to hang them in trees for good luck. When the wind blew just right, you could hear the damn things all over town. You don't remember that?"

Thea shook her head.

"Before your time, I guess."

"Have you ever seen any of those chimes out in the woods?" she asked.

"Haven't seen them anywhere in years, but your mama used to have some hanging from that big old oak tree in her backyard. I could hear them all the way across the street when a storm was coming in."

Thea was silent for a moment, deep in thought. Something else had come back to her. It wasn't just the dog that had awakened Maya that night. It was the sound of Reggie's wind chimes.

I'm scared, Sissy.

Why?

I heard something.

It's just a coonhound out in the woods. See? Mama opened the window.

It's not a coonhound, Sissy. Listen.

The dog had stopped baying and the music and laughter seemed to fade away as Thea lay on her back staring up at the ceiling. The wind chimes outside their window crackled loudly as if a shoulder had accidently brushed against them. Then the sound died away as a shadow moved across the ceiling.

"Somebody's out there," Maya whispered.

Thea shivered as she stared up at the shadow. "Nobody's out there," she whispered back. "Stop being a fraidy-cat and go back to sleep."

But somebody had been out there. Someone who had watched from the edge of the woods—or the safety of his front porch—before creeping across the backyard to climb through the open bedroom window.

Chapter Eleven

Thea showed her credentials to the guard outside Reggie's room and then lingered just inside the doorway. Her mother's head was turned toward the window. She lay so still that Thea assumed she was sleeping.

"Are you going to gawk at me all day or are you coming inside?" she grumbled, still with her head turned toward the window. Thea decided she must have seen her reflection in the glass.

"I thought you were sleeping. I didn't want to wake you." She moved to the foot of the bed, feeling awkward and at a loss. *You shouldn't feel that way at your own mother's bedside.* She couldn't help it. The discovery in the cavern painfully underscored the reason for their years of estrangement. "I'm sorry it took me so long to get here. How are you feeling?"

"Everything considered, I can't complain." Reggie pushed herself up against the pillows and adjusted her hospital gown. "How are you?"

"Me?" Thea shrugged. "I'm fine. Just a little sore is all."

Reggie searched her face. "Didn't get much sleep last night, did you?"

"No. But that's not unusual."

She frowned. "You need to take better care of yourself. You won't be young forever."

"I'm fine," Thea insisted as she idly smoothed her hand across the covers. "I need to talk to you about something."

"I'm not going anywhere," Reggie said.

Thea nodded absently. "The reason I'm late—"

"Oh, I know why you're late." Her mother's hard gaze tracked her as she came around to the side of the bed.

Thea said carefully, "What do you know?"

"You don't have to tiptoe around any of it. I know about Derrick Sway and what he did to poor Taryn." She paused. "I know what was found in that cave."

Thea released the breath she hadn't realized she'd been holding. Her heart had started to race despite her efforts to keep her emotions under control. "I'm sorry you had to hear about it from someone else. I should have come as soon as I found out, but I wanted to go to the cave first. I...needed to go to the cave. I needed to be close to her. I know how crazy that sounds—"

"No, it doesn't. Not to me. I would have done the same."

"Still, I'm sorry I wasn't the one to tell you," Thea said.

Reggie stared at her for a moment then lifted her chin in that stubborn way she had. "Doesn't matter how I found out. It's not her."

Thea stared back at her. "You can't know that for certain. You should prepare yourself. We both need to."

"It's not her." Reggie's blue eyes glittered like shattered glass. "Don't you think I would have known if my baby was that close? I'm telling you it's not her."

Thea sat on the edge of the bed. "But what if it is? At least we'll know. At least we can finally say our goodbyes. Don't you want closure?"

"Closure? How will that help anything?" Reggie balled her pale hands into fists on top of the covers. "You think we'll feel better if we can have a service and give her a headstone? All that will do is take away my hope." She turned her head back to the window. "As long as we don't know any different, she could still be alive. Someone good could have found her and taken her in. She could be happy with a family of her own by now. Don't you get it? She could still be alive."

Yes, now she got it. Thea put her hand over Reggie's.

Her mother's face crumpled at the contact. "My poor baby."

"I know, Mama. I know."

She clutched Thea's hand. "Somebody buried her down in that awful place and left her there all these years." Her eyes spilled over. "I can't bear it. I don't care how many years have gone by, I can't stand to think of her alone and suffering. It's too much. No mother should ever have these images in her head. No child should ever have to suffer the way Maya did."

"And yet so many do," Thea said.

Reggie reached for a tissue. "I don't know how you do what you do. I truly don't. You got the short end of the stick when it comes to mothers, but just look at how you've turned out."

"I'm not sure what to say to that."

"Don't say anything." She placed her hand on Thea's arm. "Just let me get this out. Tomorrow everything will go back to the way it was, but right now I need you to know that no matter what happens or how many years go by, you'll always be my little girl."

Thea's throat tightened painfully. "Sometimes it seemed as if you didn't want me around anymore."

"I know. And you don't know how much I've come to regret that. I've thought about my behavior a lot over the years," Reggie said. "Why I withdrew from you the way I did. My only excuse is that I carried a lot of guilt on my shoulders. After what happened to Maya, I didn't think I deserved to be your mother. My misery was my punishment. That's why I stayed in Black Creek and put up with all the gossip and accusations even though we would have both been better off somewhere else. No matter what anyone said about me, it was never as bad as what I thought of myself. I just never stopped to consider that by staying here I was punishing you, too."

"That's all in the past," Thea said. "We can't go back and change things."

"No, and at least something good came from all that heartache. You help save kids like Maya every single day. She'd be so proud of her Sissy."

"I hope so." Self-conscious, Thea glanced away and, after a moment, Reggie released her hand. She sank back into the pillows, looking exhausted and unbearably fragile.

"Are you sure you're okay? Are you in pain?" Thea asked. "Physical pain, I mean."

"I'm okay. Doctor says I might be able to go home in a day or two." She didn't sound optimistic. Little wonder, Thea thought. Reggie was a trooper, but she'd been through hell in the past few days. A car wreck and surgery coming on the heels of another child's abduction would take the wind from anyone's sails.

"You're too thin." Thea voiced her worry. "You work too hard."

"I'm as strong as an ox," Reggie scoffed. "I can still sling hash with the best of them."

"I'm sure you can, but it's backbreaking work."

"It's all I know." She closed her eyes.

"Are you tired? Should I go?"

"You don't need to be so careful around me, Althea. And no, don't go. I like having you close."

"Then rest. I'll be right here," Thea said.

She used the ensuing silence to get up and hang her bag on the back of a chair. Glancing out the window, she thought how normal everything seemed three stories below. The sun was still shining. People hustled to and from the parking lot, while deep inside a cave a few miles away, divers searched an underground pool for a little girl's body.

"What's the weather like?" her mother asked.

Thea turned away from the window. "Hot and humid. Just as you would expect in Florida this time of year."

"I don't mind the heat," Reggie said. "It's the end of summer I can't bear."

"Why?" Thea walked over to the bed. "Cooler weather should be a welcome respite."

"Not for me. I don't like the end of things," her mother said. "I already dread the end of your visit."

"I'll try to be better about staying in touch."

"Don't make promises you won't keep."

"You could always come see me," Thea said.

Reggie gave her a half-hearted smile. "Maybe I will. That would surprise you, wouldn't it? Your old mama showing up on your doorstep."

"Yes," Thea replied candidly. "Give me some notice and I'll make your travel arrangements."

Reggie sighed. "It's a nice dream."

Thea sat on the edge of the bed again. "I hate to bring this up, but there's something else we need to talk about if you're up to it."

Reggie nodded. "You want to ask me about Derrick."

"How did you know?"

"It's all over the hospital what he did to Taryn. Lord only knows what would have happened if you hadn't been there to stop him."

"I didn't stop him," Thea said. "I'm just glad she's going to be okay despite my incompetence."

"She won't be okay until they find Kylie. Even then…" Reggie plucked at the blanket. "Anyway, what do you want to know about Derrick?"

"When was the last time you saw him?"

"Before he went to prison. He used to come into the diner and sit in my section so I'd have to wait on him. I could have switched tables with one of the other girls, but I didn't want to give him the satisfaction."

"You haven't seen him since he got out?"

"No, and up until today, I was grateful he'd kept his distance. We didn't exactly part on the best of terms."

"What happened between you? I never really knew," Thea said.

"I guess the short answer is that I came to my senses." She couldn't quite meet Thea's gaze. "I never should have taken up with him in the first place, but I always did have a thing for the bad boys. Even your daddy had a wild streak despite June's coddling." She paused, her brow wrinkling as she thought back. "After Maya went missing, I cut a lot of people out of my life. Not just Derrick, but friends I'd known for years. Some of them didn't want anything to do with me anyway, what with all the gossip and suspicion."

"What about your suspicions?" Thea asked. "Did you think Derrick had something to do with Maya's disappearance?"

Reggie seemed uncharacteristically reluctant to speak her mind.

"Just between you and me," Thea coaxed.

"Of course, I thought about it, but there was never anything connecting him to her abduction. Not that evidence or motive mattered to some. So many people around here made up their minds about me as soon as they heard the news." Her eyes burned into Thea's. "You've had your doubts at times. Don't bother denying it. I've seen it on your face."

Thea started to refute Reggie's accusation but then decided to come clean. Get everything out in the open. "I'll admit there's something I've always wondered about. Why didn't you tell the police you came back into our room that night to open the window?"

Reggie stared at her in confusion. "What?"

"In your official statement, you said the window was open because it was hot inside the house. That was true. But you never mentioned that you made a special trip to our room to open it after you'd put us to bed."

Reggie looked stumped. "Why does it matter when I opened the window?"

Because it does. "I'm just curious."

A shadow darkened her mother's eyes but she didn't turn away. She gazed at Thea without flinching. "You think I came back to open the window for the kidnapper?"

"No, of course not. I just—"

"Don't lie. Tell me the truth." Reggie grabbed her arm so quickly that Thea recoiled before she caught herself. "That's why you've doubted me all these years? Because of that window?"

Thea was the one who flinched. "I doubted you because you pushed me away. Because you acted as if you couldn't stand the sight of me. Because you would never let me talk about Maya."

Reggie's grasp tightened around Thea's arm. Her eyes flared a split second before the anger drained out of her and she fell back against the pillows. "That my own daughter could think that of me."

Thea rubbed her arm. "I'm sorry. I was just a kid. I didn't know what to think."

"It's not your fault. I just wish you'd come to me, is all."

"Would it have made any difference? Would you have talked to me?"

"I don't know," Reggie replied honestly. "But I'm going to tell you now what I should have explained back then. I couldn't look at you at times because you reminded me of Maya. It was just too much. I couldn't talk about her without reliving all the terrible things that went through my head every night when I closed my eyes. As for the window, I didn't mention it to the police because I didn't remember. I didn't remember because I was drunk that night. Too drunk and too high to protect my little girl. So, no, whatever you thought of me wasn't your fault. You were right to have doubts. I didn't hurt my baby, but what happened to her was every bit my fault."

The raw emotion in her voice tore at Thea's poise, but she had to hold it together. There was still too much to get through. "I believe you."

Reggie sighed. "We should have cleared the air years ago."

"Yes."

"That's my fault, too."

"I could have forced the issue," Thea said. "It was easier just to build walls."

"All that time wasted. We'll never get it back."

"We can't worry about that right now," Thea said. "I know this is hard. It is for me, too. But we need to stay focused. Kylie is still out there somewhere, and I still need to ask you some questions."

"I can't tell you what I don't know," Reggie said.

"Then we'll focus on what you do know. Was Derrick ever violent with you?"

She spoke quietly but fiercely. "He was a violent man, but he never laid a hand on me or you girls. If he'd ever so much as thought about hurting either of you, he wouldn't have lived to see the inside of a prison cell."

Thea felt a prickle of apprehension as she studied her mother's expression. There was still so much about Reggie she didn't know or understand. A few tender moments didn't change that. "Is there anyone you can think of who might have had a reason for kidnapping Maya? Someone who held a grudge against you? Or anyone you suspected at the time whether they had motive or not?"

Reggie turned her head away, as if considering the question.

"What is it?" Thea prompted. "I can tell you thought of someone."

"You have to understand, I was out of my head with worry and grief after it happened. A lot of bad things went through my mind."

"Like what?"

Reggie frowned, thinking back. "It was something June said to me after your daddy's funeral. Everyone had gone back to her house after the service. She met me on the front porch and told me I wasn't welcome. I knew she blamed me for Johnny's accident. He'd been with me earlier and we'd both been drinking. I never realized until I saw the way she looked at me that day how much she truly despised me. She told me if it took the rest of her life, she'd find a way to make me feel what she felt at that moment."

"She's hateful and vindictive," Thea said. "That's not news. But you don't seriously think she had anything to do with Maya's disappearance, do you? She certainly wouldn't have any reason for abducting Kylie Buchanan."

Reggie's head whipped around. "You think the same person took both girls?"

"They disappeared through the same window. As you noted yesterday, that can't be a coincidence." Thea paused. "You said Derrick was never violent toward you, but when I saw him in the woods earlier, he told me flat out he has a score to settle with you. Do you know why?"

Reggie shrugged. "No man likes to be rejected. Especially a guy like Derrick Sway. He always thought he was God's gift to women."

Thea didn't buy her explanation. "You'd been broken up for years when he went to prison, so I don't think rejection is a motive. Maybe he thinks you're the one who turned him in to the police. Were you?"

"If I'd turned a guy like Derrick Sway into the police, I'd know enough to keep my mouth shut about it," Reggie said.

Thea took that as a qualified yes. "Do you have any idea where he might go to hide out? Any friends you know of that he remained close to?"

"Since I don't associate with any of the old crowd, there's no way I could know that."

Thea fell silent, contemplating Reggie's responses.

"Are we done now? My painkillers are wearing off and my head is starting to hurt."

"There's just one more thing I need to ask you."

Reggie rubbed her temples. "It can't wait?"

"No. I'm sorry, it can't. I hate having to bring it up, but I need to ask about the box that was found in the woods after Maya went missing."

Reggie closed her eyes. "What about it?"

"It had Maya's DNA inside and yet all this time you still believed she was alive?"

"Of course it had her DNA," Reggie said. "Someone put her doll and blanket inside so the cops would believe I murdered my own child and buried her in the woods. That box was a prop. A way to point the finger at me."

"Are we back to June as a suspect?"

"No. As much as she hates me, I don't think she would have done anything to hurt Johnny's children."

"Hates? As in the present?"

"I've made my peace with her," Reggie said. "I can't say she's done the same."

"Do you ever see her?" Thea asked curiously.

"I stop by now and then to see how she's getting on. She never invites me in. She likes to stand on the porch looking down on me the way she did that day after Johnny's funeral."

Thea felt unexpectedly defensive of her mother. "Then why do you bother going over there?"

"Somebody has to," Reggie said with a shrug. "Her friends are dead. The neighbors have all moved away. You're the only blood kin she has left. Besides, I've come to accept her for who she is. She's too old to change. I know she must get lonely rattling around in that big house. You should go see her while you're here."

Thea bristled at the suggestion. "I'm not here to socialize."

"She's your grandmother. She has a right to see her only grandchild."

Thea could hardly believe her ears. "Are we talking about the same June Chapman who once called me an abomination?"

Reggie muttered under her breath. "I won't make excuses for her behavior."

"Good."

"But I know what it's like to lose a child. How the grief festers and spreads until you're all but consumed by the pain."

"Your circumstances were completely different," Thea argued.

"Loss is loss. Grief is grief. Go see her, Althea. Make your peace before it's too late."

"Why does it matter to you so much?"

Reggie drew a long breath. "Because I hope someday a child of yours will show me the same charity."

Chapter Twelve

Thea sat with Reggie for the rest of the afternoon, waiting for a phone call from Jake that never came. She'd known it might be morning before they heard definitive news, but as twilight fell and the dinner trays came and went, she began to grow jittery, imagining all sorts of life-threatening scenarios at the cave.

"Althea, stop that pacing! You're getting on my last nerve," Reggie complained. "Go back to your hotel and get some rest. We'll know when we know."

"Are you sure you don't want me to stay the night?"

"I'm fine. There's a cop right outside my door if I need anything. Now go. You look as if you're ready to keel over."

Thea finally relented. Reggie was safe in the hospital. Might as well go back to her room and try to get some sleep. Besides, a hot shower and some food would go a long way to boosting her morale. She said good-night to Reggie and walked outside to a full moon and a mild breeze. *Jake, call me*, she implored as she climbed into his SUV. Her phone had been smashed in the confrontation with Derrick Sway, but he knew to reach her at the hospital or her hotel.

As soon as she got back to her room, she checked for messages and then took a shower and ordered dinner. Stretching out on top of the covers, she closed her eyes. Sometime later, a knock on the door startled her awake.

She straightened her robe and smoothed back her tangled hair as she got up to glance through the peephole. Not room service, after all. She opened the door and silently stood back for Jake to enter.

"I didn't expect you to show up in person," she said anxiously as she followed him into the room. "I thought you'd call if there was news. The divers—"

"Found nothing."

She closed her eyes. "Then why are you here?"

"I have other news." He seemed on edge as he turned to face her. "I tried to call you at the hospital. Reggie answered. She recognized my voice when I asked for you. I'm sorry, but I couldn't hold off. I had to tell her."

Thea's heart thumped painfully. "Tell her what?"

"It's not Maya."

Thea let out a harsh breath and dropped to the edge of the bed. "You know for certain? I didn't expect a definitive answer until tomorrow."

"Yes, we're certain. The skeletal remains are that of a male Caucasian. We won't know much more than that until Dr. Forrester and her team can examine the bones in the lab." He sat on the other bed, facing her.

"What about the etching on the rock and the wind chimes in the tree?" Her hands were trembling so she clasped them together in her lap. "They weren't placed above the cavern randomly. The stick figures are too much like Maya's drawing to be a coincidence."

"Yeah, I've been wondering about that myself," he said. "My only guess is that someone else thought the remains were Maya."

Thea glanced up. "Or maybe there's another grave nearby."

He met her gaze and nodded. "I won't lie, I thought about that, too." He paused. "Are you okay?"

"Yes," she said numbly. "I'm not even sure how I feel

at the moment. We've waited so long to know what happened to her. Then when we thought she'd been down in that cave all these years…that someone may have been visiting her grave for God only knows what purpose…" She shuddered. "It's not an image you want in your head."

"I'm sorry," he said again.

"So now we're back where we started." She took a moment to gather her thoughts. "Do you have any idea who he was? The man in the grave?"

"Not yet. Chief Bowden is checking the local database for any missing persons in the area that match the general description. The digital records only go back so far and then someone has to comb through the physical files. We're checking our own databases, of course, but that's also a process."

"Is it possible he got lost in the cave?" Thea asked. "Maybe he was homeless or a runaway who crawled inside to get out of the elements."

"Not likely. Dr. Forrester found several cuts on at least six bones of the rib cage, suggesting our John Doe was stabbed."

"Brutally, by the sounds of it." Thea let that sink in. "And then his killer dragged the body into the cave and buried him underneath a mound of rocks and debris."

Jake looked grim. "More than likely, the victim was lured into the cave. I don't see a body being dragged through all those narrow tunnels. You don't remember any other disappearances in the area?"

"Not that I recall, no."

"I didn't expect you would. By all indications, the remains have been down there for decades. Maybe longer than you've been alive."

"Do you think the remains could be the reason Derrick Sway has been hanging around in the area?"

Jake shrugged. "Impossible to say since we don't yet know the victim's identity."

Thea grew pensive. "It's just that Sway said something to me earlier I haven't been able to get out of my head. He said he was surprised Reggie Lamb had raised a cop because, when he knew her, she wasn't the law-and-order type. Then he asked if I remembered sleeping in the back seat of his car. When I said no, he said it was a good thing. I might have seen something that was bad for my health."

"What do you think he meant by that?"

"No idea. He was neck-deep in a lot of criminal activities back then. Maybe he talked Reggie into helping him with something illegal and she brought us along."

Jake looked skeptical. "She would do that?"

"Not the present-day Reggie, but she was a different person back then. It's possible she got in over her head with Sway. Maybe Maya woke up in the back of his car and saw something she shouldn't have. Maybe that's why she was taken instead of me."

"That's one theory. But it's just a theory."

"I know." Thea bit her lip. "I guess I've wondered for so long why my sister was taken instead of me that I'm willing to reach for any explanation."

His gaze softened. "I can understand that."

"Still, no matter how willing Reggie was to skirt the law, she would never have been party to murder, much less to hurting her own child. I'll admit, I've had my doubts over the years, but I saw her face today when she thought Maya had been found in the cave. If Sway took my sister, he either acted alone or had another accomplice. It wasn't my mother."

"Reggie's neighbor made an interesting observation about her yesterday," Jake said. "If she knew Sway had done something to Maya, she would have kept silent only if he threatened to hurt you."

Thea felt a pang in her chest at the possibility. Had she misjudged Reggie all these years? "Maybe that's why she turned him in years later for a crime unrelated to the kidnapping. She needed to find something that wouldn't blow back on her or me. But someone talked and Sway decided to retaliate by taking Kylie. Whether he thought she was my child or not, he had to know how deeply her abduction would hurt Reggie." Thea got up to pace. "We have to find him, Jake."

"We're doing everything we can."

"I know, I know. It's just…"

"The clock is ticking."

She jumped when a knock sounded at the door. Jake glanced past her to the entranceway. "Are you expecting someone?"

"Room service."

He rose. "I'll get out of your hair and let you have a peaceful dinner."

"No, stay," Thea said impulsively. "That is, if you haven't eaten yet. It's just a burger and fries, but I don't mind sharing."

He looked doubtful. "Are you sure?"

"Yes, stay." She got up to answer the door. The young man who brought in the food laid everything out on the table by the window. Thea signed for the meal and then closed the door behind him. She sat and motioned for Jake to take the seat across from her. She divided the order and handed him a plate. He sat and dug in.

"This hits the spot," he said between bites. "I didn't take time to eat earlier. I cleaned up and came straight here."

"We can order something else if this isn't enough."

"It'll do for the moment."

Thea devoured a fry, finding herself likewise ravenous. "The neighbor you mentioned earlier. Would he happen to be Lyle Crowder?"

Jake glanced up. "Yes, why?"

"I talked to him earlier. He was looking in the windows of your Suburban when I came out of Reggie's house."

"Why the face?" Jake asked.

"Did I make a face?"

"Subtle, but yeah. You don't like him?"

"I never had anything against him personally, but he always gave Reggie the creeps. She told me I wasn't to let him in if he ever came to the door when she wasn't home."

"But she had no problem letting someone like Derrick Sway into her house."

"It does seem a contradiction," Thea agreed. "But like I said, she changed after Maya's disappearance."

"Did she give you a reason for her distrust?"

"She said she didn't like the way Lyle stared across the street at our house. The funny thing is, he never seemed to be looking at me. I assumed he had a thing for her. A lot of men did. She was an attractive woman back in her day."

"Your mother is still an attractive woman," Jake said. "I can see a lot of her in you. Same bone structure and coloring. Same fearlessness."

Thea had gone silent.

He frowned across the table. "Did I say something wrong?"

"What? No. I was just wondering where Lyle Crowder was the night Kylie disappeared."

"He was on a fishing trip with his brother. He didn't return home until Monday afternoon."

"You've checked out his alibi?"

"Of course. Why? What are you thinking?"

"He used to work on offshore oil rigs when I was a kid. He was sometimes gone for months at a time."

"So he told me."

"He had an old bluetick coonhound with him when we talked earlier."

"Okay," Jake drawled. "I'm a little lost here. What does one have to do with the other?"

Thea felt a tingle of excitement along her backbone. "He's had that breed for as long as I can remember. He told me he left his dogs with his brother when he was working. But the night Maya went missing, we heard a hound baying in the woods."

"I doubt Lyle Crowder was the only one around here who had a coon dog."

"No, of course not, but I've had the same feeling as you that we're missing something hidden in plain sight. Could the clue that solves both cases be something as simple as a dog baying in the woods?"

Jake eyed her across the table. "It seems a stretch."

"Maybe, but just think about it. He's been living across the street the whole time, watching from the shadows of his front porch. He would have known about Reggie's party the night Maya was taken. He could have easily assumed that she and her friends would be so inebriated no one would think to check on Maya and me for hours. Twenty-eight years later, he would have seen Taryn and Reggie leave the house last Sunday morning. He could have walked across the street, removed the key from the flowerpot and let himself in the front door to unlock the bedroom window. Then all he had to do was wait for the lights to go out later that night."

She expected Jake to shoot down her theory, but instead he sat back in his chair with a contemplative frown. "He told me he used to go exploring in the cave. He even offered to go down with his dog and take a look around if we needed him to."

Thea leaned forward. "Are you sure his alibi is airtight?"

"Worth taking another look," Jake said as he rose. "I need to make a couple of calls."

"Of course. I'll go freshen up and give you some privacy."

"I don't want to chase you out of your own room."

"You're not. We both know I have a conflict of interest in this case, and you need to be able to speak candidly."

"This won't take long."

"No worries." She went into the bathroom and closed the door. As tempting as it was to listen in, she turned on the tap and washed her face, brushed her teeth, and then pulled the hair dryer from under the sink to blow out her damp hair. Then, with nothing else to do, she used the little bottle of lotion on the vanity to moisturize her hands and sat on the edge of the tub to wait. After a good ten minutes, she got up and opened the bathroom door.

"Jake?"

She stepped through the door and glanced around. The bedroom was so silent she thought at first he must have left, but instead he'd stretched out on one of the beds and fallen asleep.

Thea started to wake him up, but then she realized how exhausted he must be to succumb so quickly. Draping a blanket over him, she left him to rest as she took care of the dinner tray and then turned out the lights. Crawling into her own bed, she lay on her back and stared up at the ceiling until the sound of Jake's breathing lulled her to sleep.

THE ROOM WAS still dark when Thea woke up. For a moment, she had that disquieting sensation of not knowing where she was or how she'd gotten there. Then she shook away the cobwebs and pushed herself up against the pillows. The window was open. She could feel a warm breeze against her skin as she kicked aside the covers.

A shadow moved out on the fire escape. She reached for her weapon as she called softly, "Jake? Is that you?"

He crawled back through the window. "Sorry. I didn't mean to wake you."

"You didn't. I rarely sleep through the night." She glanced at the clock on the nightstand. Just after midnight. "What were you doing out there?"

"Listening to the wind chimes in the courtyard across the street. You can hear them up here, by the way. You didn't imagine the sound last night."

"Good to know."

He turned back to the window, still listening to the night. "What is it with this town and wooden wind chimes?"

"According to Lyle Crowder, a local woman used to make them. People hung them in their trees for good luck. He said when the wind blew just right, you could hear them all over town."

"Interesting tradition."

"He said Reggie used to have them hanging from a tree in her backyard. I'd forgotten until now, but I think that sound is what awakened Maya. She thought someone was outside our room. I told her not to be a fraidy-cat." Thea sighed. "That was the last thing I ever said to my sister."

Jake turned and leaned against the window frame. His eyes glinted in the dark. "What happened wasn't your fault."

"I know. But if I'd called out to Reggie, maybe she would have come to see about us. Maybe she would have scared the kidnapper away."

He moved across the room and sat on her bed, draping a casual arm across her legs. "Kylie's disappearance has stirred up a lot of painful memories for you, hasn't it?"

"Yes. I can't help thinking there's something more I should be doing to find her. Something I should remember that could reveal the kidnapper."

"If this were another case, you'd tell the family members not to torture themselves. You'd say obsessing over what could or should have been done does no one any good, least of all the missing child."

"And I would know better than anyone that it's easier said than done not to dwell."

"None of this is easy. For the families or for us."

"But you wouldn't want to do anything else," Thea said.

"Would you?" There was a hushed, intimate quality to his voice in the dark.

She shivered. "I don't think either of us has a choice."

He thought about that for a moment. "Why did you move to Cold Cases after I left Washington? You were on a fast track. You had a lot of people in your corner, including me. It was only a matter of time before you would have been assigned a team."

She shrugged. "Somebody has to keep looking for those kids after the CARD team goes home."

"Even if Cold Cases is the place where careers go to stagnate and die?"

"Yes, even if," she said with conviction. "None of us do this for the glory."

He fell silent. Except for the gleam of his eyes, he was little more than a silhouette at the end of her bed. Yet Thea felt so physically attuned to him, she could almost hear the beat of his heart in the darkness.

He straightened. "I should go, let you get some rest."

"You don't have to. It's late. There's plenty of room here, and besides…" She trailed off. "This isn't a good night to be alone."

He didn't say a word, but instead rose and, ignoring the second bed, went around to lie down beside her. They weren't touching, but Thea felt closer to Jake than she had to anyone in a very long time.

After a moment he said, "Do you ever wonder what would have happened if you'd come with me to Jacksonville?"

She turned in surprise. "To my career, you mean?"

"To us."

She closed her eyes. "What's the point in wondering? You never asked me to come."

"You never asked me to stay."

She drew back. "How could I ask that of you? You'd worked so hard for so long. No one deserved that promotion more than you. Besides, when you finally told me you'd accepted the offer, you acted as if you couldn't leave town fast enough. I thought part of the attraction of the new assignment was getting away from me."

"You couldn't possibly have thought that."

Something in his voice caused her to tremble. "We'd come to a crossroads in our relationship. It was either commit more deeply or break up. Your leaving town made the decision easy for us."

"It was easy for you?" He turned to stare at her in the dark.

"You know what I mean." She scowled up at the ceiling and tried not to feel such deep regret. Tried not to think about the cold, empty apartment that waited for her back in DC. "It wasn't easy, but it was inevitable. We always said the job had to come first."

"That was a mistake," he said. "It worked for a while, but what we do can't be all that we are. It's too dark. There has to be light at the end of the tunnel." He paused. "I can't help wondering if you've found that light."

"Are you asking if there's someone in my life? No. What about you?"

His slight hesitation caused her heart to sink. "No."

"You hesitated," she accused.

"No one serious," he said. "No one who gets me the way you do."

She slid her hand down his arm and clasped his hand.

He squeezed her fingers. "I've missed this. I've missed you."

"After all this time?"

His voice deepened. "You have no idea how often I think about you."

Thea didn't know how to respond to that. She felt overwhelmed and a little unnerved.

"Am I being too honest?" He brought their linked hands to his mouth. Such a soft, sweet kiss and yet Thea felt a shudder go through her as she rolled to her side.

"I've missed you, too," she said. "I just didn't want to admit it."

"That stubborn streak." She heard a smile in his voice a split second before he threaded his fingers through her hair and kissed her deeply, stirring a longing she'd tried to bury since the day he'd left DC.

Nothing stays buried forever. Not secrets. Not longing. Not love.

Yes, love, although maybe she was still too stubborn to take her confession that far.

They kissed for the longest time and broke apart only to undress slowly, without frenzy or desperation. Just two old lovers comfortable in their familiarity. Two injured souls needing to find momentary light at the end of a very dark tunnel. But when their bodies joined, it was shockingly dynamic. Electric. Like the sizzle of two live power lines in a lightning storm. Thea could hardly catch her breath. Everywhere Jake touched turned to fire. Her neck, her breasts, the insides of her thighs. Clutching the covers, she arched into him, matching his rhythm until they collapsed against one another, gasping and quivering. Even then, Jake didn't let her go. He rolled onto his back and nestled her in the crook of his arm. She fit perfectly. As if she'd never been gone.

Chapter Thirteen

Jake was already dressed when Thea woke the next morning. "What time is it?" she asked sleepily when he came out of the bathroom.

"It's early. I need to go back to my room and grab a shower and shave before I head over to the command center." He sat on the edge of the bed. "If you meant what you said yesterday about finding something for you to do, come by later and I'll put you to work."

She rose on one elbow, squinting at the slash of sunlight streaming in through the window. "I need to go see Reggie first. I also promised her I'd visit my grandmother."

Jake quirked a brow. "I didn't think the two of you were close."

"We're practically strangers. I can't even remember the last time I saw her. She never wanted anything to do with me when I was growing up, and I don't expect anything has changed for her. But I'll make the effort because it seems important to Reggie and because, I'll admit, I'm curious."

"Do you need a lift?"

"I've arranged for a rental car. Should be here by nine or so. Hopefully, I'll have my new phone by then, too, if you need me."

He nodded. "I have a new phone, too. Same number." He reached for his keys on the nightstand before turning back to Thea. "Should we talk about what happened last night?"

She straightened the covers. "Yes, we probably should, but later. Our priorities haven't changed. There's still a missing child out there."

"A fact I don't forget even for a second." A mask dropped as he stood. He was already thinking about Kylie and about what he and his team needed to do in the coming hours to find her. "I'll keep in touch," he said briskly. Then he bent and brushed his lips against hers. "And we *will* talk," he promised.

She waited until the door closed behind him before throwing off the covers and climbing out of bed. A shower came first. She dug fresh clothes from her suitcase and quickly dressed. By the time she'd called the hospital to check on Reggie, her cell phone had arrived. She went downstairs and sat on a bench outside the hotel to familiarize herself with the new model while she waited for the rental car to be delivered.

A movement across the street caught her attention. Grace Bowden stood at the bay window in the Indigo Dollhouse, staring out. Thea waved, but the woman didn't respond. Her gaze seemed fixated on the street as if she were waiting for someone.

Curious, Thea got up and crossed the intersection. She pecked on the window and, after a few moments, Grace opened the door.

"Thea! What are you doing here so early?" Grace looked pretty and summery in a floral dress and sandals, but there was still something about her bright smile that didn't quite ring true to Thea.

She motioned behind her to the hotel. "I was sitting outside just now and noticed you in the window. I thought I'd stop by and say hello."

Grace cast an uneasy glance toward the curb as her

fingers toyed nervously with the delicate gold necklace at her throat. "That's nice of you. I didn't expect to see you again before you left."

Thea gave her a surreptitious scrutiny. "Am I interrupting something? You must be expecting a client. You said you only open on weekends these days unless you have an appointment."

"Yes, I have a collector coming in later. The meeting has the potential to be a lucrative transaction for me."

"Then why do you look so upset?" Thea asked. "Forgive me if I'm being too nosy, but I can't help wondering if something is wrong."

Grace glanced once more at the street before she stepped back and motioned Thea inside. "A woman called my house this morning." She closed the door behind them. "She said she was looking for an antique doll for her niece. I explained I had a meeting today and suggested she come in on Saturday to look at my inventory. She insisted on coming in first thing this morning. She said she's leaving the country today and won't be back for quite some time."

"Did she give you her name?"

"Valerie something-or-other. I jotted it down, but it was probably made up. I think she was calling for Russ Buchanan."

Thea frowned. "What makes you think that?"

"The woman was very specific about the doll she wanted for her niece. Her description was nearly identical to the antique doll Russ bought for Kylie's birthday."

"What did you tell her?"

"I couldn't give her an exact match. Most of my inventory is one of a kind, but I told her she was welcome to come in and take a look at my collection. When I inquired about her niece's name and age, she hung up. I know it sounds crazy, but I can't stop thinking about that call. I can't help wondering…"

"What?" Thea prompted.

"I know this sounds crazy, but do you think Russ Buchanan and that woman could be taking Kylie out of the country?"

"One phone call isn't much to go on," Thea said. "Have you told Chief Bowden about the call?"

"No, not yet. He's just so busy at the moment." She bit her lip. "You don't think I'm overreacting? The last thing I want to do is waste Nash's time or send him on a wild-goose chase."

"I think it's always better to be safe than sorry," Thea said. "Tell him what happened and let him decide how to proceed."

"You're right, of course." Grace hurried around the counter to grab her phone. "I just can't stop thinking about poor little Kylie. She was so shy and nervous the day Taryn brought her into the shop. A child deserves better than a philandering, abusive father and a mother who's so neglectful she allowed her own child to be taken right from under her nose." She glanced up, stricken. "Oh, Thea, I'm so sorry. I wasn't thinking."

"It's fine. Should I leave while you make the call?"

"Oh no, please stay. I'd rather not be alone if the woman shows up. Or, God forbid, Russ Buchanan himself. Besides, I could use the company. Go on into the kitchen and help yourself to a cup of coffee. I won't be but a minute."

Thea walked into the back and glanced around. Something was different about the space. She tried to pinpoint the change as she listened to Grace's low voice in the other room. Then she had it. The child-sized table and chairs was missing from the corner.

She glanced over her shoulder into the shop. She hadn't noticed earlier, but the shelves were even emptier than when she'd been in the day before. Was Grace clearing out her merchandise for some reason?

Taking out her phone, she called Jake. He answered on the first ring. "I was just about to call you." He sounded tense.

"What's going on?"

"I'm at the hospital with Reggie." Thea's heart jumped to her throat, but before she could respond, he said quickly, "She's okay. I wanted to talk to her about Derrick Sway."

Thea's pulse was still thumping. "Are you sure she's okay?"

"Yes, she's fine. I'm just leaving her room now."

"Was she able to tell you anything?"

"About Sway, no. But she did tell me something interesting about the Bowdens."

Thea's gaze shot into the outer room. "That's...a co-incidence."

"Why?"

She turned away from the doorway and lowered her voice. "I'm with Grace now."

"At her shop?"

"Yes. She said someone called earlier looking for a doll identical to the one Russ Buchanan bought for Kylie a few months ago. She had the impression the woman was calling on Russ's behalf. The woman said she needed to buy the doll this morning because she's leaving the country and won't be back for some time."

"Where is Grace now?"

Something in his tone sent a prickle of fear up Thea's spine. "What's going on, Jake? What did Reggie tell you?"

"Don't react, just listen. Your instincts were right about the Bowden marriage. Grace and Nash Bowden were separated for a long time before they finally divorced over a year ago."

"Okay," Thea said in a neutral tone.

"Reggie said when Grace was a kid, she seemed to have an unnatural obsession with Maya's disappearance. She was always asking questions about her, always wanting to see pictures of her. Reggie would sometimes catch her in your room going through the dresser drawers and closet while you were outside playing. She put up with the behavior for a while because no one else was allowed to come to the house and play with you. Then things went missing. She eventually told Grace not to come over anymore."

"I don't get why this is important," Thea whispered into the phone.

"Five years ago, Grace lost a baby. She never got over it. The child, a girl, would have been the same age as Kylie. Grace has intimate knowledge of Reggie's house and Maya's disappearance. And she misled you about the state of her marriage. It's not proof of anything, but it's enough to make her a person of interest."

"I see." Thea's gaze flicked around the space while they talked. The back door opened to the patio and a second door led to, presumably, a storage area. The building was ancient. There might even be a cellar with walls thick enough to drown out a child's cry for help.

"Thea, are you there?"

"Yes."

"Keep her talking if you can, but be careful what you say to her. She may be volatile and possibly dangerous. I'm on my way to the shop now."

"Okay." Something had come back to Thea as she fixated on that closed door. She could almost hear Reggie's voice in her ear.

That girl is a thief and a liar, Althea. A bad seed if I ever saw one. I don't want you hanging around with her anymore. Every time she comes over, something turns up missing. Hairpins, books, a picture from my dresser. I'll bet you anything she's the one who took my wind chimes.

The memory was so vivid that for a dangerous moment, Thea became lost in the past. Jake's voice in her ear and the creak of a floorboard startled her back to the present. She whirled a split second before the Taser barbs connected with her skin and every muscle in her body started to spasm.

THEA DIDN'T REMEMBER losing consciousness, but she must have. When she opened her eyes, she found herself on the floor in a strange room, one hand cuffed to an old iron bedstead. The blast from the Taser wouldn't have incapacitated her for more than a few seconds. Long enough to drag her outside and heft her into the back of an SUV? Then what?

As her mind cleared, the images came back stronger, along with the hazier sensation of a needle prick in her arm.

She straightened on the floor and jerked at the handcuffs as she craned her neck to glance out the window. The landscape was wooded, and she could see the gleam of a lake in the distance. They were no longer at the doll shop. No telling how many miles they'd traveled from Black Creek while she'd been unconscious. She had no idea how long she'd been out, but judging by the brightness of the sun, no more than a few hours. It was still broad daylight outside.

She tried to quell the roiling in her stomach as she took stock of her surroundings. The room was sparsely furnished with a bed, dresser, nightstand and lamp. Nothing within her limited reach that could be used for a weapon or lockpick.

Directly across from her was an open closet. Inside the shadowy recess, a child hunkered with her head buried against her knees and her arms clasped around her legs. She was so still and silent that, for a moment, Thea thought she might be sleeping.

"Kylie?" She said the name so softly the child didn't appear to hear her. "Kylie Buchanan, is that you?"

The child kept her face buried as she tried to push herself deeper into the closet.

"It's okay, sweetheart. I'm not going to hurt you. I want to take you home to your mommy."

Still no sound or reaction.

"Do you know Reggie?"

The head finally bobbed up.

"I know she's a friend of yours. I'm her daughter, Thea."

Kylie dropped her arms from around her legs and scooted to the edge of the closet, poking her head out to survey the room before she scrambled to her feet.

"Is my mommy dead?"

Her quivering voice tore at Thea's heart. "No, honey, she's not dead. She's worried sick about you, though. She misses you very much."

The child inched closer. "She said Mommy died. She said my daddy killed her."

Thea tamped down the horrified gasp that rose to her throat. "Your mommy is fine, I promise."

"Will you take me to her?"

"Yes, just as soon as I can. I may need your help, though, okay?"

A reluctant nod.

"Do you know where we are?"

She shook her head.

"Are you okay? Have you been hurt?"

Another headshake. "I want my mommy."

"I know, sweetie, I know. I need you to do something for me. Go back into the closet and see if you can find something sharp, like a safety pin or a belt buckle. Anything metal. Can you do that for me?"

The little girl went back over to the closet and dropped to her knees to explore. A few minutes later, she crawled back out with something clutched in her fist. She approached Thea shyly and held out her hand, displaying a child's hairpin adorned with a pink plastic flower.

"Is this yours?" Thea asked, then froze in recognition. She and Maya had had nearly identical hairpins. Thea's had been yellow. This one was pink. "Is there anything else like this in the closet?"

Kylie shook her head.

Thea stared at the pink plastic rose. Had Grace taken the keepsake when she was a child or had she entered Reggie's house more recently to unlock the bedroom window?

She glanced back outside. Where were they? Surely not at Grace's home. She wouldn't take the chance on hiding Kylie where she might be spotted by neighbors. No, they were someplace remote, but close enough to town that Grace could easily drive back and forth while she made arrangements.

A car pulled into the driveway just then. At the sound of the engine, Kylie dashed across the room and scooted back into the closet. A few minutes later, a door closed in the outer part of the house. Thea slipped the hairpin underneath the mattress and lifted a finger to her lips as her gaze met Kylie's. A split second later, the bedroom door opened and Grace Bowden stepped inside.

"I didn't expect you to be awake so soon. I thought you'd be out until after we left. Not that it matters all that much. Everything is still going according to plan."

"What plan is that?" Thea asked. "Where are you taking her?"

"Somewhere safe for both of us." She glanced around the room. "Come out, dearest. Don't be shy. I've brought your favorite lunch. It's waiting for you on the table along with a little surprise. Come on, now. Don't you want to see what I've brought you for our trip?"

Kylie stared out from the back of the closet with wide, frightened eyes.

"It's okay," Thea coaxed. "Go eat your lunch. I need to talk to Grace."

"Don't tell her what to do," Grace snapped. "You're not her mother."

"Neither are you."

"Don't listen to her," Grace said to Kylie. "I am your mommy now. I'll take such good care of you. You'll love where we're going. It's warm and sunny, and we can swim every day if we want to. Please come out and eat your lunch. We need to get on the road soon."

Thea caught Kylie's eye and nodded. The child crawled out and reluctantly followed Grace into the other room. Thea could hear a TV or radio from another part of the house. A few minutes later, Grace came back into the bedroom and closed the door. "I know you must have questions. Not that I owe you any explanations, but I always liked you."

Thea stared up at her. "Yes, I have questions. Why are you doing this? You know you won't get away with it."

Grace smiled. "You might be surprised. People have always underestimated me. As to the why...it's very simple. Every child deserves a mother who will love and protect her unconditionally."

"Kylie has a mother who loves her."

"But she couldn't protect her, could she? Not even from the child's own father." She knelt, putting them at eye level but keeping her distance. When Thea shifted away from her, Grace said, "Oh, don't worry. I've no intention of hurting you. We were friends once. I always thought we could have been best friends if Reggie hadn't been so mean to me."

"You stole things from our house," Thea said. "She didn't like that."

"She had no proof that I took anything."

"But you did, didn't you? You took her wind chimes

and hung them from a tree over an opening that led into the cave. How did you even know the opening was there?"

"I stumbled across it one day. My parents didn't care what I did so long as I stayed out of their way. My aunt Lillian meant well, but she was clueless when it came to precocious children. Sometimes when I got lonely or felt sorry for myself, I'd spend hours in the cave exploring. That's how I found Maya's grave. I hung Reggie's wind chimes in the tree to keep her company."

"And the stick figures etched into the rock?"

Grace shrugged. "She needed a headstone and I knew she'd want you close."

"You saw her drawing on our refrigerator. That's where you got the idea for the stick figures."

"I always loved that drawing. You and Maya holding hands for all eternity. I used to wonder what it would be like to have a sister. To have *someone*."

"Why didn't you tell anyone about the grave?" Thea asked. "If you truly considered me a friend, you would have told me."

"I wanted to," Grace said. "But I liked having a secret too much."

"It made you feel special. Important…?"

"Yes," she admitted candidly. "Oh, I fully intended to tell you someday. I imagined how I would do it all the time. I'd lure you into the cave and lead you back to the cavern. You'd be awestruck when you realized what I'd found. But you were always such a fraidy-cat. You wouldn't even climb over the fence, much less go down into the cave with me. Then, after Reggie told me I couldn't come over any-more, I didn't want you to know. I didn't want her to know."

"You decided to keep Maya all to yourself. Except it isn't Maya in that grave."

Grace looked momentarily surprised before she shrugged. "It was still a good secret."

"When did you decide to take Kylie?"

"I'd noticed her for years. Sometimes when Taryn would take her to the park, I'd close the shop early and walk down the street so that I could watch them through the fence. She's such a lovely child, with a sweet, shy disposition. After a while, it became painfully obvious how desperately unhappy she was. It wasn't fair that she should have to suffer or that I should be so lonely when the two of us could have each other.

"When I heard that she and Taryn were staying with Reggie, I started to make plans. Even then, I wasn't sure I could go through with them. Then that night—Sunday night—I drove back to the church after the service just to catch another glimpse of her. I saw Taryn get out of her vehicle and go into the building without Kylie. She left her alone in the car after dark. Anything could have happened to that child. I knew then it was up to me to protect her."

"So you took her. You planted Maya's picture in Derrick Sway's bedroom and you hung those totems in the woods so that everyone would assume he'd kidnapped both Kylie and Maya. Then you told him that Reggie was the one who'd turned him in to the police, knowing he'd come after her."

Grace sighed. "People are predictable, for the most part. The plan worked perfectly until you showed up. But I knew eventually you'd remember how I tried to get you to go into the cave with me. You'd remember my curiosity about Maya's disappearance and the keepsakes that went missing from your house. You'd get just suspicious enough to start asking uncomfortable questions, so I needed to throw you off the scent until Kylie and I were safely out of the country."

"You drugged me that first night," Thea said. "How were you able to get into my room?"

"Security is nonexistent in that old hotel and people are

trusting in a small town. I've watched that place for years from across the street. They all have their routines. It was easy to get your room number from the front desk and grab a key card from housekeeping. A little ketamine on a piece of glass and you wouldn't feel quite yourself for days."

"You won't get away with this," Thea said again. "I was on the phone with the FBI when you attacked me. They're probably already tearing your shop and home apart. It's only a matter of time before they figure out where we are."

"No one knows about this place. Not even Nash. My aunt inherited the cabin years ago and never changed the name on the deed."

"The FBI will find it, trust me."

"Eventually, but by then it'll be too late. Kylie and I will be far, far away."

"You're delusional," Thea said.

"I'm what my parents made me." She gave Thea a sad smile as she rose and moved to the door. "It's a shame, really. We could have been such good friends."

THEA WAITED TO make sure Grace wasn't coming back into the room before fishing the hairpin from beneath the mattress. Popping the plastic flower from the clip, she bent the wire to make a short L shape. Placing the long end of the L inside the handcuff lock, she turned it like a key, rotating the pin to push down the inside ridges. She had to stop more than once to quell her impatience so as not to break the thin wire. As she worked, she could hear the front door opening and closing as Grace made several trips from the cabin to the car and back. Thea had no idea of their immediate destination. Probably to the coast to board a ship somewhere. If Grace had somehow acquired passports so that they could leave the country, Kylie might never be found.

When the lock clicked open, she could have wept with

relief. She flung off the cuff and stood to glance out the window. The SUV was still in the driveway. Grace was busily arranging suitcases in the cargo area.

Thea left the bedroom quickly, taking a quick survey of the living area. Kylie lay curled on the sofa with her head turned toward the TV. She seemed so absorbed in the cartoon that she didn't notice Thea when she tiptoed into the room. She didn't even react when Thea whispered her name. Then Thea realized that the child had been drugged to keep her docile for the trip.

She scooped Kylie up into her arms, nestling the child's head against her shoulder as she moved to the back of the house, searching for another way out. All the while, she expected to hear Grace burst through the front door at any moment. Hurrying through the small kitchen, Thea fumbled with the back door lock for an impossibly long time before they were finally outside. She held Kylie close as she sprinted for the trees. A shot sounded behind her and then another. She dove for cover, turning so that her body protected the child's.

"I don't want to hurt you, Thea, but I will if I have to!"

She lay Kylie gently on the ground. The child roused and whimpered.

"Shush. It'll be okay," Thea soothed.

"You can't outrun me," Grace warned. "I know these woods like the back of my hand."

Thea hunkered behind the tree and waited. After a moment, Grace grew impatient and strode into the trees. Thea braced herself, willing Kylie to silence as she waited. Grace came into view, but still Thea waited until the distant sound of a car engine captured Grace's attention. Thea sprinted forward, lowering her shoulders and crashing into Grace with enough force to take them both down. They landed hard on the ground, momentarily dazed before they each scrambled for the weapon.

The car engine drew closer as they fought. Doors slammed. Voices sounded from the back of the cabin. Thea tried to tune out the distraction as she focused on the struggle. Grace was a lot stronger than she looked, and she fought like a cornered animal, kicking, scratching and then landing a punch that sent Thea sprawling backward. Grace grabbed the gun and rolled, taking aim a split second before someone kicked the weapon from her hand and ordered her to lie facedown on the ground. Then Chief Bowden knelt and cuffed his ex-wife.

"You okay?" Jake put out a hand as Thea scrambled to her feet.

"How did you find us?"

"We're the FBI, remember?" He glanced around. "Kylie…?"

"She's over there." They both rushed to the child's side and Jake lifted her tenderly in his arms.

Chapter Fourteen

A little while later, they were back at the hospital, standing outside Taryn's room. Kylie had been examined as soon as they'd brought her in and then she'd been taken straight up to her mother. The reunion brought tears to Thea's eyes.

"This never gets old," Jake said. "This is what we live for."

"Yes, but it's not an entirely happy ending," Thea said. She moved away from the door. "I'm worried about Russ Buchanan. He won't give up his family without a fight. I'm afraid Taryn is in for a rough time if he sues for sole custody."

"She may have some leverage," Jake said. "One of his former clients swears he was hired by Buchanan to harass Reggie. We think he's the one who ran her car off the road. His testimony will give Taryn some ammunition in a custody fight."

"I hope so. After everything she and Kylie have been through, they deserve a little peace."

They moved down the hallway toward the elevators.

"Buy you a cup of bad coffee?" Jake asked.

"Thanks, but I'm on my way to see Reggie. Rain check?"

"I'll be heading back to Jacksonville in a couple of hours. Our work here is done." He punched the down arrow button. "What about you? When will you go back to DC?"

"I'm not sure. Reggie will need some help when she gets out of here. I thought I'd stick around for a few days."

"Maybe I can drive down on the weekend," Jake said. "We haven't had our talk yet. Or better yet, come see me in Jacksonville. I'll show you around the office. Let you get the lay of the land."

She frowned. "Why do I need to get the lay of the land?"

"There's an opening on my team. I'd like you to come work with me again."

"I don't know, Jake. That's a generous offer, but I've got my own work. What I do is important, too."

"I know it is. I don't see any reason you can't do both." The elevator door opened. He ignored it. "I left once without asking you to come with me. I'm not about to make that mistake again. Just think about it, okay?"

The door slid closed. Neither of them reached for the button.

Thea drew a deep breath. "Did you mean what you said? I could do both jobs?"

"Yes. I wouldn't want it any other way."

"Then I don't have to think about it. This may surprise you, but I've been considering a move for quite some time."

"You always manage to surprise me," he said.

"I have a lot of unfinished business down here. I never would have admitted this before, but I'd like to be closer to my mother."

"You both deserve a second chance."

"Yes, but Reggie isn't my only unfinished business. I need to find out what happened to my sister and to somehow make peace with my grandmother." She slipped her hand in his. "And then there's you, Jake."

The tender gleam in his eyes was like the light at the end of a very dark tunnel.

* * * * *

COLTON 911: UNDER SUSPICION

BONNIE VANAK

For the real Harry in my life, my heroic dad,
Harold Fischer. Love you, Dad. Miss you.

Chapter One

On some days, life was worth living again. This wasn't one of them.

Lifting the sheet covering the victim, Detective Harry Cartwright squatted down by the body, the eyes staring skyward at nothing. A neat round hole punctured the victim's forehead and a small-caliber firearm rested near his outstretched right hand. Christmas lights adorned the red-brick mansion and several reindeer decorations grazed near a red sleigh filled with brightly wrapped boxes.

"How can anyone hate Santa Claus?" he mused, his gaze scanning the red suit, the immaculate white ruff ringing the cuffs.

He dropped the cloth over the body. Out of habit he touched the gold medal he always carried in his trouser pocket. The last thing he expected before coffee was a dead Santa Claus. Naperville was a peaceful suburb of Chicago, a place where Santas were more than likely to bounce kids on their knees for photo ops than end up with slugs in their foreheads. But Jimmy had driven him out here, a stop on the way to where another vic—Axel Colton—had died.

Though it wasn't his case, Harry could no more resist a quick look at a crime scene than a dog could resist a meaty bone.

Jimmy Curry, lead investigator with Major Crimes in Naperville, thrust a steaming paper cup at Harry. He gulped the coffee gratefully, glad for the warmth scalding his throat. A veteran of the force, Jimmy had been his old partner in Naperville before Harry moved to Chicago.

"Who called it in?" Harry asked.

Jimmy jerked a thumb at a patrol cop standing nearby. "Junior here. First week on the force."

The cop, who looked all of eighteen years old, flipped through a notebook. "Vic's name is Devin L. Duell. Ex-con, in for breaking and entering, paroled last month. Neighborhood security guard shot him. She was making rounds and saw him trying to break in around oh six hundred. He turned, lunged at her and she fired. Single shot to the head. Homeowners are Mr. and Mrs. Henry Ladd, away for the week at a convention."

"Where's the security guard?" Jimmy asked.

The uniformed cop gestured to a woman standing nearby. "Maureen Markam. Robber meets security guard armed and ready."

Harry glanced around at the snow dusting the elegant sweep of driveway, the immaculate lawn, the house locked up tight.

"You think this was a burglary?" he drawled to the patrol cop.

"Miss Markam said there's been break-ins over the last few weeks. Some guy in a Santa suit. Meets the description."

"Security cameras?" Harry pointed to the house behind them.

"Blacked out with spray paint. Just like the ones at Axel Colton's house." The newbie's eyes brightened. "Hey, you think this has to do with the Axel Colton murder?"

Harry resisted the temptation to roll his eyes. He

pointed to a red sack a crime scene investigator photographed. "What's in the bag?"

The newbie frowned. "A soccer ball and a kid's toy truck. I still think this is a robbery gone wrong."

Jimmy sighed. "Harry, why don't you give the kid an education?"

"Why not?" Harry squatted by the body, lifted the sheet again. "Look here, kid. This is execution style." He pointed to the bullet wound. "See the gunpowder residue? Close range, against the forehead."

He dropped the sheet again, dusted off his hands. "You know the drill, Jimmy. Have your team check reports of local burglaries to see if the vic's description matches. Interview all the neighbors. Check all incoming emails, letters, phone calls and visits to our Santa in prison before he was paroled."

He narrowed his gaze at the security guard talking to another detective. "Something in Miss Markam's story doesn't match. See if she had a relationship with Santa."

As Jimmy shooed off the newbie cop, Harry saw a familiar face among the gathering throng of bystanders outside the crime scene tape.

His day went from mildly bad to excruciating.

"Harry Cartwright!"

Dominic Anthony Russo the Third. Shock of white hair neatly swept back, his coat impeccable. Snow melted soon as it touched the man's shoulders. Funny about Dominic making anything melt. Harry always thought the man was as icy as Chicago in winter. Even when Marie and John were alive.

Never one to obey rules, the old man ducked under the tape, ignoring the protests of the uniforms guarding the scene. Harry walked toward him before Dominic trampled all over the crime scene. He touched the medal again. It was a family heirloom, had belonged to his wife.

"Dominic." Short and clipped greeting, hoping the old man wouldn't cause a scene this time.

"Harry. I can't say it's a pleasure to see you back here." Russo flexed his fingers as if he longed to punch him.

Again.

"I'm here on official business and this is a crime scene." Harry pointed to the sheet-covered body, one black boot sticking out from beneath it.

"Right. Cop business." Russo shook his head. "Low pay, chasing criminals. You screwed up, Harry."

Here we go again. Harry remained silent. Russo couldn't say anything worse than what Harry had said to himself over the past two and a half years.

"You could have had all this, Harry." Russo swept a hand up and down the tree-lined street and the multimillion-dollar mansions. "You should have stayed in Naperville and taken that job with my firm. Head of my security. And then Marie and John would still be alive."

Russo fisted his hands in Harry's jacket, bunching his tie. "You killed them as much as that crook who was after you did."

Harry shrugged off the man's grip. He smoothed down and straightened his tie. "I'm not a rent-a-cop. And I told you, I'll live with their deaths on my conscience as long as I breathe. But I'm not your lapdog, Dominic. I don't answer to you. In fact…"

He narrowed his gaze at the older man. "Where were you this morning around 6:00 a.m.?"

His ex-father-in-law sputtered. "How dare you…"

"This is an official homicide investigation." He crooked a finger at Jimmy, who hurried over. "I asked a question. Where were you?"

"I was home with my wife! I'll call my lawyer…"

"Call your lawyer, but that makes you look even more suspicious," Jimmy drawled.

"Jimmy and the major case squad may have more questions for you. Don't leave town." Harry walked off to a string of curses from Russo that would make a sailor proud.

Harry felt a wave of relief as a uniform pulled Russo back behind the tape. Not his case. Not his problem. Not his town anymore.

He stared at his reflection in the window of a police cruiser and straightened his tie. Tiny, scowling Tasmanian devils peppered the black fabric. Marie had given him that tie for his birthday. She thought it was whimsical and fun, something he needed in his life. And then a few weeks later, a car crash ended her life and John's and anything whimsical and fun died with his family.

Jimmy joined him, shutting his notebook. Jimmy, bless him, knew the strained relationship with his ex-in-laws.

"Intense."

"Yep. He can be." Harry rubbed the nape of his tensed neck. He withdrew the medal, staring at it.

Marie's great-grandmother brought it over from Italy, passing it down to Dominic, who gave it to his only daughter. Treasured family heirloom and his wife had given it to Harry on their wedding day.

"St. Jude is the patron saint of hopeless causes, darling," Marie had told him with an impish smile. "Our marriage is a lost cause, according to Dad, so you might as well have it for protection."

Damn, he felt like a wrecking ball smashed into his guts the day she died. Every time he touched the medal, it reminded him of her, but along with the good memories came the bad, the guilt…

Jimmy popped a piece of chewing gum into his mouth as Harry pocketed the medal once more. "We'll handle this. What did you dig up on the Colton case?"

Axel Colton. Blunt force trauma, his head bashed in in his luxurious Naperville home recently. Out of Harry's jurisdiction, but Naperville's major crimes unit asked him to be point man on the case. With Christmas coming up, Naperville's police department had their hands filled. The murder of wealthy Axel Colton took prominence, but the department was slammed, so they called in a favor and asked Harry to be lead detective on the investigation. The sooner Colton's murder was solved, the sooner good citizens could sleep easy.

Didn't hurt that Harry had met the Coltons while dating Carly Colton, Ernest and Fallon Colton's daughter. Carly's father and her uncle Alfred had been murdered by a serial killer Harry had helped to collar.

Harry glanced around. Too many ears and mouths, and he knew how this neighborhood gossiped. He inclined his head at Jimmy's car. "If you're done here, let's roll."

Jimmy nodded, left the investigation to two other detectives and soon they were driving away. Harry felt another wave of relief, as if he'd escaped the yawning jaws of a steel trap.

His old partner guided the car down a tree-lined street. "Why do you want to visit the crime scene again? Got any leads?"

"Maybe. Whoever killed Axel Colton wasn't Santa Claus."

Jimmy slid the car into a parking space before Axel Colton's mansion. The house loomed, silent and dark in the snowfall.

Harry pulled out his phone, showed Jimmy a photo he'd come across.

Jimmy whistled. "Your latest love conquest?"

"Hardly. Her name's Sara Sandoval. Came across her photo when I was checking out Vita Yates, Axel's ex-wife. Met her at Yates' Yards, the nursery where she works, when I was chasing a lead on Nash Colton, when we thought he might have killed Axel."

"Quite a looker."

"Yeah, reminds me of Carly Colton." Harry pocketed his phone. "I used to date Carly."

"Lucky you. You questioning this Sara? What connection does she have to Axel?"

"I plan to talk to her." Harry rubbed his beard, his jaw tight. "I did a little digging. Found something at the crime scene as well."

He laughed.

His former partner glanced at him. "What's so funny?"

"The Coltons." Harry snorted. "Everywhere you turn, there they are."

But in this case, his dating Carly, and attending a couple of family dinners with her, proved beneficial to the case.

Because after meeting her at Yates' Yards, he realized Sara Sandoval wasn't just a pretty face who reminded him of Carly Colton. But unlike with Carly, he'd felt instantly smitten, the chemistry between them like an electric shock.

Harry knew he had to forget the attraction he'd felt upon seeing her. The family resemblance was plain. Sara was related somehow to Axel Colton.

He'd made it a rule to never get involved with suspects.

Especially during a homicide investigation.

WHAT DID YOU do when all your hopes and dreams shattered like brittle glass?

You picked up the pieces and started all over again. Survived. She knew how to survive. Hadn't she done exactly that since the day her mother told her the truth about her real father?

Sara Sandoval took in a deep breath of the chilled Chicago air. Paste on a bright smile, push forward. But first…

The Yates were kind enough to give her time off after Sara requested it for personal reasons. She insisted on working from home. Go home and rest, they'd said.

Vita and Rick, her employers at the nursery, thought she simply had a stomach bug. They didn't know her connection to the dreadful news about Axel Colton's death.

No one did. Easy enough to hide in plain sight from everyone with her last name. Her marketing expertise had gained her a job while she'd watched the Coltons from a distance.

She'd gone home but had not rested for the past few days. She'd worked on the accounts she'd scored for the nursery and between working, tried to reconcile herself to what happened.

Shivering, Sara used her key to open the lobby door to her apartment building and shouldered her way inside before the door banged shut. She took the stairs to the third floor, the bags filled with groceries feeling like lead weights. But the elevator was finicky again, and she didn't want to get trapped.

At Apartment 302 she knocked loudly. Widow Pendleton was slightly deaf.

The door opened to reveal an elderly woman, a yellow knit shawl draped around her shoulders, her rheumy blue eyes peering behind spectacles. The woman brightened upon seeing Sara.

"Sara my dear! Come in!"

Sighing, Sara went into the kitchen and set one bag down on the cracked linoleum table. "Mrs. Pendleton, I told you, you need to use the peephole before answering the door and find out who is there."

"No one comes much to visit these days, dear. Except you." Her face crumbled. "My Amy never visits, not since we had a falling-out last year."

The widow reached into a cookie jar and withdrew some worn dollar bills. "How much do I owe you, dear?"

"Keep it. It wasn't much." Sara thought of her slim budget and winced, but it seemed more important for the widow to have food than she did.

Vita will probably ply me with chicken soup when I go back to work at Yates' nursery tomorrow. Her kindhearted employer was like a second mom to Sara.

"Now, Sara…you're always doing everything for me. Please, take the money."

Pride was a tough thing to swallow. Sara knew about that, and sensed the elderly woman disliked handouts. "I'll tell you what. Make me one of those delicious apple pies you enjoy baking and we'll call it even."

Mrs. Pendleton frowned. "You can't have apple pie for dinner."

"Says who? The apple pie police?" At the woman's chuckle, Sara added, "I love to eat homemade apple pie."

The woman beamed. "I'll get started on the pie right away."

After they said their goodbyes, Sara walked down the hallway to her own apartment. When she was inside, she set the bag down, shrugged out of her winter coat and then put away the few purchases.

Though it was almost noon, she had no appetite. Instead, she made coffee and paced the kitchen. Before it finished dripping, she poured herself a cup.

Sara picked up her mug of coffee and brought it over to the postage-stamp-sized table. On the table a scrapbook lay open.

She hadn't looked at this album in a long time. So very long, until this morning.

The mug was warm beneath her fingers. She read the inscription, her throat tight.

WORLD'S GREATEST DAUGHTER!

She'd taken the cup home from Yates' Yards and planned to return it. The Yateses had an assortment of customized coffee mugs in the employee break room. Sara had gone through the entire collection. Her favorite proclaimed WORLD'S GREATEST DAD. She always selected that cup when it was clean and she wanted coffee from the break room. But she hadn't seen it for days now, so she'd settled for WORLD'S GREATEST DAUGHTER!

The irony of the sentiment wasn't lost on her.

Sara cut out the photo of Axel Colton from a recent newspaper article on his death. Snip, snip, the scissors moving methodically as if she were cutting wrapping paper for a gift and not a photo from a news article about a murder.

Four quick strokes of the glue stick across the back. She placed the photo on the empty page.

Something splashed onto the newspaper cutting. Sara swiped a hand across her face. No tears. *Don't let anyone ever see you cry.*

Axel Colton was dead, along with her dreams of ever knowing her real father.

Since February, she'd been observing the Coltons. A few times she'd seen her birth father from a distance.

Every time she saw him, she tried to work up the courage to approach him, tell him the truth about her origins.

Each time she'd failed.

Now she had nothing but regrets, and a photo album filled with clippings.

With an angry swipe, she sent the album sailing off the table. It landed on the cheap linoleum and lay open, like a wound.

Hands shaking, she sipped her coffee and stared out the window at the streets of Chicago below her. Snow had fallen, then stopped. It would be another cold winter.

Was this move here, and the changes she'd made, all for nothing?

You have cousins. You have other family. Confess to them who you really are and there's a chance they'll accept you. It's not too late.

Her throat squeezed tight as she realized her mother might not like the idea of Sara cozying up to the Coltons. She'd been less than enthusiastic when Sara told her she was moving to Chicago to finally meet her birth father.

Now Axel was dead. Her mother had been mysteriously out of reach since Jackson, Myles Colton's son, had been kidnapped last month. The little boy had been safely found, the thirty-million-dollar ransom paid with fake bills and the man who picked up the ransom money found dead.

Vanishing like this after Axel's death didn't bode well for Regina. If anyone had reason to kill Axel Colton, it was her mother.

Sara called Regina and left another voice mail.

"Mom, call me. It's urgent. Please call me as soon as you get this message!"

Sara hung up and began to pace the tiny kitchen, sidestepping the album. She couldn't bear to look at it anymore.

She needed to come clean with the Yateses and tell them who she was, and hope for the best. They'd hired her for her expertise in marketing the nursery. Maybe they wouldn't fire her for her origins.

Sara glanced at the clock hanging on the wall above the window. Almost noon. She couldn't simply stay here any longer. She had to get out, clear her head.

As she headed for the winter coat hanging on a peg in the hallway, the downstairs buzzer rang. Sara frowned.

Surely Mrs. Pendleton couldn't have baked a pie that quickly. Few people knew she lived here. She hadn't made many friends since moving in, simply because she'd been too busy with work...and stalking her birth father.

I'm a father stalker.

Not anymore.

Sara pressed a button by the door. "Yes, who is it?"

"Detective Harry Cartwright, Chicago Police Department. I need to talk with you."

Her heart did a happy dance for a minute. The detective who'd been at Yates' Yards when he informed Vita about Axel's death. Sara had fainted and had woken up to see his handsome face furrowed with concern.

After buzzing him through, Sara smoothed down her cranberry sweater and opened the door the length of the chain lock when he knocked.

He put a badge up for her inspection.

"Sara Sandoval? I have a few questions. May I come inside?"

Sara unhitched the chain and opened the door, letting him inside. The rush of pleasure faded as a cold chill rushed down her spine. The detective wasn't here to pay a social visit.

"What's this about?"

"Axel Colton. I'm investigating his murder."

Sara bit her lower lip so hard she tasted blood. Sooner or later, she knew it would come to this.

The sharp-eyed detective seemed like the type who would never stop until he got the answers he wanted from her.

Chapter Two

Harry had been chilled before, now he was hot. Surely it wasn't the surge of pure male interest that slammed into him as he entered Sara's apartment.

No, it was the heat coming from her radiator, bathing him in warmth as he walked into her apartment hallway. Though it was December and not the icy cold of a true Chicago winter yet, she had the thermostat turned way up.

And Sara Sandoval wore a sweater. A cranberry-red sweater that clung to her curves like glue. He gave a brief, appreciative look. Polished and professional, even while relaxing at home. But she looked anything but relaxed.

At first glance, he recognized the slight resemblance to Carly Colton. But it was like comparing a skyscraper to the pyramids of Giza. Sara was nearly as tall as he was, and had a classic beauty with her honey-tinted skin, black hair and high cheekbones.

She looked like a model, not a potential murder suspect. Vivid green eyes that could snap with passion, now narrowed in suspicion. Hair bound in a braid, as if she needed it off her face. For a single moment, he wondered what she looked like with all that silky hair free of restraint. Maybe fanned out across a pillow as she lay in bed, relaxed, her arms lifting upward to pull him down atop her...

Don't go there.

Harry turned off the very male part of him and focused on the surroundings as she led him into a small living room. Sara hugged herself, finally looking at him.

"What can I help you with, Detective?"

He almost told her to call him Harry. Keep it friendly, personal. Keep her off guard, unbalanced. Get her to talk. Then turn up the heat, so to speak, and get the information he wanted.

For some odd reason, he disliked playing good cop, bad cop with her. She seemed frail and vulnerable. But he'd met homicidal people who acted the same.

Honesty was the best approach.

"I have some questions for you. May we sit?"

Silently she gestured to a sofa that looked like a Goodwill donation. Harry sat, watching her perch on the edge of an equally frayed armchair.

"How are you feeling? You gave everyone a scare when you fainted at Yates' Yards."

She shrugged. "I'm better now. I didn't eat much that day, so I guess the lack of food made me faint."

Or perhaps news someone close to you had died. That can also cause a fainting spell.

"How long have you worked for the Yateses?"

She blinked, as if the ordinary question caught her off guard. "Eight months."

No more information. His guard went up. Most people were eager to talk about themselves, offer information before he even asked. She was closemouthed, quiet.

"And you do what for them?"

"Marketing."

Any more clipped answers and he'd have nothing more

than when he'd walked into the apartment. Harry did a cursory scan of the surroundings.

"What kind of marketing can a nursery need, especially in winter?"

She blinked again, but this time his question didn't shut her down.

"Plenty of marketing. That's when business naturally slows down, so nurseries need that extra push. I'm working on a large account, the Richardson-Davis wedding. They requested a theme wedding for Christmas and we're supplying all the flowers to their florist."

"Let me guess, holly and Christmas trees," he said dryly.

Sara smiled, a genuine smile that added a sparkle to her eyes. "Far from it. Vita and Rick have been courting this account for a while, but had no idea how to cater to the couple's requests. They wanted something different, big, larger than life that would be the talk of the social set. If they liked Vita and Rick's ideas, the Yates nursery would land all the flowers for the wedding and the engagement party and the florist will use our stock before going elsewhere for large orders. I suggested a tropical wedding. Hawaiian. Birds of paradise, ferns, leis, everything. I made the contact and suggested the theme, and the couple loved it."

Now he had her warmed up like a Cubs pitcher before a big game. Sara became animated, her hands moving in the air as she described the floral arrangements for the wedding of the season.

Then she looked at him, her skin darkening, and her mouth opening. "Oh, you didn't come here to learn about planning a Hawaiian wedding."

Charmed, he grinned. "No. Sounds fascinating, though."

He flipped open his notebook. "Have you ever met Axel Colton?"

The switch from flowers to the vic made her pretty mouth wobble. "Um, no. Never."

She fisted her hands on her lap. Now they were getting somewhere.

"Am I under investigation?" she blurted out.

Harry gave her a level look. "I'm looking at all angles and possibilities for everything and anyone connected to the victim."

He began firing off questions at her, the hard stuff, asking where she was the night of the murder, was she familiar with the vic, all standard things. Sara had no alibi. She was home alone the night Colton was killed.

Flushed now, her hands so tight they appeared bloodless, she finally unclenched her fists. "It's warm in here. I need a glass of water. Would you like one?"

Shaking his head, he watched her stand, race into the kitchen as if eager to escape him. *Sorry, not going to happen.*

Harry followed her into the kitchen and watched her fish a glass out of the dishwasher.

He glanced down, saw the album lying open. *This is interesting.*

Axel Colton's face from a magazine clipping stared back at him. Harry picked up the album.

"You dropped this."

Sara's green eyes widened. Her pulse beat faster as she carefully set down the glass on the counter as if afraid of dropping it. If he'd wanted any indication his suspicions were on target, he had it now.

He watched her bring the album to an empty drawer in the kitchen, shove it inside and slam the drawer shut.

"Miss Sandoval…"

"Sara."

"Sara, I must ask. What are you doing with a photo album of the victim?"

Caught.

Sara swiped a bead of sweat away from her perspiring forehead. She'd never been adept at lying or even evading the truth, up until the day she'd decided to move to Chicago to get to know her birth father better.

If she'd felt icy cold this morning and wondered how she could endure a tough Chicago winter, she was on fire now. Maybe being in the hot seat under the scrutiny of this detective was a way to save on heating bills. Sara almost laughed, caught herself and gathered her lost composure.

She indicated a chair at the table. "Please sit."

He sat, arms on the table, his eagle-eyed gaze centered on her as she took the opposite seat.

"You're related to Axel Colton."

The detective's statement felt like a gut punch to her stomach. "Oh? I am?"

He gestured to her face. "There's a family resemblance."

Sara touched her mouth. "There is?"

His mouth twitched, as if he struggled to hide a smile. Maybe he knew what she was doing. Surely someone as savvy as Harry Cartwright knew when one was evading direct questions through asking questions of her own.

"You came here to Chicago, perhaps to meet him. Not so much for a marketing job." He flipped through his notebook. "You were the assistant director of multimedia for Caymen Reynolds, one of the largest marketing firms in the Midwest. One doesn't give that kind of high-powered position up to take a job advertising ferns for a local nursery."

Sara felt her stomach roil. "Maybe I wanted a big change of scenery."

"In Chicago?" He arched a dark brown eyebrow. "A big change of scenery is moving to Miami. You haven't been living here long, and it looks like you're unsure about settling in."

"What makes you think that?"

His mouth twitched upward in a brief smile. "I've never seen such a clean junk drawer. There's no signs of a real home, nothing on the walls. Only a few books and knick-knacks on the bookcase. There's also plenty of boxes still unpacked in the living room."

Despite her trepidation, she had to admire his skills. "Yes. I moved here not long ago from St. Louis. You're quite good at detecting, Detective."

Gone was the small smile, replaced with intensity. He leaned across the table.

"Yeah. That's my job. So tell me the truth. What are you doing with Axel Colton's photos in that album?"

Sara folded and unfolded her hands. "It's not a photo album, not really."

Photos were in a photo album. She had no real photos of Axel. No happy family gatherings, no father-daughter dances at school, no photos of Axel and her mother together. Just the one photo Regina had back in her house of Axel, tucked away in a drawer.

If Sara hadn't found that photo, maybe she never would have known. Never would be in this mess.

"Semantics. May I see it, please?" He pointed to the drawer.

Biting her lip, she went to the drawer, jerked out the album and all but threw it on the table before him. "Here. I should burn it now that he's dead."

Detective Cartwright didn't flinch. Instead he began

flipping through the album, his expression neutral. Finally he closed it.

"Magazine and newspaper clippings. No photos. Why were you stalking Colton? Because he's related to you?"

"I don't have any photos of him because he never knew I existed." She folded and unfolded her hands again, this time in her lap. It was hot in here. "He, he's, um, my birth father."

"Ah."

That was it? A one-syllable word? No inflection, nothing to hint what he thought or if he accused her of being more than a curious daughter. She'd never been grilled by the police before. Never had reason to, either.

Not until Axel was murdered.

Life wasn't fair. All she'd wanted was a chance to meet the man she'd dreamed about her entire life. Even though her mother warned that Axel and the Coltons in general were nasty people one did not want to know, Sara had to find out for herself.

Sara looked down at her hands again. Offer as little information as possible, yet she was already a suspect and she didn't want him asking others personal information to find out about her origins. Not before she had a chance to level with Vita and Rick. They'd been so kind to her, treating her like a daughter.

"My mother was his mistress, but they severed ties years ago, before I was born. My mother, Regina, blamed Axel for my brother's death. After my brother died, she left Axel, changed her name from Perez to her mother's maiden name, Sandoval, and moved to St. Louis to begin a new life before my birth."

"Why did you really move here?" Cartwright's voice seemed almost gentle.

Pride made her sit up, look him square in the eye. "To

meet him. I never knew Axel Colton was alive until I found a photo of him in my mother's drawer. She told me years ago he was killed in a boating accident, along with the brother I never knew. It was only when my mother finally confessed the truth that I set out to find him. Axel was alive. My brother drowned in a swimming pool because Axel was too busy to watch him."

It had seemed like a crazy quest, to quit her plum job and leave behind her friends to start over in Chicago. *Call me Don Quixote, tilting at the windmill of Coltons.*

But she'd never questioned herself on the decision. Maybe some people would have taken time to think about their actions. But some people might also never grab the chance to realize a dream.

She had, and knew nothing would stop her from pursuing it.

"You got the job at the Yateses' nursery to spy on the Coltons?"

Sara's temper began to rise. "Not spy. Observe. Figure out how I could get close enough to meet my father."

"Why not just ring his doorbell?" Cartwright's gaze sharpened.

To someone as skilled and experienced, and perhaps normal, as this detective, it seemed like an easy decision. Ring the doorbell, introduce yourself. He and the others had no idea how long she'd pined to have a father and a family, and how she feared discovering the father whom she'd idolized in death would never live up to the expectations she'd built around him.

It was like dreaming of meeting a celebrity, only to have the celebrity slam the door shut in one's face. If Axel had done that, Sara didn't know what she would have done.

"Miss Sandoval? Answer my question, please."

"Sara."

"Sara, why didn't you simply ring his doorbell or call your father? He wasn't a private person."

He waited. Silence.

"Sara?" He leaned forward. "Are you all right?"

"Fine. I'm having a Forest Park moment," she murmured.

Now he seemed caught off guard. "Forrest... Gump moment?"

She laughed, a loud, sharp laugh that contrasted to the ugliness she'd mentioned. "Forest Park. It's the largest park in St. Louis, where I'm from, but you already know that, Detective, since you did a thorough background check on me. I used to walk there to gather my thoughts."

"Don't think," he shot back. "Tell me the truth. No need to think about what the truth is. You and I both know it. You were in Colton's house. Don't lie to me."

If he'd reached out and slapped her, she couldn't have felt more shocked... "What...no! Never. I never set foot inside his house. I never even met him!"

"Then why was a coffee mug with your fingerprints found in his kitchen?"

Confused, she shook her head. "What coffee mug?"

He scrolled through his phone, showed a photo. Sara's heart sank.

WORLD'S GREATEST DAD.

"Don't deny using this cup." He tucked his cell phone back into his trouser pocket. "We ran the prints. Yours and Colton's were the only ones we lifted off the mug."

More confusion. She shook her head. "I mean, no, yes, I used it! It belongs to the Yateses, they have it in their break room at the nursery where I work. But I was never in Axel Colton's house! How did you get my fingerprints?"

Calm. Cool. Confident. The detective was in charge

and he didn't need to assert any authority. It practically oozed from him. "You're in the system. Your mother fingerprinted you as a child in case you were ever abducted."

Slow rage began to build. "My mother did that to protect me and now the police are using it against me?"

"We use whatever resources are available to us to do our job, Miss Sandoval. Why were you in Colton's house?"

"I wasn't! I never even came close. I couldn't…"

"The truth."

Her temper finally snapped. "Fine! You want the truth? You want to know why I didn't simply ring his doorbell or call him up like an old friend? Confront him and say, 'Hi, Dad. It's me, the illegitimate daughter you never realized existed, I'd like to get to know you.' Why didn't I do that? Because I was afraid, all right? I was afraid he'd shut the door in my face!"

The dam burst and she spilled everything pent up inside since discovering her father had been murdered. "I was afraid he'd throw me out, or accuse me of wanting his money, and then what would I do? I'd dreamed about meeting him, dreamed about having this stupid life where he actually cared about me. I couldn't face that kind of hard rejection. I had to mentally prepare myself for it and then when I finally did work up the nerve to ask Vita and Rick to introduce me, he's dead. Gone forever. I'll never have that chance. I don't know how that coffee mug got in his house, but it wasn't me who put it there. Someone else did."

Sara slumped against the hard vinyl chair, burying her face into her hands. This was all wrong. The detective was doing his job. He wasn't a therapist or a friend. He didn't care about her lost hopes and dreams.

A hand settled gently on her shoulder. Sara uncovered her face to see him holding out a wet paper towel. She murmured thanks, scrubbed the tears from her cheeks and then carefully placed the towel into the trash bin. Threw it away, like her lost chances in life. But by the time she turned back to the detective, she felt more in control.

"Thank you." She expelled a breath. "I apologize. You're just doing your job."

His blue-green gaze seemed less harsh, but he still gripped the pen in his hand. "I am sorry for the loss of your father."

The simple condolence, so commonplace with the Coltons who could claim a legitimate family connection to Axel, eased the tightness in her chest. Part of her stress, she realized, was that no one knew she secretly mourned him. No one knew she had the right to mourn such a sharp loss.

"You're the first person to say that." Now she looked him straight in the face, not caring if her emotions showed like snow on blacktop. "Not even my mother would care."

If her mother even knew Axel was dead. But again, Sara didn't know, because Regina had been out of touch for days.

"Did your mother say anything about Axel's death?"

"No, I don't know." She gave another bitter laugh. "That's another problem. I haven't talked to her since the night little Jackson was kidnapped. I had called to let her know Myles's son had been taken and the kidnapper wanted thirty million as a ransom. It was so upsetting, I had to talk to someone who understood. Mom has a soft spot for children in trouble."

He ceased scribbling on the little notepad. His gaze sharpened again. Gone was the compassionate man, replaced by the suspicious detective.

"You haven't called your mother to tell her your father is dead?"

"I've called. Left messages. She hasn't answered. She could be gone on a company business trip...left her personal cell phone at home."

"Most people always have their phones with them on business trips." He glanced at her. "I have to contact her."

Sara rattled off her mother's cell phone number. He shut his notebook. "Thanks. Did you contact her employer?"

"Yes, but the office has been shut down for renovations the past two weeks. Roof leak. Everyone is working remotely from home and I don't have the home number of my mother's boss."

"Huh."

His tone indicated he didn't believe her. How could this detective know that she and Regina had fought about Sara's moving and her mother had pleaded with her to let the past go?

Don't go see your father, Sara, please, he's not a good man...

"Is my mother a suspect?" she blurted out.

His gaze turned level. "I'm afraid I can't say. Official police business."

Sara frowned. "My mother is not the type to end someone's life. She's a kind, caring soul."

Doubt on his face said it all. *Right. Why should I believe you?*

He nodded at her. "Don't leave town, under any circumstances. I need to be in touch with you at all times. I will have more questions."

She showed him out the door and when he left, she sagged against it, her knees weak.

Official police business. She liked this detective, against her better judgment. He had flashes of real compassion, and his rugged body and penetrating blue-green gaze could make a woman feel safe but wanting to get past that hard exterior. Secrets filled those amazing eyes. For a moment when she mentioned her dead brother, they had filled with his own personal pain before his expression turned guarded once more.

Harry Cartwright was investigating her father's death and now Regina turned into a suspect. If anyone had reason to kill Axel Colton for the misdeeds of his past, it was her mother, who blamed him for Wyatt's drowning.

A mother never forgot a child who died.

Worry built inside her again. Where was her mother and why wasn't she answering her phone?

Chapter Three

Long ago, Sara learned to set aside personal problems to focus on work. It served her well as she flipped open her laptop to work on coordinating the floral arrangements for the Richardson-Davis wedding. In two weeks, everything had to be delivered to the florist's exact standards.

With this account and the prestige of the wedding, Yates' Yards was certain to land other prime business.

She worked quietly, trying not to let Detective Cartwright's visit distract her. Oddly enough it wasn't the fact he considered her a suspect in her father's murder. It was the man himself she couldn't quite erase from her mind.

In another time and place, she'd fall hard and fast for Harry Cartwright. It wasn't so much his good looks. It was his manner, the flashes of compassion and kindness she'd seen, even when he grilled her.

Sara sighed and pushed back from the kitchen table. She stood, did a series of stretches and was shocked to see the kitchen clock read nearly 5:00 p.m. Grabbing her cell phone, she dialed Vita Yates.

"I'm so sorry," she blurted out when Vita answered. "I'll be in tomorrow. I've been working on the spreadsheets for the Richardson-Davis wedding. How are all the arrangements?"

"Don't worry, Sara. Everything's under control here. Are you feeling better?"

Vita's warm, caring tone made Sara suddenly vulnerable, wanting to dissolve into tears. Faced with a tough cop like Harry Cartwright and she could hold her own, but the moment someone as sweet as Vita showed concern, she melted like snow in Florida.

She gripped her cell phone so hard her knuckles whitened.

"I'm so much better, thanks." *And under investigation for the murder of your ex-husband.* "I'll be back tomorrow at eight, ready to work."

"Thanks, dear. You're such an asset to us. Make sure to rest plenty tonight. Thanks to you, we have many more clients to plan events for. Oh, by the way, our Instagram account has dozens of new followers thanks to your ideas!"

Sara wished her a good night and hung up, feeling like a rat for lying. Honesty was best. How many times had her own mother lied to her over the years about her father and brother?

Tomorrow morning, she would come clean with Vita and Rick about her identity. If they threw her out on her butt into the cold street, well, she wouldn't blame them.

She'd be jobless, though. Not as if she'd been through worse.

She checked the nursery's Instagram account on her phone, pleased to see all the likes and comments on the latest post. Sara had suggested to Vita and Rick to take a few selfies as they worked in the greenhouses and caption them with little stories about themselves to drive home the point that Yates' was a family-owned and -operated nursery that specialized in personal touches. Not only had they done so, but Lila, Vita's daughter, had snapped one of herself in a stylish green sweater, peeking out from an arrangement of poinsettias in the humid greenhouse. The cheerful Christmas blossoms accented Lila's wide grin, resulting in the most traffic.

Pocketing her phone, Sara stared out of the window at the windswept street. Harry Cartwright came to mind again. *Don't leave town.* She was stuck here. Not that she wanted to leave. She wanted answers as much as he did. When she found out who killed her father, maybe she'd finally have closure.

Outside, a man and a young girl of perhaps five scurried down the street. The girl had a pink winter jacket, unzipped. She slipped and nearly fell on the sidewalk, but the man caught her. Laughing, he swept her up into his arms and they continued on their way.

Her mouth wobbled as she stared after them. Memories struck like icy knives. Ten years old, father-daughter dance. Her teacher telling her with a sympathetic look only fathers and daughters were permitted. Perhaps she had an uncle who could escort her?

Remembering the white-hot embarrassment of the entire class staring at her as she'd shaken her head and mumbled she had no male relatives.

Someone had tittered.

Someone else gave her a new nickname—All Alone Sara.

Billy Barton, who had a mother and father and endless family, even made up a song about her, "Sara, Sara, all alone. No daddy to hug her when he gets home!"

She scrubbed her face with her chilled hands. At least the nicknames and singing had stopped after she'd slugged Billy Barton on the playground two weeks after the dance. She'd gotten three days detention as a result of Billy's black eye. Oddly enough he stopped teasing her and began tagging after her, giving her gifts of a Twinkie from his lunchbox or pencils with the end chewed off.

If only it was so easy to erase the hurt her own mother caused with the lies she'd told Sara "to protect her."

Her cell phone jingled softly. Maybe her mom finally decided to check in. She grabbed it, recognized the number and answered.

"Ernie, hey, how are you? What's up?"

Her former boss blew out a breath. "Finally! I had to ask my secretary to look up your number. You changed phones."

A pinch of guilt. When she'd moved to Chicago, she'd cut most of her ties in order to focus on her new life and goal of finding her father. "Yeah. I was tired of you calling me and begging me to come back and rescue you."

He laughed. "Changing your phone wouldn't ever work with me, Sara. I'm a bloodhound."

"No, your secretary is." She found herself smiling. "What's going on?"

"I'm in Chicago for a few days. Want to have dinner?"

"Hey, what are you doing in town?"

"I'm here for a client meeting. It's not until tomorrow, though. Flew in tonight."

"Who's the client?"

"Stafford & Son Electronics."

She made a whistling sound. "Impressive. All of their Midwest division?"

"That and the East Coast as well. I know you were working on nabbing that account, they expressed interest and you left us."

True to Ernie's good-natured personality, he didn't sound bitter about her abandoning ship. Ernie didn't care, as long as the client eventually landed with their company.

"They're a good client, but make sure you address the father and the son when meeting with them. The father is old-world, demands respect, and the son is always pushing social media advertising on the father."

How hard she'd worked on that account, slogging until late at night to brainstorm ideas they'd find acceptable. Now they were signing, finally, and she'd lose out on the healthy bonus. But money wasn't as important as it once was.

"Hey, have dinner with me and give me some pointers. I could use your advice, Sara."

She hesitated a minute.

Ernie Livingstone was a vice president in the firm, a gregarious man happily married with two adorable daughters. She'd always felt comfortable chatting with him. Ernie had begged her not to leave, and promised the door would remain open if she wished to return.

He knew something bothered her and prompted her departure, but didn't pry.

Suddenly the prospect of being alone in her apartment all night seemed as appetizing as swimming in Lake Michigan in winter. Dinner was too long and intimate with Ernie, who could wheedle and cajole her into returning to the firm, but a drink couldn't hurt. And maybe Ernie could even check on her mom when he returned to town.

Sara hated admitting to herself she was beginning to worry more than usual. All the scenarios playing out in her head ended up with Regina feeling guilty over Axel's death, guilty over not telling Sara the truth, maybe even guilty because she'd been the one to kill him.

She couldn't bear to think about the latter.

Sara pulled herself together. "How about a drink instead? Where are you staying?"

"The Four Seasons."

Sara laughed. "On a company expense account, of course."

"What else? You think I could afford the bill otherwise? I have two kids to put through college."

She laughed again, feeling the day's tension slide away. "Ernie, you've been using that excuse since the day they were born."

"Can't start saving soon enough. Do you know how much it costs to send one kid through Harvard? What time?"

She glanced at the clock. "It'll take me a while to catch the train and get there. How about seven?"

"Train! Girl, you need to move downtown, be where the action is!"

Rolling her eyes, she shook her head. "I'm not a veep in a billion-dollar marketing firm, Ernie. I'll meet you in the lobby."

As she hung up, she ruefully thought of her old life. Instead of a cheap one-bedroom in Evanston outside Chicago, she could have afforded a small but elegant apartment downtown on her old salary. Maybe even with a prime view of Lake Michigan.

So much she'd sacrificed simply to meet Axel Colton and call him Dad face-to-face.

What was more important? A large salary and the fast-track career path to making partner? Or trying to establish a relationship with the man you've dreamed about since you were little?

She glanced around at the secondhand furniture and cramped space. "Here's your sign, and your answer."

For meeting Ernie, she chose elegant black silk pants, an emerald green cashmere sweater and cute designer ankle boots with sturdy heels. At least her wardrobe screamed style, if her surroundings did not.

She unbraided her hair, brushed it out and stared at her reflection. Definitely a haircut was in order, but there hadn't been time. Maybe now she could find a good stylist.

The air was crisp and cold, but it had stopped snowing. Sara walked to the train station, thinking about her life back in St. Louis. She'd commuted into the city with her car, had her own parking space. Now, like thousands of other commuters, she hoofed it to the L to save on gas and parking downtown.

But there was something to be said for the time it took to reach Chicago's downtown. It gave her plenty of time to reflect.

When she finally reached the Four Seasons, she was more than ready for warmth and a drink with Ernie. She eagerly anticipated catching up with her former boss, and getting news about her coworkers and her former staff. Penny, her assistant, had cried the day Sara announced her resignation plans to move to Chicago.

The elegant lobby made her sigh in appreciation. With its majestic view of Lake Michigan and downtown Chicago, and the welcoming atmosphere, the hotel boasted a contemporary charm that catered to both businesspeople and tourists. Small wonder Ernie chose to host a client meeting here. Impressions were important, especially in their business.

Not her business anymore. No, her business was dirt and potted lilies, not multimillion-dollar clients and a healthy expense account to wine and dine them.

Ernie waited for her in a chair in the lobby. Always a stocky man who had his suits tailor-made to fit his height and girth, he seemed to have gained a few pounds. More gray feathered his hair, though he was only in his early forties. For a moment she wondered if the same would happen to her if she had stayed in her lucrative but high-pressured career path at the firm.

He waved, and when she approached with a big smile, whistled.

"Looking good, Sandoval. Real good. Have I told you lately how beautiful you are? Man I miss you!"

The praise made her squirm. Sara turned so his intended kiss on the lips landed on her cheek. She wrinkled her nose at the distinct smell of bourbon.

"Starting without me, Ernie?"

His smile dropped. "I'm celebrating. What's wrong with a little celebration?"

Sara was glad she committed only to a drink, not dinner. She patted his arm, as one would reassure a sullen child. "You have the right to celebrate. It's a big account. Let's have that drink and you can tell me about it."

A few people were in the lounge, scattered at the booths and tables. Only a few were at the horseshoe-shaped bar. Lamps on each table added a quiet, intimate effect. Maybe too intimate. Ernie ushered her toward a corner booth and took her coat, draping it on the opposite seat. She slid into the booth with her purse and he joined her on the same seat, putting distance between them at least.

Until she realized he was staring at the bar like a pointer dog at a rabbit.

"I'll get our drinks. White wine for you? Chardonnay, right?"

She waved at the seat. "Let the server do it, Ernie. No rush, no need to order from the bar."

And something about the way you're acting makes me feel better about a server handing me a drink instead of you having it.

Ernie was happily married, and always respected her, but Sara had learned to trust her instincts when socializing.

He pouted again, but settled back against the leather banquette. Sara scanned their surroundings. A few couples sitting at the bar leaned close, and a man in a black suit at the far end of the bar studied the television sandwiched between lighted glass shelves filled with liquor bottles. He was too far away to see clearly, but he had a good view of everyone who entered the bar.

Probably waiting for his date.

A waiter scurried over, took their drink orders. Sara decided against alcohol. She needed to retain her wits, and cut her ties short. She ordered seltzer with a twist of lime. Ernie a double bourbon.

When the waiter left, her former employer shook his head. "I invited you for a drink, Sara. When did you stop drinking wine?"

"I have an early day tomorrow." True enough.

"Right. Working for that nursery. What do they have you doing, digging in the dirt?"

She clamped a lid on her temper. "They're a large business in Chicago."

"Chicago doesn't need you as much as we do. You really should return to us, Sara. You're sorely missed."

She felt a pinch of guilt and smiled. "It's good to be needed."

Ernie grinned. "You sure are pretty, Sara. I almost forgot how pretty. Since you left, we don't have any account managers whose good looks are an asset with clients."

Her smile dropped. "I always thought my brain and my business acumen were my biggest asset with clients."

He waved a hand. "Of course, of course. You were the best. You're stylish, and what you're wearing proves it. Can't have a frumpy account manager meeting with high-end prospects."

Tension knotted her stomach. All the years she'd worked with Ernie, had she missed this underside of him? Had she been so invested in the opportunities the firm offered she ignored this?

Respect was important, especially for her. Appreciation went far, and credit as well. For the first time, Sara wondered if Ernie gave all three at the office. Rumors had stirred about how he swiped accounts from younger account managers eager to climb the ladder.

Was she one of them? Did it matter now?

No. But working for Vita and Rick, who truly appreciated her skills and not the designer labels on her clothing, made her see Ernie in a new light.

Setting aside those concerns, Sara started asking questions about the office and the account.

"You should have seen me. I hooked and reeled him in. You did an okay job gaining his interest, Sara, but he needed a professional touch, a man's sales pitch."

As he talked, bragging about how he'd coaxed the client into signing with the firm, her eyes glazed over. Had Ernie always been this pompous and overbearing? Perhaps she'd excused or never noticed his behavior in her eagerness to advance at the office.

When the waiter set their drinks down, Ernie grabbed his. "Here's to the new account!"

She raised her glass, watching him down half the contents of his drink. Sara sipped hers, wondering how she could slip away. Her lonely apartment was starting to look more and more appealing.

"Sara, hey!"

She glanced up, saw Nash Colton and Valerie Yates, Rick Yates's niece. Sara did a double take. Nash held

Valerie's hand in a proprietary way, signaling his intent. It made her glad. She liked Valerie, who had been kind to her each time she saw her and gone through pure hell when Nash was suspected of Axel's murder. Security cameras at Nash's house showed the heavy candlestick in his car's trunk had been planted there by a stranger.

Now Nash was cleared. *And I'm under suspicion.*

"Nice to see you again." She made introductions. "My former boss, Ernie, is in town. This is Valerie Yates and Nash Colton. They're related to my current employer."

"But not to each other." Valerie gave a little laugh. "Only through marriage. Uncle Rick is Nash's step-uncle."

Ernie didn't get up or offer to shake hands, only nodded. "Oh right, the nursery people."

Sara's smile tightened. "We're catching up on my former company."

"Interesting coincidence," Nash murmured. "All four of us being here at the same time."

"Four?" Sara asked.

"You, us and Harry Cartwright. He's over there." Valerie gestured to the solo man at the bar.

Craning her neck, she realized the detective wasn't wearing a suit, but a silk tuxedo. Dinner dress. Intrigued, she watched him. Even from a distance, he cut a nice figure, the jacket stretched across broad shoulders, his hair and short beard well groomed.

Sara's heart raced. "Yes, interesting coincidence. I hope he didn't bother you, Nash. I mean, you're not a suspect in Axel's murder anymore."

Nash's jaw tightened and his gaze hardened. "No, I'm not but I want to find who did kill him, as much as the rest of my family does."

Why was Harry Cartwright here? Stalking any Coltons who happened to stop by?

Or worse, was the detective tailing her because he thought she was guilty of killing her own father?

Chapter Four

She'd hoped for an entertaining evening away from her small, stuffy apartment. Not this kind of potential drama. Sara fisted her hands in her lap.

"Sara? Are you okay? You look lost." Valerie sounded amused. "You should go over and say hello to Detective Cartwright."

No thank you. We already had an interesting conversation.

Ernie leaned forward, took another slug from his glass. "Sara didn't come here to pick up men. She's with me."

An uncomfortable silence descended. Sara's stomach tightened. How she wished she could throw her seltzer in Ernie's face, but creating a scene, especially in front of the detective, made her pause. She didn't want to draw any unnecessary attention to herself.

"This is a nice place," she said lamely, ignoring Ernie. "Do you both come here for a drink often?"

Goodness, she sounded like an idiot.

Nash's gaze softened while Valerie rested her head against him.

"No. Nash wanted to celebrate being cleared of Axel's murder, so we booked a room."

Too dark to see Valerie's flush, but Sara suspected it was

there all the same. She smiled. "Good reason to celebrate. You both deserve it. Romance, roses and candlelight."

Valerie's expression blanked. Sara wanted to bang her head against the table. She'd forgotten about the heavy candlestick planted in Nash's trunk by whoever wanted to frame him for Axel's murder.

"No candles. Or candlesticks," Nash said dryly. "But we'll manage the romance without them. We have theater tickets, so we'd best get going. See you, Sara."

Nash took Valerie's elbow and ignored Ernie.

She waved goodbye.

Feeling the unexpected weight of someone looking at her, she glanced at the bar to see Harry Cartwright studying her. She flushed, resisted the temptation to touch her hair or smooth her sweater. He nodded at her and turned back to his drink.

For a wild moment, she wished she was sitting at the bar with him, instead of sequestered with her former boss.

"Hey, Sara. Let's go somewhere more private to talk about the account."

She glanced over, saw his glass had emptied. Then she felt a sudden quick pressure on her leg.

He was touching her. Sara squirmed away, but he slid closer. Fumes invaded her breathing space as he leaned close. She turned away, feeling trapped.

"C'mon, Sara, let's have some fun. You were always so serious at work. I've got a room upstairs."

In your dreams. Sara felt an urgent need to leave, now, before this escalated. Ernie had never been this obnoxious. Then again, she'd never been alone on a business trip with him and seen him drink like this.

"I can't go anywhere until you slide out of the booth, Ernie."

He beamed, threw two twenties on the table and then

slid out of the booth, holding out his hand. Grabbing her purse, she left the booth and ignored his hand, snatching up her coat instead.

"I have to leave. Good luck with the account, Ernie."

Harry turned in his seat, watched her. He tilted his head, as if trying to figure her out.

Nothing to see here, Detective. Only a woman trying to dump a drunk former employer who grabbed her thigh.

Ernie's mouth turned down. "You owe me, Sara. You owe me for all I did for you."

His fingers laced around her arm, preventing her from leaving.

"Let go of me." She kept her voice low. The desire to avoid a scene was rapidly fading, replaced with the urge to kick him in the shins.

Or someplace else.

"So damn pretty," he muttered and yanked her close. "Just one little kiss, Sara."

Just as she was about to wrench free, a deep voice interrupted them.

"The lady asked you to leave her alone. I suggest you listen to her."

Sara looked up into the expressionless face of Detective Harry Cartwright. No, not expressionless. Fury simmered in his blue-green eyes, though he seemed calm. Collected.

Ernie sneered. "None of your business, buddy. Take a hike."

"It became my business when you started to assault her. Step away from the lady now."

So polished and cool. Sara's heart skipped a beat.

"Stop hassling me. This is business between myself and my girlfriend. Beat it now before I rearrange your face with my fists. I'll have you on the ground long before the cops arrive." Ernie's sneer widened.

"That would be impossible, seeing that I am the police."

Harry lifted the corner of his dinner jacket, showing a badge and the glint of his sidearm. Ernie paled and dropped Sara's arm.

Seizing the moment, Sara stepped out of range of Ernie's grasp. "You're intoxicated, Ernie. Go upstairs and sleep it off if you want to close that account." She lifted her chin. "Or do you wish me to call Bill Myers and tell him you'll be indisposed and he should look elsewhere for representation? No, that wouldn't be professional. But I am concerned for you, Ernie. I could call your wife and let her know you're not feeling well, judging from your behavior toward me."

Ernie's jaw dropped. He rubbed his eyes as if awakening from a bad dream. Behind her, she felt the large, imposing and oddly comforting presence of the detective, as if he were her backup.

If she needed rescuing.

She did not.

But it was sweet of him to try.

Without another word, Ernie bolted. If they had been on a dirt road, he'd have left dust in his wake.

Detective Cartwright's mouth twitched. "I see you're more effective than a gun or a badge."

Sara's fingers tightened on her purse. "Only with married men who fear their wives finding out what they do at night on business trips."

It sounded as if she'd made a habit of doing this. Sara flushed. "I mean, I know him. He's my former boss at the firm where I worked in St. Louis. He was never this… this…"

"Obnoxious?"

Sara sighed. "Yes. When he called and wanted to meet me for a drink, I thought he really did want to talk business, this account the firm had been eyeing for a long time that I was working on, I mean it's a huge business deal and he said he wanted advice so I thought, why not meet him for a drink…"

"It's okay, Sara," he said quietly. "You don't have to explain why you were with him. I didn't mean to embarrass you. I saw you looking like you were in trouble, and wanted to help."

"You're very observant."

What a lame remark, when she really wanted to thank him. How did one thank a police detective who had you under the microscope as a possible murder suspect?

For a moment they stood in awkward silence. Sara couldn't help but stare. Gone was the ruggedly handsome and hard-nosed detective who had questioned her earlier. In his place was a charming man in an elegant silk tuxedo. She glanced downward. Even his black patent leather shoes gleamed.

His short hair was combed, his beard trimmed. He looked like a dream date or a man about to sweep a woman off her feet as he escorted her into a formal gala.

Then he nodded. "Have a good night."

Finding her voice, she touched his arm as he turned away. "Thank you, Detective Cartwright. Thank you for saying something. Many men would not."

He looked down at her hand and then at her face. "Call me Harry. If you're not ready to go home yet, would you care to join me?"

It would be lovely. But did he plan to grill her some more about Axel Colton? She had already had enough subterfuge tonight.

"To talk about the case and Axel Colton?" It was hard to keep the bitterness from her tone.

He shook his head. "No. Just to talk, let you get your composure back. You're trembling."

She glanced at her hand still on his arm. Dismay filled her as she realized her hand shook. Sara pulled it away and gave a little laugh. Of course he would notice. The man noticed everyone. Came with the job, she guessed.

"Thanks. Yes, repressed anger does that. I'm quite good at leashing my temper. I suppose it's a good thing as it wouldn't look right on my résumé to say I punched my former employer when he got fresh with me."

A smile touched his face. Really he was quite handsome, especially with the smile, which made him look more human.

Sara drew in a breath. "Thank you for asking, but I don't want to take you away from your dinner date. Or whatever plans you had."

To her surprise, sadness pulled his mouth down, thought she could see him struggle against it. He looked back at the bar and his abandoned drink. "I don't have plans, or a dinner date."

Harry stretched out his hands. No wedding ring, but there was a slight tan line on his left ring finger. "It's my wedding anniversary. I come here…every year tonight… to honor a promise I made."

Her stomach tightened. This was not going to be good.

"You're married."

"Was. She died." He didn't look at her and that alone made him seem less of a confident police detective, more like a man who'd suffered loss.

"I'm so sorry." Hard as it had been to lose a father she never knew, she couldn't imagine losing a life's partner.

"She died in a car crash a little over two years ago, along with our little boy." He shrugged, and the gesture seemed to hide a wealth of pain. "We got married here, and she loved it so much we spent every anniversary here. We would dress in formal wear and have dinner, and after our son was born and money was tighter, we settled on one drink in the lounge. She made me promise we would always meet here on this date. It meant…a lot to her."

Her fingers stopped trembling. She'd been thinking of him as a police detective perhaps tailing her to grill her for more information and he was here simply to observe a heartfelt promise.

Sara's heart ached for him. Not merely the tragedy, but the loss of all those years ago, the loss of a child.

"It's a sweet tradition," she said softly. "It shows how much you loved her."

Harry glanced away and nodded.

She squeezed his arm. "Yes, I'd love to have a drink with you. But not at the bar. Can we get a table?"

He lost the sad look and his mouth twisted upward. "Yes, a table. Not a corner booth so if you wish to leave, you won't feel trapped."

Sara smiled. "As long as we avoid talking about work, I'll be fine."

Harry escorted her over to a table closer to the door. It was private, but offered easy access out. He pulled out a chair for her. After she sat, he took the opposite seat, his eye on the entrance.

"Are you looking for someone? You had the same kind of position while at the bar, as if expecting someone to arrive."

"And you called me observant." His mouth quirked upward again. "It's habit. I seldom sit with my back to the door. Lots of my kind don't."

"Your kind?"

"Cops. Military types as well. It's self-preservation. You want to see who is coming into the room."

"You mean you want to know if a suspect is coming into the room," she said slowly.

Harry's expression turned guarded. "Something like that. Or an enemy."

Which am I?

"But we agreed not to talk about work." He signaled for the waiter, who brought his untouched bourbon over. Harry glanced at her.

"Club soda with a twist of lime," she said.

"Shall I start a tab?" the waiter asked.

"No," she and Harry said in unison.

They looked at each other. He chuckled and she smiled.

"Not that I want to drink and run, but I do have an early start tomorrow." Sara hooked her purse on one of the tabs beneath the table. "I have to check on a client."

"Ah, work again." He grinned.

Sara sighed. "Yes, it's a hard habit to break. Especially when you're accustomed to your work being your life."

"Then you need to get out more often, see the city. Or do you like staying at home at night, kicking off your shoes and watching a good television program?"

"Not always. Back home, well, where my mother lives, I was active, had lots of friends who lived around St. Louis and I seldom stayed at home. But it's different here."

For reasons she didn't want to explain to him, reasons that had to do with her dead father.

"Chicago has a lot to offer. Theater, museums, winter sports," he told her.

"I do like ice-skating."

"Have you ever skated with Santa?" He leaned over the table. "Every Christmas, there's a skating Santa downtown. The kids, and even the adults, love it."

"Is he accompanied by eight tiny reindeer?"

"They're on vacation. Too many hooves to fit skates for."

This whimsical side of him was fun, and he was quite sober, which settled her raw nerves.

Her stomach rumbled, reminding her she hadn't eaten dinner, or lunch. Sara flushed as he tilted his head.

"If you're hungry, they have a good restaurant here. Or you can order sandwiches from the bar."

So tactful. She'd planned to take an Uber to the train station tonight. She thought of her budget, inwardly winced. "I'll be fine. I'll grab something from the freezer and nuke it when I get home."

"Sounds like my dinner when I'm on the run. Bless the invention of the microwave."

She laughed, and they began conversing about favorite foods. Harry Cartwright was charming and had an engaging smile. Certainly he was rather dashing, not traditionally handsome, but rugged, with compelling eyes.

He seemed interested in her opinion and looked at her, really looked at her, unlike some of the men she'd dated in the past.

Date?

He's a detective, Sara. Not a boyfriend.

But after the tension of the past few days, it felt good to talk about something normal like food and cooking shows, which led to a heated discussion about the merits of deep-dish pizza versus regular crust. Sara liked all kinds of cooking shows. Harry liked them as well, especially the volatile ones.

"Have you ever cooked with cast iron?" He leaned back.

"Never."

Harry shook his head. "A cast-iron frying pan is amazing for cooking. Not just frying, either. I can make a terrific chicken cacciatore with my cast-iron frying pan."

In back of the lounge on a raised dais, a band set up

instruments—drums, electric piano and acoustic guitar. She sat up and watched. A blues tune soon rippled through the air.

"Does the music bother you?" he asked. "Some people dislike the blues."

Sara rolled her eyes. "How can anyone not like the blues in Chicago?"

"You'd be surprised. Probably the same people who like putting ketchup on a Chicago hot dog or think thin-crust pizza is best."

Hiding a smirk because she did love ketchup on her hot dogs, she shook her head. "I love music. I play the acoustic guitar, when I'm not immersed in a big project. I used to play in a band."

Harry leaned forward, his arms resting on the table. "A garage band?"

"Afraid so. Just my friends and me. More a creative outlet than anything, though we did get one or two paying gigs at local schools."

She wondered about him. Was he all work? "How do you relax? Do you have a hobby?"

"Art." Harry flexed his fingers. "I paint. Acrylic, mostly, but sometimes sketching when I don't have the time."

They began talking about art, art history. Harry surprised her with his in-depth knowledge of the classics. He'd even exhibited a few paintings at a local gallery.

"Ever think about doing it for a living?" she asked.

Harry laughed. "Become a starving artist? No, I'm too good of a cop. Plus my job interferes with my paintings. I end up blending the two. I also do quick sketches for witnesses at the scene sometimes if they can't get to the station to work with the police sketch artist. It helps to sketch out a rough drawing while their memory is fresh."

Back to his work as a police detective again. Disappointment stabbed her. She had started to forget about his professional life.

"Did you find it hard to leave St. Louis? You spent your entire life there." Harry sipped his bourbon, his gaze sharp.

A casual question from anyone else, but this man was a police officer investigating a homicide. Sara wondered if he was turning their conversation toward more of a casual interrogation to discover her background.

"It was, but in an odd way, it was time. I do miss Mom's house and her yard. She has a huge yard. I had a vegetable garden—amazing zucchini and carrots. I loved gardening in the backyard. So it was a little tough trading all that space for a tiny apartment of my own."

Lost in thought, she remembered all the promises she'd made to herself while in college, studying hard and working her way through school. "I needed to break free of routine, see a world outside the microcosm of my hometown where everyone knows everyone else."

Sara swept a hand across the air. "Look at these people. Everyone has a story to tell, experiences to share. I always wonder what their stories are, and back home, I already knew those stories, heard them hundreds of times before. I find people in a large city like Chicago fascinating. Don't you?"

Harry leaned back, studied her. "You're different, Sara Sandoval."

She tilted her head. "Different how?"

"Most people are interested only in telling their own stories. Or hiding secrets." He tugged at the silk tie at his throat, as if it felt too tight.

What secrets did he hide? Sara wanted to know, but the question seemed far too intimate for this cozy setting.

"Oh, come on. You mean to tell me you've never people-watched and wondered where they came from, what drives them, what they're all about?"

"Usually when they're sitting down in an interrogation room, yeah." His mouth twisted into a smile beneath his beard.

Sara changed tactics. She needed to know, for her sake, and they were back to discussing work again, so why not? "Detective Cartwright…"

"Harry."

"Harry." She drew in a breath. "Why do you think someone killed my father?"

She halfway expected him to brush aside her question, or make excuses about having to leave. Instead he looked straight at her.

"Discovery of motive is half the battle in narrowing down the list of suspects."

Now was the time to pin him down. Get real answers. "I told you I don't have an alibi for the night Axel was killed. Am I considered a suspect?"

Harry studied her, his green-blue gaze piercing. "Yes."

"Why? Because I don't have an alibi?"

His gaze never left her face. "That, the coffee mug evidence and you came to Chicago on an ulterior motive, not for a change of scenery. I can't rule out that you did meet your father and got into an argument with him and acted out of anger."

"I didn't!"

"Can you prove it?"

"Can you prove I did?"

For a moment they didn't say anything. Sara sipped her drink and gave a bitter laugh. "I suppose we should have stuck to avoiding talk about work."

"It does seem to ruin an evening out." He traced a droplet of condensation that rolled down the side of his bourbon like a raindrop. Or a tear. "Then again, after a long day investigating a homicide, it's hard to disassociate myself from the job."

"Shoptalk can ruin a night."

He considered. "Yes. Especially when conversing with an intelligent woman such as yourself. You fascinate me, Sara."

Her anger died. Such a contradiction. Harry Cartwright irked her one moment and charmed the next. Men had called her several things—mostly complimenting her looks. None had ever complimented her mind. Harry barely knew her. They'd had only three encounters and yet she felt more alive and energized with him than with her former boyfriends.

They'd been immature, interested in sports and advancing their careers, not in justice. Or in her life.

Maybe that was what attracted her to Harry. His depth. A man who honored a promise to a wife who died certainly had much depth. And heart. Even if he thought she was a murderer.

It was certainly an odd place to be in.

She thought of Ernie, who only wanted to use her. "Thank you. Some men would not be as complimentary."

"Like your former employer?" Harry's mouth turned down. "He's a piece of work. Not only because he was drunk. There's something about him I wouldn't trust."

The fleeting impression he'd had of Ernie bothered her. "You can't tell much about a person in one encounter. He really isn't like that. He was drunk."

Harry toyed with his glass. "I don't need more than one encounter. I'm a cop. This Ernie is ambitious, but slovenly, eager to take the easy way out, arrogant bully but backs down when faced with confrontation. Dangerous, even."

Sara paused in lifting her glass to her mouth. "Dangerous?"

"Yes. Watch it with him, Sara. Not only is he a sexual predator, but he doesn't seem like one. And he does have the mannerisms of someone who will go after you if he doesn't get his way."

His warning sent a chill down her spine.

"Huh." She made her voice noncommittal. "And what is your impression of me?"

"I'm still figuring you out."

"Because I'm a murder suspect," she said slowly.

"No, because I can't figure out how anyone can live in Chicago and not like deep-dish pizza."

She laughed and he grinned. The previous tension between them evaporated. Sara liked Harry, maybe a little too much. Harry smelled faintly of aftershave, pleasant and spicy, but not overwhelming. Even interviewing her at her apartment, he'd looked polished and professional.

Her laugh died. As much as she found him charming and attractive, Sara knew there could never be anything between them. He was a cop and she was...

A suspect.

She glanced down at the gold watch her mother had given her on her sixteenth birthday and was stunned to see it was nearly eleven. Sara pushed back from the table. "I need to call it a night. I have a date with a frozen dinner waiting for me."

He grinned. "A first for me. No woman ever left me for a microwave dinner."

Sara smiled back. "Quite the opposite of a hot date."

Harry stood and tossed some money on the table. "Did you drive?"

"Train."

"May I drive you to the train station?"

She sensed he would be the protective type loath to leave a date alone to find her own transportation. "No, that's quite all right. The station isn't far and I like walking."

"Good night then."

"Good night, Harry. Thank you for the drink, and intervening for me with my former employer."

Instead of shaking her hand or nodding, he took her hand in a gentle grip and then brushed a kiss against her knuckles. The touch of his warm mouth electrified her, sent a thrill rushing through her.

So gallant.

"Thank you, Sara Sandoval, for rescuing me from what promised to be a rather lonely and melancholy evening. I'm sure we will be talking soon."

He released her hand, nodded, and then headed out of the lounge.

She'd learned two things from him tonight. Detective Harry Cartwright was a gentleman, something few men were these days. And he had her listed as a suspect in her father's murder.

Harry Cartwright had engaged her interest. Funny how time passed with him and dragged with Ernie. Once she could have talked for hours with Ernie, but that was all about work.

It was different with Harry. She really liked him, found him attractive and interesting. Too bad he thought she killed Axel Colton.

Shrugging into her coat, she headed for the lobby doors when a voice halted her.

"Sara, hey, Sara, please wait!"

Groaning, she stopped. If Ernie desired to make a scene or worse…

She turned, saw him heading for her, hurrying as if afraid she'd slip away. This time he didn't look drunk or eager to haul her upstairs to his room. He looked…

Scared.

Gathering all her patience, she stopped. "What is it, Ernie? I'm through with you. And the firm."

"I'm sorry, Sara. I truly am. I screwed up." Ernie's jaw tightened as he stared into the distance. "I got drunk and tried to take advantage of you. It won't ever happen again, I promise."

"Of course it won't, because I'm not returning to the company, Ernie. Good night."

She started for the door. Ernie beat her to it. "Wait, please, Sara."

He ran a hand through his hair, his skin sallow, his jaw tight. "I'm in a jam since you left. All those times you helped out with the accounts, I can't manage it all. I need you back."

She would have sidestepped him but for the raw honesty in his voice. She'd seen Ernie desperate only once and at that time, Sara had stepped in to smooth things over with the client.

They'd nailed the account and Ernie returned to his confident, breezy self. Uneasy, she wondered how many times she'd missed the telltale signs Ernie had leaned too heavily on her.

He seemed ready to fall to pieces now.

"What are you saying, Ernie? The truth."

Not meeting her gaze, he rubbed a hand over his face. "It was you, Sara. You were a manager, but hell, aw hell, you were more than that. You kept our department functioning. There's at least five high-end clients I've screwed up with—oh, not big items. But every day I'm losing track of details. I can't replace you."

He finally did look up. Shocked, she realized tears swam in his eyes.

"If I don't get you back to the firm, I'm in danger of losing my job. All the clients are starting to complain I'm not following up on their needs. You always made things easier, made them run smoothly. It was you all this time, Sara. Damn, I'm sorry I never acknowledged that, but without you I'm toast. My career will sink. You know how word of mouth is important in our business. I'm too old to get back into the marketplace, not with a bad rep following me. I need you back, Sara."

She stepped back. "Ernie, I can't."

"I'll do anything." Now the tears vanished, replaced by a wild look in his eyes. "I swear, I'll do anything. You have no reason to stay here anymore. Your birth father, that Axel Colton, he's dead. There's no reason you shouldn't return, go live with your mother again…"

Had he slapped her, Sara couldn't have felt more shocked. "How do you know about my birth father?"

Ernie made an impatient gesture. "I was in your office before you left, looking for the spreadsheet for the Geckel account, and came across some notes you had about Axel Colton."

Heat suffused her, pure anger that made her want to shake him. "That was private, Ernie. It was in my computer bag, not a place for anyone to look through."

"Then you should have locked it away! You told me the spreadsheet was in your office and I couldn't find it."

"You're lying." She struggled with her rising temper. "The spreadsheet was in plain view."

"Doesn't matter. Too late. I know why you really came here to Chicago and now you have nothing to keep you here. That nursery job, it can't pay much. There's no real career here for you. Not like you had with me."

"*Had* is the word, Ernie. I doubt I could work for you again."

"You have to! Don't leave me high and dry again, Sara. You may regret it." He grinned as if the smile erased the threat. "Come back to the firm. I'll double your salary, and put you on the fast track to becoming a vice president. You don't even have to work with me, just manage the accounts the way you once did."

Instinct urged her to soothe him and get away fast. "It's something to think about, Ernie. Good night."

She fled out onto the street, turned and saw with relief he headed toward the bank of elevators.

Ernie wanted her back.

No, he desperately *needed* her back.

The idea stripped away her composure, leaving her shivering from more than the December chill as she scurried toward the train station.

Ernie knew about her birth father and the real reason she left the firm. How badly did he want her back to cover for him as she'd done in the past?

Bad enough to kill Axel Colton?

Chapter Five

From the shadows near a potted plant as he fished into his wallet for the valet slip, Harry watched the exchange between Sara and her former employer. He unknotted his tie and tugged at his shirt collar. This tradition each year was one few understood. He'd loved Marie with his whole heart, and losing her and his son shattered his world. Women he'd dated, hell, none of them understood this tradition. One had been angry he couldn't escort her to the theater because he had to have a drink in honor of his dead wife.

Sara Sandoval understood. Not only understood, but appreciated it.

He couldn't figure her out. Wanted to figure her out. She intrigued him, pulled at him in a basic sexual way he understood well. He was a guy, and guys were hard-wired to respond to a lovely woman. What he couldn't figure out was why the sexual chemistry felt deeper, more visceral than mere desire, a spark that could easily burst into an inferno and settle into a steady burn promising to last a long time.

Harry knew he couldn't afford to get involved with Sara. She was a suspect. But his protective streak refused to let her walk out of the hotel without watching to make sure she was all right.

He didn't like the way that Ernie talked to Sara and the wild look in his eyes. Harry had seen other men equally desperate, usually right before they confessed to a crime.

He also didn't like the fact she was walking outside into the dark night with the subtle threat lingering around her like smoke.

As Sara stepped outside the lobby, he followed. True enough she didn't linger, but walked across the street in the direction of the train station. Not so fast.

Sprinting across the street he easily caught up with her. "Sara," he called out, not wishing to scare her. She'd already been scared enough tonight.

She stepped off the sidewalk. Out of seemingly nowhere, a dark, late-model sedan accelerated…right at her.

Cursing, Harry reached out, grabbed her arms and yanked her toward him. She fell against his chest, gasping.

Sara looked up at him. She felt so good, so right in his arms. Softness and yet beneath he sensed pure steel. This was a woman who knew what she wanted and went after it.

With some reluctance, he released her. Harry couldn't resist brushing back a strand of hair from her cheek. "Are you okay?"

She gave a breathless laugh. "I am now. For a moment, I saw my life flash before my eyes."

He wondered about that. Was it a coincidence that car happened to speed up and pass just as she stepped off the sidewalk? Harry wished he had gotten the license plate. Then again, perhaps he was being paranoid.

Harry glanced down the street. "Forget the train. My car is parked in the hotel lot. I'll drive you home."

"It's more than a thirty-minute drive."

He nodded. "I know."

"But I don't want to take you away from your plans."

Harry sighed. "Sara, my plans consisted of going into the station to catch up on paperwork. Do you know how much cops hate paperwork?"

"Probably as much as I hate walking alone at night to the train station?"

He blew out a breath, frustrated with her. "Why didn't you let me drive you? Or at least walk you there?"

She bit her lower lip, drawing attention to its lush curve. "Maybe because it's best we put space between us. I am under investigation."

"No matter. You shouldn't walk by yourself this late at night." His jaw tightened as he glanced back at the hotel. "Especially with certain undesirables around."

She shivered. "You overheard."

"Everything." *And my assessment of that jerk was right. He is dangerous.* He held out his hand. "Come on. I'll drive you home."

He thought for a moment. Maybe she would open up more in a less formal setting. Food always helped.

"You hungry? Want something better than a frozen microwave dinner?"

Sara tilted her head. "Such as?"

"The best hot dogs in Chicago."

She threw him a questioning look. "At this time of night?"

"It's an all-night joint. You in?"

For a moment he thought she'd say no. Then she put a hand to her stomach. "I am really hungry."

"I'll drive, and then drive you home. It isn't far."

Harry waited for her reaction as the valet brought his car up front. His car wasn't what most people expected a cop to drive, such as a sedan, or an inconspicuous black four-door. When the valet pulled up in a cherry-red 2019 Mustang, Sara's eyes widened.

"Wow. Lovely."

Her taste in cars equaled his own. Harry tipped the valet, then escorted her to the passenger side. He ensured the door was closed before taking the driver's seat.

"Cold?" he asked.

"A little." Sara touched the leather seat. "Seat warmers. Nice. Classy car. Standard issue for all homicide detectives?"

He chuckled. "My personal vehicle. Call it a teenage wish finally fulfilled. I don't get to drive her much since my department-issued car is what I usually drive."

"You should put flashing lights on it and get to crime scenes faster."

Harry put the heater on. "Not in this state. Illinois law forbids police equipment in personal cars."

The hot dog restaurant wasn't far. Fortunately, they had inside seating. Wicked cold out.

Harry parked the car. Sara got out as he did and walked with him to the entrance. He opened the door for her, hoping she wasn't the type who would bluster or protest at this simple courtesy. Sometimes when he did this on a date, he got a ten-minute lecture.

Instead of protesting, she smiled and thanked him. Okay, good first step.

No one else was inside except a bored-looking teen wiping down the counter. They paid for their own dogs, hot tea for Sara and coffee for Harry, and took them to the counter for garnishes. His eyes widened. Couldn't believe it. Just as he started to like her, against his better judgment…

"You aren't seriously doing that?" He stared in incredulous amazement.

She blinked. "What? I like ketchup on my hot dogs."

"No." He shook his head. "No. I'll have to arrest you."

Her jaw dropped. "What?"

Harry pointed to the sign hanging above the counter. "See? You're violating all kinds of rules."

She looked up, laughed, such a cheerful and carefree sound, it made his heart turn over. "That's just a frivolous sign."

They took their dogs to a nearby booth and sat.

Harry bit into his dog and chewed, swallowed. "That sign is real. It's against the law, and good taste, to put ketchup on a hot dog within the city limits of Chicago."

Grinning, she bit into her dog. Chewed thoughtfully, and wiped her mouth with dainty motions with a paper napkin. "Since we're on the subject, what do you do with suspects who put pineapple on deep-dish pizza? Lock them in prison? Beat them with a wooden spoon?"

"Worse." Harry finished his dog in two quick bites. Wow, he was hungry after all. "Send them to Miami and force them to watch a Dolphins game."

She laughed again and sipped her tea. "Might sound like torture to some, but Florida in the winter would be worth Dolphins tickets."

"Not for me. I like the cold." He did. Even on the worst days, when the wind cut through you like a steel blade slicing through warm butter, he felt alive. Invigorated. Sometimes the weather, more than humans, reminded him of one simple rule.

Stay alive.

But he was tired of surviving. So he stuck to the job, to the facts, and ignored the past, pushed aside the idea that there could be more than what life had dished out to him.

Dished out things that tasted much worse than ketchup on a hot dog.

Harry drank more coffee, had a sudden craving for a beer. As if they were on a date and he wasn't trying to coax information from her, this pretty suspect with the wind-chime laughter. As if there could be more between them than his suspicions.

He was about to ask her about her mother's relationship with Axel when Sara turned her head to look out the window. "Such a sweet car. It's too bad you don't have much chance to drive it, except when you're off duty. Must be horrendously expensive to garage it."

He shrugged. "I leave it at a friend's house. Let him drive it in exchange for free parking."

"You're a trusting soul."

Odd remark. Trusting? He was a cop. Harry glanced at her. "Only with close friends in my personal life. Life can be damn hard without them to get you through. Even more than family."

"I don't know about that. I always thought family was more important. If I had to sacrifice friendships for family, I'd do it. That's what happens when you're brought up to think you're an only child, no relatives except your mother."

Detecting the note of bitterness in her voice, he decided to follow it. Now was his chance to dig further into her life, and a motive for killing Axel. If she did kill her father.

"I'm sure it was difficult growing up without a father, and then finding out you had one all along."

But Sara was intelligent, as he'd already noted. She didn't fall for the bait. She drank more tea before answering.

"Look, Harry, what my childhood was like and what my life is now are two separate matters. You mentioned motive is important to a homicide investigation. I'm sure you think I had a motive, and that's why I'm still considered a suspect."

Harry stayed quiet. Let her talk, get it out.

"I have no motive—in fact, I have only the motive for him to be alive. I didn't kill Axel. I know that's a lame thing to say to you, a police detective, but it's the truth."

Sara stared out the window. "I'd have given anything to at least have met him, had the chance to tell him he was my father. Even with all the bad things I've heard about him, and how my mother feared him…he was still my dad. Now he's gone. I'll never have the chance to determine for myself what kind of man he was."

"Perhaps you found out what type of man he was and decided you were better off without him permanently."

She scowled and shook her head. "It's not in my nature. You assessed Ernie and determined his personality by observing him just for one evening. Do you really think I'm a person capable of killing another human being? No matter how vile that person is?"

His chest tightened. "I don't know you, Sara. I've only met you. You can tell me everything about your past, but I rely on evidence, motive and facts. It's how I operate. The fact is, we found the coffee mug on Colton's counter with your fingerprints on it."

"And I have no motive, forget the coffee cup! You have no evidence I killed him and those are the facts." She spat out the words in a staccato rush, and then took a deep breath.

"I want to find out who killed him as much as the Coltons do. I'm family, even if not acknowledged. If you want to look at a Colton, consider this. Maybe whoever did this was simply greedy and wanted their inheritance from Axel. Had you considered that angle?"

He wondered about that. Sara had not been named in the will. Of course not. Axel hadn't known of her exis-

tence. What she said made sense. But he had to rule out
every single suspect. The family was demanding answers.
Carin, Axel's mother, had complained long and loud to
the media about Naperville and Chicago PD's tortoise-like
progress on the case. The brass was starting to squeeze
him as well. They wanted Harry to solve this and work
on the backlog on his desk.

"I've considered all angles." He crushed the hot dog
wrapper in his hand. "Still considering. There are thirty
million angles to consider, now that Dean Colton's new
will is in probate, naming your father and his brother as
his heirs. Thirty million dollars is a lot of money. People
have killed for less."

Sara finished her tea, took his crumpled wrapper and
hers, and dumped them into the trash.

"If I did kill my father, it wouldn't have been for
money, certainly not for money still tied up in the courts."

"But you have other reasons," he stated calmly. "Like
I said, I have to consider all angles."

"Can we go now? I have an early day tomorrow."

In the car, she said nothing more. Harry doubted she
would spill anything. She was too much on guard, too
smart.

Harry switched on the heat and turned the satellite HD
radio to a blues station. The soothing wail of music filled
the empty space between them.

He was exhausted, and even fortified with food, he
was letting his guard down around her. Sara smelled like
fresh flowers and sunshine. He wondered if anyone ever
told her that.

She smelled like paradise. For a wild moment he remembered that old Meatloaf song, "Paradise by the Dashboard Light," and wanted to laugh.

Sex with Sara was as unlikely as snow in Miami. But

Miami, ah, the beach and the turquoise water, Sara in a little blue bikini, her sexy, slumberous gaze on his as she waded into the ocean, playfully splashing him…

He shook his head. Damn, he was tired. These fantasies, they had to stop. Yeah, she was a beautiful, intelligent woman, but he had a job to do.

"Detective Cartwright?"

He blinked. Guess they were back to formal names again. "Sorry, I was focusing on the road."

And other things.

"Like I was saying at the restaurant, you need to look at other suspects. You seem like a methodical person. Who was that man who planted the candlestick in Nash's trunk? Did he do it? It seems logical."

Logic had nothing to do with that act. "I can't discuss that."

She blew out a breath. "This is my street. Turn here."

"I know. I've been to your apartment, remember?"

He pulled up to the curb before her building, started to turn off the engine. She shook her head.

"Don't bother. I can see myself in."

Sara sounded angry. He didn't blame her. Still, his protective streak wouldn't let her simply go. He'd seen too many women who'd been victims of violence.

Harry pulled out his cell phone. "Give me your cell phone number."

He had it already, but wanted to be polite.

Sara frowned. "Why? We're not dating. I mean, you're nice, and maybe, but it just wouldn't work…"

He almost laughed. So he wasn't the only one thinking about them being more than a cop and a suspect.

"So you can text me when you're inside your apartment and I'll know you are safe."

By the dashboard light he saw her skin darken with an obvious flush. "Oh."

Harry pointed to the keys in her hand. "You've already done one thing right. Always have your keys ready before going into a building or a car. You can use a key as a weapon, strike an attacker in the eyes."

She sighed. "I know. Trust me, I'm a single woman. I know how to protect myself."

He pressed harder, hoping to find an answer he hadn't seen all night. "Use the key to open the door and then pull it open with your left hand."

Sara shook her head. "Sorry, Detective. I'm hopelessly right-handed."

He tilted his head. "Oh yeah? Some people are, but you can learn to use your left hand. I did when training for the police academy. I learned to shoot with both hands. Is your mother right-handed as well?"

Suspicion flared in her pretty green eyes. Sara wasn't stupid. "She uses both. What do you care?"

"Just asking."

He tucked away that bit of information for later. Right-handed. Not left-handed. *Check that homicide file on Axel Colton.*

When she texted her number to him, he plugged it into his contacts. "Good night, Sara. Remember. Don't leave town."

Best to leave her on that professional note. Funny how they'd both not wanted to talk business and then ended up like this.

He watched her storm off into her apartment building. She did not look back. Still, he waited until she headed for the stairs.

Less than five minutes later, he received a text. I'm inside my apartment, you can leave now.

Then another text, as if an afterthought. Good night. Thank you for driving me home and seeing I'm safe.

Harry pulled away from the curb and headed back to his precinct. Sara seemed eager to find out who had killed her birth father. Did she express that interest to clear herself?

Or did she have something else to hide…or someone to protect? Like her mother?

Instead of heading to the precinct, he drove to Axel Colton's Naperville home.

The mansion was cordoned off as a crime scene. He had a key. Harry parked on the street and let himself into the house, flipping on the lights.

The air inside seemed heavy and smelled like fingerprint powder and blood. Triangles still marked where Axel's blood had pooled on the floor. He walked over to one and squatted down.

Axel had been killed by a vicious blow to his head with a heavy object. Blood on a marble candlestick planted in Nash Colton's trunk matched Axel's. No fingerprints. It had been wiped clean.

They had the murder weapon.

They did not have motive.

Security cameras on Nash's home showed a man planting the murder weapon in Nash's trunk. They'd identified the man as Dennis Angelo, a petty thief. Before they could bring him in for questioning, Angelo was killed in a car crash as he headed home…to St. Louis.

Harry stood and walked around the living room. He couldn't let Sara know that she had soared to the top of the suspect list not only because of the coffee mug, but also because the man with the murder weapon was from her hometown.

Dennis Angelo had no known association with Axel or any of the other Coltons. It might be a coincidence.

He didn't believe in them. But he hoped, for Sara's sake, he'd be proven wrong.

Chapter Six

Sara decided to come clean with the Yateses. It might cost her the job, but she had to do it. She only wished she'd been able to tell the truth earlier. The next morning, she dressed in a violet sweater, black silk trousers and ankle boots, and added a purple-and-red pashmina scarf with sparkling strands woven through it. Instead of braiding her long hair, she left it loose.

One should always look stylish and presentable when being fired.

She arrived at the nursery around 7:30 a.m. and parked on the street. The Yateses lived in an upscale Chicago suburb.

At least the day was warmer than yesterday and she didn't have to worry about slipping on an icy walkway. Sara opened the iron gate and marched along the brick pathway leading to the office building. The nursery grounds were speckled with light snow. Several greenhouses scattered throughout the expansive property protected delicate plants from cold Illinois winters.

Since the business didn't open until 8:30, she wasn't surprised to see the lights off and the building locked. Probably Rick and Vita were either having coffee in their house much farther behind the nursery grounds, or more likely, checking on the plants to ensure they'd survived the cold. The landscapers had their hands full, ensuring the flowers would blossom and no insects would dare show their face on the tiny buds.

Much easier to deal with plants than people. More predictable. Plants don't have motives. Or lie.

Using her key to open one of the double doors, she made sure to lock the door behind her. Sara headed for her office and closed the door, breathing a sigh of relief. At least she'd have time to organize files before facing Vita and Rick.

If they fired her today, she wanted to make sure they had all the sales contacts she'd made at this job.

Sara placed her laptop bag and paper cup of coffee on her desk. After shrugging out of her coat and hanging it on the coatrack by the door, she powered up her computer and got to work.

She was so absorbed, she almost didn't hear the knock at the door. Sara glanced at the clock on the wall that featured a whimsical arrangement of yellow daisies. Nearly 8:30!

"Come in," she called out.

The office door opened and Lila, Vita's daughter, strolled inside. Sara brightened. "Good morning, stranger."

Lila smiled. "Hi, Sara! Good to see you again. You look better than the last time I saw you. You feeling okay now?"

Not really, but that has nothing to do with my physical health.

"I'm good. Are you having breakfast with your mom and Rick?"

Lila nodded. "They asked me and Myles to stop by this morning. Mom said they needed to talk with us. Something about Axel's death."

Sara's heart beat faster. She sipped her coffee, hoping Lila couldn't detect her surprise. "Oh. What's going on?"

"Good news. The police are narrowing down a list of possible suspects in Dad's death." Lila wandered over to the window overlooking the nursery grounds. "Mom said Detective Cartwright has a new suspect and he has more questions for her this morning."

What time did police detectives arrive at work? Harry had said last night he was going to do paperwork after he dropped her off. Did he remain at the station all night?

She had to meet with Valerie and Rick, and include Lila and Myles, before Harry could out her.

Bad enough she was Axel's illegitimate daughter. That alone would present a shock, but to find out she was suspected in his murder?

Sara felt like a spy whose cover was about to be blown, except she would be the one revealing her secret.

Lila pulled out her cell phone. "I've got an important meeting at ten at my art gallery and have to return to the city. I'll talk to you later, Sara."

Sara pushed out from her desk and stood so fast the chair almost toppled to the floor. "Wait. I need to talk with you, your brother, and Vita and Rick. It's important."

"You're not going to quit on us, I hope." Lila gave a little laugh. "Just when Mom was so excited about the possibility of new business for winter. She and Rick are even talking about expansion."

Not quit. Not willingly.

"It's better if I explain when you're all together."

"Sounds serious."

"It is."

Worry clouded Lila's pretty face. "I'll call everyone together. They're still at the house."

"I'll meet you in the conference room in ten."

Ten minutes later, refreshed by a new cup of coffee Lila had brewed earlier, Sara sat at the elegant mahogany table in the conference room used for conferring with clients. Rick had told her he'd found the table in an estate sale. He loved the hand-carved rosettes on the sides. Perfect for a nursery.

Sara traced one of the flowers now with a trembling finger. This was tougher than she'd expected. When she'd taken the job months ago, she'd been cool, confident in her abilities and absolutely neutral about her father's family.

Now she'd come to regard them as friends, even more.

Rick had last used this room to plan a funeral with a busy florist client. Someone had left a pot of lilies in the corner and the heavy fragrance filled the air.

Leaves still clinging with stubborn insistence on a majestic oak outside the conference room window fluttered in the wind. *I'm like those leaves. I refuse to accept the inevitable and move on. But at some point, I'll be forced into it.*

The conference room door opened and Vita and Rick entered, followed by Myles and a worried-looking Lila.

They sat across from her. *My firing squad.*

"Sara?" Vita's voice was gentle. "Lila said you had a matter of great importance to discuss with the family. I gather it isn't business."

The family. Once she might have regarded them as her family. "No." She drew in a deep breath. "It's got nothing to do with the business. This is personal."

As personal as it gets...

HARRY HADN'T BEEN able to sleep much after he drove home from Axel's house. The department would soon release it to the family, after Carin, Axel's mother, had pestered the brass.

He couldn't stop thinking of Sara, and went over in his mind all the angles and motives she would have for killing her own father. Each one unraveled like a stray thread on a sweater.

Doubts filled him the next morning as he showered and mulled over her involvement. Was he being entirely objective?

Or had Sara enchanted him so much with her intelligence and beauty that he searched for an excuse to eliminate her as the top suspect in her father's death?

Yesterday he'd stopped by Yates' Yards and questioned Vita Yates about the coffee mug collection in the employee break room. Vita told him sometimes employees took the mugs home. Sometimes clients used them as well if they came into the nursery for meetings. They didn't keep track of them.

He'd gotten a list of all the employees, clients and visitors for the past two months. It was extensive. It included the murder victim—Axel Colton.

Colton had been there on a day when Vita and Rick were gone. In fact, he'd insisted on meeting Lila there before taking her to lunch at his house.

After he contacted Lila, Colton's daughter told Harry she couldn't remember if Axel had taken the coffee mug. He might have. She was too focused on hustling him out of the nursery before Rick or Vita returned. Rick in particular did not hold any fondness for Axel.

When he'd further questioned her on what they discussed, Lila told Harry the lunch was peculiar. Axel acted as if he wanted to discuss something of great importance, but in the end, he only asked about her business and if she was happy with her life.

If Sara told the truth and hadn't visited her father, and Axel himself hadn't used the mug, someone else must have planted the coffee mug in Colton's house. Someone who had known she used the mug, and had been watching her.

The last fact bothered him on a visceral level. If Sara had a stalker, she was unaware of it.

The station was busy today, swarming with people, but he had no time for chatter. Enough pressure squeezed him to try to solve this case.

To his surprise, Sean Stafford was at his desk. Now this was worth a stop. Sean had been on leave for more than three weeks. He and his fiancée, January Colton, had eloped shortly before she'd given birth to the couple's twins.

Busy with a file, Sean didn't look up. Harry rapped on the detective's desk. "Hey, papa."

Sean glanced up, grinned. "Harry! Good to see you."

"Welcome back. I thought you were taking an extra week of paternity leave."

"January's mom is helping out and the captain asked for everyone who can spare time to work on the Colton murder case." Sean leaned back, yawned.

Harry grinned. "And you needed to get away from the crying. Twice the crying. Welcome to the joys of parenthood and never sleeping again."

"Never?" Sean rubbed his cheek. "Ever?"

"Probably not for the next twenty years," Harry said a little too cheerfully. "How are the twins?"

Sean's expression softened. "Man, they're so little but growing so fast. Already have personalities. Leo's demanding and if he doesn't get what he wants right now, you'll hear it. Laura's a sweetheart, doesn't fuss, waits her turn."

"So Leo's like you and Laura takes after her mom." Harry mock punched Sean's arm.

Sean beamed. "Yeah. Oh, thanks so much for the two bouncy seats. Awesome gift, Harry."

"I figured they would come in handy."

"They are. You knew just what to give us. Last night the twins kept crying and January put them in the bouncy seats for the first time and they loved them. I remember you saying how John never wanted to leave his bouncy seat except when Marie fed him. Seems the same with Leo," Sean said.

His former partner went on talking about the twins. Harry kept his smile, but his guts did that little twist the way they always did when anyone or anything reminded him of his own son. It wasn't Sean's fault. The man was caught up in the glow of being a first-time father.

He clapped Sean on the back. "Congratulations again."

At his own desk, he could focus on work and forget his personal life and the bite of his painful past. Harry opened Axel Colton's file and read through it, searching for anything he could use to tighten leads on the case.

A few minutes later, Sean came over, sat on Harry's desk. "I thought I looked tired, but you look absolutely beat. What's going on?"

Harry didn't look up. "You're sitting on my desk."

"All the chairs are taken. Carin Pederson was here a while ago. Good thing you missed her."

A paragraph in the notes stood out. Harry took a yellow highlighter and circled it. The candlestick used to deliver the killing blow to Axel's skull weighed a little less than eight pounds. Its mate sat on an elegant table near the spot where Axel died.

Axel and Sara were about the same height. She was slender, her arms toned. But strong enough to lift an eight-pound marble candlestick and hit her birth father over the head?

When she claimed she had not even met him, and only wanted to face him in person?

"Thought I'd update you on what's happening. The Coltons are putting pressure on the brass about this case, Harry, turning up the heat. Carin was complaining not enough is being done to find her son's killer. She was practically screaming she wants more police on this case to bring her son's killer to justice or she's holding a press conference and accusing the Chicago PD of dragging its heels," Sean said.

Harry flipped through the autopsy report. Axel died from a blow to the right side of his head.

Sara admitted she was hopelessly right-handed.

Her mother, Regina, used both her hands.

It was nearly impossible for Sara to face Axel and hit him with her right hand on the right side of his head. Unless Sara had been walking away from Axel and turned... striking him on his right side. Didn't make sense. The vic had collapsed to the polished floor face flat. As if struck where he stood, by someone standing in front of him who was left-handed or at least ambidextrous? Axel faced his killer. Harry felt a chill rush down his spine that had nothing to do with the gush of relief he felt.

Sara couldn't have killed her father.

But her mother might have.

Was he grasping at straws to find ways to clear Sara instead of doing his job? Harry rubbed his eyes and set the highlighter down.

"Harry?" Sean waved a hand in front of him. "Did you hear anything I said?"

"What?"

"I heard you were having a drink with Sara Sandoval at the Four Seasons."

The tone in his former partner's voice made him finally look up. "So?"

"You had a drink at the Four Seasons, and not that landscaping place where she works. Sounds social. Get anything out of her?"

"No." Harry leaned back, the chair creaking in protest. He didn't like where this thread was headed. Much better to listen to Sean talk about his newborn twins.

"Huh."

"Huh what?"

But Sean didn't go there. "I went over that file again and again. The chief asked me to work with you because Carin is yapping she wants answers. Brass wants them, too, and the sooner we, or Naperville, solves this, the happier everyone will be."

"You think I'm dragging my heels?"

A heavy sigh. "No. I'm telling you the heat is growing on this, Harry."

No kidding.

"Okay, here's a recap." Harry sat up. "I have a candlestick used to kill Colton, no prints, no DNA except for Colton's blood. I have a dead suspect who planted the weapon in Nash Colton's trunk. And I have security cameras that were damaged in Colton's house so there's no evidence of anyone entering and leaving his house around the time of the murder. If Sara visited her father, we don't know."

"It wasn't premeditated. Whoever killed Colton used the candlestick that was available," Sean mused.

"Right. This was a crime of passion." Harry pointed to the file. "Someone got mad at Colton and hit him. They didn't visit his house to kill him. It happened spontaneously."

"If you're going to kill someone, a candlestick isn't a good weapon," Sean said dryly.

He nodded, glad his ex-partner followed his line of reasoning. "Knives, guns, hell, poisoning is much more reliable than trying to hit someone over the head."

"Someone had to have seen something. Did Naperville check the neighbors? That's a posh area. Security patrol."

Harry laughed, but there was no humor in it. "They did. My old friend Jimmy talked with all the neighbors and the security patrol. He's working another case now—a Santa Claus shot and killed outside a house. Looked like a burglary gone wrong, but Jimmy and I had the feeling it wasn't."

"And there's no way the two cases are connected."

"Not that we know, but Jimmy's checking all angles." Harry drummed his fingers on the desk. "We need more than forensic evidence, not that we have much of that. We need motive to seal this and get a conviction. But right now we have little to go on."

Sean shook his head. "Tough break. What do you want from me?"

Harry picked up a ragged piece of paper. "Neighbors across the street from Colton do have security cameras. They're out of the country, supposed to return today. Soon as they do, check their footage. Might get at least a glimpse of a license plate."

He shut the file. "I'm headed out to do a little more digging."

Sean held up a hand as Harry pushed back from his desk. "Harry, I'm here to help you. I have a full caseload of my own. I'm glad you're back at Homicide. You're a damn good cop. We need you here."

He held his tongue. Things had been distant for a long time between him and Sean.

"I'm glad you're getting your life back together. But

remember, Sara Sandoval is a suspect. Don't get personally involved."

Harry rubbed his jaw, suddenly weary beyond belief. "Don't go there, Sean. Because I sure as hell won't."

Sean nodded. "Deal. I'll let you know what I find out about that security footage."

He nodded, and then looked over the file again. His phone buzzed. Incoming text from his sister, Linda, who lived in Rogers Park.

When are you coming over for dinner? Amelia misses you and Elliott and I do, too.

Soon, he texted back. I'll be in touch.

The weight of several pairs of eyes sat upon him as Harry left the squad room. He sure as hell was impartial in this investigation. No matter how much he was attracted to Sara Sandoval. Justice had to be served.

Besides, he really wasn't getting his life back together. Sean was wrong.

Didn't matter now. He would find out who killed Axel. No matter what.

GROWING UP AS the child of a single, busy mother who worked long hours as an office manager, Sara had long ago learned to deal with problems head-on. Facing this family, who had treated her like one of their own, was no different.

Why then did her insides feel as if she were on a roller coaster and the track ahead was missing?

Taking a deep breath for courage, she looked at all four of them. "I asked you here because I need to tell you the truth. I'm sorry I wasn't open with you before. I wanted…to get to know the Colton side of the family…

my father's side, before I announced my connection. Axel Colton was my father."

Their expressions were blank. Lila's mouth opened and Myles's gaze narrowed. But it was Rick and Vita she focused on the most.

Her employers, who had treated her with such fairness. Such kindness.

Rick blinked and made a pursing motion with his lips as if to whistle, then thought better of it and sat back. He glanced at his wife.

Oddly enough, Vita did not looked surprised. Her expression composed, she studied Sara with the same thoroughness expressed during Sara's employment interview.

"My mom is Regina Sandoval. She was Axel's mistress and changed her name after leaving Axel when my brother died. I was born after she moved to St. Louis to begin a new life. Mom never told Axel about me, and… only this year did I find out my father hadn't died in a boating accident with my brother, as my mother always said. She finally told me the truth. I came here to meet Axel…to see what the Coltons were like. I suppose some might call it spying, but for me, it was trying to work up the nerve to announce my parentage to my father, and get to know him from a distance."

She threw back her shoulders and thought about everything that had happened since getting hired. "I understand the shock you must feel. If you wish me to leave, I don't want you to lose all the accounts I lined up for your business. I have all the information on a spreadsheet in your server's cloud, as well as the information on the contacts, meetings with potential accounts, and of course the clients I already signed on."

Dignity was so important. She did have a professional reputation and standards. Any transition would be as smooth as possible for whoever assumed her marketing responsibilities. She wasn't certain where she could work next. Certainly not her former job, not with groping Ernie lurking about. Too bad she had deceived them because she genuinely liked Valerie and Rick, and their kids. Her half siblings. The work provided a challenge she hadn't felt in a long time.

Myles drummed his fingers on the table. "Wow. Great news, Sara. Welcome to the family, sis."

She dared to hope she heard him right. Sara glanced at Lila, who beamed. "Yes, welcome, Sara. This is great. You're family!"

Vita was unreadable, but Rick's expression softened. "I understand why you remained quiet, Sara. I'm glad you told us. Your skills here are exceptional."

"Does that mean Sara now has to take a cut in pay? I mean, she is family," Myles teased.

She smiled, the first real smile of relief felt since walking onto the property this morning.

Then she remembered the other part of her news and her spirits dropped.

Her hands trembling, she fisted them in her lap, hiding them from view. Sara mustered her strength.

"There's something else you need to know…something you must know while I'm here." Sara licked her lips. "Detective Cartwright, the lead detective on the case, considers me a suspect."

Silence descended, as thick and cloying as the scent of lilies in the corner. Funny how she always associated that smell with death.

Myles sat up. "Wow. That's… He thinks you killed our father?"

"*Your* own father?" Lila blurted out. "Why?"

Nodding, Sara stared out the window, unable to meet

their shocked gazes. "I have no alibi. I was home the night of the murder. He said I could have gone to confront Axel and became enraged when he denied my claim, or sent me on my way. Or laughed in my face."

For the first time, Vita's blank expression cracked. Her mouth thinned. "Yes, Axel was capable of all that. He was not always a pleasant person."

"I don't know." Sara brought her hands to the table, wondering if she had the same elegant fingers as her father. "I never did meet him. I didn't kill him. But there's no evidence I didn't."

"There must be no evidence you did, either, Sara." Lila blinked rapidly. "I mean, the police seem like they are grasping at straws these days. Grandmother Carin is putting extreme pressure on the department."

Best to tell them everything. "I'm higher on the suspect list because they found a coffee mug with my fingerprints in Axel's house. It was one that came from the employee break room."

Vita frowned. Rick and Lila looked bewildered, while Myles the lawyer looked thoughtful.

Myles spoke slowly. "That's not evidence you killed our father, Sara. It's circumstantial evidence that merely puts you in the house. That's all. Someone could have taken the mug and put it there."

She had to level with them. "The mug only had Axel's fingerprints on it, and mine."

Little frown lines deepened on Vita's face. "That's why Detective Cartwright wanted a list of all our clients who'd visited the nursery over the past two months. He's probably trying to make a connection to whoever put the mug there."

The tightness in her chest eased. "He is? That must be a long list."

"Quite long," Vita said, leaning forward. "If someone is trying to frame you, Sara, we may be able to help."

"Unfortunately, everyone uses that break room and it's hard to narrow down who might have taken the mug. We only have security cameras on the outside of our business." Rick's expression tightened. "Do you remember what day you used the mug? That might narrow it down."

She shook her head. "I did like using it. So it wasn't one time or anything like that."

Silly of her, having a little fantasy that she'd given the mug to Axel, for Father's Day, perhaps.

Doubt flickered in the gazes of Myles and Lila. Rick glanced at his wife, who nodded.

"Sara, please come with me. I'd like to have a word with you in private," Vita told her.

Lila threw her a sympathetic look, while Myles sighed. Rick left, presumably to oversee the landscapers.

This is it. She swallowed hard.

She followed Vita to the back of the building, where Rick had built a sunroom to accommodate high-end clients. In contrast to the stark, sleek conference room, this room was light and airy. Oak-paneled ceilings gave it a warmth and richness, while the floor-to-ceiling glass windows overlooked the lush grounds outside. Ferns and other plants filled in the corners, showcasing the nursery's plants. Instead of stiff leather chairs, a cream-colored sofa and a few matching chairs were arranged around a glass-topped coffee table. A smaller table and chairs sat near the door leading to the gardens.

It was a peaceful place where the Yateses encouraged staff to take their breaks and relax.

She could not relax.

"Please sit, Sara."

Vita indicated a chair by the sofa. Sara perched on

the edge, every nerve taut as piano wire. She crossed her legs at the ankle. Despite the lack of warmth in the room, sweat poured down her back, pooling in the waistband of her fine silk trousers.

Here it comes. They're going to fire me. I deserve it for not telling them the truth. Maybe I can get a job somewhere in Chicago...there's plenty of good marketing firms.

Vita sat in the chair opposite Sara and folded her hands into her lap.

"I knew Axel had a mistress."

Not the words Sara expected to hear. She watched Vita's face, the careworn lines and usually friendly gaze growing hardened. Vita stared down at her hands.

"I knew he had a mistress even before the truth of my husband's affair with your mother emerged. A wife... knows. I should have divorced Axel back then when I discovered he was sleeping with Regina, but I waited, for the sake of Lila and Myles. Then Regina's son, your brother, Wyatt, drowned. It was Axel's fault for not watching the baby."

Vita folded and unfolded her hands. "I felt for your mother, but I was more than scared for my own children. Axel was careless and responsible for Wyatt's death, the death of an innocent child. What about our children? It needed to end. Myles and Lila needed to feel safe, and protected. I didn't care what the cost or the price I'd pay for leaving him. I had to do it. It was not easy being a single mother. Eventually I met Rick and he was everything I dreamed about in a husband, and he became a good, loving and caring stepfather."

Silence draped between them. Knowing the struggles her own mother faced raising one child on her own, Sara ached for Vita.

"I'm glad you found happiness with him."

Vita lifted her head. Stunned, Sara watched the tears swimming in her employer's eyes.

"I truly was sorry for your mother's loss. I can't imagine…the horrific pain she felt at losing her child. I could forgive Regina for sleeping with my husband. But I could never forgive Axel for Wyatt's death, even if it was an accident. Axel had ruined lives, not merely mine and my children's."

Emotion clogged Sara's throat. Her grip on the armchair rests tightened, making her hands bloodless.

"When my mom told me everything, about Wyatt, I went into the bathroom and sobbed because I've always wanted a brother. A brother to hang out with, and play catch with, to tease and maybe I wouldn't feel so alone. When Mom told me Wyatt drowned and Axel was partly responsible, I felt so hollow. Empty. And yet I still wanted, I needed, to see Axel. I needed to look him in the face and tell him I was his daughter. Only then could I have closure. Only then, after he either rejected or embraced me, could I move on with my life."

She felt a hand on her shoulder. Glancing up through her blurred vision, she saw Vita holding out a box of tissues.

"I suppose we both deserve a good cry. It's why I thought privacy was best."

Sara took a tissue, wiped her nose, blew her nose and struggled to regain her lost composure. Vita wiped her own eyes.

She crumpled the tissue and crossed the room to toss it out. Sara turned suddenly.

"Vita, did Axel have a lot of enemies?"

Her employer sighed. "He wasn't one for making friends. My ex had a tendency to drive people away with his selfish streak. But an enemy who would go to such extremes? I don't know."

Sara had to know. More than anyone else, Vita knew her father well. "What was he really like? My mother only told me he was not a good person."

Vita stared out the window. "Axel was a selfish, arrogant and irresponsible man. But he was once a good man—otherwise, I never would have married him."

Nodding, she drew in a deep breath. "I kept hoping… for something different. I'll never know now. Vita, if you want me to resign today, I will. I don't want to cause you or your family any more grief or trouble."

To her surprise, Vita joined her at the window and took one of her hands. Her employer's hand was warm and slightly calloused. No one could ever accuse this woman of fearing hard work.

"Axel became greedy and selfish over time. I sense you only wanted to know your birth father and the relatives from his side you never met."

From what her own mother had said, Sara knew Axel Colton was a hard man. Hearing it from Vita drove home the point.

"I did," she said quietly. "I've always wanted a family."

Vita nodded. "I did not know, no one did, that your mother was pregnant with you when she left. I was simply relieved she had moved away to start a new life. But now that you are here, with us…"

Vita's voice dropped to a whisper. "I hope you'll stay. I've started to grow fond of you."

Tears welled up in Sara's eyes all over again. She stepped into Vita's warm embrace. "Thank you."

Seemingly overcome with emotion herself, Vita patted her back. "No, we're the ones who need to thank you for increasing our business and making us think outside the box when it comes to filling client needs. You're very good at your job, Sara, and I would hate to lose you, especially over Axel. He's done enough damage in my life."

Sara wiped her eyes as Vita released her. "I do like it here, and I hope you'll consider me like family. Well, not the same as your own children, but…"

"I already do." Vita smiled. "Now, shall we go see about those spreadsheets you've been working on while you were at home?"

Vita believed her. The other Coltons might have their doubts, but Axel's ex-wife did not. Sara only wished the rest of the family would have Vita's faith in her.

How would all of them react when they discovered her real identity?

Chapter Seven

The next morning Harry headed out to Yates' Yards to further question Vita about her ex-husband's lifestyle. Might provide a clue to who could have killed him.

Though Sara Sandoval remained a suspect, he needed to explore other connections. For all his partying lifestyle, Axel had come into contact with many people. Each one presented a thread leading to the main tapestry. His job was to trace the dozens of threads that made a complete picture.

When he reached the nursery, the cold, crisp air hinted again of snow. Harry headed into the office. He was in luck. Vita was in the front office with her assistant going over paperwork. Her manner was relaxed, her smile wide and professional.

Seeing him, he noticed a slight tension, though the smile remained. "Detective Cartwright. How may I help you?" she asked.

"I need to talk to you in private." He didn't want others overhearing Mrs. Yates's personal past with Axel.

Vita led him down the hallway to a spacious office with leather chairs pulled in front of a mahogany desk. A matching sofa sat off to one side, along with a table and other chairs, providing a more informal setting. Vita didn't invite him to sit there, but indicated one of the leather chairs before the desk as she sat behind it.

Amused, he sat. He knew the message she handed out—putting her in a position of power behind the desk. Vita Yates might be a good-hearted, sweet woman, but she was strong.

Had to be, to have married and divorced Axel.

She offered him coffee, which he refused. Harry didn't want to waste time with social niceties. He needed answers. Already this morning the department brass had grilled him on progress on the case. They wanted this one solved and off the books so they could call a press conference and look good.

It took less time than anticipated. Vita was forthcoming and honest about Axel. She'd separated from him after the affair with Regina and sought out a high-powered divorce attorney to ensure her children would receive the support they needed. Axel wasn't a bad person, only a neglectful father and husband who liked to party too much. His work ethic was questionable.

"If you're looking for Axel's enemies, anyone who might wish to hurt him, I'm afraid I can't help you. He's been so far removed from my life I wouldn't know. Have you talked with his brother?"

Harry consulted his notes. "This morning I did. It was a short conversation."

One thoroughly unpleasant. Erik Colton was rude and arrogant, testing Harry's temper to the max.

Vita touched a silver photograph of her children on her desk. "Axel was careless and irresponsible, but Erik has been unhappy for as long as I've known him. He's an angry person. Always angry. I recall a few times I invited him over for dinner. Once all he did was argue with anything we talked about. I stopped inviting him over afterward."

Interesting. Could Erik have been angry enough to fight with his brother and in a fit of temper, hit him over the head? But Erik had a solid alibi. That night he had been at his club. Several patrons had seen him there all night, drinking.

Harry tapped his pen against the notebook. "I talked with Erik briefly. He said Axel had changed."

Now it was her turn to look surprised. "Axel changed, how?"

"He wasn't clear, just said his twin had gone soft." Harry didn't tell her Erik had scoffed as he relayed this information.

There was also the matter of Dean Colton's will, which was in probate. Harry had his own theory about that will, though anything had yet to be proven. Dean Colton's wife, Anna, said her twin sons, Ernest and Alfred, had been the legitimate heirs to the estate. Carin Pederson, Dean's former lover, had produced two illegitimate twins, Erik and Axel, and both had a healthy trust fund their father had set up for them. Now another will had popped up to complicate matters.

"You heard about the earlier will Dean Colton left, Axel and Erik's father? The one where half of the corporation's assets were left to Axel and Erik?"

Vita's expression grew troubled. "Of course. But I don't believe it."

"Was Axel the kind to commit a crime to get what he wanted? Such as forge a legal document?" Harry leaned forward. "Think hard, Vita. Because if he was, then this puts a new spin on the investigation."

"No. My ex-husband was many things, Detective, but he wasn't a criminal. His brother..."

Following that thread, Harry pressed harder. "Erik might have forged the will to get the thirty million it said he and his brother were owed?"

Vita got up, walked to the window, her back to him. "I don't know. Erik isn't a pleasant person, but I hate accusing him of anything."

"You know him, Vita. You've sat at the dinner table with him. Would you say he might be capable of forging the will?"

A heavy sigh. "Yes. Erik tended to blow through his money, even more than Axel. I heard a rumor he was hard up for cash."

If Erik had forged the will, then argued with his twin after confessing the act, Erik stood to inherit the full thirty million dollars upon Axel's death if no one discovered Erik's deceit.

Twins, yet so different.

"Did Axel contact you in the past few weeks, apologizing for anything he did to you? Want to see his children more?"

She kept staring out the window. "He had been in touch with Myles and Lila. I wished no contact with him."

"Why?" He made a mental note to ask Lila, who seemed to be less angry with her father than Myles.

Vita turned to face him and touched the photo again. "Axel was part of my painful past. I learned to forgive him to move forward, but I had no wish to revisit any part of that past."

"What about your husband? Would Axel have contacted him?"

A small, knowing smile touched her lips. "Axel knew if he ever tried to contact Rick, or contact me through Rick, he'd get a much ruder response. My husband is very protective of me, Detective."

"Of course." He wondered how Vita would absorb the news he had for her. "I wanted to give you an update on Jackson's kidnapping."

She nodded.

"The FBI has questioned all known acquaintances of Donald Palicki, the man who picked up the ransom and was later found dead. No new leads. They're still searching for the suspect who shot Myles with the tranquilizer dart during the ransom exchange. The prints we lifted from the dart aren't in the system."

Vita bit her lower lip. "I'll let Myles know. This is troubling to know the other kidnapper is still out there."

Snapping his notebook shut, he nodded. "I need to talk with Sara now. Where is she?"

Her polite smile dropped. She folded her arms across her chest. "Why must you question her?"

Accustomed to hostility while he investigated family members, he decided directness was best. "She's a suspect."

"I believe you're misguided, Detective. Sara couldn't have killed my ex-husband. I can't see any good coming of you grilling her over the death of a man she longed to know, but never met."

"Leave that to me."

"I consider Sara family now."

"So you know her background."

Vita gave him a long, level look. "Yes, she told us. Sara explained everything about herself and Axel. You should know, Detective Cartwright, as protective as Rick is of me and my children, I am equally protective of my family. I will not stand for Sara getting hurt."

"Yes, ma'am." He liked her own directness. Oddly enough, he also liked Sara having someone stand up for her. "But this is an official police investigation."

"Very well. Sara's in the greenhouse."

Harry craned his neck and gazed out the window at the scattering of greenhouses on the grounds. "Ah, which one?"

Vita laughed. "Yes, that would help, wouldn't it? Come with me."

As they walked toward a door leading to the nursery outside, she glanced at him. "Sara's been a tremendous asset to Rick and myself. She brings a wealth of marketing ideas and knowledge to our business and has helped us to increase our income. I value her not only as a family member, but as an employee."

He nodded. "I won't take up much of her time."

"I would appreciate that." She opened the door and pointed to a distant glass building. "We have an event later she is helping to arrange at the new greenhouse my husband finished renovating. Follow the stone pathway outside to the left."

The cold outside was far warmer than the chilly reception he'd received from Vita Yates. He got it. Couldn't blame her. Talking about your former spouse, dredging up a painful past wasn't on his Top Ten list of fun activities, either.

The greenhouse where Sara worked wasn't large, but it was set among several trees, shading it from direct sunshine. Even to his inexperienced eye, he could tell this one had been designed for more than cultivating plants. The pitched glass roof and clear glass walls allowed in plenty of natural light, as well as allowed those inside to see the trees and ivy-draped terraces. Bare trees stretched out their limbs skyward, yet he could appreciate how pretty they'd look in spring and even more in the fall with vivid colors.

Lately, he appreciated glimpses of beauty wherever

he could find them. They were an oasis for the grim moments on the job, the sweet stench of death, the slick red of bloodstains...

The darkness of a human soul.

He paused for a moment to observe Sara through the glass. This greenhouse was different. Instead of rows of potted plants and irrigation tubes, it was mostly empty but for saplings lining the walls. Potted red and green poinsettias hung from beams overhead, and green ivy draped tastefully over support beams holding up the roof.

In her bright red sweater and a dark skirt and boots, Sara moved gracefully inside, waving her hands, pausing to help arrange the white linen–draped chairs.

Sara didn't look up when he opened the glass door. She directed two workers as they arranged circular tables in the room, and placed red linen cloths over the tops.

"Yes, like that. Good. Can you go get the silverware and place settings? I'll take care of the music system. We'll wait to set up the side table Chef Rysen required," Sara told them.

As the men trotted out, she finally noticed him. Her demeanor changed, and he sensed the temperature drop as much as he had with Vita. So much for the artificial warmth inside the greenhouse.

"Detective. You're here to ask more questions?" She palmed her cell phone. "Vita called and said you were on your way. I hope you don't mind if I continue to work as we talk. I'm on a tight deadline."

Sara walked over to a small table with what looked like wireless, portable speakers and fiddled with a laptop. Instrumental Christmas music began playing over the speakers. She turned down the volume.

No element of surprise here, but he didn't want one. Instead of delving into the interrogation, he decided to focus on the unusual greenhouse. Maybe warming her up would lower her guard.

Not that he wanted to focus on that solely to coax out answers, but for some reason he couldn't fathom, Harry wanted to converse with her without the pall of a murder dangling over their heads like the sword of Damocles.

"Amazing greenhouse. I see you're not using it for plants. What are you planning?" He pointed to the speakers. "Or are you playing Christmas music to make the plants grow faster?"

Sara looked puzzled, then smiled. "That's a gardening theory I've never heard before."

She swept an arm around, gesturing at the greenhouse. "This is partly Rick's idea. He finished customizing it for winter plants, but it's not really needed now, so he wondered if we could use it for customers. I found a ladies' Purple Hat Club in need of a different venue for high tea. They wanted to host one outside, but it's far too cold. I suggested renting them the greenhouse for a small fee, as long as they handled the catering. They were thrilled and convinced one of the ladies' husbands, a popular chef, to serve the food and tea."

Harry looked around. "Sounds impressive, but a lot of work for a simple tea."

"Oh no, not one tea, but a series of them. Each week they plan to rent the greenhouse. Not only that, they're posting the event on their social media sites. Word of mouth means Yates' Yards will pull in even more business, especially when these ladies begin their spring gardening. Most belong to a garden society as well. I arranged to have Rick speak to their club next month. It's a terrific cross-promo opportunity."

Smart and efficient. Sara had definitely brought her marketing ideas to the nursery. Suddenly doubts filled him. He looked at her slender arms, her slim figure. Sara seemed too delicate to lift a heavy candlestick and bash in someone's brains.

Then again, he'd seen stranger things in Homicide.

"I need to know," he began, then frowned as he realized she stared upward. "What are you looking at?"

"Oh good, it's happening!"

He glanced at the roof. "What?"

"Look at the sky!"

Expecting to see a meteor, or hell, considering the way this investigation was going, he saw nothing but gray skies and snow.

"Yeah? I'm looking."

She pointed upward and clapped her hands. "It's snowing! I was hoping it would snow. The ladies said it would be wonderful for their holiday theme. I have the perfect music for this."

Bemused, because it was Chicago and snow was as common as, well, snow in Chicago, he shook his head. Sara went to the laptop and switched the music to a holiday waltz.

Twirling, she laughed, arms stretched upward. "This is amazing. I'm so glad Rick renovated this greenhouse."

Enthralled, he watched her dance in the space between the tables, twirling like a ballerina, her long hair flying out, her skirt billowing. Harry almost forgot the reason why he'd visited. He could stay here all afternoon and watch her celebrate the snowfall.

"So beautiful."

"Yes," he mused, unable to tear his eyes away from her. "Quite beautiful."

Sara held out both hands. "Dance with me, Harry. I've always wanted to dance in a snowfall."

He shook his head, part of him wishing to capitulate

to her spell and waltz with her around the room. "I enjoy watching you," he murmured.

Dancing alone, she whirled around the tables as she smiled, almost caught up in the winter magic of fat flakes dusting the greenhouse roof. The music swelled and rippled in the still air as Sara danced, her head gazing with rapt attention upward, her body swaying in sinuous grace to the haunting melody.

Such a lovely contrast to the grim crime scene of her father's death… Sara lifted his weary spirits. How he wished he could bottle this moment and uncork it, like champagne, when the world became too dark and ugly to bear. For the first time since Marie's death, he felt a deep connection with someone, a moment that soothed his weary spirit.

Hard to believe a man as self-centered as Axel had fathered this enchanting, beautiful woman.

Axel…the reason he was here. Harry's grin dropped. He cleared his throat.

"Miss Sandoval, as I said, I have more questions for you."

She stopped dancing. He hated this part of the job that drove away the joy on her pretty face, replacing it with sheer disappointment and then wariness. He could almost hear internal walls dropping around her as self-preservation, like a castle dropping an iron gate to keep out enemies.

"Of course. I got carried away by my work."

Her polite, tight tone swept away any lingering magic between them, as if whisked outside by a stiff broom.

"No problem." Harry flipped open his notebook and forced himself to focus on the job. Always the job.

He began hammering her with questions. What she

knew about her father, or if she'd ever run into him anywhere by chance?

Hard to believe the woman had spent months studying
a man she wanted to meet and never once tried to arrange
an accidental meeting.

Sara admitted seeing him from a distance, but never
had formally met him. Harry made a notation.

Had she ever been inside his home? Sara folded her
arms across her chest.

"Never."

"Are you absolutely certain your father knew nothing of your existence? Never tried to contact you or your
mother?"

Sara sighed and shook her head. "Never. I told you, I
was working up the nerve to meet him."

"What about any other Coltons contacting you?"

"No." She blew out a breath. "If you have anything, any
other evidence that connects me to my father's murder
other than a coffee mug, I want to know about it. I have
the right to know. Are you going to haul me into the station? Arrest me? Should I hire a lawyer?"

"That's up to you, and no, you are not under arrest. But
as I said before, do not leave town. It won't look good for
you." Harry felt his chest constrict. He hoped he would
never have to arrest her.

Because as much as he hated admitting it, he liked Sara
Sandoval. He liked her very much.

And that made doing his job much harder, along with
being impartial regarding her involvement. It was far safer
to remain distant and objective.

No matter what he felt inside, or how much he did
want to waltz with her beneath the falling snow. Integrity meant everything to Harry. He'd sworn to be objective and honest as a cop.

If he lowered his guard around her and cut her slack because he felt attracted to her, and Sara Sandoval turned out to be a killer, he might not only lose his job.

He felt he would lose part of his heart as well.

As much as she enjoyed working at Yates' Yards on arranging the nursery's first afternoon tea, Sara was relieved to finally make it home to her apartment. It had been a nerve-wracking day, going from the joys of dancing inside the greenhouse as Harry Cartwright watched with a soft smile on his face...

To his grim expression as he grilled her once more on her involvement in Axel's life, and possibly his death.

Her thoughts were in turmoil. She didn't want to like the hard-nosed cop who thought she could have killed her father. Answering his questions had made her feel like a criminal and she wanted him gone.

Yet she liked having him close. Never had she felt this confused about a man.

No use denying the attraction. It flared between them in a rush of pure chemistry. Her heart leapt and her lady parts nudged her, reminding her that she was getting older, hey, time to settle down and have babies.

Each time she drew near the good-looking detective, she had to sternly remind herself it was strictly business. Even when, and she knew it would be a matter of when, not if, he cleared her as a suspect, there could never be anything between them.

Work was everything with him. Harry Cartwright was the kind of guy who would always put the job first.

For once, she wanted someone to put her first. Someone who wouldn't neglect her the way Axel had neglected her mother, and eventually, the brother who died.

Sara unlocked the outside door of the building and

checked her mailbox. Nothing. She'd halfway hoped for a postcard from Regina. Her mother used to enjoy writing. She once said handwriting thank-you notes and postcards was a lost art.

Smells of roasting beef and peppers wafted through the hallway as she climbed the stairs, along with the ever-present musty odor of a well-trafficked carpet seldom cleaned. As she walked toward her apartment, exhaustion feeling like twin weights on her shoulders, the door to #302 opened. Emma Pendleton stepped out, waved at her.

"Sara!"

She almost groaned. *Please, not now.* Lonely and seldom leaving her apartment, Emma loved to chatter. But after an emotional and physically exhausting day, Sara had looked forward to a quiet evening alone without company. She had planned to order pizza and then settle back in her favorite flannel pajamas to binge-watch cooking shows. Odd how she liked them more now that Harry admitted they were also a guilty pleasure.

Too late, she heard the shuffling down the carpet. Sara mustered a smile as she turned.

"Hi, Mrs. Pendleton. I've had a really long day. Can this…"

Her voice trailed as she saw her elderly neighbor's smile wobble. Mrs. Pendleton clutched a pink envelope in one blue-veined hand.

"I'm so sorry, dear. I wanted to tell you I haven't had the strength to make the pie for you. But I should have it soon. I do apologize."

"It's quite all right. Honestly, whenever you can. No rush. If you'll excuse me, I'm quite tired and I need to rest."

"Of course, dear. I wouldn't have bothered you otherwise, but I found this and it's addressed to you."

The woman waved the envelope like a flag.

"The postman must have delivered it to me by mistake a few days ago. I set it aside to give to you and simply forgot. I'm so forgetful these days. I am so sorry."

The widow wrung her hands after handing Sara the mail. "I hope it isn't important! It isn't a bill, is it? It looked personal, but if it's a bill, I'll gladly pay the late fee, I am so sorry…"

The pink envelope looked like it contained a greeting card. It was slightly rumpled and a silver sticker sealed it shut at the flap. The postmark was smudged. Sara stared at the return address.

Her mother's address.

Breath caught in her throat. "It's okay, Mrs. Pendleton, thanks, don't worry about it, I've got to go."

Barely had she gotten into her apartment and locked the door when she flipped on the light and dropped her purse onto the floor. Sara stumbled to a chair and tore the envelope with shaking hands.

A single sheet of white paper rested inside. She removed it and began to read.

Dearest Sara,
I've tried to find a way to say this, and every time I go to pick up the phone or text you, I fail. This is so difficult for me. I wish we hadn't parted ways with anger. I love you so much, Sara.
    I suppose this is why every time we've talked since you left I haven't been able to ask much about your life or your attempts to contact your father. When Wyatt died, part of me died inside. This is why I could never forgive your father and why I felt it necessary to move away and change my name, so Axel or any of the Coltons could never find me.

I did not want them to know about your existence.

I know you have your heart set on meeting him, Sara. I fear I didn't say enough because I didn't want you to hate me.

But when I found out you wanted to finally introduce yourself to Axel, I had do something. It's hard for me to talk about this.

I called Axel today for the first time since I left him. I told him about you, Sara. I begged him to treat you with gentleness.

He laughed at me. Axel told me there is no way you could be his daughter. He said cruel and intolerable things. He didn't care, the same way he had little remorse after Wyatt died.

Axel Colton will break your heart the same way he broke mine. He deserves to die for all the misery he's caused me, and how he hurt my baby.
I need to get out of town for a while so I can forget Axel and everything he has done. I'm so sorry I didn't have the courage to say this earlier. I love you.
Mom

The paper fluttered to the floor. Sara collapsed against the chair.

"Oh, dear heavens, Mom, what did you do?" she whispered. "Mom, how could you?"

Her mother hated Axel Colton and wanted him dead. She had to tell the police. It was the right thing to do.

Heart racing, her fingers trembling, Sara fumbled in her purse for her cell phone and dialed Regina's number one more time. This time, the voice mailbox was full.

She dropped the phone into her purse and then buried her face into her hands.

With one letter, Regina had cleared Sara of being a suspect.

And put herself at the top of the list as the person most likely to have murdered Axel Colton.

Chapter Eight

Harry had told Sara not to leave town because he might need to question her further.

He never expected her to call him with questions of her own.

He'd kicked off his shoes, loosened his tie and cracked open a well-deserved beer as he flopped onto the sofa to watch a cooking show when his cell rang. Harry glanced at it and did a double take.

"Sara. What's up?"

A small silence. Then she spoke in a clear, strong voice. "How did you know…oh, right, caller ID." A small laugh. "Um, how are you?"

"Good." He sipped his beer, wondering if this was a social call or if she had something to confess. Hopefully the former.

Not that he planned to date her, but Harry sincerely didn't want her to be the killer. For only the second time in his life, he wanted to be proven wrong.

The first time was after Marie and their son had been in the car crash and Harry had given up all hope they might make it. He'd prayed he was wrong.

He was right. They died shortly after arriving at the hospital.

"Is there something I can do for you?" *Keep it profes-*

*sional. Don't blow her off if she needs to talk, maybe she's
decided to level with you.*

"I need to talk with you, but not over the phone. I have
to show you something. Can we meet someplace?"

He looked with longing at the television and the beer
in his hand. Harry set down the bottle and switched off
the television. First time he'd allowed himself to relax at
home in days. "Yes."

Not at her home. Not at his. Someplace neutral. Judging from the emotion in her voice, whatever she had to
tell him, it was heavy.

"Do you know Mira's Diner off the interstate in Evanston?" he asked.

"No, but I can find it. Meet me there? When?"

He calculated the drive. This time of night, traffic
wouldn't be too bad. "Give me twenty minutes."

"Yes. I'll see you there."

He hung up, gave another longing look to his beer and
headed for the shower to clear his head. Minutes later, he
was dressed in a blue striped dress shirt, his favorite jeans,
boots and a navy sports jacket.

He took his department-issued car in case he had to
haul her into the station. Harry hoped not, but he was too
jaded. After thirty-four years on this earth, dealing with
all kinds of personalities, he learned to expect the unexpected. So he made a call to his former partner.

Mira's Diner was a greasy spoon where local cops
could get a decent meal and a great cup of coffee. It was
no gourmet restaurant, but it served the purpose. Best of
all, he could talk with Sara in private while still having
other cops' eyes upon him. Just in case.

He didn't think she would pull anything, but Harry's
spidey sense warned him something was up. That instinct
had saved his hide a time or two, like when a pretty and

seemingly sweet cashier under investigation for an inside robbery gone wrong had asked to meet him just to talk. She'd been terrified and didn't want to go to the station.

He'd met her in the industrial area where she worked. With patrol as backup. The cashier had been quick with her handgun, but Harry was quicker. He had her in cuffs as she screamed obscenities at him, before she fired a single shot.

Harry pulled into the diner's parking lot and switched off the engine. A neon red sign blared out Mira's Diner like a lighthouse beacon. Cars crowded the parking lot, including two patrol vehicles.

Frying hamburgers, bacon and freshly brewed coffee odors hit him as soon as he walked inside, reminding Harry he hadn't eaten lunch or dinner yet. He asked the hostess for a booth near the back. He recognized two patrol officers from his station and nodded at them in passing, but did not stop to talk.

Spying Sean at the counter near the door, he shook his head. Damn, that man was fast. But it felt good to know he had eyes on him during this meeting with Sara.

When seated, he eyed the door. This booth gave him a good view of the diner, and was private enough so they could talk without eavesdroppers.

He ordered hot coffee, black, and then texted Sean. Amused, he watched his former partner pick up his phone.

Did you get the security footage from the neighbors? Harry asked.

Yeah. Nada. Camera angle only goes to the end of the driveway and shows a little of the street.

Anything on the street?

I did see one vehicle parked on the street at 7 p.m. the day Colton was killed. It left fifteen minutes later. Dark Range Rover, late model. Got lucky, it backed onto their driveway when they left. Plate's fuzzy, but our IT guy is cleaning it up.

Let me know when you have something. He pocketed his phone.

Sara walked into the diner as the waitress served Harry's coffee. For a moment he looked at her, really looked at her, telling himself he was only assessing objectively without her seeing him. Same as he'd do for any other suspect.

Yeah, right. That wasn't a little skip-beat of his heart the moment she strolled inside, her hair mussed, her cheeks darkened by the winter chill, her long legs encased in tight jeans. She brightened up the diner with her colorful dark pink coat and a pink-and-red scarf with sparkling strands.

Harry added a few spoonfuls of sugar to his coffee, stirred, and then waved to her. She hurried over. The two uniforms he'd nodded to previously gave Sara an appreciative once-over. Harry scowled.

Sara was a suspect, nothing more. Yet he felt protective of her. Maybe it was a lingering effect of seeing that bastard ex-boss of hers manhandle her. He couldn't ignore his gut feeling this was something more. An undeniable chemistry sparking between them as certain as lake-effect snow in the winter.

She slid into the booth opposite him and shrugged out of her coat. "Thanks for meeting me. I hope I didn't interrupt anything."

"Only the best home-cooked meal I've ever seen."

Her mouth pulled downward. "Oh, I'm sorry."

"I taped it."

Her dark eyebrows knitted together. "Taped…oh!" Sara rolled her eyes as he chuckled. "On your DVR. I see. Well, I hope it's worth the wait."

Some things are.

"Did you eat dinner?"

She shook her head.

"I'm starved. Go ahead, order something. My treat."

"You always treat suspects to a last meal?"

"Only if it's not something created on the Food Network," he told her.

She smiled and picked up a menu. They gave the waitress their orders and Sara settled back.

"Do you always eat here?" she asked. "No wonder you like cooking shows."

"Sometimes. They have a great cup of coffee."

"I've always liked diners. Mom and I used to go to one every Sunday for breakfast. Fresh blueberry muffins made in cups. Mom's the one who turned me on to British comedy. We loved watching Monty Python movies. When I would scrape my knee or take a fall riding my bike—I was such a klutz as a kid—she would calm me down by telling me it was just a flesh wound, like the Black Knight, and I'd live."

Sara was babbling, but he could wait. He knew how nervous she was, taking a chance in meeting him here. Sara twisted the ends of her scarf, fiddled with her silverware as she talked about favorite foods and British television shows. Finally he asked her.

"Sara, what's wrong? Why did you need to meet?" His mouth quirked. "As enjoyable as it is listening to you, something is weighing on you. Talk to me."

"I don't know why, but I trust you, Harry." A small laugh. "I guess I have no one else I can trust right now.

I mean, I am a suspect, but I believe you truly do want justice for my father's murder."

"Yes." It had gone beyond merely doing his job. He itched to close this case, bring resolution for the family.

For Sara as well, if she wasn't the killer. It appeared less and less likely she was.

"Tell me what's wrong. What do you want to show me? New evidence?" he asked.

Sara blinked. "Uh, not exactly."

The waitress brought their food—a chicken salad for her, grilled Brie on rye for him. He dug into his food, famished, while she picked at hers.

"I have something that may incriminate someone else in Axel's murder, but I need your professional opinion. Right now all I have is a theory and a letter."

Harry stopped eating and leaned forward. Whoa. Out of everything he'd expected her to say, this certainly was not it.

She opened her purse and withdrew a pink envelope, setting it on the table. He listened as she explained about receiving the letter, and the smudged postmark.

"At first, I thought the letter genuine. It would explain why my mother's been out of touch." She brushed back a strand of hair from her face. "I, I wasn't certain if I should show you, seeing as the letter is incriminating to her."

Harry sat back, waited.

"And then I took another look at the letter. It's printed by a computer, which isn't odd, considering my mother hated to handwrite letters. With her Christmas card letters to friends, she printed them out. Only with clients would she handwrite notes because those drew more attention and were more personal. And Mom didn't sign it. She only printed her name."

She frowned. "I mean, she always liked to write letters and said it was a lost art, but why send one instead of calling me? We've always been able to talk before."

The letter did cast Regina in a new light. Picking it up with the edge of his napkin, he read. Pretty damning against her mother.

If Regina had killed her ex-lover and then sent this letter, it would explain many things.

"Why are you picking it up with your napkin? Can you get fingerprints off paper?" she asked.

"You'd be surprised what the lab can extract. Envelope seals contain DNA if the person licked it. If it is a forgery, whoever sent it would be smart and find another way to seal it. I'll have to take this in as evidence."

Sara bit her bottom lip, the move signaling distress, yet oddly sensual on her. "I understand. I was so relieved to hear from my mother, but you must know, this is not like her."

Harry dropped the letter on the table and polished off his sandwich in three quick bites. "Sara, what did your mother tell you during your last conversation with her? When was it?"

"About two or three weeks ago. I lost track. I told her I was finally going to confront Axel. She was worried about how he would react and said she didn't want me to get hurt. She was also worried about my apartment, wondering if it was in a safe neighborhood after I told her it looked like someone jimmied the kitchen door. It leads to a fire escape."

Whoa. This was news. Harry narrowed his gaze. "Someone tried to break into your home? When?"

"Right before I talked with Mom. I remember because she urged me to contact the police."

"Your mother was right. Did you?"

She sighed. "No. I noticed when I went outside to water a plant I had forgotten I'd placed out there."

A head shake and another sigh. "Here I am, working for a landscape and nursery company and I let plants die. I picked up the plant, it was dead already, and noticed the back lock. I couldn't be certain the marks were from a previous break-in or attempted break-in. I reported it to the building super, but he never responded. So I put a table and chairs by that door, just in case."

Harry pulled out his phone and made notes, reminding himself to check out the building manager as well. "Sara, did anyone see you entering or exiting your apartment the night your father was killed? A nosy neighbor?"

Sara frowned and then a wide smile touched her face. It was like watching sunrise after a long night. "My neighbor Mrs. Pendleton. She's always watching me. Sweet lady, all alone, I think she's lonely. She frequently stops me in the hallway. In fact, she's the one who gave me this letter. It was delivered to her mailbox by mistake."

"I need to talk to her."

"So, Harry…is this letter a fake? Or does my mother have something terrible to hide. Please tell me this letter doesn't incriminate her."

Pushing aside her half-eaten salad, Sara looked at him with her incredible green eyes. Pleading and wide, those eyes could lure the toughest man into a confession. He was made of stronger stuff but felt himself melting a little.

Only a little.

"What kind of car does your mother drive?" He could look it up in the DMV, but this would save time.

"A 2019 black Range Rover."

Not good. He felt bad for her but steeled himself.

"Most likely Regina did visit your father the day he was

killed. We don't have conclusive evidence, but it doesn't look good for your mother, Sara."

She did not meet his gaze. "My mother didn't kill Axel. She doesn't have that kind of temper. She's a gentle soul who wouldn't hurt anyone."

"And yet you haven't heard from her and she indicated in the letter she was leaving town."

Now she did look up and anger tightened her expression, her mouth thinning. "I told you that letter is probably fake."

"I'll be the judge of that." He beckoned to the waitress, who brought over the check.

"You're infuriating at times, Harry."

Pleased she used his first name, he handed over his credit card. "I've been told that."

"By whom?"

"My mother." He grinned and finally her ice-cold look melted. Yeah, he coaxed a smile from her.

Harry asked for an empty baggie. When the waitress returned with one, he dropped the letter into it. "Preserving evidence. I'll drop this off at the lab later. Come on. We're going back to your apartment."

A becoming flush darkened her skin. "Um…why?"

Intrigued, he leaned forward. "So I can make passionate love to you all night."

What the…where did that come from? He'd thought about teasing her, but this was too much, totally unprofessional. He took a deep breath, ready to apologize for being an ass when she gave a soft smile.

"Kind of hard to do in my apartment. The bed has a broken spring. Not very romantic. And I think the heater doesn't always work. We'd end up shivering under the covers all night."

Relieved she didn't accuse him of harassing her, he

nodded. "Then let's settle for me checking out your apartment's back door. I want to make sure that lock is sturdy in case that burglar returns for you."

Her smile faded. "You think someone tried to break into my place when I was there?"

Should he alarm her? Harry settled for a compromise. "I don't know, but in any city, always best to be cautious. Landlords tell you the lock is solid, but they don't like spending extra money."

Sara shrugged into her jacket. "True. This apartment was vacant and I didn't need much money for a deposit. The rent is inexpensive and I'm on a month-to-month lease. Since I wasn't certain how long I would remain in Chicago, I grabbed it."

He followed her back to Evanston. A restful and relaxing night off had been shot, but this was worth it. Harry had a gut feeling Sara's apartment might yield some answers.

When they were inside, walking down the hallway, he stopped.

"No security cameras." He scanned the hallway. Lighting wasn't bad, but he didn't like the shadows. Bad people could hide there, jump out and harm innocents like Sara.

Innocent?

Yeah, he was beginning to think she was, at least innocent of killing her own father.

"I know. I'm always aware of my surroundings. I never take the elevator except if I have heavy bags and even then, I'm careful." She frowned. "I have to be these days. There's all kinds of criminals out there."

At least she showed some city savvy in taking precautions when arriving and leaving her apartment.

Once inside her apartment, he headed for the kitchen. They pulled out the table and two chairs she had jammed against the kitchen door. Harry examined the inside lock. It was solid and up high enough to prohibit anyone trying to unlock it if they broke the window on the door. He hated these kind of entrances to the fire escape. They were pretty and allowed in natural light, but also beckoned burglars and provided an easier way to break inside if one didn't have the proper locks.

Harry opened the door and stepped out onto the fire escape. He glanced down. Terrific. Fire escape backed up to a dark alley. Perfect for burglars.

Using his cell phone flashlight, he examined the latch and the wood doorjamb. Someone had definitely taken a screwdriver to the wood, trying to break the door open. Judging from the freshly splintered wood, it was recent, too. Maybe last month.

Sara needed to know.

But why this apartment? Was the person who attempted this targeting Sara to rob her? Or worse?

He climbed down the fire escape to check the alley. It crossed to another alleyway that dead-ended to the left, but dumped out onto the street that paralleled Sara's building. Easy access. Too easy.

Good rabbit warren for anyone trying to sneak in and out of the building.

As HE CLIMBED back up the fire escape and reached Sara's landing, the tinkle of glass breaking jerked his attention to the right. A shadow on the fire escape five doors down, one floor above.

Bingo.

The kitchen door opened. Sara stepped outside, hugging herself. "Find anything?"

He lowered his voice and withdrew his weapon. "Go back inside, call 9-1-1 and tell them there's a robbery in progress at your building. Lock the door and do not come out until you hear from me."

Sara retreated, closed the door. It wasn't until he heard the quiet snick of the lock turning that he turned around.

The suspect crept down the fire escape stairs, grunting as he hauled a sack over one shoulder. Dim yellow lights from the apartment windows glinted off metal the perp held in his right hand. Gun.

Harry called for backup, possible armed robbery in progress at the address, and waited.

He climbed down the fire escape, hitting the alleyway the same time the suspect did. Sirens screeched nearby. Two patrol officers entered the alleyway.

"Police, drop your weapon," he barked out.

The perp turned, fired. Harry dropped, rolled but not fast enough as the hot burn seared his upper arm.

"10-1, 10-1, shots fired at police," a patrol officer yelled into his shoulder mike. "Officer down."

"I'm okay," he yelled back. "He's headed west toward Johnson. Go around the building."

The suspect took off running down the alleyway. Burdened by the heavy sack, the perp was fast, but Harry was faster. He ducked behind a dumpster as the perp turned and fired again. Then the perp hooked a right and sure enough, headed for the open street, right toward the patrol car blocking the entrance. As the perp raised his weapon, Harry jammed his gun into the suspect's back.

"Drop your weapon now or you'll get a bullet in your spine," he told him.

The gun clattered to the ground along with the heavy sack. Harry kicked the weapon aside as two patrol officers rushed forward to make the collar. Only then did Harry grimace.

Damn. He examined his arm. Just a graze, but it would make showering a bitch.

A patrol officer radioed for an ambulance. Harry shook his head. "I'm fine."

Then amid the flashing blue and red lights, the chatter on the patrol unit's radios, the stream of uniforms into the alley as he sagged against the redbrick building, he saw an angel emerge from the direction of Sara's apartment. An angel with dark hair bound back in a braid, wide green eyes and a worried expression.

He groaned. "I told you to stay inside and wait for me," he barked out at Sara.

"I waited until the police arrived. I saw him shoot at you, Harry!"

"I'm fine."

In the dim alleyway light, he saw her pretty eyes widen. "That's blood. You're hurt!"

"I'm fine," he snapped.

"No, you're not."

Oh, damn. More trouble. He knew that voice. Sure enough, Sean emerged from the sea of uniforms.

"You following me? You're not my mother," Harry grumbled.

"I heard the call go out. Yeah, I followed you from the diner." Sean shook his head. "You're going to the hospital, Harry."

"It's just a flesh wound." Warm blood seeped through his fingers. He winked at Sara.

"Flesh wounds get infected. Come on, stop arguing." Sean crouched down next to him.

"Tell that to the Black Knight. You know, the guy from Monty Python." He watched Sara's mouth quirk, and then her lips wobbled.

"You're no knight." Sean beckoned to the paramedics walking toward them.

"He is indeed a knight," Sara said so softly Harry wondered if he heard her right.

His ex-partner studied Sara. "Sara Sandoval. One of the suspects in the Axel Colton murder case. We've not met…yet. I'm Detective Sean Stafford."

Sara narrowed her gaze. "Yes, I am a suspect. But that's not important now. Harry's wound is."

Harry sighed, knowing Sean would lecture him about Sara and playing the hero. Right now his arm throbbed too much to care.

"Bastard ruined my jacket," Harry muttered, and then he glanced at Sara. "Sorry."

Her expression tightened. "*Bastard* is too nice of a word for him. Do you think that's the same man who tried to break into my apartment?"

"Maybe. Hey, wait, don't cut that, it's a good shirt," he protested as a paramedic brought out scissors.

"It was. Got a tear in it now. Stop complaining. I'll buy you a new one," Sean told him as he helped Harry shrug out of his jacket and shirt.

Bare-chested, he watched the paramedic treat his graze. It bled freely, but he'd had worse. Harry glanced upward at Sara, staring at him.

Her gaze centered not on his wound, but his chest. Harry wanted to laugh. Had they been alone, he'd have teased her that this was so not the way he'd wanted to get half-naked with her. But with Sean hovering over him like an anxious mama bird, he didn't dare.

Not only was his ex-partner worried, he'd warned Harry not to get involved with a suspect.

Too late. His interest, and his emotions, were already engaged. Hell, he hadn't felt this much sheer desire for a woman since Marie died. Not exactly the way he'd thought he'd feel something in his long-dead heart again. Certainly not here in a dirty alley smelling of rotting trash and spilled beer, blood trickling down his bicep.

Life sure was strange. But lately, he'd learned to accept that fact.

The paramedics finished dressing his arm. He flexed it as they handed him a blanket.

"It's cold out," the EMS guy told him. "We highly recommend you go to the hospital, but if you refuse, you have to see your doctor tomorrow. You're risking an infection."

Man, he hated feeling like a victim. He shrugged off the blanket and grabbed his shirt and jacket. "I'm fine and I'll go see my doctor tomorrow."

Forget the shirt. He tried to shrug into his jacket, but the bulky bandage prevented that. Without words, Sara picked up the blanket and gently placed it around his shoulders. Grateful for the warmth, pride preventing him from admitting he was freezing, Harry clutched it tight around him.

She turned to the paramedics. "I'll make sure he visits his doctor."

Oh, damn. Sean tilted his head. "Yeah? I was going to offer. Do you know who his doctor is?"

"I can find out. Right now he needs a hot drink and warmth." Sara looked more like a warrior than an angel right now, fierce and protective. "Officer…"

"Detective," Sean said.

"You can join us if you're worried I might poison his drink. I have plenty of hot coffee and tea for the whole department if you want. Or you can return to Mira's Diner for a refill, since you're so familiar with the place, unless you only go there when you're watching Harry meet with a suspect."

Harry closed his eyes. Sara was a hellava lot more observant than he'd given her credit for.

"Okay, okay." Sean huffed out a breath as Harry opened his eyes. "He's all yours. Harry, get yourself to the doctor tomorrow to get checked out or I'll have the chief drag you in."

"I will," he muttered.

He'd collared a dangerous thief, had gotten his sorry ass shot and now he felt like a kid caught with his hand in the cookie jar. As he and Sara headed toward her apartment, using the hallway this time, the door to Apartment 302 opened and a white-haired woman in a pink knitted shawl stepped out.

"I heard all the police sirens, Sara, oh my!" she gasped, seeing Harry.

"Everything's all right, ma'am. Please return inside. The police have this handled. Patrol officers may stop by to ask you questions."

"Oh dear. Sara, are you all right? I was so worried!"

Sara wrapped her arm around Harry's waist. Warmth seeped into his bones, and it felt damn good.

"I'm fine, Mrs. Pendleton. Please do as Detective Cartwright asks. Please stay inside."

When the door shut behind the elderly tenant, he shook his head. "She does a much better job at listening than you do."

"Hush or you'll get no sugar for that cup of coffee. In fact, forget the coffee. Hot cocoa for you, and I need a cup of chamomile tea."

"Sounds terrific," he murmured. Right now he could drink motor oil and it would taste good, wash away the ugly smell of gunpowder and blood.

Too often he'd come close to biting it. Tonight he wasn't close, but the wound served as a grim reminder he needed to be more careful, especially when chasing down a perp on foot.

No longer did he have a wife to weep over his casket or a son to ask questions no widow wished to answer. But he knew people would miss him, knew he had to get his head straight because even on days when life didn't seem worth living again, he had to push on.

So others could live their lives.

Inside her apartment he gratefully sank onto her too-soft sofa as she busied herself in the kitchen. Then she emerged, vanished into her bedroom and returned carrying a large pink fleece jacket with red hearts embroidered on the sleeves.

He raised his brows. "I hope that's for you."

"Mrs. Pendleton donated it to me. It belonged to her daughter. I didn't have the heart to tell her it was far too large. But it might fit you."

"Pink?" His nose wrinkled. "With hearts? I'll look like a deranged Cupid."

"It will keep you warm and I don't have anything else you can wear. Better than wearing a blanket."

He gave a dubious look at the jacket as he shrugged off the blanket. "I don't know. Do you have any manly sweatshirts, like a basic gray or navy that a guy could wear?"

Sara sucked in a breath and he frowned, then realized she stared once more at his bare chest. His blood surged, thick and hot. Yeah, the chemistry was there between them, sizzling like electricity arcing on a live downed wire.

Now was not the time to entertain the idea of exploring that further. He put the jacket on, zipped up and the interest faded from her gaze.

Yeah, nothing like wearing a girly jacket to douse desire. Maybe he should ask her for a pair of bunny slippers with floppy ears. Or wear flip-flops with white socks.

"What's so funny?" she asked.

Harry caught himself grinning. "Not much. Just… this." He gestured at the jacket, winced at his sore arm.

A soft smile touched her lips. "You look good in anything. Even a silly pink jacket."

He removed the medal from his trouser pocket. Hopeless cause, indeed. That was him. Maybe the medal stopped the bullet from hitting him someplace else, like his heart.

Sara held out her hand. "May I?"

He gave her the medal and she turned it over, examining it. "St. Jude. My mom has one. She never wears it, though. It's lovely. Looks like an antique."

He pocketed the medal as she returned it to him. "It is. An heirloom belonging to my wife's family. Marie, my wife, she gave it to me on our wedding day. After she died, her father asked for it back. I refused. I guess… I keep it because it reminds me of her."

Sara smiled softly. "Then don't give it back. It is yours, after all, family heirloom or not."

She switched on a table lamp next to him, so close he could smell her light perfume. Her fingers were long and elegant. She looked pale, too pale, as if witnessing his shooting had drained all the blood from her. But he sensed a solid core of strength in her that had gotten her through past tough times and served a purpose now.

Sara Sandoval wasn't someone who fell apart in a crisis. He could appreciate that, just as he appreciated the soft sway of her hips, the classic beauty of her face and the curves hidden beneath wool and denim.

Sara glanced at the kitchen. "I promised you hot cocoa. I'd better go fix it."

She headed back into the kitchen. Whoa. Harry moved his sore arm, welcomed the throbbing. It took his mind off the throbbing much lower. He could fall hard and fast for Sara if he wasn't careful. Focusing on the job helped as a good distraction.

He called Sean for an update on the perp, left a voice mail when his friend didn't pick up. Sara brought him steaming cocoa in a mug that read Coffee Is My Boyfriend. He grinned.

"Nice sentiment."

Her face darkened in an obvious flush. "My friend gave it to me as a Christmas gift when I skipped her party because of work. She was trying to fix me up on a blind date with this guy she raved would be perfect for me."

"Oh yeah? Did you ever go out with him?" He wondered about her social life. Did she have a boyfriend? From his background checks, Sara seemed happily single and relationship free.

"No. But she did, and ended up marrying him." Sara shook her head. "When I finally met him, I don't know why she thought I'd fall in love with him. He had money and maybe she thought that made a good match. But he was far too arrogant and this sounds petty, but…"

She laughed. Intrigued, Harry leaned forward. "What?"

"Oh, it is petty, but it's a pet peeve of mine. He wore too much cologne. Bathed in it. It made my eyes water. In my line of work, I've learned to be more sensitive to people's needs. I try to wear a light scent in case people are allergic. Does mine bother you?"

"No," he said in a husky voice. "It's perfect."

Sara gave a soft smile. "Scents are so important, and they can leave a lasting impression. I remember when I first met you, after I fainted and you were leaning over me and helped me recover. I smelled this amazing scent, spicy, but not too heavy. So intriguing and yet comforting, like the smells of home."

"I'm glad you were okay. I…was worried something bad happened to you."

"It was embarrassing. I hate looking weak in front of anyone. I've never done that before, but I was light-headed from not eating, and the news, it was too much for me." Sara touched his hand. "Thank you for looking after me."

The connection between them felt stronger than ever. Harry sipped his cocoa, his gaze centered on her. Funny how hot cocoa never appealed to him, but the scent now, along with the light fragrance of her perfume, made him think of autumn nights lazing on a wide porch, the crisp scent of wood smoke and home…

His cell rang. Harry set down his cocoa and picked up.

"Hey, how's the arm?" Sean asked.

"Fine. What's going on with our perp?"

He listened to Sean's report, deeply troubled, all his earlier peace vanishing. "I'll check in with you tomorrow after I go to the doc."

Harry hung up, toying with his cell phone, lost in thought. Sara waved a hand before his face.

"Harry? What's going on?"

He set down the phone, stared into his cooling chocolate to get a grip on reality. Reality wasn't a beautiful woman who cared about him getting hurt on the job. Reality was Sara Sandoval's questionable past and her connection to Axel Colton's murder.

"The guy they caught robbing your neighbor. He's a real creep, but dumber than a bag of rocks. Loved to brag about all his heists to his ex-cell mates. Name's Eddie Angelo. Ever hear of him?" he asked her.

Sara shook her head.

"You never heard of him?" Harry picked up his cell,

scrolled through messages and found the mugshot of Eddie Angelo that Sean had texted him. The guy looked like roadkill, his hair mussed up and sticking up on end, his beard long and scruffy.

He showed it to Sara, who frowned. "He doesn't look familiar."

"They ran his name through CODIS and he's got five priors of B and E in Chicago."

At her blank stare, he added, "The federal database for DNA. Guy's been convicted five times of breaking and entering. Paroled three months ago. Lives in St. Louis." Harry set down his mug carefully on the nicked coffee table.

"That makes sense, if he was here in this building now, stealing again."

Harry drummed his fingers against his thigh. "He's the brother of Dennis Angelo, the same guy who planted the murder weapon in Nash's trunk."

Sara's mug rattled as she set it on the table. "Are you saying this Dennis and Eddie…were working together? Or is it a coincidence?"

"I'm a cop. I don't believe in coincidences." He gave her a long, level look. "You sure you've never heard of either of them? Saw them in St. Louis?"

Sara shook her head. "It's a large city, Harry. Why would I have heard of them unless they were on the news?"

"You tell me, Sara. Or is there something you aren't telling me?"

"I've told you the truth so far."

The truth. Or a muted version of it? Little white lies that seemed harmless but omitted the full story?

His arm began to throb, a pulsing ache that warned he'd get little sleep unless he took a painkiller.

"Okay. Thanks for the cocoa. I need to get home."

"You barely touched it," she protested.

He offered a bare smile. "What I did drink was good. Make sure you lock up behind me."

When he was downstairs in his car, he took in a deep breath. This night had truly been revealing. He felt glad of Sean's news about the perp. It served as a slap to his face that no bullet grazing ever could.

He needed a grim reminder that this was an active homicide case and Sara was still a suspect.

Because Eddie Angelo and his equally seedy brother, Dennis, weren't any ordinary ex-felons who lived in St. Louis and committed crimes in Chicago.

They had a real and damning connection to Sara and her mother, Regina.

Sean had traced the brothers' history and discovered Eddie had done odd jobs for Regina around the yard. The same yard Sara used to garden.

She lied to him. It was pretty damn obvious.

He'd started to believe Sara Sandoval hadn't killed her father.

With this new information? Maybe not.

Chapter Nine

Sara couldn't focus the next day at work. Harry had been warm and friendly one moment, enjoying her company, and the next, he turned as icy as a Chicago winter.

As soon as he discovered someone named Eddie Angelo was the man who shot him and broke into Sara's building, Harry's attitude changed. Maybe because Harry thought she knew him? But St. Louis wasn't a small town where everyone knew her name.

I guess I'm still a suspect. But why won't he level with me?

Time to do her own sleuthing. She could also play detective. Sara typed the name Harry had mentioned into Google, didn't get much. Her mother might know this person.

Sara tried calling her mother again. Nothing. She couldn't even leave a voice mail.

Her hand shaking, she set down her cell phone on her desk. The cursor on her screen kept blinking like an accusation. Guilty. Guilty. Guilty.

Did her own mother kill Axel Colton?

Ridiculous. Regina lacked a fierce temper…

Except when it comes to protecting you.

Pushing back from her desk, she went to the window to look out at the gardens. Vita was outside with a woman who had her back turned to Sara. Two gardeners dug up a young sapling for an order while another waited with a cart. Curious, Sara returned to her computer to look up the order.

Cold dread skated down her spine as she read the name.

Carin Pederson. Axel's mother. Her own grandmother.

She'd met her at Axel's funeral, but Carin had been cold and dismissive. She'd know Sara as a lowly nursery employee. Not family.

Suddenly she didn't want Carin to know the family connection. Not yet. Sara printed out the order form and grabbed her jacket. She scurried outside. A bitter wind nipped at her cheeks, but it felt nothing to the icy numbness in her heart.

If on the remote chance her own mother had killed Axel, how could she claim any kind of relationship with Carin? A mother's love ran deep. She knew this from her own mother, and watching Vita and her loving relationship with Myles and Lila.

As she reached Vita, the woman with her turned around. Her heart raced. She wasn't ready for this. Too late to back away now, though she felt as if she'd rushed headfirst toward the jaws of a tiger.

"Hi, Vita. Here's the order, in case you need it," she said lamely, handing her employer the paper.

"You told me there would be no charge, Vita. Or are you determined to leech money out of me, despite my grief?" Carin ignored Sara.

"It's okay, Sara. The paperwork is merely for documentation," Vita said tightly.

"Oh, that's good to know. I'll mark the file."

Vita cleared her throat. "Carin, this is Sara Sandoval. I believe you met her at Axel's funeral."

The woman sniffed and nodded.

"It's a lovely tree," Sara said, smiling at Carin. "But it is a little late in the year to plant a sapling. You should make certain to water it and fertilize it at the right time."

"It's for my son's grave. Of course I'll make sure it's watered." Carin turned away from Sara and began snapping orders at the two gardeners.

Sara wanted to back away slowly, but part of her, the same human half fascinated by train wrecks, even the one in her own life, decided to remain. She'd had so little contact with Carin. Maybe there was something, a spark of compassion or friendliness, that could connect them. Carin was her paternal grandmother.

Certainly Sara didn't inherit her grandmother's height, for Carin was short, and quite thin. But perhaps her sense of style. Beneath her coat, she wore a red Chanel suit and red designer heels. Her white hair was uncovered, pulled into a tight bun.

But her green eyes were the same as Sara's.

Family.

Sara remembered all those holidays where it was just Regina and Sara. No matter how much they'd decorated the house, it was always too quiet. Her friends all had big families, sitting around a large dining table, laughing and exchanging tales.

Their neighbors the Millers always had cars crowding their driveway, overflowing onto the street. Carole Miller, who was in Sara's science class and friendly with her, had five brothers and sisters and endless cousins, uncles and aunts. All of them always celebrated Christmas at the Millers'.

One year Mrs. Miller came over and knocked on their door. Sara had held her breath, eagerly hoping Mrs. Miller would finally ask them over for dinner. Maybe even share dessert.

Mrs. Miller had asked Regina if the relatives could park their cars in their driveway. Sara had hung back behind the front door, hoping Mrs. Miller would finally issue the sacred invitation. They wouldn't eat much, but it would have been lovely to bask in the warm glow of holiday cheer with lots of people, maybe sing Christmas carols at the big Steinway piano Carole Miller played "Chopsticks" on, and Regina would bring over her home-made apple pie...

Her mother had glanced at Sara and swallowed her pride. She'd told Mrs. Miller it was just the two of them for Christmas and since Sara was an only child and Regina had baked too many pies this year, maybe they could bring one over for dessert...

Mrs. Miller thanked Regina for use of their empty driveway, murmured something about having to get back to her simmering cranberries and rushed across the street.

No invitation.

Sara didn't cry.

Regina looked at Sara, and her expression had hardened. She followed Mrs. Miller and told her that she'd changed her mind. No cars. She had to leave because they were heading out of town for a special Christmas celebration.

Regina had taken Sara to an expensive dinner at a luxurious restaurant. Before leaving, she'd blocked the driveway with rocks to prevent the Millers from parking there.

Regina had a fierce love for Sara. Sara didn't want to upset her mother and acted happy and surprised about the gourmet Christmas meal.

Later, in the privacy of her bedroom, she cried for the father and brother drowned in a boating accident, the family she never had...

Carin was her grandmother. Blood was blood. *Grand-*

mother. Maybe she could call her Grandmother. Regina's parents died years ago. Carin was a living, breathing connection. Maybe she could finally have that dream come true...

"What are you staring at?" Carin snapped.

Sara blinked and looked away, her stomach clenching as if the woman had slapped her. She pasted on the same polite smile used for unruly customers. She crumpled the order form in her hands and shrugged. "Nothing, Mrs. Pederson."

Her grandmother turned to Vita. "Vita, tell them to hurry, for heaven's sake. I don't have all day. I have a hair appointment this afternoon."

Doubtful she could feel any worse than Carin already made her feel, Sara started to back away.

Vita threw Sara a questioning look and mouthed, "Do you want to tell her who you really are?"

Bless Vita for asking before blurting out the truth. Sara shook her head.

A small smile touched Vita's mouth. As Carin turned away from both of them, Vita winked and twirled her finger near her temple, the sign for "crazy." Tension fled Sara's shoulders as she stopped feeling sorry for herself. Carin was not a pleasant person. Surely she was not an easy ex-mother-in-law to have in Vita's life.

The two men lifted the sapling out of the ground and placed it on the cart. One landscaper hauled it toward the driveway, Carin and Vita flanking the cart like pallbearers at a funeral.

Axel's funeral.

Suddenly she became too aware of the cold creeping into her bones, the pretty heels that provided no protection from the light snow dusting the ground. Her ears hurt. Or maybe it was all a reaction to seeing this.

Sara went inside, headed into her office. Once there, she picked up her coffee mug with a trembling hand.

A knock sounded at her doorjamb. She peered up to see Lila's troubled expression.

"Are you all right? I saw what happened."

Sara set her mug down carefully. "Yes. It was unexpected. Thanks for asking."

Lila sat in one of the chairs before Sara's desk. "Uncle Erik was in yesterday to pressure Mom and Rick about that tree for Axel's grave. He's always in here to pick out flowers for the girlfriends he thinks no one knows about because he gets them at a discount. So cheap."

"I know." Sara had met him a few times, though Erik had never realized she was Axel's daughter.

Her half sister made a face. "I saw Carin was coming into the nursery and I hid. She may be my grandmother, but she's difficult."

Throat tight, Sara nodded.

"Well, more than difficult." Lila leaned forward, her gaze filled with sympathy. "Sara, she isn't the grandmotherly type. In fact, I don't know if she's anyone's type. She's never been a nice grandmother to me or to Myles. I'm sorry if she made you feel awkward."

Sweet Lila. Such nice words. Sara shrugged away a lifetime of rejection. "She's a client. I would rather Carin not know my relationship with Axel. I don't think she'd take well to it."

"No, she probably would not. She's too absorbed in her own grief. I mean, Axel wasn't a terrific father to us, but Axel was her son. It's different for her."

Such honesty felt refreshing. Sara toyed with her now-cold mug of coffee. "Lila, I don't know if you or anyone else believe me, but I didn't kill Axel. I only wanted to introduce myself and get to know him."

Lila closed her eyes. "I believe you."

"You...do?"

Her half sister's eyes flew open. "Yes. I know we don't know each other that well, but I like to think I'm a good judge of character and your character doesn't seem to have it in you to commit such an act of violence. Even if Axel provoked you."

The lack of censure from Lila suddenly meant more than if Carin had expressed joy at Sara being a long-lost granddaughter.

Lila stared out the window, and Sara sensed she wanted to say something but found it hard.

"Lila, what's wrong?"

Her half sister sighed. "I'm sorry you never knew Axel. He was your father, too, but you need to know something, Sara. It was never easy around him. I don't want you getting dreamy-eyed, thinking he was this amazing dad. He wasn't."

Sara leaned back. "What was he like as a dad growing up?"

"Self-centered. Not really mean, but he was more absent than around. He was there for birthdays. Sometimes. He wasn't the kind of dad you could talk with or ask advice. Myles and I were lucky when Mom met Rick. Rick became everything Axel wasn't."

A heavy sigh from Lila. "I guess that's why I didn't feel angry or upset when I found out you were our sister. Maybe not even surprised. Axel hurt Mom a lot when he had an affair with your mother. But in a way, he was already separated from her. At least, that's how it felt for me. I learned to get along without him. As for Carin, she's not grandma material. If she even caught us calling her grandmother, she'd get angry and walk away."

"Sounds like her Chanel panties were too much in a wad," Sara said dryly.

Lila laughed. "Yes, that is a good description of Carin. Don't ever feel bad about being on the wrong side of the sheets, Sara. Because of Carin having an affair with our grandfather, Dean, everyone Axel and Erik Colton fathered has that dubious background."

"Thanks," she said, feeling as if a burden had lifted. "Thanks for not hating me for my connection to Axel."

"Hate you? You're kind and smart and you've helped Mom and Rick with new business. I'm glad you came into our lives."

For the first time since last night's fiasco with Harry, Sara felt a genuine smile touch her lips. "I'm glad, too."

"Families are so complicated at times." Lila sighed. "Especially with the Coltons. I hope your mother's side of the family is normal."

A short laugh. Normal? What defined normal anymore? Since Lila opened up to her, she told her the truth.

"Not exactly. My mom was an only child. Her parents died when she was in college. The few aunts and uncles on her side are either long gone or never acknowledged my mother after she had an affair with Axel and I was born."

She thought about the cold attitude of her mother's relatives and how they judged Regina instead of reacting with kindness when Regina asked them to visit for the holidays.

Regina never did reveal how her relatives had reacted, but Sara could see the hurt in her mother's eyes. It made her determined to never make contact with that side of the family. *I guess I'm as protective of my mom as she is of me.*

"They considered me to be a stain in their eyes because I was illegitimate. I never discovered this until much later, when Mom told me the truth about my origins. They never were close to us growing up, would only send a Christmas card, when they remembered."

"It's just you and Regina?" Lila's eyes widened. "I wouldn't know how that feels. But I bet it was nice at times, having your mom's undivided attention."

Now that she thought about it, Lila was right. Sara smiled. "My mother had a way of making every holiday special. I think she did it because I always wanted brothers and sisters, and a father. So she lavished lots on me each holiday."

Lila grinned. "Well, now you have a lot of Colton cousins and relatives. Maybe too many. I have to get back to work. Maybe we can do lunch tomorrow?"

If Carin had been icy, Lila was positively warm, shattering the cold Sara felt. "That would be lovely. I'll text you."

After Lila left, Sara looked at her cell phone, considered calling Harry Cartwright. Her mother had been gone for a long time. If she had left town, she'd have informed Sara.

It simply wasn't like her mother to leave and not call, or at least text. Sara thought of the letter and shivered.

If Regina had murdered Axel, even in a fit of rage, would she take the coward's way out and flee town?

Or face up to what she had done and turn herself over to the police?

Sara honestly didn't know. She had no real inkling of the kind of relationship Regina had shared with Axel until this year. But losing a child… She could understand the grief and rage her mother felt when Wyatt died due to Axel's carelessness.

She needed to find Regina. Now. Only one person she knew had the ability to track her like a bloodhound.

With great reluctance, Sara picked up her phone and called Harry Cartwright, hoping he could help.

He answered on the first ring. "Hey."

His deep, rugged voice soothed her the way no warm drink could on a cold night. "Hi. You left in a hurry last night."

"Sorry. My arm was hurting." He snorted. "And me being a manly man, I couldn't let you know it."

Sara smiled. "Consider this your daily nag call. Did you see the doctor?"

"Yes, I saw the doctor."

His impatient tone sounded like all the men she'd ever encountered who loathed visiting the doctor. So much that she could almost consider him as just another guy.

But he wasn't. He was extraordinary, funny, compassionate, courageous, dedicated...and quite possibly the man who'd break her heart.

"And?"

"And it's a flesh wound." He sighed. "I was ordered to rest for a couple of days."

Sara suspected he was not the type to follow orders that restricted him. "So you're working."

"Yeah, you got me. From home. This is the age of high-speed internet and computers. Not that I'd know. I'm still on dial-up," he joked.

"Lucky you. At least you have a phone. I'm calling you from a tin can and a string."

He chuckled and warmth spread through her. Harry was the kind of guy she'd want with her in a crisis, who could navigate through floodwaters and ease panic with a joke about getting his shoes wet.

If this didn't qualify as a crisis, nothing would.

"After I left your place last night, I talked with your neighbor, that nosy Mrs. Pendleton. She wasn't helpful, but admitted she goes to bed early and you come home late at times, so the night Axel was killed, you could have come home and she wouldn't have known it."

Sara searched her memory. That night she'd left work on time at Yates' Yards and picked up takeout from a local restaurant. So much for having a neighbor who could provide an alibi. Then she brightened. "Wait! I still have the receipt. I got Chinese takeout that night. What time was Axel killed?"

"You save your receipts from Chinese takeout?" Harry sounded amused.

"Habit from when I took clients out for dinner. Let me call you back."

She hung up, scrolled through her phone to find the photo of the receipt, then called Harry. He answered immediately.

"The coroner puts the time of death between 7:00 and 9:00 p.m. What does your receipt say?"

Gazing at the receipt, she sighed. "I guess having a receipt that proves I was in a Chinese restaurant at 6:00 p.m. doesn't clear me."

"Not exactly. Unless you can claim a bad case of heartburn that took you to the ER."

He sounded too lighthearted and upbeat for such a serious conversation. Sara frowned. "Well, am I still high on the suspect list?"

Instead of answering, Harry changed the subject. "Since I'm housebound, I did a little checking on your former employer, that POS Ernie."

This sounded interesting. "You think he had something to do with Axel's death?"

"Hardly. I was more interested in his involvement with getting you to work for him again, and how desperate he is." Harry made a growly sound. "He's slime, Sara. The guy is up to his eyes in debt. He actually took a loan from his 401K and now has to pay it back. The company president has been breathing down his neck for new business. Business, it seems from talking to others in the firm, that you were responsible for obtaining."

"Why did you go to all that trouble to look into Ernie if he's not a suspect in Axel's death? Is he a threat?"

"His behavior makes him a threat to you."

Touched he would be so protective, she smiled. "Thanks. I can handle Ernie. He's a bully and like all bullies, they usually back away from direct confrontation."

"Usually. Be careful. I don't like this guy."

I don't, either. But more and more against my better judgment, I'm beginning to like you.

She cleared her throat. "What did you find out about my mother's letter? Did she write it?"

Somehow she knew what the answer was, though it made her heart sink.

"It was definitely her DNA on the envelope. Your mother wrote that letter and mailed it to you."

Gripping the phone so tight in her hand her knuckles whitened, she licked her lips. "How could you know? How could it be a match? Her DNA shouldn't be in the system."

"It wasn't." Harry sounded calm, and she wanted to scream. "I did a little digging and your father's attorney helped. Your mother willingly submitted a sample years ago to Axel Colton's lawyer when your father underwent a paternity test that proved he fathered your brother."

If he had reached through the phone and struck her, she couldn't feel more shocked. "My father didn't believe the baby was his?" she whispered. "You had no right to invade my mother's privacy."

Harry went silent for a minute. "I have the right, Sara. I have a killer to find and I'll go to any lengths to find him."

"I assume that since you have the proof my mom mailed that letter, which is pretty incriminating, that eases your suspicion of me?" She couldn't help her bitter tone. "Or do you think we're the murdering dynamic duo?"

"Less likely you did it." He drew in a breath, as if wincing. "Sara, Eddie and Dennis Angelo both have connections to your mother."

Oh no. Sara shook her head. "Impossible."

"Dennis worked for the same office as your mother, and as the office manager, she would have paid him, or even hired him. Eddie did odd jobs for Regina."

Sara blinked. "No, he couldn't have... When?"

"Five years ago. We checked his bank and found checks from your mother written to him. She hired him to clear the snow from her driveway. He was running a small snowplow business. Then she hired him again to haul away a dead tree stump in the spring."

"Mom told me she hired a guy to help her with a couple of projects, but she never mentioned names. I don't remember her saying anything about him."

The sound of shuffling papers. "Both times you were away at college. I can't find a connection to you."

"So that's why you've cleared me, more or less, as a suspect," she said slowly.

"Right. Except for the mug. That may have been placed in Axel's kitchen." Harry's voice deepened. "By whoever wanted to frame you for his murder. Or at least divert suspicion to you. Or it could have been a simple case of someone taking the mug and visiting Axel."

"You said my fingerprints and Axel's were the only ones on it."

"Yours were the only prints we found that we could lift. The others were smeared. So it might have been an innocent case of whoever took the mug put it there and forgot about it. Maybe even Axel himself. He visited the nursery a couple of times before his death."

Relief and fear mingled in her stomach. Relief she'd been cleared. Fear Regina might have killed Axel.

The little cursor on her computer screen seemed to taunt her. *Gone. Guilty. Your mother is guilty.*

Your mother killed Axel Colton, your father.

"I can't believe this," she whispered.

"She may have run away," Harry said gently. "Sara, you have to be prepared for the eventuality your mother killed your father."

The words came out in a rush. "I still can't reach my mother. Not through her cell phone, or emails. Her office has been closed the past two weeks for renovations and they're moving. Mom thought this was a good time for well-deserved vacation. She promised to call me with the new office number."

"The fact that no one can reach your mother is not good for her, Sara."

"Then go find her." She stared at her computer screen. Footsteps sounded outside her door. She was supposed to be working, and she didn't want Vita to find out Regina had been moved to the top of the suspect list.

Sara bit her lip against the grief welling inside her. "I'll have to find her a good lawyer."

"Can you think of any places, favorite vacation spots, a cabin loaned to you by a friend, where Regina would go?"

"No." She started to protest that her mother wasn't the type to run from trouble and then remembered how Regina told her how she'd fled Axel while pregnant with Sara, and changed her last name.

Fleeing definitely fit Regina's personality. Especially if it meant keeping her only living child safe.

"I can't think of anywhere she'd go. Most of all, I know

if she did go someplace, Harry, she would call me. If her cell phone was broken, she'd buy another. This isn't like her."

"People do unusual things under stress."

"Not my mother," she snapped. "She would never cut off contact with me."

"Even to protect you?"

The question made her pause. *Oh, Mom, what did you do?*

"I don't know. It doesn't matter. I want her found safe, and alive. That's what matters most."

"I will. Sara, be careful. Eddie Angelo broke into your apartment building, but he may have been targeting you if your mother used him as an accessory and failed to pay him off. Criminals know the easiest way to blackmail victims is through a family member."

"I'll take extra precautions. Go find my mom."

"I will find her. Take extra precautions, but remember, don't leave town. It won't look good for you with the district attorney if your mother is guilty and you aided and abetted her." He paused. "I'd be forced to arrest you, Sara, and I really, really do not want to be put in that position."

A lump clogged her throat.

He hung up.

Sara felt as if she rode a high-speed roller coaster. She should be happy about being cleared as a suspect, but more and more, it looked bad for Regina.

Where could her mother have gone?

Chapter Ten

Harry hated light duty. He itched to be on the street again, but the doctor ordered him to rest for two days after he was wounded.

The following day, his phone buzzed. Harry rolled over, groaned as he rolled onto his sore arm and grabbed his phone. He groaned again.

Sean. Texting at 4:30 a.m.

You okay? How are you feeling?

Harry texted back. I was feeling great until you woke me up. Go get some sleep.

Can't. Twins are up. Did you tell Sara about her mother's letter?

Might as well make coffee and get up. He was too awake now to fall back asleep. Harry padded into the kitchen, put on coffee and sat at his kitchen table, texting Sean about the letter and Sara's reaction and how Sara was no longer a suspect.

He also told Sean he'd started to worry about Sara's safety.

Sean texted back. The Angelo brothers are bad news

but now out of picture. Sara should be fine if Regina hired Eddie. She wouldn't hurt her own daughter.

Bristling, Harry texted back. Not taking chances. The Angelo brothers may have accomplices. Sara could still be in danger.

The coffee machine dinged and he poured a mug, added several sugars. When he returned to the kitchen table, his phone blared out two words.

Huh. Interesting.

What? Harry texted back.

You and Sara.

Drawing in a breath, he texted back, Go help your wife and babies then grab some sleep. TTYL.

The last thing he needed was his former partner speculating about a possible romance between him and Sara. That was on the back burner, and that burner wasn't even lit.

I'm only trying to protect her as I would any citizen.

But his conscience warned otherwise.

He drank the coffee, made breakfast and did some work on his laptop. By ten o'clock he shut the laptop and contemplated his day. He felt fine, if not a little sore.

Until Sean called him with bad news. Someone had stabbed Eddie Angelo in what looked like a jailhouse fight. The DA had been ready to cut a deal with Angelo in exchange for what he knew.

Now their prime source of information was lying on a morgue slab. Harry thumbed off his phone, itching to do something.

Instead of following orders, he decided to circumvent

them. It wasn't technically going into work if he met someone for a meal.

After showering and dressing, Harry drove to Naperville to meet with Jimmy Curry, his friend and the lead investigator on the Santa Claus homicide. Brass warned him not to come into the station, fine, he was just having breakfast with an old friend.

An old friend who could fill him in on details about any progress Naperville made on the Colton case.

The breakfast crowd had dissipated by the time he pulled into the parking lot of Belle's Eatery. Too early for the lunch crowd. Harry jingled his car keys in hand as he walked into the restaurant and slid into a green booth by the window. He ordered coffee with two sugars, and pocketed his car keys. If Jimmy, who prided himself on arriving on time, was late, it meant he nailed something.

Harry scrolled through his cell phone while he waited. He glanced at emails and then through his photos, stopping at a photo of Marie and John.

Breath caught in his throat. Damn. He'd forgotten he had this. Left it on his phone when he transferred all his data to the one phone he'd bought a year ago.

A colorful Christmas tree behind them, Marie's wide smile and sparkling eyes met the camera as she held a squirmy, giggling John. He remembered that day…hell, how could he forget? The first Christmas where John really got into opening gifts, tearing at the boxes, playing with the bright, shiny paper. His laughter and Marie's as they tried to keep their baby from eating that same shiny paper. The three of them alone. Her parents had taken a cruise to Europe and he'd felt such relief they had privacy, instead of his father-in-law descending into the usual lecturing about how Harry's salary couldn't provide Marie with everything she needed, how Harry should take the offer to be head of security at her old man's firm…

They'd had a wonderful day. Took John to try skating in downtown, and Harry and Marie had gripped his hands, delighting in his squeals as they lifted him up while they skated. Later as John finally slept, he and Marie had made love downstairs before the fireplace as snow softly fell outside and Christmas carols played over their sound system…

He touched the phone's screen, his throat tight, his appetite vanishing. How quickly life could change in an eye blink. One minute you're worried about the kid's college fund and how you can afford that dream vacation to Disney in the summer. The next, you're spending your vacation money on two coffins and a burial plot…

"Hey, Harry! Good to see you!"

Blinking, he shoved his phone back into his pocket. Jimmy slid into the booth opposite him. Harry pretended absorption in his coffee to hide his face. While Jimmy shrugged out of his coat, Harry grabbed a paper napkin and wiped his wet eyes.

When he looked up, he deliberately winced and crumpled the napkin, stuffing it into his jeans pocket.

"Hurts still, huh?" Jimmy sounded sympathetic.

"Like a bitch. But I hate taking any pain pills." Blame his loss of composure on the gunshot wound. Not on his past.

While they placed their orders, Harry's thoughts drifted to Sara. He felt a tug of deep connection with her, something he hadn't experienced since the day he lost Marie. That spark, that chemistry, was undeniable.

But impractical.

Who was he kidding? Even if she was cleared as a suspect, Harry couldn't begin a relationship with her. The wounds in his heart were too raw, taking too long to heal. He'd dated plenty of women over the past two years to try to forget about Marie. Each relationship ended with him gently breaking it off.

Some had tried to get him to talk about his family. Those women were the ones who lasted longer because they genuinely cared, but in the end, it didn't matter. Who wanted to date a guy who was deeply in love with a memory?

"Got some news for you. Not what you want to hear, but good news all the same." Jimmy stirred sugar into the steaming coffee the waitress poured. "Remember the Santa thief?"

"Yeah." Seemed like a lifetime ago.

"We made an arrest."

Harry's head jerked up. "Yeah?"

"Like you said. Not a simple burglary." Jimmy showed him a cell phone photo. "Maureen Markam, aka Maureen Duell. Vic was her ex-husband. He dressed as Santa, burglarizing homes, but that night he'd planned to visit her and surprise the kid with toys after he did a few homes. She admitted everything. Went to see him before he was released, begged him to stay away from the kid. Turns out Mr. Duell used to beat the crap out of her. He got released, targeted the homes she patrolled. She saw him at the Ladd house while on duty, he threatened to tell the cops she was in on the burglaries and their kid would be sent to social services. He hit her and she shot him, point-blank."

Harry's disgust rose. Men who assaulted women were pond scum.

"Looks like the DA will cut her a sweet deal. She did get the guy responsible for the break-ins."

Harry nodded his thanks as the waitress brought their

meals. He toyed with his oatmeal, not hungry anymore. "Glad that's closed. Any news on Colton? Anything?"

"Nothing." Jimmy frowned. "Colton was a lazy bum who lived off his trust fund, made a few enemies but this doesn't make sense. Whoever did it was mighty pissed off, but who hits a guy over the head with an antique marble candlestick? That seems so…"

"Angry?"

Jimmy sat back. "Yeah. It was convenient. So we know it was a crime of passion, no prints or DNA on the weapon, except for the vic's. But it wasn't even in easy reach."

Harry's mind sorted through the details of the crime scene and suddenly it dawned. After taking out his phone, he scrolled through the photos of the crime scene he'd stored for referral.

The candlestick. The markings on the bottom.

"Damn. Why didn't I see this before?" he muttered.

"What?"

"This candlestick…" He showed his phone to Jimmy. "Antique, marble, with real gold. Expensive. What did the other one appraise at?"

"Around $6,000 each. But a lot of stuff in Colton's home is expensive. He was rich."

"Yeah, but most of the things in his home, they were not antiques. His decor was modern." Harry snorted. "I know about this stuff from my ex-mother-in-law. She prides herself on her traditional French Provincial home. I couldn't tell Asian from mid-century modern, but heaven forbid you dare gift Arlene with an Art Deco photo frame for her antique desk. She actually lectured me for half an hour after I gave her that frame before Marie and I got married. I liked it, thought it would look great on her writing desk."

Jimmy shook his head. "Beats me. I don't know how you put up with your in-laws, Harry."

I did it for Marie. Because I loved her and when you love a woman that much, you'd do almost anything for her.

"Those candlesticks at Axel Colton's…they're ornate, almost as if they don't belong. Colton's living room was all high-end contemporary. Lots of glass, look at this living room."

He showed Jimmy the photo he'd taken of the pristine cream sofa and the mirrored coffee table with matching end tables. "The candlesticks don't fit in. They don't match."

Jimmy shrugged. "Maybe Colton liked them and was trying to figure out a place for them. We never could trace their origin. Family said they always saw them around."

"His immediate family. Colton was from the wrong side of the sheets, remember? Maybe one of the Coltons on the right side of the sheets wanted them back, family heirloom and all that, and thought it a fitting demise for Colton…beaming him with a candlestick he refused to hand over." He stared at the candlestick photo and it jogged a memory.

"I keep all the photos from past crime scenes, and the vic's houses, on my phone," he muttered. "There. Look at this house. Italian decor. Fits right in with the candlesticks."

"What house is that?"

"Alfred Colton's. One of the twins murdered by the serial killer earlier this year."

Jimmy's eyes widened. "Damn. So what's the connection?"

"None right now. But what if Axel, being an illegitimate brother, stole something of his father's that was an antique that had been in the Colton family for years?"

"And this would make the murder not about Axel, but about the candlesticks. Personal property. But why not simply take the candlesticks after killing Colton?"

"Because if this is the motive and the suspect used the candlestick to kill Colton, whoever did this knew they could be traced back to them." Harry tapped his phone. "I remember the Alfred and Ernest Colton case. Sean's wife, January, would know. She's Alfred's daughter."

He texted Sean, knowing his ex-partner would probably yell at him for being out instead of home resting. So what? He told Sean he needed to talk to January at their home. Set up the time.

Harry set his phone down and dug into his now-cold oatmeal. "Jimmy, I need you and your guys to go over every inch of Axel Colton's home one more time. See if anything else looks like it doesn't belong. If Colton took the candlesticks, chances are he might have taken other things."

"It's still the same with you, huh, Harry? All work and no play. Always the job."

Jimmy's voice was quiet, but Harry sensed a deeper meaning. "So? I'm working a hot case. Same with you, buddy."

"Not anymore. Pauline and I are getting married."

Harry set down his spoon carefully, his stomach tight. "Whoa, that was quick."

"Eight months? Naw, I'm getting older. I'm thirty-four, same as you. I want to settle down, have a family. Have someone to grow old with."

"I used to have that." He shrugged. "Not anymore."

"You can have it again. You're not dead, Harry."

Part of me feels that way at times.

"Congratulations. She's a nice girl."

"I wasn't gonna tell you, didn't want you to feel like I was rubbing it in your face."

"I'm happy for you, I really am." He was happy for Jimmy, who'd been a bachelor his entire life. Jimmy had sworn he'd never get married because he never wanted to make someone a widow, and uncertainty always filled a cop's life.

"Then stop feeling sorry for yourself and stop living in the past."

His guts churned. Harry felt his temper start to rise. "Who says I am? And who are you to tell me how to live my life?"

"A friend. A friend who knew Marie long before you did, buddy. She wouldn't want this for you. Harry, you have to let it go and start living again." Jimmy's voice caught. "She was a sweetheart and there'll never be anyone like her again. But Marie wouldn't want you to live like this."

"Don't go there, Jimmy. Not into my personal life. Not if you want to stay friends."

"Someone has to go there. Harry, it wasn't your fault. It wasn't anyone's fault except the con who killed her and he's never seeing freedom again."

Harry leaned back against the booth and snorted. "You mean, live the high life like this? I've moved on, Jimmy. Back in Homicide where I belong. Sean and I are friends again and work together again. I'm focused on the job. To protect and serve."

"The job. Always the job." Jimmy sighed and dug into his eggs.

He ate a few forkfuls quickly, the way cops always did when they needed to eat fast because you never knew when a call would blare over the radio. Never knew when you'd have to rush off to investigate a fresh lead or provide backup during a gun battle.

Never knew when you'd get a dreaded call to come to the hospital to say goodbye to a fellow officer or in Harry's case, say goodbye to your wife and little boy...

Suddenly no longer hungry, Harry pushed his bowl aside. He drained his coffee and threw some bills on the table. "I have to run. Keep in touch, let me know what you find in Colton's house. Text me a photo of any suspicious items so I can show January."

Jimmy nodded. "Take care of yourself, Harry."

The words seemed to have a double meaning, which Harry ignored. But as he slid behind the wheel of his sedan, he hesitated in turning on the engine. Thoughts of Sara kept entering his mind.

Maybe Jimmy was right. He focused too much on the job, never made time for a personal life. Sean had moved on, married and now had a family. Jimmy was moving on as well.

I'm stuck in the past.

It was time to push forward.

Then he remembered the internal screaming in his mind when the doctors grimly informed him Marie and John were dead. The pain so deep and sharp he couldn't breathe, couldn't even cry. When he did cry, he clung to the grief as if it were a living thing because they were connected to the grief. He feared the moment he stopped grieving, his memories of his wife and child would fade into twilight. Only work had saved him from dissolving into a puddle of depression. Work had nudged him each day to get the hell out of bed, shower, keep putting one foot in front of the other. The world hadn't stopped spinning and criminals still broke the law. He found a solitary comfort in that routine, even if it proved cheerless at times.

When all else failed, he had the job.

Gritting his teeth, Harry switched on the ignition. Time to move on? Not today.

He had a murder to solve.

Chapter Eleven

Sara wasn't certain meeting another Colton cousin was a terrific idea, but she couldn't resist the temptation. Especially when the invitation came from January Stafford, the daughter of Alfred Colton, who'd been murdered by a serial killer.

January had been so sweet when she'd phoned Sara and expressed interest in meeting her. Sadly, they had something in common more than being Coltons—both their fathers had died at the hands of killers. At least January had closure, unlike Sara.

Her new husband, the father of their twins, was Detective Sean Stafford, who happened to be Harry's ex-partner.

Sara smelled something fishy when January mentioned something about Colton heirlooms and how perhaps Sara could be a help in recalling anything her mother said about Axel's lifestyle.

She drove straight from work to the Stafford home, releasing a sigh of relief. Harry's car wasn't here. Dusk had started to drape the sky with vivid colors of lavender and rose, streaking the clouds that scuttled past. A hint of snow lingered in the air.

The house had a wide front porch with twin Christmas trees flanking the double doors. Gold light from a brass overhead fixture highlighted the homey touches on the porch—a basket of pine cones, white rocking chairs and a table sporting a Santa Claus on skis. Garland adorned the porch railing, along with strings of Christmas lights.

Impressed they had time to decorate with the whirlwind of having twins, Sara rang the doorbell, knowing it was one of the high-tech security ones and they could answer from their smartphones. But instead of a voice speaking from the doorbell's microphone, a good-looking man with a rag over one shoulder opened the door.

Sara stuck out her hand. "You must be Sean. I recognize you from the other night in the alley when Harry was shot."

He shook her palm. "Come on in. January just finished feeding the twins."

"And you got burping duty."

Sean frowned, looked down at the towel where Sara pointed. He beamed. "Yeah, Leo's a little piggy."

He led her into a spacious formal living room with elegant furniture, a brick fireplace and a large portrait of Sean and a pretty blonde woman hanging over the mantel. Garland threaded with lights adorned the mantel. A fir tree sat in one corner, fully decorated with lights, red and green ornaments and tinsel. Several colorful packages with Christmas wrapping sat beneath the tree. The tree and decorations softened the formal look of the room.

"Have a seat. I'll be right back."

"Nice house."

"Thanks. It's all so…shiny still." He glanced around the room. "January sold her town house and her mom bought us the house and new furniture as a wedding gift, seeing we needed more space with the twins. She also helped to decorate, insisting the twins needed to experience their first Christmas with a real tree and all the trimmings. Bought a bunch of gifts and wrapped them as well."

He shook his head. "Good thing she did because we barely have time to eat, let alone get a tree and decorate it. It's not as if they'll remember, because they're so small. But January loves it, and it makes her happy, so it makes me happy, too."

He vanished up the stairs as Sara sat on one of the matching striped silk chairs. She touched the fabric, smiled as she thought of how the elegant furniture would soon sport signs of ordinary wear and tear with their new family.

Sara scrolled through phone messages while she waited. Nothing from her mother yet. She tried to ease the tightness in her stomach that warned something bad had happened. Regina wasn't a killer, but what if someone had hurt her?

She needed to find out and Harry refused to allow her to leave town. Riddled with worry, she texted Harry.

I need to go to St. Louis and find out what happened to Mom.

A terse text back. No. I told you, do not leave town.
Fuming, she texted back. Does your arm hurt?

Yes.

Good. Maybe it will knock some sense into your head. My mother did not kill Axel, but God only knows if something happened to her.

She shut off her phone as it pinged again, indicating an answer.

I don't care what you say, Harry. Sara drew in a deep breath. She seldom fought, but when she did, she gave it everything she had. If Harry Cartwright thought she'd meekly sit back and not search for Regina, he had a surprise in store.

She would fight for her mother. If only she could reach her!

Footsteps sounded on the stairs. Sara stood as a pretty blonde woman in a casual green blouse and dark slacks descended. The woman glowed as if motherhood and twins agreed with her.

The happiness on January's face heightened all Sara's own concerns. *This is motherhood. Mothers care about their children and most would do anything for them. My own mother wouldn't go this long without contacting me. Oh, Harry, can't you see? Something is terribly wrong.*

Sara stuck out her palm. "January? Hi, I'm Sara Sandoval."

"Sara. No handshakes here with family. I'm not formal." January hugged her and then released her. "It's a pleasure to meet another cousin. Welcome, Sara."

Tremendous relief filled her. January was yet another Colton who didn't frown on her origins. "Thanks. I'm happy to meet you."

"I thought we could have tea, or coffee, if you'd like." January started for the kitchen.

Sara followed. "Tea is fine. Please, let me help. You have enough on your hands with the little ones."

January beamed. "They're asleep. Their feeding seemed to take forever, but once they're down, they stay fast asleep for at least four hours. Don't worry about me, it feels good to do something other than breastfeed or change diapers or grab quick meals."

She listened to January chatter about her twins as Sara

helped set out the teacups, sugar and cream on a serving platter. January frowned and began measuring out coffee for the coffeemaker on the counter.

"Oh darn. I forgot. Sean's cutting back on caffeine, he gets so little sleep these days, and Harry drinks only coffee, not tea."

"Harry's on his way here?" She felt that little flutter in her chest that had nothing to do with apprehension, only excitement. Then she remembered that last text she'd sent and stifled a groan.

Bad timing. Terrible.

When the drinks were ready, Sara brought the service out to the living room and set it on the coffee table as Sean padded down the stairs carrying a baby monitor. January followed with a platter of chocolate chip cookies.

"I didn't know Harry was coming here. Maybe I should leave…" Sara sat on one of the chairs and wondered if it wasn't too late to make her escape.

Setting the monitor down on a nearby table, Sean peered out the window. "He's parking his car right now."

She pasted on a polite smile as her heart did little skip-hops. Harry didn't bother with the doorbell. He came right inside, pounded Sean on the back with a guy slap and then walked into the living room as if he belonged there. He wore jeans and a navy sweater and carried a small satchel.

He kissed January on the forehead, took a seat and only then did he realize Sara's presence.

Harry stared.

"What are you doing here?" His voice came out as a deep growl. "Or are you determined to annoy me in person and not just through texting."

Sara stirred sugar into her tea. "I was invited, same as you were."

"I thought Sara would like to meet a Colton cousin."

Sean handed Harry a mug of steaming coffee and sat on the sofa next to his wife. "Besides, you crossed Sara off your suspect list. I thought the four of us could brainstorm. Sara might have valuable information her mother passed on about Axel's habits and if he were brazen enough to steal family heirlooms from Alfred or Ernest. Maybe Axel said something in passing to Sara's mom that Sara can remember."

Dead silence.

"And since you and Sara seem to be so…involved in the case, we thought it would be good to have both of you over at the same time," Sean added, sounding less convinced.

Right. You couldn't come up with a better explanation? She began to realize just why January and Sean had invited her over.

She looked questioningly at Harry, who kept his expression placid, but his eyes spelled fury as his jaw tensed beneath his well-trimmed beard. Oh yes, this was a setup if there ever was one. Harry didn't want her here and could have kicked his friend for inviting her.

Softly, Sara began humming, "Matchmaker, matchmaker, make me a match…"

Sean and January looked at each other. "Oh dear," January murmured. "Are we that obvious?"

For a moment, no one said a word. Then to her surprise Harry threw back his head and laughed.

"As obvious as coal on snow, January honey, but you're forgiven." He glared at Sean. "Your husband, on the other hand…"

Sean threw up his hands. "I thought it was a good idea. Besides, you needed to meet January, Sara. And you do have a unique connection to Axel and why Harry's here."

"Right. Sara has many unique things about her." Harry sipped his coffee. "In case you're wondering, Sara, my arm is much better thanks to a delightful painkiller I took earlier. Sorry to disappoint you."

Sean and January threw her questioning looks. She felt a flush of guilt. "That was rude of me. I lost my temper, Harry, and I apologize."

He raised a dark brow. "Apology accepted if you'll accept mine for being a jerk. Pain puts me into a bad mood."

January brightened. "Now that we're all friends, Harry, what did you need to discuss? You sounded so mysterious over the phone."

"Business in a few. First, tell me how you're doing. You look radiant. Twins good?" Harry asked.

For a few minutes January talked about the babies while they listened. Harry leaned forward, expressing real interest, not mere politeness. His attentive attitude was refreshing. Sara had not met many men genuinely interested in a new mother talking about her babies.

When January finished, Sean chimed in. "She's a real pro at this. Her mom has been fantastic in helping out, but we're thinking, hoping, she'll go home soon. We appreciate her help, but we would like to be alone with the twins to get ourselves into a routine."

"I can appreciate that." Harry rubbed his chin. "I remember after John was born and Marie's mother seemed like she wanted to move in with us permanently. I thought she would never leave us alone to be a real family. Not that we had a lot of time to enjoy being one before…before I lost them both."

Silence descended in the air. Sean and January both looked uncomfortable. They said nothing, and Sara's stomach tightened. She smiled to cover the sudden tension in the air.

"Babies are quite demanding, from what I know. They set their own schedule. My best friend from high school had a baby two years ago and it was amusing how she and her husband were insistent their lives would not change. That didn't last long."

Sean and January seemed to breathe a sigh of relief. Harry reached into his pocket as if fingering the medal he kept there, then he dug into his satchel and brought out some photos.

"Okay, let's get down to business and the real reason I'm here, January. I need your help to identify some items found in Axel Colton's home," Harry told her.

January looked over the photos and frowned. "Yes, I know these. The candlesticks were my grandfather's. Dean bought them in Italy on a business trip and later, he gave them to Mom and Dad. They weren't special, just he thought they would like them since Mom was into Italian decor."

January stared at the photo. "I can't believe Axel had them. How would he get them?"

"Sara, did your mother ever say anything about Axel giving her anything that had been in his family?"

She shook her head, guilt stabbing her at January's woebegone look. Even though she had no connection to Axel other than by blood, it was a horrible thing to learn the father you'd dreamed about idolizing was a thief.

"My mom never wanted anything of Axel's. She only wanted to be as far away from him as possible after my brother, Wyatt, drowned. She even changed her name to protect herself, and me. I didn't know until earlier this year that Axel was my father," Sara told them.

"Maybe Dean asked Alfred for these items back and gave them to Axel because he felt guilty for neglecting him?" Sean asked.

"As far as I know, my grandfather never did that." January examined the photos of the items as Harry explained what they were.

The two candlesticks. A silver serving platter that had also been in the family for more than two generations.

"Then there's this…something not as expensive."

From a plastic bag marked Evidence, Harry withdrew a wooden box. He opened it to display a pretty Christmas scene of a white-topped house, a gazebo, snow-topped trees and tiny people dressed in winter clothing.

"Jimmy found this music box tucked away in a dresser drawer. It doesn't seem as valuable as the silver platter or the candlesticks, but seemed out of place, so he put it in as evidence."

Sara craned her neck and gasped. "I have one just like that. It's a Thomas Kinkade music box."

All three turned to look at her. Sara felt heat creep up her neck to her cheeks. "I like to collect music boxes. I have since I was a child."

Harry turned it over in his hand. "A trait you may have inherited from Axel. January, do you recall seeing this in your father's house?"

January reached for the box. She examined the interior. "Not really, but Dad liked to surprise Mom with things like this…he enjoyed engraving special messages to her. Honey, can get you get the magnifying glass from the junk drawer?"

When Sean returned with it, January studied the box with the glass. "Yes, here it is. It's so small you can barely read it. There, on the inside of the box. To my darling Farrah, love eternally Alfred."

Sara fisted her hands in her lap. This definitely proved her father was a thief. Why would anyone give away such a personal, precious memento?

"So this means Axel broke into my parent's house and

stole these things?" January looked confused. "I don't understand. Wouldn't Dad have reported them missing?"

"Was Axel ever inside your house? Did Alfred ever have him over on a social occasion?"

January tapped her head. "Sorry, let me think… I have baby brain."

Sean encased her hands in his. "Take your time, honey."

"Let me call Mom. She's out shopping."

A few minutes later, January hung up. "Mystery solved. Dean came by shortly before he died and asked Dad if he could have the candlesticks back, and the silver platter. He said he needed them, but didn't say why. Mom and Dad told him they didn't mind, they were his to begin with. I guess Dean gave them to Axel, maybe he felt bad Axel had no family heirlooms?"

For a moment, silence descended into the room, broken only by the soft crackling over the baby monitor.

"It makes sense," Sean murmured. "So there goes your theory, Harry."

"Well, that clears up the mystery about how Axel got them. But not about the music box." Harry put the box back into the evidence bag.

"Mom did say she had no idea the box was missing. She thought maybe the domestic worker had broken it and thrown it out and was afraid to tell her. That particular domestic worker had done something like that before and Mom caught her."

Harry leaned forward, and judging from the glint in his eye, his mind was clicking over a possibility. "Who was the domestic worker? Does she still work for your mother?"

"Mary Martin. She wasn't very good. Mom had to reprimand her a couple of times and finally let her go after she caught her stealing from the liquor cabinet."

"I'll check her out." Harry glanced at Sara. "I don't want to take up any more of your time…"

A soft wail sounded over the baby monitor. January brightened.

"But you're here so you need to meet the twins. Wait and we'll bring them down," she told them.

Sara's heart sank at the tight expression on Harry's face. *Don't, January. Please don't. He's not ready for this…it's too soon. Give him time…*

He glanced out the window as if desperate to escape, and then shrugged. "Ah hell," he muttered.

Sean and January came downstairs, each carrying a sleepy twin, one wrapped in a blue blanket, the other in a pink blanket. The pride and joy on their faces as they gazed at their children touched Sara's heart.

January beamed at her. "Would you like to hold Laura?"

Although she had little experience with babies, she held out her arms. January instructed her to keep Laura's head upright. The baby slept peacefully, her little fingers close to one cheek. She smelled heavenly and for a wild moment Sara felt a tug of wistfulness.

Growing up as an only child, without any family, she'd missed out on moments like this with family members. Only when her friends started marrying and having babies did she experience them. Even then, relatives took precedence over friends.

Maybe someday she'd have children of her own. It would be lovely to have a family.

Sean handed Harry the twin in the blue blanket. "Here. Alfred Leo Stafford, meet the best cop in Chicago, your uncle Harry."

Harry held baby Leo, staring at the newborn as if he were the most unique and precious thing in the world.

Tension knotted his entire body. Sara realized it wasn't a person's natural tension at fearing to hurt the little one, but something else.

Something much more personal.

"I forgot how tiny they are," he mused. "So small… John was this small… I counted all his fingers and toes. I was afraid to hold him when he was first born."

He shrugged and kissed Leo's forehead. "Welcome to the crazy world, Leo. You picked good parents."

Beaming, Sean took baby Leo from Harry's arms. "You're great with babies, Harry."

"I was," he murmured so softly Sara knew they didn't hear him.

But she did and her heart ached for him. How did you ever recover from losing your child?

When Sean returned downstairs, she was more than ready to leave. She liked the Staffords, but they had moved into a different stage of life, while she was still single and Harry…

Harry had experienced a dual loss no husband, or father, ever should suffer. Her heart went out to him. Beneath his beard, his jaw tightened, but he offered a smile as he clapped Sean on the back.

"Congratulations again, man. Best of luck to you."

"Sorry the visit wasn't a success," Sean told him, and then he shook Sara's hand.

They said their goodbyes and headed outside. A scent of pine and crispness layered the cool breeze ruffling the fringes of her scarf. Inhaling the fresh air, she felt glad to be free from the tension inside. Sean and January were proud new parents, joyous because of their babies, and oblivious to Harry's quiet pain.

She was not unaware.

Instead of heading directly for his car, Harry lingered

by her vehicle. Sara didn't open the door, but turned to face him. Someone had to acknowledge what he endured. Even if he didn't want to admit how much it hurt.

"That was tough for you," she murmured.

Harry jammed his hands into the pockets of his jeans and leaned against his car. "I guess."

Shutting down. Any light had vanished from his blue-green gaze. He looked cold and distant.

The hard-nosed attitude might work for interrogations, but she sensed something deep struck a nerve with him.

"He's your good friend, but it's got to be hell seeing him so happy with new babies."

Harry blinked. "Ah, hmmm."

"Especially when you hold one of them, and you remember holding your own child."

His brow furrowed. "Don't go there, Sara."

"I don't want to cause you more pain, Harry. I only want you to know I see you…" She pointed to her eyes. "Here."

Taking a gamble, she stepped forward and touched his chest. "And here."

Harry looked away. "I'm fine. I'm a cop, Sara. We learn to deal with death."

"Death of strangers, yes. Death even of your friends at times. But a wife and child…that's something you never get over. You only get through it."

At first she feared she'd overstepped her bounds, for he scowled and started to pull away. Harry took two paces, stopped. He brought out the St. Jude medal and looked at it, returned it to his pocket as if putting away fragile glass. He rubbed the back of his neck and suddenly he seemed to emotionally crumble.

"I miss them," he whispered. "Damn, I really miss them, and seeing the babies, holding Leo…it brought it all rushing back. It was always supposed to be me who never walked through our front door again. Me. Not them. I even bought a funeral plot because I'm a cop in Chicago and I warned Marie there might come a time when she'd lose me. I wanted her to be taken care of and get through something like that without having to worry about arrangements or expenses. I never imagined…using it for my wife and kid."

She could never understand what he felt or the depth of his grief. Sara approached him, took his icy hands into hers. "She must have been a wonderful woman. Tell me about her and your child."

Harry stared at their linked hands. "Marie was quiet and shy, but had a fierce streak when it came to protecting those she loved. The proudest I ever was of her was the day she told her parents we were getting married. Her old man blew a gasket, said I wasn't good enough and I was marrying Marie for the family money. Marie told him she'd live with me in a run-down trailer because she loved me and no one would stand in her way."

Moisture glistened in his eyes, making them brilliant. "John, he ran us ragged at times. So curious and alive… everything fascinated him. His personality started to shine through. He was only two, but you could see he was smart and loved puzzling things out and putting them back together. Marie was a terrific mom, loved John with all her heart and when they pulled her out of the car wreck, she'd been twisted around, as if trying to shield him in the back seat from the impact."

Now her own eyes dampened. Sara didn't dare let go of him. If she did, she had the funny feeling he'd vanish back into himself, sinking as if immersed by a body of water so deep he couldn't find his way to the surface.

"I'm so sorry," she whispered.

Harry's jaw tightened. "I wish it had been me instead of them, oh God, why wasn't it me who died that day? Maybe I shouldn't have gone on living."

She shook her head. "No, don't you go there. I don't know why ugly things happen, or why our loved ones die and there's nothing we can do to save them, but, Harry, I know life is worth living. And each day you're aboveground, breathing and placing one foot in front of the other, it's a victory. We don't know the answers. All we can control is getting through times like that as best as we can."

Sara cupped his face in her hands. "You're not alone. You're never alone. I never met her, but your wife sounds like a wonderful, loving woman. Marie wouldn't want you to join her and John. She'd want you to go on living and be happy."

Acting on instinct, she kissed his cheek. He lifted his head, stared at her and suddenly kissed her on the mouth. Harry cupped the back of her head and devoured her lips, kissing her as if his next breath depended on hers. She opened her mouth to him, welcoming the surge of passion and heat.

Needing it as much as he did, she wrapped her arms around him, giving in to the feelings she'd suppressed ever since the moment she'd awakened from a dead faint and saw him administering aid to her. He kissed her as if he never wanted to release her.

When he finally did, Harry leaned his forehead against hers. "Damn, I didn't mean to do that."

"I'm glad you did."

A slight knocking drew their attention to the house. Sean and January stood at the large picture window. Both beamed. Sean did a thumbs-up sign.

Harry swore softly as Sara flushed, then she laughed.

"I guess they consider the visit a success after all," she mused.

"I'll say." Harry kissed her mouth again, gentler this time. "Thank you, Sara. I'll be okay now. I just had a moment. Someone warned me, I forget who, that grief is like a river that trickles down to a low creek as the months and years pass, but there would be times something triggers a memory, or a thought and it comes bursting out like a broken dam again, as painful as the day you lost them. Today was one of those days."

She touched his cheek. "I understand. The day I found out my father was dead, I guess all that grief rushed forward and overwhelmed me. But he was a stranger. Your loss is greater."

Harry took her hand, turned it over and studied it. "You have such lovely hands, Sara. Mine are big paws."

That made no sense. She frowned as he kissed the inside of her wrist.

"Don't ever make comparisons, Sara. Comparing your loss to mine is like comparing your hands to mine. You suffered a huge loss. I have memories to comfort me."

The familiar tightness rose in her throat. Sara tried to stem the flow of tears, but they leaked out of her eyes and began trickling down her cheeks. The harder she tried to stop crying, the worse it got.

"Aw damn, I didn't mean to make you do that." Harry took the edge of her scarf and gently wiped away her tears.

"I'll be fine. I'm just overwhelmed, oh no, are they still watching?" Sara couldn't bear to look.

Harry did. "No, fortunately. We must look like a couple of crying fools in their driveway."

She smiled and wiped her eyes. "Falling apart in the cold."

He studied her a minute. "You okay?"

Nodding, she drew in a deep breath and opened her car door. "Thanks, Harry. I haven't really permitted myself to do that in front of anyone. I needed it."

He kissed her cheek, his mouth warm and slightly wet. "You'd best get home, get warm."

Solid advice, and yet he lingered. Sara ached for him. She knew what it was like to head into an empty apartment, the quiet so dense it made the air heavy, when all you wanted was company. Because being alone with your own haunting thoughts made the loneliness even worse.

On impulse she made a decision. "Do you want to go with me and grab a bite of dinner? Or just sit and talk? Nothing expensive, but good, homemade food. It's not exactly in an upscale area, though."

For a moment he said nothing and she thought she'd misread the torment in his gaze. Then he nodded. "Thanks. Yeah, that would be great. I'm not eager to go home yet."

"I'll drive and then drive you back here to get your car."

"Or you can follow me and we'll leave from the restaurant. It's closer to my house." Sara thought the idea of returning here might be too much. All he needed was to pull into the driveway later and see Sean and January silhouetted by the living room lamp, cooing to their bundles of joy.

"Sounds fine." Harry glanced at the house. "Too many memories right now. Let's go."

NEVER HAD A woman read him so thoroughly as Sara had this evening. Even Marie, as much as she loved him, sometimes got upset when he'd distanced himself because of the job. She had wanted to be part of his life, every part of it, even the ugliness of crime. Sometimes Marie had missed cues from him after a particularly grueling day when he'd desperately wanted her company, but didn't want to discuss his job. She'd end up hurt, and he'd end up comforting her and failing to be comforted himself.

Not now with Sara. Astute and empathetic, she'd realized how difficult being around Sean and January had felt for him.

The restaurant Sara selected was a diner in a questionable part of town. But it was well-lit, cheerful and had plenty of security cameras. Instead of getting out of her car and heading inside, Sara popped her trunk. She removed a small bag of dog food.

"I have to do something first. Want to come with?"

Curious, he nodded, and then walked with her to the building's rear. Sitting against the building in a spot shielded from the wind was a man sitting on the ground with a large, shaggy dog. Both the man and dog had seen better days and were obviously homeless. Harry's guard instantly went up and then relaxed when he saw the man jump to his feet with a big smile.

"Miss Sara! I was hoping you'd come by. I'm almost out."

"Hi, Rob." She petted the dog and then handed Rob the bag. "Here you go."

"Thanks, Miss Sara. Here. Just like we agreed." Rob handed her two crumpled bills.

She took the money and stuffed it into her coat pocket. "Rob, it's cold out here. Why aren't you inside?"

The man scratched his graying beard. "I'll bunk down later."

"Did you eat yet?" she persisted.

A shrug. "Naw. They told me it was okay to eat in the kitchen, but I can't leave Rex alone out here."

"This is my friend, Harry. Harry, Rob."

"Pleasure to meet you." Harry squatted down and petted the dog. "Hey there, buddy."

The man cast a dubious look at Harry's badge, glinting in the parking lot light. "His name is Rex. Are you here to arrest me?"

Harry stood, and shook his head. "Nope. Miss Sara promised me a hot meal of good food. That's why I'm here. Food good here?"

"The best," Rob said gravely.

"Great. I'm starving." Harry took Sara's arm and nodded at Rob. "Thanks."

The diner inside was informal and cheerful. A silver Christmas tree sat near the counter and garland threaded with white lights decorated the tops of the booths. A few patrons ate at the counter, and more crowded the booths.

Harry looked around. "Need to wash my hands."

"Me, too," Sara told him. "The restrooms are back this way."

After they emerged from the restrooms, the hostess led them to a quiet booth in back. Harry helped Sara remove her coat, and then took his off, hanging both on the hooks by the booth. He took the seat opposite her, watching the door as always.

She studied him with her amazing green eyes. Such a beautiful woman, inside and out.

"Thanks for helping me with Rob and Rex. It's my way of making sure his dog gets fed and Rob has a little pride. He hates taking charity, but when it comes to Rex, he'll do it."

"The restaurant owners don't mind? That's good of them."

Her face fell a little. "Vinnie and Lorraine have been wonderful to Rob and Rex. Rob came here over the summer, asking for a job. He washes dishes for them at night.

During the day he works at the garage across the street as a mechanic, which is what he used to do in the Army. He's terrific at repairing engines. That's how I met him. He fixed my transmission."

A homeless vet. Harry was sadly familiar with their plight. "Does he sleep here on the restaurant grounds? Some homeless people prefer being outside."

"No. He wants a place, but with the cost of housing, especially with a dog, he can't afford an apartment. The repair shop owner lets him sleep in the garage and store his things there, but he doesn't want the heat run at night. Now that it's getting cold, I'm worried he could freeze."

Harry watched Sara as she talked. So animated and fierce in her conviction of helping others. It was insightful seeing this side of her.

Their waiter came over and took their drink orders, leaving them to peruse the menu.

"I love their mushroom risotto. It's how I found the place on the way home from work one day. They had a special."

He considered. "A diner that serves risotto? Impressive."

Sara grinned, her green eyes sparkling. "Isn't it? Vinnie is from Italy. Lorraine is Greek, so you'll find lots of cultural favorites on the menu. They consider you family if you eat here more than once."

"You sound like me. You eat out a lot or you nuke something at home." Harry scanned the menu.

"I like finding different restaurants with good food that doesn't cost a month's paycheck." Sara shrugged. "Even when I was making better money, it became a fun hobby. You can find little, tucked-away places where the cooking is excellent, served with a dash of culture and friendliness."

"Same here. I like gourmet dining once in a while, but would rather eat someplace less pretentious." He pointed to his jeans. "In case you can't tell, I'm not a pretentious kinda guy."

Sara smiled and looked pleased. "Me, too. I never had the need to Instagram my food to show the world what upscale restaurant was worthy of my money. Guys I've dated in the past who tried to impress me left me cold when they bragged about how much they knew about dining out or wine pairings. It's not my style."

Harry loved that Sara wasn't afraid to voice her needs. She knew what she wanted and liked and how to assert herself.

A guy would always know where he stood with her.

With a start he realized Marie was far different. With his wife, he always wondered if she went along with him simply to please him, much as she had pleased her parents.

When the waiter came, they both ordered the mushroom risotto.

"What's your favorite winter sport?" he asked when the waiter left.

"I like to ski when I can save up money for trips. I do have a friend who has a time-share in Aspen. Comes in handy."

They talked about winter sports for a few minutes. Lost in thought, Harry recalled a time when he tried to get Marie to ski.

"She never got off the bunny slope. Marie preferred sitting by the fire with hot cocoa. But she tried to learn, to please me, I guess. We had some good times on vacation, but the snowball fights and snowshoeing, especially after John was born, made them even more special because those were things we could do as a family."

"She sounds like a wonderful wife and mom," Sara said softly.

Harry toyed with his water glass. "I don't talk about their deaths much, but I need to talk tonight. I'm happy for January and especially Sean. For a long time, Sean blamed himself for their deaths. As if I wasn't blaming myself enough."

Sara reached across the table and gripped his hand. "How did they die?"

Oddly, the question didn't bother him as it once had. In the past when someone asked, he didn't give details. It was too intense and personal.

"She and John were killed in a car accident. The brake lines to my personal vehicle were cut. The man who did it was John Andrews, an ex-con suspected in a murder case Sean and I were investigating for vehicular homicide."

Harry slid his hand out from Sara's to drink water, amazed his hand was steady. Once, he never would have been able to talk about their deaths without shaking.

Tears filled Sara's eyes. "I'm so sorry. You had to deal not only with losing them, but the anguish of knowing it was at the hands of a dangerous criminal."

He had to keep talking, get it out. Sara was different. She seemed to understand he wasn't being maudlin or agonizing over every detail of the accident. Hell, he'd done that more than two years ago. He simply needed to get it out, let her know he carried a lot of baggage with him. Because he truly liked her, and if that kiss was an indication of the way things were going, he knew where they would end up.

Harry felt like he'd been walking in a snowstorm for a long time and suddenly spotted a warm, welcoming inn with a crackling fire and warmth.

"Marie was a wonderful wife and mother, but she never

told me she had seen Andrews watching the house. It was only later that her best friend said Marie confided in her that a strange guy was always parked near the house. Marie didn't want to burden me. I didn't know anything was wrong. I was cocky and arrogant and thought nothing could penetrate my home life. If she had told me, I would have driven her and John to her parents', told her to stay there. But she acted as if nothing was wrong."

Harry rubbed his chin. "I should have known she was afraid. I should have known Andrews would have done something like this."

"Are you a mind reader?"

Startled, he frowned. "No."

"Of course not. So how could you have known? You had no indications Andrews was watching your home. You had no idea he'd go to such lengths to hurt you and your family. You had no way of knowing Marie was afraid. It's not your fault. It's not her fault. The only person to blame is Andrews."

Sara's green gaze held his. "I'm not telling you how you should feel, Harry. But blaming yourself is pointless. In your profession, danger comes with the job, even if you don't ever fire your gun."

For a moment, he considered. "I guess you're right."

"I know I'm right."

He looked up as she flushed. "Tell me how you really feel."

"Well, if you insist."

They both smiled at each other, the tension breaking. Harry drank more water.

"I tried to break her out of her shell. I tried to get her to go out and do things she always said she wanted to try, like painting. Actually, that's how I started—it was to encourage her. But she was too shy to join the classes when I had to drop out because of work commitments."

He sighed. "Sometimes I wondered if she married me because she was afraid of life and having a cop as a husband was having someone to lean on."

Life after they died had gone on, though he'd felt imprisoned in grief he didn't know how to release. Being a cop meant keeping emotion in check in order to do the job and solve the crime. Life taught him to be zealous when solving crime. It didn't teach him how to heal his shattered heart.

The art helped. Painting allowed him to express all the rage and sorrow, and if not mend his broken heart, at least start to piece it together again. He started to paint to encourage his wife to learn and grow and continued after her death as a means of washing away the tears he could not shed.

To his relief, their meals arrived. He didn't mind talking about his past with Sara, but he wanted to know more about her. As they dug into their risotto, which Harry praised as some of the best he'd ever had, he asked Sara about growing up in St. Louis. He wasn't surprised to find out Regina had encouraged her to volunteer for charities and had instilled a sense of civic duty into her daughter.

"We're given responsibility to give back to society. I think more parents should teach that to their children. Then again, my mom was extraordinary. Always volunteering, despite her schedule, but always had time for me." Sara's gaze grew troubled. "I wish I knew where she was. She couldn't have killed Axel, I mean, it just isn't like her."

"I'll find her." When Harry made a promise, he kept it. "One way or another, I'll find her, Sara."

She nodded and toyed with her fork. "I know you will. As long as she's safe."

He changed the subject to talk about the city and what they liked best about Chicago. The more lighthearted conversation coaxed her out of her funk.

Harry ordered a hot dog, sans bun, to go, and insisted on paying the check. When they got outside, he clasped her hand and steered her to the back of the building.

Rob and Rex were still there, huddled against the cold. Harry opened the carton and handed the hot dog to Rex. The dog gulped down the treat.

Harry put a hand on the man's shoulder. "Go inside, Rob. There's a hot meal waiting for you."

Rob shook his head. "Not without Rex. I can't bring him into the restaurant and I won't leave him. What if someone steals him?"

"Go inside," Harry said gently. "I'll stay out here and watch him while you eat."

"Promise? Rex is all the family I have. Me and him, we're all we have."

"I promise." Harry sat on the ground and petted the dog.

When Rob headed inside, Harry glanced up. "You don't have to stay, Sara. You can go home."

Sara sat on the ground beside him. "I think Rex needs two bodyguards."

While some women he'd dated might have fed the dog as Sara had, they would have been horrified at the idea of sitting on the cold ground in elegant silk trousers to watch the dog while his owner enjoyed dinner inside. Not Sara. His admiration for her rose.

Harry removed his cell phone and dialed a number. While it rang, she scratched the dog's ears. Never mind that the dog might have fleas. Sara didn't care.

He was beginning to realize exactly how special and compassionate Sara Sandoval was.

Two phone calls later, everything was arranged. Harry thumbed off his cell, his fingers slightly frozen. But inside he felt warm all over.

Gaze rapt with admiration, Sara studied him as if he'd given away his last dollar instead of finding a place for Rob and Rex.

When Rob came outside, Harry jingled his keys in his hand. "Come on, Rob. I've found a warm place for you and Rex to stay. Buddy of mine has a small, furnished studio for very low rent. Utilities included, though not cable, just electric, heat and water. It's not in walking distance, but on the bus route so you can get to work."

It was sort of a white lie, for he'd promised his friend he'd pay the security and first month's rent in exchange for Rob having a lower rent for the annual lease term.

He didn't do it to look like the white knight in Sara's eyes.

But he had to admit, it felt damn good to see her happy he'd helped.

HARRY CARTWRIGHT SEEMED like a kaleidoscope of colorful layers. At first she'd wanted to dismiss him as a cop who might be a thorn in her side. Now she was getting to know the real man behind the badge, and the compassionate soul within.

Finding a home for Rob and Rex had cost him. Rob never could have saved enough for the security or first month's rent.

They packed all Rob's belongings in Sara's trunk. Harry drove Rob and Rex himself to the studio apartment. It didn't take long to move in Rob's few things. Sara made sure to turn up the heat as Rex ran around, sniffing the small, but comfortable space.

Turning to Harry, Rob stuck out a hand, his mouth

trembling. "Nobody cares about me and Rex except my bosses and Miss Sara here. Rex would have starved if not for Miss Sara. Thanks, Harry. You're not a bad sort yourself."

Harry made sure to escort Sara out to her car and lingered as she got behind the wheel. She rolled down her window and pressed her gloved hand upon his.

"Thank you, Harry. Not many people would care about the fate of a homeless man and his dog."

He nodded, as if such a magnanimous gesture was an everyday occurrence for him. Maybe it was.

"When you get home, make sure to lock up behind you, Sara. Someone is out there who may be targeting you. I'm determined to find out who killed your father. It may be your mother and you'd best prepare yourself for that."

Sara put her keys into the ignition. "I'm prepared. But first we have to find her."

He tapped her nose. "No, sweetie. I have to find her. I'm going tomorrow, first thing in the morning when the doc clears me. I'll find her, I promise."

Relief washed through her. It felt like someone had taken a heavy load off her back. All this time she'd fretted and worried alone. Now she had Harry at her side to help. Harry didn't seem the type to make such promises easily.

He's also going to find Regina to question her and perhaps arrest her.

The flicker of doubt winked on and off like a neon sign. Sara took a deep breath. Later, she would deal with those consequences, like she had with other matters ever since she made the decision to move to Chicago and introduce herself to Axel Colton.

Harry dropped a brief but sweet kiss on her mouth, leaving her lips warm and tingling. When she returned home, Sara went straight to her apartment and locked the door, making sure to check the locks.

That kiss swept her breath away. She still felt the pressure of his mouth against hers, the blood humming in her veins, desire zinging all the way down to her toes.

Frustrated, she roamed around her apartment, too restless to settle down.

Harry had shared a special part of himself, showed what kind of man he really was and had awakened passion he'd stirred inside her that sparked into an inferno. One kiss. Sara hugged herself, thinking about how he'd be in bed. Desire sparked again. She wanted him.

He wasn't right for her. He was a cop with a job to do.

But he was the only one she did want.

Her phone chimed. She glanced at the text and smiled. Harry, checking on her.

Lock up?

Sara smiled. Yes, I locked up.

Good night, Sara.

Then, as if an afterthought, I miss you.
Miss you too, she texted back.

Sara set down her phone and picked up a book to read about landscape ideas in winter. Finally she went to bed. But for a long time she lay awake, thinking about Harry and how they desired each other.

And how he might end up finding her mother tomorrow, and arresting her.

Chapter Twelve

The next morning after the doctor cleared him to return fully to work, Harry wasted no time.

An urgency drove him onward, more than yesterday. He'd run Mary Martin's name in a thorough background check. Alfred and Farrah Colton's domestic worker was married, had two children and was clean, no priors, but digging deeper, he discovered a disturbing connection.

Mary was the sister of Dennis and Eddie Angelo.

The threads on this case were twisting together in a pattern that made sense. But he knew someone had to be the driving force behind all of this. Trouble was, that person remained elusive.

Harry set out to find Regina Sandoval, but decided to take a detour first. He needed to follow the thread on Dennis Angelo. Wasn't as if he delayed the inevitable.

No, not because he couldn't forget kissing Sara. Last night after he got home, he'd fallen asleep, dreaming about her. He'd been wandering in a dense fog, the scent of rain and tears on his cheeks, and she emerged from the mist like a beacon lighting the way. Sara had taken him into her arms and melted against him like she had last night.

For the first time in months, he'd awakened feeling hopeful and energized about something other than the job.

It was the kiss. The best mistake he'd ever made.

But man, if he ended up arresting her mother, the relationship was over before it ever began. Maybe he needed to end it. Cut it off before it progressed. He hated admitting he cared about her, more than he thought he would ever care about a woman again.

If he wasn't careful, Sara Sandoval could hurt him more than any bullet graze could.

Harry drove on the exact same route as Dennis Angelo had on his last trip after the ex-con had planted the murder weapon in Nash's trunk. Most people drove I-55, the quickest way to St. Louis. Dennis Angelo had not.

Angelo had driven a less traveled road, I-57, stopping at a no-tell motel north of Kankakee. The manager had already told Harry and other investigating officers the motel's security cameras were broken. However, he'd seen Angelo's old, rattling Buick. He had noted it because the muffler was broken and the car thundered into the motel parking lot.

Not very inconspicuous.

A few miles down the road, Angelo had crashed his car, dying almost instantly.

Something warned Harry the manager neglected to be totally honest and forthcoming with the police.

The Love Inn looked seedy and sagging as he pulled into the parking lot. A pink neon sign blared out Rooms By The Hour. He'd been here at night after Angelo was killed. Daylight didn't improve its appearance.

A musty smell of cigarette smoke and stale body odor hit him as he walked into the office. Yellow tinted the white walls and ceiling, signs of a heavy smoker. Using his knuckles, Harry dinged the grimy front desk bell a few times.

Out of a back room came the same rumpled man he'd interviewed right after Angelo was killed. His eyes bleary and squinting, he waddled to the counter. A greasy brown spot stained his blue T-shirt beneath his frayed sport jacket. Harry immediately detected the odor of old cigar smoke, stale beer and the unmistakable smell of pot.

"Room for a night or an hour?" the manager asked, scratching his belly.

Harry flashed his badge. "Chicago PD. I'm back to ask you about a motel patron. Dennis Angelo."

"Oh. That guy." The man scratched his nose. Harry stepped back in case the guy had something contagious, like scabies.

"Yeah, that guy. You said…" Harry flipped through his notebook. "Angelo was here, alone, the night he was killed. You spotted his car, but he did not check in."

"Yeah, I was taking a smoke break."

Judging from the walls and smells in the office, the guy took too many smoke breaks.

"You're absolutely sure Angelo was alone? Here, in a motel most people rent rooms by the hour?" Harry made his way around the counter. Got close. Forget the contagion. He could shower later. Answers were more important.

The man blinked and backed off. "Maybe someone else was with him."

"Who? What kind of car?"

"I didn't see the car. But I did see Angelo with a woman."

Harry swore under his breath. "And you didn't tell me this earlier because…"

The man shrugged. "We see a lot of men here with women. My boss would fire me. I'm paid to collect money, not spy on customers. We pride ourselves on discretion. It's our reputation."

Harry got into the man's face and fisted his hands in

the manager's worn coat lapels, scabies or no scabies. "Listen, you lying shyster, I want the truth. I don't give a damn about your customers or your rep. Tell me what I need to know or I'll go over this place inch by inch until I find something to haul you in for."

The manager swallowed. "Okay, okay, I'll tell you what I know!"

Harry released him. "Good man. Who was the woman with Dennis Angelo?"

Paling, the man swallowed hard. "I don't know! It was dark. I just saw a woman. I think it was a woman. I didn't really pay attention because like I said, there's lots of women who come here with men."

"Did they arrive in separate cars?"

"I guess. I only remember them because Angelo had paid for a room for an hour and kept pacing in the parking lot, like he was waiting for his date."

Some date.

Harry began writing notes. "What kind of dress?"

"I think, I think it was a dress. Dark. No wait, pants."

He groaned, tempted to shake the man to rattle his brain cells.

Minutes later, he had little to go on. The woman was about Angelo's height, maybe a little shorter. Or taller. Wore a hat and a shapeless coat. Or maybe it wasn't even a woman. The manager couldn't tell Harry if Angelo left before the woman did, or vice versa, because he'd suddenly been busy checking in other customers. An hour later, Angelo was gone, the key to the room left on the front desk.

It could have been Regina. Regina was tall, like Angelo. Or maybe Angelo had stopped here for a quick bout of sex, like most of the motel's less upstanding patrons.

Soon Harry was back in his car headed to St. Louis.

When he arrived at the suburban neighborhood where Regina Sandoval lived, it was nearly two o'clock.

Regina's house looked vacant. Newspapers piled up on the driveway. No car. Nice house, two-story middle income. Quiet neighborhood where kids' bikes piled up in the driveway and you didn't have to worry about anyone stealing them. He gave the house a long, appreciative look. He could envision Sara growing up here, backpack slung across one slender shoulder, her long legs coltish as she walked to school. That little frown line of concentration, maybe, as she thought about an upcoming test. Doing a background check, he'd discovered she'd been an honor student, a trait following her into college. No priors with Regina or Sara. Not even a parking ticket.

No one answered when he knocked. He went around the back, peered through the back door. Everything was too quiet. His gut warned him this wasn't going to be good. But before he went breaking inside, he needed to ask around.

Legwork served a purpose, but gave no answers. By the time he finished talking to neighbors, he learned Regina was an outstanding mother and a good neighbor, and Sara was her darling. Only the Miller family hadn't gotten along well with the Sandovals, according to the neighborhood gossips. But the Millers were known snobs who shunned others. The family had moved six years ago after the husband lost his job due to a drinking problem.

Regina seldom drank, always pitched in at PTA and school events, and whenever someone in the neighborhood needed a helping hand, she was there.

He walked down the sidewalk, feeling he'd either received the snow job of his life or Regina had been respected and liked by everyone. Except the Millers.

No one could tell him where Regina was, though. She'd

said something to Carla Harrison, Regina's friend, about taking a vacation since her office was closing for renovations.

Time to check with the Harrisons.

Harry knocked on the Harrisons' door. A sullen teenager answered. "What?"

He flashed his badge. "Chicago PD. Your mom or dad home?"

"Should they be?"

Normally he had lots of patience dealing with unruly, sarcastic teens. Not today. "Where are they?"

"Dunno." The girl started to push the door shut. Harry shoved his foot inside, preventing her.

"I asked you a question. Where are your parents?"

He caught the scent of pot. Ah. No wonder the kid was trying to shove him out the door.

"I'm not here to check up on you," he said, softening his tone. "I'm investigating the disappearance of Regina Sandoval."

No answer.

"No one knows where she went. Her daughter says she's missing."

A blank stare.

He sighed. "Look, I won't tell your parents what you're doing. Just tell me where your mom is."

Relief flitted across the teen's face.

"Regina Sandoval. Your neighbor," he said helpfully.

"Oh her." The girl made a dismissive gesture. "My mom's visiting her. The Good Samaritan thing, you know? She's in the hospital. St. Good Hope."

No wonder the woman hadn't answered her daughter's concerned phone calls. "What happened?"

"Some kind of freak accident. Coma, I dunno. Mom just found out today and went there."

Harry plugged the hospital name into his cell. "There's no hospital in St. Louis by that name."

"Duh. 'Course not. It's in Springfield, where Regina was staying."

Harry gave her a level look and the kid had the good sense to look away. He plugged in the name and city, got an address and directions. "Why aren't you at school?"

"Half day today."

"When is your father getting home?"

"He texted to say he's about a half an hour away. Why?"

"Because you shouldn't be alone. And don't smoke. You'll ruin your lungs."

The sullen expression returned. "No, I won't. Everyone says that. And you promised you wouldn't tell my parents."

"I did promise. I won't tell them. However..." Harry grinned. "I may stop by the station, have a chat with their narcotics division. I used to work Narcotics."

Blood drained from the teen's face. She scurried inside and slammed the door shut, locking it.

Oh yeah, a little fear did wonders for the younger law-breaking set.

The hospital wasn't too far, but traffic already started to build up. Harry thought of all the moms and dads heading home to their children and maybe a good meal around the dinner table. Small talk, maybe someone had earned an A in math or their daughter had scored a winning goal in soccer.

His throat tightened. Once he'd thought he might have the same happy suburban life. He'd thought about it, considered quitting the force so Marie wouldn't wait up, worrying, wondering if he would make it home. Always the worrying when you were a cop's wife.

He was going to tell her he would consider her father's job offer as head of security.

Going to…but that night she and John were killed. For weeks, his world had spun on its axis in a crazy tilt, like a ride he desperately wanted to abandon, but was strapped in for the duration.

He finally reached the hospital, a sterile three-story building that looked like every other hospital he'd visited. Harry pulled into a parking space reserved for police and shut off his engine. For a moment, he sat in the car, staring at the hospital.

Damn, he hated hospitals. Nothing good there. Even after Marie gave birth…that had been a happy memory, but now it only reminded him of the vast hole in his heart. The emptiness he still felt when he examined his personal life.

Dating hadn't helped.

Meeting Sara Sandoval had.

He rubbed his chin and then climbed out, heading inside to find out what the hell happened to her mother.

After paying a courtesy visit to the chief operating officer and explaining the purpose of his visit, he entered Room 405. A woman, her head wrapped in bandages, lay on a hospital bed near the window. Another woman, plump and middle-aged, sat reading a book in a chair by her bed. The woman glanced up.

Harry showed his badge. "Harry Cartwright, Chicago PD. I'm here to see Regina Sandoval."

The woman shut her book and set it on the hospital table next to the bed. "Thank goodness. I was frantic with worry when the Springfield police called me and told me she was here. I'm Carla Harrison, Regina's friend and neighbor."

Though the woman in the hospital bed was pale, he

saw the resemblance to Sara in her high cheekbones and heart-shaped face. "What happened?"

"She hit her head falling down some stairs at a house she was visiting. The cleaning lady found her and paramedics brought her here. The police think it was a robbery gone wrong, or a home invasion. Her purse, cell phone and wallet were stolen. If not for the cleaning lady finding her…" Carla brushed at her eyes.

"Why was she in Springfield?" Made no sense. If Regina was guilty, she'd be halfway across the country.

"Her firm is opening a satellite office here. Regina had taken a vacation and on the way home, stopped at the house."

Harry gave Carla Harrison a long look. "How did the police find her and contact you?"

"I contacted them. Regina was due home two days ago for the neighborhood meeting on the Christmas parade. She's the honorary chairwoman. She hasn't missed a parade in twenty years. I knew something was wrong, but she didn't answer her phone. So I started making calls and gave the St. Louis police a photo to circulate. The Springfield police finally reached the homeowner where she was found. He's going to be the manager in charge of the satellite office. He had no idea who she was, but called the company president. The president said Regina had a key to the house and was overseeing the furniture being moved inside. It was typical of her to go into the house to stock it with drinks and some food before the family moved in, to help them feel welcome. She is thoughtful and organized that way."

Carla wiped at her eyes again. "Look at her. Who could tell who she is by using a photo to identify her, with her face all bruised and her head banged up? The only good thing is Regina has a distinctive birthmark on her right arm, like the map of Italy. I used to tease her that was the reason why she loved making Italian food because I didn't think it was in her blood."

At Harry's stare, she added, "Regina is Hispanic. But that doesn't matter… Are you investigating who robbed her?"

Harry touched the medal in his pocket, thinking of how the murder of Axel Colton was turning into what seemed like an impossible case to unravel. He needed to focus on each thread and unravel it and not get distracted.

"Do you have the address of the home?" he asked.

"The police have all that information. Don't you work together?"

"I'm here on another matter, ma'am."

"Such as?" Carla sounded hostile. He couldn't blame her.

Harry decided on a partial truth. "Her daughter, Sara, has been desperately trying to reach Regina."

Blood drained from Carla's face. "Oh dear, I didn't even think about that. Poor Sara! She must be frantic. She and Regina are quite close. I'll call her now. Oh no! I don't have her phone number, I think she changed it when she moved."

"Leave that to me." He removed his cell phone, texted Sara that her mother had been found and was safe, and he'd call her later.

"Mrs. Harrison, please have a seat. I need to ask you some questions."

Knowing that even though Regina was unconscious, she might be able to hear, he decided to question Carla in front of her. Maybe it would coax her into waking up. He couldn't get all softhearted now just because he could imagine Sara here, crying over her mother, wondering if she would ever wake up, crazy with worry and guilt over not reaching her earlier…

Harry took out his notebook and pen and remained standing at the opposite side of Regina's bed so he could see her in his peripheral vision. He grilled Carla about Regina, and any association she had with Eddie and Dennis Angelo. Carla told him Eddie had done odd jobs around the neighborhood after Regina recommended him, but no one ever heard of his brother. Or their sister, Mary Martin.

"Eddie was down on his luck, a nice, polite man, and Regina helped him out by hiring him to do some odd jobs around the yard. But he ghosted her after she needed him to help move some inventory at the warehouse and she had to formally fire him. I had the feeling Eddie wasn't cut out for a regular job." Carla kept glancing at her cell phone.

"How did Regina find Eddie? Was he knocking on neighbors' doors, asking for work?" Harry scribbled notes.

Carla's thin blond brows narrowed as she thought. "No, it was almost odd…he found her at her office at first. He was hoping for day labor after he moved from Chicago to St. Louis. He said he came with recommendations from some rich person in Chicago."

Harry stopped writing. This was peculiar. "Who was this person?"

The woman shook her head. "I can't remember. Regina mentioned it in passing and laughed, but she was a little startled. I remember that. I had the feeling she was bothered this acquaintance knew where she lived. As if she had run far away from something bad in her past and didn't want to be found. Do you think it was an ex-husband? Regina's my friend, but she's a private person and I never did find out if she'd been in an abusive relationship. She did act like that when we first met, always looking over her shoulder."

Looking over her shoulder to see if her old lover, Sara's father, would ring the doorbell after finding out about the daughter Axel didn't know existed? Yet another thread he had to follow.

"You have absolutely no idea who recommended Eddie to Regina? Try to remember, Mrs. Harrison. This is important."

"I don't see why. Eddie was just a down-on-his-luck man who couldn't quit drinking."

"He may have been more than that," Harry said grimly. "Was this person's name Axel Colton?"

Carla wrinkled her forehead. "Colton, that sounds familiar. I saw on the news about him, isn't he the one who was murdered?"

"Yes. Was it Axel Colton?"

"I don't think so. But the last name may have begun with a *C*. She was rather vague."

He had only more questions and no real answers. He needed to check out the house where Regina Sandoval had her accident.

This time, he needed to bring Sara along. She knew her mother and just might provide a link to all the broken threads in the case until Regina regained consciousness.

Chapter Thirteen

Sara felt as if someone had put her on a turntable and spun her madly around. Her life had flipped in hours. Sheer relief at discovering her mother had been found. Extreme worry knowing she was unconscious and injured in a hospital.

And now Harry wanted her along with him as he checked out the crime scene where Regina had been injured.

Vita graciously gave her the day off to accompany Harry. Shortly after seven o'clock in the morning, he picked her up in his sedan in front of her apartment and handed her a cup of hot coffee prepared exactly as she liked.

She accepted the coffee with grateful thanks as she settled into the passenger seat. Harry looked different this morning and then she realized why.

"You shaved off your beard!"

"I thought it was a good idea." Harry rubbed his clean cheek. "The beard was sort of an act of rebellion and when I was working in Narcotics, it helped with undercover work."

Sara scrutinized his cheeks. "It makes you look younger."

To her surprise, he flushed. "Yeah, just what I need, the look of a baby-faced cop."

"Not baby-faced. Just younger. I like it."

He smiled. "Feels strange not having it. But I'll get used to it."

As they started for Springfield, Sara mused over her mother being found. "I don't understand why the police didn't inform me sooner about finding my mother. Or why they didn't contact anyone at her office. Wouldn't they have asked the home's owner right away who my mother was and identified her that way?"

Harry nodded. "The house was recently bought by the new hire taking over the satellite office. They contacted the real estate agent, who told them the owner and his family are driving across the country from California. The Springfield police had trouble reaching him. When they finally did, he said your mother's company had a skeleton key because they had all his furniture delivered to the house. When the police called your mother's company to get more information, the president said it was probably Regina found in the house. She oversaw that project. There was a car there that matched the description the president gave the police."

Sara sipped her coffee. "Are you allowed to bring me onto an active crime scene?"

A side glance. "I called Springfield PD and told them. It's not much of an active crime scene now, plus the vic is still alive."

Vic. Her mother. "You mean if she dies the police will change their minds?" She couldn't help the bitterness in her voice.

"They have priorities just as every other PD does. Right now your mother's case is a robbery. They're not even calling it a home invasion because there's no signs of forced entry. Your mother knows whoever did this."

A shudder snaked down her spine. Hard to believe

someone would want to hurt her mother that badly, let alone someone Regina knew well enough to admit into the house.

"How did this person find her?" she asked.

"That's what I'd like to know," Harry said grimly. "It would have to appear that whoever did this contacted your mother and she arranged to meet him at the house. But we won't have solid answers until she wakes up."

Harry finally pulled into the driveway of a two-story green house with white shutters. It was in a solid middle-class neighborhood, not unlike the one where she and Regina lived. Regina's car was nowhere in sight.

"My mother's car is gone." Sara's hands tightened on her now-cold cup of coffee.

"Springfield had it towed to their impound lot. We'll get it back soon." Harry unbuckled his seat belt and turned, facing her. "Sara, you should know something. This wasn't a home invasion. Your mother was deliberately targeted. The only things stolen belonged to her. Nothing else was taken, not the new electronic equipment worth thousands, or the home computer, or anything else in the house of value."

Maybe such knowledge would help the police narrow down leads on her mother's attacker, but it only made Sara more uneasy. Whoever did this to Regina had wanted her dead. It was the only explanation.

The house was still and too quiet when they went inside. The carpeting smelled new and she detected a hint of pine. Tears welled in her eyes as she spotted the Christmas tree in the corner with tinsel, lights and decorations.

"Mom must have done that. She would want the family to feel happy and welcome here. It's one reason she's so good at her job—she oversees so many details and knows moving is tough on a family."

Harry pointed to the kitchen beyond the living room.

"Your mother was working in the kitchen and she was found lying on the basement stairs. Stairs are right off the kitchen."

The kitchen was modern with polished granite countertops, stainless steel appliances and a farmhouse sink. Several bar stools were arranged along the island.

"Do you see anything that would belong to your mother? Anything?"

Sara shook her head. "If she was here helping out, Mom wouldn't have many personal items inside. She respected someone else's space."

The kitchen was tidy, but for a stack of papers on the island that immediately caught Harry's interest. He clasped Sara's hand. "Don't touch them. I need to process this."

Harry pulled gloves from his pocket, snapped them on and picked up a pink flyer from a neat stack. "Grand opening of Larkspur Insurance. Come see us for all your home, auto and personal property needs!" the flyer advertised.

"Pink," he mused.

"One of the owners of Larkspur Insurance is a woman. That's her signature color—in fact, Mom said this satellite office is targeting busy businesswomen who don't have time to shop for insurance. They planned to decorate the office with pink accents."

But Harry's attention was elsewhere. He began opening bottom cabinets.

"What are you looking for?" she asked, bemused.

"Trash." He pulled out a bin under the sink. "Not here. Empty. Come on."

He led the way outside to the attached garage and handed her a pair of surgical gloves. "You allergic to latex?"

When she shook her head he instructed her to don the gloves.

"Put the gloves on. Start looking through the trash cans, see if there are envelopes. If you see any or anything else odd, tell me," he instructed.

But only newspaper and bubble wrap littered the trash bin she saw. Then she heard Harry call it. "Got it, you bastard."

Glancing up she saw him hold up a pink envelope in one gloved hand. He turned it over. Sara's breath caught. "That's like the pink envelope my mother used to mail my letter!"

Harry held the envelope up to the light. "Whoever did this is clever, but sloppy. Or in a rush. They forgot to check all the trash."

"But you said my mom's DNA was on the envelope seal and she must have written it."

"It was her DNA, but I'd bet a month's salary she did not write that letter." Harry dropped the pink envelope into a bag marked Evidence. "You know your mother and her habits. You said she liked to write letters and always mailed notes to clients that were handwritten. Think, Sara. Did she seal them and then address and stamp them?"

Sara nodded. "Usually she used a software program to print out mailing labels."

It dawned on her. "You think someone else mailed that letter to implicate my mother? How did they open a sealed envelope?"

"Freeze a sealed envelope for about an hour or two and the glue will unstick. All you have to do is pry open the envelope, slip in whatever you wish and reseal using a sponge to avoid fingerprints. The glue gets tacky again after it thaws out."

Harry shook his head and quietly swore. "The DNA the

lab lifted was just enough to incriminate her, but slightly compromised. They did lift a fingerprint that matched Regina's as well. Whoever is behind this is determined to make it look like your mother killed Axel."

"And that person is the real killer." She shuddered, fear skidding down her spine on crawling legs.

She was horrified someone tried to frame her mother for the crime. Her mother, who lay in a hospital bed.

"Maybe. I doubt Regina killed Axel. Not with what happened." He peeled off the gloves and stuffed them into his pocket. "Let's go inside."

Harry showed her how to peel back the gloves. Sara placed them in her purse so as not to leave anything behind, same as Harry had done.

"Why would anyone want to hurt my mother? She'd never harm anyone. She has no enemies and she's a good person." Her voice caught and she struggled to prevent her emotions from taking over.

"I don't know, but trust me, Sara. I will find out. I promise this." Harry's quiet, reassuring voice settled her raw nerves a little.

"I have to call and see how she's doing. Maybe…oh I hope so…she woke up."

The cell phone shook in her hand as she dialed the hospital for a status update on Regina. Her hopes crumbled as the nurse relayed the news.

Sara thumbed off the cell. "No changes. The nurse said it takes time with a head injury. She had woken up a couple of times previously…"

She had to hold it together for her mother's sake. Believe that Regina would pull through and everything would be okay. But it was really tough when you were alone.

Harry put a comforting hand on her shoulder. She felt

grateful for the touch. It centered her, made everything less hectic and terrifying. He reminded her she wasn't entirely alone.

"Let's go outside for some fresh air," he told her.

They walked onto a wood deck overseeing an expansive yard. Playground equipment sat off to the side. Sara hugged herself.

"Look at that. Typical of my mother. I bet she told the movers to make sure the equipment was set up, even though it's winter and the kids wouldn't use it for a while. But that was a detail Regina specialized in overseeing. She was like that at home as well, always making sure I was comfortable."

Cold penetrated her bones, a deep cold that had nothing to do with the weather. She stared at the yard, trying not to see her mother lying in a hospital bed, never fully waking up.

"I love her so much. She's my only family. I don't know what I'll do if she dies," she whispered.

Suddenly she was in Harry's arms as he engulfed her in a warm, comforting hug. He rested his cheek against her head. "Never think like that, Sara. She's alive and as long as she's alive, there's always hope. Always cling to that hope."

The softness in his voice, edged with a slight pain, told her Harry spoke from experience. Harry, who had suffered a tremendous loss, but still had the capacity for compassion and understanding. Some people might have turned hard from grief and lost their sense of humanity.

Harry had not. He was a good cop who sought to do the right thing, and seemed to honor that goal. He always seemed to be working and focusing solely on solving cases. But moments like this gave her glimpses into the real Harry Cartwright, a man who cared about more than the job. Even if he didn't like showing it.

They stood motionless on the deck, the icy wind billowing the edges of her scarf still penetrating her thin coat, but the chill inside her lessened. It felt wonderful to be held with such tenderness.

He stepped back and she lost the wonderful warmth of his arms. Harry brushed aside a strand of her hair, his fingers warm against her chilled cheeks. "You're not alone, Sara. You do have other family now. Vita thinks of you like a third child. You have a lot of family members now."

She smiled, glad he reminded her of the possibilities. "Yes. Vita's family are wonderful."

"I'm sure the other Coltons would welcome you as much as Vita has." Harry kept stroking her cheek and his touch sent delightful shivers down her spine. Delicious warmth filled her.

"A few might. Maybe not Uncle Erik or my grandmother."

Harry raised his eyebrows. "Carin is something else. Not the milk-and-cookies type."

"My grandmother…" She gave a humorless laugh. "No, more like the Rodeo Drive sort. I bet she never has a hair out of place."

"But she does seem like she has a hair up her butt."

Sara laughed as he grinned, and she mock punched his arm. "Harry!"

"Got you to laugh," he said softly. "Knocked that sad look off your face."

She stepped closer to him, leaning against him. "Yes, you did. Thanks."

"Sorry, shouldn't have said that about Carin. It was inappropriate, even though she's been a pain to the department, saying we're working too slow to solve Axel's murder. She's grieving in her own way. She lost a son."

His voice grew quieter. "I know what that's like. It's something you never get over."

So true. Sara felt a brief stab of guilt. She may have lost a father she didn't know, but her grandmother lost a child. It was the wrong order of life. Most parents expected to die before their children did.

"It's cold out here. I used to like winter before I heard Axel died. Now winter reminds me we're all mortal," she mused.

Harry took her bare hands into his and rubbed them.

"My grandmother was getting a tree for Axel's grave when I saw her at Yates' Yards. Carin doesn't know who I really am, and I'd like to keep it that way. She seems like a cold person and I don't think she'd welcome me with open arms." Sara snuggled into his coat as he wrapped his arms around her once more. "Not like Vita and her family have done."

"Maybe you should give her a chance." Harry tilted her chin up with one finger so she gazed into his face. "Everyone deserves a second chance."

Sara had the suspicion he was talking about himself, not Carin. She wrapped her arms around his neck and parted her lips.

He needed no other invitation as he brushed his mouth against hers. His lips were slightly cold and firm, but as they sank deeper into the kiss, sparks leapt between them. Sara was no longer chilled. She was heating from the inside out, the amazing warmth searing her as she pressed closer, needing and wanting more.

Groaning, he took her deeper into the kiss. Sara felt as if she stood on the edge of a cliff, ready to skydive. The parachute strapped to her back assured her she would not fall, but the thrill of the experience overrode any natural fears. She'd been kissed by experts—men who considered themselves great lovers and knew how to please a woman in bed.

But this was different. This wasn't a kiss of seduction and pleasure. This was a kiss of comfort and reassurance, a kiss in the middle of a crazily spinning world that calmed the vertigo. She knew it would be great in bed with Harry not because he was a good-looking man she was wildly attracted to.

She knew when they finally ended up in bed it would be amazing because he had a good heart and he would make love with the same dedication and intensity he showed with everything in life. Harry wasn't a one-night stand. Not with her. Not with this blazing passion and intensity that was far deeper and richer than she'd felt with any other man.

He would give everything, body and soul, when he tangled with her between the sheets.

They broke apart and he gave a small smile. "Cold still?"

"No. I'm warm." A little laugh. "Nice and warm."

Harry made her feel as if everything would turn out all right. *But will he stay? Will he break your heart because you're starting to fall in love with him? All those other men meant nothing to you. Not like he does.*

Hard as it was to ignore the voice whispering doubts inside her, for now she would. Sara needed Harry.

His hands grazed her jacket and he frowned. "Sara Sandoval, you need to get a thicker jacket if you're going to survive winter in Chicago. This isn't St. Louis anymore."

She smiled. "I suppose I should."

When she first arrived in the windy city, Sara had no intentions of really staying. Settling here seemed unlikely, especially if Axel had wanted nothing to do with her. But lately she thought she could learn to live here on a more permanent basis.

It has nothing to do with Harry, right? Oh no, nothing at all...

Right. She gave a little laugh. "I suppose we should go inside. Much warmer in there."

Harry turned serious. "I need your help. I'm going to search every inch of this house to see if your mother's attacker left anything else behind, and you can identify any personal objects as your mother's."

An hour later, they had covered every inch of the house except the basement. Sara couldn't bring herself to explore the area where her mother had fallen. The only questionable item Sara found was a business card advertising Larkspur, with Regina's name on it. She'd spotted it on the bedroom dresser.

Harry's nose wrinkled. "Smell that? Heavy, spicy... like perfume."

Sara inhaled. "Not really, but Mom liked to freshen the air with scent, especially if she knew the family's preferences. It's not unusual."

"Strange choice for an air freshener. I think I've smelled this before...more like men's aftershave."

She marveled he could detect such a faint fragrance. "You have a good nose, Harry. Does it come with the job of being a detective?"

His mouth quirked upward. "More like it comes with the territory of being an epicure. Although with my beer, I'm much more pedestrian."

The fact he'd caught it was a grim reminder they were

in a crime scene. Sara gazed around the kitchen and wished they could leave. Right now. She couldn't help but feel the ghost of violence remained here.

His gaze sharpened. "Stay here. I want to check out the basement."

Lingering in the kitchen, she studied the flyers on the counter. Then she remembered something she'd seen in the trash that she'd dismissed.

Harry trudged up the stairs. "Nothing. No smell of cologne."

"These flyers." She pointed to the stack. "When I was going through the trash in the garage, I saw a cardboard box from a printing company. Could it mean anything? Mom wouldn't have tossed the box for the flyers once she finished mailing them. She always orders extras and would have stored them in the box."

"Which means someone else, maybe her attacker, threw it away and there could be fingerprints. I'll call Springfield, ask them to dust the box and everything else in the trash for prints."

She pulled out her cell phone. "One more thing I remembered. If she was in someone else's house, Mom would never open the door to anyone, even someone she knew, without warning. She made a rule they had to call her first on her cell phone. She didn't care if it was the company president."

"Whoever attacked her called her first." Harry pulled out a notebook and scribbled something. "I can pull the phone records for Regina's cell and find out. Good job, Sara."

Not that she'd done anything spectacular.

"You ready to leave here?" he asked. "I have to go to

the Springfield PD to let them know what we found, but after, I thought we could stop at the hospital."

Her breath hitched and her heart beat faster. "To see Mom?"

As he nodded, she threw her arms around his neck and hugged him tight. "Yes, please, thank you!"

Harry patted her back. "As long as I'm with you, it's okay. But I don't want you making any trips back there without me."

His gaze turned hard. "Whoever did this is upping their game and they may target you next. I want you to promise me you'll go to work, go straight home and if you need to go out, call someone to go with you."

Her joy faded a little. "You're really worried someone might come after me?"

"They've already attacked your mother, for what reason, I don't know. Regina is still under suspicion, Sara." He framed her face with his warm hands. "I want to make sure you're safe."

So protective and concerned. Sara understood his reasons. It didn't make it easier. She was accustomed to freedom and living her life as she pleased. But she knew he was right.

"I promise."

He kissed her palms, one by one. "Good. Let's go see your mother. Then after, we'll stop by a hardware store. I need to copy your front door key."

Sara's heart fluttered. "Why, Detective Cartwright, do you plan to take liberties with me?"

Harry's mouth twitched briefly. "Not right now. Later, perhaps. Will you be at work all day tomorrow?"

"Yes, why?"

"I plan to try to break into your apartment. I'm not convinced that building is secure. After I'm finished, I'll stop by your place after I have dinner at my sister's, and we'll get the locks changed if they don't meet my satisfaction."

Sara felt another flutter, mixed in with rising indignation. Pushy much? "That's extreme, Harry."

"These are extreme circumstances, Sara. You're under my protection now and I do everything I can to make sure those under my protection are safe." His jaw tightened. "I'm not going to fail like I did last time."

Anger faded as she realized the implication of his declaration. Last time, meaning when his wife and child died. "Okay, we'll make you a copy of my keys. I'll do it because I get it. I do, Harry. But I'm not someone you can wrap up in a cocoon, shielding me from the world. I won't live like that. I cherish my life and my privacy."

Then because she had begun to care, and wanted to start a real relationship with him, she added, "I like you, Harry. A lot. I want to see if we can be more than friends. So if you plan to swaddle me in cotton wool and put me away in a box like a gemstone, know this. It won't work out so we might as well stop before we take any kind of romantic leap."

She took a breath. "Into anything, including intimacy."

Harry's eyes darkened as if he liked the idea of being intimate with her. He took the key and stared at it a moment. Nodded. "I know. Give me a chance, Sara. If I know you're safe, I can relax a little. Right now things are moving too fast with us, and too slow and complex with this case. I need to control…something…not you, but knowing you're safe will let me sleep at night. I'm not the domineering type who wants to keep you on a leash. If I think the locks are secure, I'll meet you at your place tomorrow night and return the keys."

He gave her a long, lingering look that had her heart doing backflips. Oh yes, the chemistry between them grew more intense. "I need to level with you, Sara. I don't consider us the cop and the former suspect, or even friends. I'm starting to care, Sara, and it's scary for me to do that with another woman. Let me do this one thing to make sure you're okay in your own home. Just trust me, okay?"

Sara bit her lip. "Okay. Will you at least let me know when you plan to enter my apartment and let me know when you leave?"

His mouth twitched. "Of course. I plan to call you and keep you on the phone the whole time."

That made her feel better. It wasn't as if he planned to sneak inside and comb through her belongings. "Good. Stay away from my bedroom, though. Mornings get hectic and I seldom have a chance to tidy up the way I wish."

"Of course." Then his voice deepened and he got that intent look in his eyes once more. "I don't plan on entering your bedroom until I'm asked, and then I have no plans to leave right away. I'm the kind of guy who likes to take his time in bed, Sara."

There it was, the sexual gauntlet thrown down. She felt another flutter much lower, signaling she was up to the challenge. She smiled slowly, and licked her lips, knowing he tracked the move. "Good. I like things that…last all night long."

For a moment they regarded each other, and then he tucked the key away and turned brisk and professional once more. "Thank you for trusting me on this. Let's go see your mom. Maybe, by some miracle, she'll have awakened."

As they drove away from the house she couldn't imagine who Regina would have allowed inside the house. Whoever it was, it was someone her mother trusted.

Someone who might turn out to be the same person who killed Axel.

And wanted Regina dead as well.

To HIS RELIEF the next day, Sara's locks not only seemed secure, but he had a good feeling about her staying here. Her nosy neighbor, Mrs. Pendleton, had peeked outside her door when he walked toward Sara's apartment and threw all kinds of questions at him. Nosy neighbors were almost as good as security systems.

Unfortunately, he didn't have the same luck with the phone records to Regina Sandoval's cell or the box with the flyers. The box held no viable prints. Frustration filled him as he drove that afternoon to Carin Pederson's house to meet with her son Erik.

Whoever had called Regina Sandoval had done so from a cheap prepaid phone that had no records. It made her attack even more planned, and whoever had done it had meant to deliberately harm her. Even tracking the pings the phone had made had been fruitless. Regina's attacker had called her a mile or so from the satellite office her company planned to open.

Carin Pederson lived in a stately mansion in an upscale Chicago suburb. Although Erik had a condo in the city, Harry had found out Carin's son spent more time living with his mother. The condo's ownership was in question as well, since Erik had mortgaged it to the point where he had no equity in the property.

Harry had talked with Nash Colton, who admitted his father was tightly wound and even angrier than usual. It gave Harry another reason to question Axel's twin further.

But the man was hard to find. Every time he tried to pin him down for an interview, Erik either wasn't answering his phone or blew him off.

It was only when Harry left him a message that he could either answer questions at home or at the police station in handcuffs, that he was able to nail down a time.

Erik was staying at his mother's house in Overland Park. The mansion looked like a relic from the 1800s, majestic and stately once. Now it appeared dowdy and neglected, with dirt covering the antique windows like cataracts. Harry rang the doorbell. At least it worked.

A domestic worker in a uniform grayer than the front windows answered. She escorted him into a parlor and left. Harry stood by the fireplace, gazing around. He suspected the room was in better shape than most of the house. But after dealing a few times with Carin Pederson, he knew impressions were important to her.

To his surprise, Carin entered the room. In a cream Chanel suit and cream pumps, she looked impeccable and stylish, but the severe expression on her tight face spoiled the effect. No wonder Sara hadn't wanted to reveal her true identity to her grandmother. He wouldn't want that, either.

"I understand you're here to torment my only surviving son. Isn't it enough you police have put us through misery by failing to do your job and find out who killed Axel?"

Diplomacy was never his strong suit, but he needed it now. Harry summoned all his tact and thought of her tremendous loss. She had a right to demand justice.

"I'm truly sorry about your loss. Let me reassure you, we are working around the clock to solve the case and bring your son's killer to justice."

Carin sniffed. "If you worked as hard as you say you are doing, you'd have found the killer by now. I heard you're the lead detective and yet there are reports of you wasting time with Sara Sandoval when you should have locked her up already. She was a suspect, was she not?"

His temper slipped a notch, but Harry managed to keep a polite smile in place. "I wouldn't call it wasting time, ma'am. Miss Sandoval has been cleared as a suspect and she's been instrumental in aiding the investigation, especially since her mother was found attacked and left for dead. We believe whoever attacked her mother is the same person who killed your son. It's why I need to question Erik."

If Carin grew pale at the news he could not tell. The woman wore too much makeup.

"Talk to my son, but I warn you, Detective. I have considerable influence and power in this city with elected officials. If you and your Keystone Cops keep making the kind of amateur mistakes you have made, there will be consequences."

"Of course." He struggled to keep his temper in place. "I must speak with Erik. Or did he slip out from your leash again?"

Now the woman flushed red beneath her cosmetics. "Watch yourself, Detective."

You watch it, lady. Keystone Cops? "Is Erik here? The sooner I can talk with him, the sooner I can leave."

Her thin lips pursed. "Very well. I will send him downstairs."

She waved a hand. "You can let yourself out when you're finished."

Harry watched her walk toward the back of the house. Sara wasn't exaggerating when she claimed her grandmother could be icy. His blood warmed as he thought of Sara. He missed talking with her.

Erik finally trudged down the stairs and entered the parlor, looking like a sullen child instead of a fifty-nine-year-old man. In his gray trousers, neatly starched white shirt and red tie, the man looked as if ready for a business meeting. Yet to his knowledge, Erik Colton had never owned a business in his life. Like his twin, Erik preferred to live off his trust fund.

"Detective. I apologize for ah, our domestic worker's, lack of courtesy. She should have known better. You should have been offered something to drink. Coffee? Tea? Please sit."

Not the domestic worker's fault. "I'll stand. Nothing to drink for now."

He started right away with questions about Erik's whereabouts the night of Regina's attack and if Erik ever talked recently with Regina Sandoval. Erik had an alibi, albeit a weak one. He was home with his mother.

"If we're finished here..." Erik started to rise.

"Not quite. I'll take that cup of coffee now."

Erik yelled for the domestic worker, who scurried into the room.

"Coffee, please. Two sugars, no cream. And a mug if you have it, not those little china cups that barely hold a mouthful of liquid," Harry told her.

She returned with a steaming mug of coffee. Harry looked at the inscription.

WORLD'S GREATEST TWIN.

Accepting it with thanks, Harry sipped. The domestic worker left.

"Interesting cup. Seems customized mugs run in your family. Did you know one reading WORLD'S GREATEST DAD was found in Axel's kitchen after he died?"

Erik grew red-faced. "What does that have to do with anything?"

"That same coffee cup was found in Axel's kitchen with Sara Sandoval's prints all over it. As if someone were trying to set her up, planting evidence she was in Axel's house the day of the murder."

"Maybe she was. Talk to her, not me."

Erik ran a finger under his collar. Good. He was sweating. Harry planned to coax a little more perspiration from him.

"Tell me about Axel and his relationship with Regina Sandoval. When was the last time your brother saw her?"

"That slut?" Erik scoffed and brushed at his trousers. "We were glad he finally got rid of her. She was a menace, always demanding money and Axel's time. It was her fault Vita divorced my brother."

Blame the victim. Classic psychological trait. Harry locked gazes with him and switched tactics.

"Do you have any association with a man named Eddie Angelo?"

Now Erik looked away. "Never heard of the man."

"No? What about his brother, Dennis Angelo? Their sister, Mary Martin?"

Erik's gaze shifted left and he squirmed a little. "Who are these people and why are you asking me about them?"

"Leave the questions to me. You've never met a Mary Martin? She used to be a domestic worker for Farrah and Alfred Colton. Your half brother Alfred."

Erik sighed. "Why would I know her? Perhaps I've heard her name before, but that would be because my children or another relative mentioned her."

Right. *And you don't even remember to call your own domestic worker by her name.* Servants were below recognition to a person like Erik Colton.

"Did you love your brother?"

Erik blinked several times, glanced away, adjusted the hem of his trousers. "Of course."

Slow on answering. Interesting.

"You were twins. I'm sure he talked with you. Was there anyone Axel worried about, anyone threatening him?"

"There may have been. People were jealous of us and our money."

Like I'm jealous of a television detective. Such a fantasy. "Did you and your brother have a good relationship with your father? Did Dean ever gift you or Axel with family heirlooms?"

Erik looked away again. "He set up our trust funds."

Evasion.

"A trust fund is one thing. But what about personal items that your father may have wanted to give you that belonged to the family? Items that you could pass on to your own children, such as a silver platter that belonged to his mother? More sentimental than valuable."

A short laugh. "I'm not a sentimental man, Detective. Neither was Axel."

"Your father never gave you anything that belonged to him?"

"Never and I don't see where this is going. Are we finished?" Erik snapped.

Raw nerves were a good sign. "Maybe Dean gave personal items to Axel."

Erik sniffed. "My brother and I shared many things, but we were not alike. Axel craved recognition from our father and his heritage. He had started to distance himself from the family."

"Meaning you and your mother?"

A shrug. "Everyone. He talked as if he wanted revenge, although for what, I don't know. It was typical of Axel to create drama where there was none."

Harry consulted his notes, while keeping one eye on Erik. "You're certain you were nowhere near Springfield that day? Never contacted Regina Sandoval about your brother's death or anything else?"

No makeup on Erik's face, so it was easy enough to detect the flush. Rage? Or guilt?

Erik stood. "I think we are done, Detective. If you want to know anything about Regina Sandoval, ask her illegitimate daughter, not me. But I understand you've already been seen around town with her."

Slapping a lid on his temper and the urge to punch Erik Colton in his face, Harry followed him out of the room. As Erik opened the door for him, a gust of wind blew past the man. Harry caught a whiff of the man's aftershave.

He stiffened.

Damn if that wasn't the same, or close to it, cologne he'd smelled at the house where Regina Sandoval had been attacked.

Harry turned, looked him straight in the eye. "Know this, Colton. You and your mother may think we're dragging our heels on this case, but I'm damn good at my job and I always find the bad guys. Always. I've solved every case I've had. With or without help from families as obstinate and unpleasant as yours."

As Colton started to sputter, Harry smiled slowly. "Nice aftershave. I just came from a crime scene where I smelled the exact same scent. Odd, isn't it?"

Colton slammed the door behind him, but not before Harry caught the unmistakable look on his face.

The man was scared. He knew he'd slipped up.

You couldn't convict someone based on a fragrance. But he knew he was getting close, much closer, to finding answers. Even if he hadn't killed his brother, Erik Colton was looking more likely for another crime.

Attacking Regina Sandoval and leaving her for dead.

THE WEATHER HAD turned unexpectedly warm for Chicago in December, and the sudden change had many people enjoying the outdoors. At work, Sara took advantage of the warmth and strolled on the grounds of the nursery during her lunch break.

She'd found it hard to remain cooped up. She hadn't gone for a run in days. Every day when she returned home after work, the walls of her apartment seemed to close in around her, suffocating and squeezing.

Sara had promised Harry to never go out alone. She always kept her promises.

At least tonight she could open her windows and let in fresh air. Then she remembered Harry's stern warning about someone trying to break inside and sighed. He would come over tonight anyway to return her key.

The thought made her lady parts tingle in anticipation. Maybe they would make a night of it. All night long.

She trudged up the stairs and started past Mrs. Pendleton's apartment when the elderly lady opened the door.

"Sara! Wait."

Turning, she saw her elderly neighbor marching toward her with a plate in her gloved hands.

"I finally got my baking done. Here, dear. Let me put it inside for you. It's still hot, so be careful."

After unlocking the front door, Sara let Mrs. Pendleton inside. Her neighbor placed the pie on the counter.

"Enjoy, dear, and thank you again for getting groceries for me." Mrs. Pendleton beamed at her and glanced around the kitchen. "It's so warm in here. Why don't you open a window? Or better yet, go for a nice walk? I would if these old bones could handle the stairs better."

"Good idea. Thank you." Sara escorted her neighbor to the door.

Mrs. Pendleton turned, her rheumy blue gaze unreadable. "I really would get some fresh air, Sara. I know you're new to Chicago's winters. Days like this are meant to be enjoyed outside."

She thanked her again and closed the door behind her neighbor. Sara opened the living room window a couple of inches, securing it with the sturdy lock Harry had given her. She didn't dare try it with the kitchen window because of the fire escape.

After eating her take-out salad, she pushed it aside. Her appetite wasn't terrific. Maybe it was the pie waiting for her. Sara inhaled the delicious scent of freshly baked apples. Pie was her one weakness and Mrs. Pendleton was thoughtful enough to indulge.

Now I'm really going to have to make up for these calories with an extra-long run.

She cut herself a healthy slice, heated it in the microwave and settled back on the sofa to watch her favorite cooking show.

Somehow it held little appeal tonight. Maybe it was the pie. It tasted okay, not as good as she anticipated. That was life. Sometimes reality didn't live up to your anticipation.

Harry had. He'd held her attention from the moment she'd seen him gazing down at her with concern after she'd fainted from the news of Axel's death. The man had deep layers she had only begun to peel back.

She finished the pie and grabbed her phone, checking the hospital for a status update on Regina. Still no change.

She texted Lila, asking about lunch tomorrow. Lila was busy with her art gallery and a new show starting soon. Sighing, Sara clicked on an app to read a book.

Soon, her eyes started to close. She blinked, tried to focus. No use. Odd. The novel had fascinated her earlier in the week when she'd downloaded it to her phone.

Something smelled odd, too. Was that gas? Had she accidentally left the oven on?

As she tossed aside her phone and stood to race into the kitchen to check, she swayed. The room spun as if she were on a fast-moving carousel.

This was crazy. Another fainting spell? Sara turned and saw her phone on the sofa as if from a long distance away. She stumbled toward it. *Have to call Harry. Something's wrong.* Her vision blurred.

Grabbing the table for support, she knocked over the lamp. Her vision grew gray and she could no longer stand.

As she collapsed to the floor, her last thought was calling Harry for help. But her phone seemed so far away.

So very far…

Chapter Fourteen

The pounding kept up a steady rhythm outside. It had turned warm and the neighbors decided to take up the garage renovations they'd abandoned in the cold weather.

Lifting the curtain with the back of one hand, Harry peered out the dining room window. Seemed like everyone was out enjoying the weather. He dropped the curtain, musing over things.

Once he and Marie had a house like this. He'd sold it after she died and opted for an anonymous apartment in the city, closer to the station. But sometimes it was nice to visit suburbia again.

"Harry, dinner's ready," a voice sang out.

He headed into the dining room, where his brother-in-law and eight-year-old niece were already seated. Offers of help with meal preparation had been politely refused. Linda said he deserved to be pampered for a change.

He sat next to Amelia, who beamed. "Uncle Harry! I learned to skate today all by myself! I didn't even fall!"

She gave him a beseeching look. "Do you remember your promise?"

Laughing, he took a dollar from his wallet and gave it to her. "Here you go. I remember. One dollar when you learn to skate. But remember, falling is part of learning. You only need to make sure to get back up again."

Such a sweetheart. Glad as he was to have family in the city, sometimes he didn't visit enough.

Or make the time. Tonight, Linda and Elliott insisted he join them because they had news to share.

Certainly he had no news to share. Talking about a murder investigation was hardly dinner talk, even if Amelia wasn't present. Very few times did he discuss active cases with his family. Elliott still asked questions, which Harry dodged, but Linda never did.

When you grew up with your father as a cop, you learned what subjects were off-limits at the dinner table.

He dug into Linda's excellent roast as he listened to them talk about Amelia's school, and how they canceled the annual ski trip to Colorado in February. The last caught his attention.

"Why aren't you going?" he asked his sister. "All okay?"

"Better than okay." Elliott beamed. "We didn't want to risk it."

"I'm pregnant." Linda squeezed her husband's hand. "We wanted to tell you in person."

Harry squelched the hollowing feeling in his chest. Another baby. He was thrilled for them, but it was yet another reminder of his personal loss.

This was their joy and he would never spoil it. He stood and gave his sister a quick, affectionate peck on the cheek. "Congrats."

Then he hugged her. Linda and Elliott had been trying for another baby for years.

Elliott glanced at his wife. "We talked it over and we hope it's a boy and if it is, we want to name him John, after my father. We hope that's okay with you."

The excellent roast turned sour in his stomach. "Of course. It's a good name."

Simply because his own son had been named John didn't mean he couldn't tolerate a nephew with the same name. At least that is what he told himself. The pain he felt deep inside would go away eventually, certainly after Linda gave birth.

"Congratulations again."

He asked basic questions about the baby and their plans, listened as they held an animated discussion. Yet for all their joy, and Amelia's excitement about having a little brother or sister to boss around, something inside him twisted with disquiet.

What was wrong with him that his only sister's news had him feeling uneasy? Was he that much of a jerk?

As Elliott and Amelia helped Linda clear the table, insisting he relax and enjoy himself, the feeling grew more intense. Harry frowned and walked to the window again. In the past he'd followed his gut and it served him well. He stared at the neighbors pounding hammers on the garage extension. Such a nice evening out. The kind where people in the city would get out for fresh air…

Sara.

Groaning, he turned from the window. That was it. Not his sadness over his own child's death. It had to do with Sara.

He knew Sara liked to go for long runs and this weather might prove too tempting for her. Even though she'd promised him she would remain inside her apartment. Time to check up on her, letting her know he would be over soon.

Fishing out his cell phone, he called her number. No answer.

Harry tried again, left a voice mail, and then hung up. He tapped the phone against his open palm.

Something was terribly wrong. Sara always answered her phone.

On impulse, he called the dispatch in Evanston to see if anyone reported an emergency in her area. No one had. But an elderly woman with a shaky voice had reported she might have smelled gas in the hallway of her apartment building.

Harry's blood went cold when the dispatcher gave him the address. Sara's apartment building.

"Get uniforms over there, ASAP," he told the dispatcher.

Harry went into the kitchen and kissed Linda's cheek. "I have to run."

Linda turned from the sink. "But we haven't had dessert yet! I made strawberry shortcake, your favorite!"

"I'm sorry. Rain check. I have to check on something—otherwise, I'd stay." Then because he loved his sister and her family and didn't want them worrying, he added, "A friend isn't answering her phone."

"Her?" Elliott's eyes lit up. "Are you dating again?"

"Which friend and why haven't you told us about her?" Linda demanded.

"Uncle Harry, are you shagging with someone?"

All three adults turned and stared at Amelia.

"What did you say?" her father demanded.

Amelia turned beet red. "Uh, uh…"

"Young lady, where did you hear that word?" Linda demanded.

"From that show you watched." Amelia twisted her hands together. "It means getting together, right?"

Harry laughed and swept up his niece in a bear hug. "In a way, sweetheart. She's a friend I'm hoping will turn into more than a friend." He kissed her and grinned at Linda. "And you wanted another one. Good luck. I have to run."

Worry filled him as he put on his flashers and raced to Sara's apartment. Still not answering her phone. Could be she decided to silence it to read or take a snooze. Anything was possible.

But that call from Sara's building…

Outside Sara's building, a patrol unit had just pulled up. Harry used the key she'd given him and yanked open the door as he and the two officers ran inside. Heart racing, Harry took the steps two at a time. She had to be okay, she'd open the door and laugh, making an excuse about taking a bath and not having her phone close by.

Her door was locked. Harry pounded on it. "Sara? Sara!"

"I smell gas," one officer said.

Harry unlocked the door with shaky hands. Bursting inside, he whipped his gaze around, searching, calling her name. Then he came to an abrupt halt as he spotted a body on the living room floor.

Sara. His nose wrinkled as he smelled the distinct odor. Damn it.

"Get all the windows open," he yelled. "And be careful, this place can blow any minute."

Harry lifted Sara into his arms and raced out into the hallway. Gently he laid her on the hallway carpet. Not breathing.

He began CPR and chest compressions. *C'mon Sara, breathe, c'mon sweetheart, breathe…*

Someone in the apartment building down the hallway opened their door. "Is everything all right?" an elderly woman called out in a quavering voice.

"Gas leak! The whole building could go up! Get out of here!"

Ignoring her gasp, he focused on CPR. Sara's lips seemed so cold against his…when they had been warm and filled with life only hours ago. She had to live. He wasn't going to lose anyone else. Not on his watch.

After a minute she woke up, coughing. Harry's relief was short-lived as he realized the gas was still leaking. The officers were going door to door now, getting the tenants to leave.

He called 9-1-1 on his cell phone.

"I have a female victim, possible poisoning caused by gas leak." He rattled off the address. "Evacuate the building, source of the gas leak not identified. Advise caution."

No time for conversation as Sara kept coughing, and looked dazed. He stood, threw her over his shoulder in a fireman's hold and ran down the stairs. Another patrol vehicle pulled up as he carried her outside into the fresh air.

He set Sara down carefully on the sidewalk. "It's okay, sweetheart, you're going to be all right now. Breathe deep."

Harry looked at one officer and identified himself. "Watch her, I have to go back and secure the scene. Two officers are inside, helping to evacuate the building. There's still a gas leak and this whole place could blow."

The officer crouched by Sara, called for an ambulance on his shoulder mike. "What happened?"

Rage filled him, pure and hot. He fought it. Emotions did no good in a crisis. "Someone tried to kill her."

Two HOURS LATER, the building had been totally evacuated and public works gave the all clear for people to return to their apartments. From the hallway, Harry watched a forensics team at work determining the source of the leak. Much as he longed to be at the hospital with Sara, his work was here.

The ER doctor had confirmed high levels of doxylamine, an over-the-counter sleep aid, had been found in Sara's blood. Sara was resting comfortably and they planned to admit her.

He'd called Vita Yates and asked her to stay with Sara at the hospital, briefly explaining what happened. A patrol officer would also stand guard in case the suspect tried to return to kill Sara.

Anything could happen. Whoever did this was clever and determined.

The valves on Sara's stove had all been turned on. If not for the window Sara had cracked open, she might be dead.

He couldn't think about that. Had to focus on the investigation. Why did someone want to kill Sara? Was it the same person who'd injured Regina Sandoval?

Maybe even the same person who had killed Axel Colton?

He knew the threads were starting to come together to form patterns, but a clear pattern wasn't discernable yet. Harry walked into the kitchen. Though the gas smell had dissipated, he scented something else—a faint but discernable strong smell. Like men's cologne. He frowned. Damn if that wasn't the same smell he'd detected in the house where Regina Sandoval had been attacked.

"Detective Cartwright?"

A crime scene tech marched into the hallway, bearing a plate in her gloved hands. "We found this in the kitchen sink…looks like it could be the remains of dessert the victim ate. We found a pie in the refrigerator with a slice cut out."

Harry's stomach tightened as he sniffed the plate. "Apple, maybe. Inform me after you get the forensics on it."

Then he remembered Sara talking about her neighbor who liked to bake pie. An elderly woman…the same one who'd poked her head out into the hallway when he frantically tried to breathe life into Sara?

He marched down the hallway, knocking on doors until a tenant told him in Apartment 302, Emma Pendleton lived alone. Sara had sometimes shopped for the elderly widow.

No answer at Apartment 302. Harry went outside and checked with the patrol officers.

Everyone had returned inside to their apartments. No one recalled seeing an elderly woman from the third floor. "Where's the building superintendent?" he asked.

To his dismay, he discovered there was no building super. The man had been laid off four months ago. Rumor had it the building's owner was in financial straits. Tenants with maintenance issues had been complaining to the attorney who collected the rent, but nothing had been done. Some had withheld rent until the problems were fixed. They were forming a group and had pooled their money to hire a lawyer to fight for them to pressure the landlord into fixing the building's problems.

He called Sean on his cell phone, instructed him to find out who the building owner was. Harry hung up, glanced around at the patrol officers.

"I need to get into Apartment 302. The woman who lives inside may have information connected to this case."

Upstairs, they pounded and pounded on the door. No answer. Harry didn't want to frighten an elderly woman, but his gut warned this wasn't an ordinary tenant. Not with the remains of an apple pie in the sink and Sara found unconscious after eating it.

He looked at the patrol officer pounding on the door.

"Break it."

The officer kicked open the door. Harry entered first, his sidearm drawn. In his experience, innocent-looking civilians could brandish weapons.

The officers checked every room. "All clear," one called out.

Harry replaced his gun and looked around. The apartment seemed innocuous if not poorly furnished. He snapped on a pair of gloves given to him by a crime scene technician.

"Detective!" an officer called out.

He went into the bedroom. The officer pointed to the closet and a battered, scratched chest of drawers.

"Clothing is missing. Looks like someone packed and left in a hurry. Probably when the building was being evacuated. Good time to slip away without being noticed." The officer shook his head.

Returning to the kitchen, Harry opened drawers and cabinets. He didn't have to look far. Mrs. Pendleton had several apples in the refrigerator and containers of nutmeg and cinnamon discarded in the trash. Both containers were full and still had price tags.

In the trash, he found an empty bottle of sleeping tablets and bagged it, telling an officer to give it to the crime scene technicians down the hall. Harry scowled as he snapped off the gloves and issued instructions to a nearby officer.

"Tell the techs to sweep this apartment. I have to go to the hospital. Put a BOLO out for Emma Pendleton. If I'm not mistaken, she's our prime suspect in trying to kill Sara Sandoval."

HER HEAD POUNDED like someone had nailed iron spikes into her skull. Pressure squeezed her right arm and a beeping sounded. Sara winced at the bright lights over her head. She could hear something outside, noise, voices droning. Something was in her nose... Sara moved an arm and felt tubing protruding from her nose. She wanted to close her eyes and go back to sleep, but someone kept urging her to stay awake.

"Sara, how are you feeling?"

That voice…it seemed familiar. She tried to focus, and realized Vita Yates leaned over her.

"My head aches." She put a hand to her throat. "Thirsty."

Vita gave her a cup of water. "The doctor said you can have this. Small sips."

Gratefully she drank it and handed it back. Her thoughts cleared slightly as she realized the tubing in her nose was an oxygen cannula. Her right arm felt pressure from the cuff attached to it, taking her blood pressure automatically every few minutes.

"Where am I? What happened?" Her voice sounded shaky and raspy.

Vita placed the cup on a bedside table. "You're in the hospital. Detective Cartwright found you in your apartment passed out. The gas from the stove was on. If he hadn't found you…"

Vita stopped talking and wiped a tear. "Oh, Sara, why would anyone hurt you?"

Harry saved her. Suddenly more than anything, she needed to see him.

"There's a police officer outside your room. He told me to get him when you're awake." Vita squeezed her hand. "I'll be right back. Don't go to sleep again. They want to question you."

Despite Vita's warning, she couldn't help closing her eyes. And then she heard a deep, gruff voice that instantly made her eyes fly open in abject relief.

"Harry," she whispered, her left hand reaching out for him.

Vita wiped her eyes again. "I think I'll search for a decent cup of coffee, and leave you alone."

Harry sat at her side, took her hand into his as Vita left the room. "Sara."

His voice sounded shaky and it made her wonder exactly how bad she was.

"Am I going to die?" she whispered.

A slight laugh and a head shake. "Not if I have anything to do with it. No, you're going to be fine, but they want to keep you overnight to make sure you're okay."

She fingered the cannula. "This…it feels odd."

"Leave it." A gentle squeeze of her fingers. "Honey, I need to ask you what happened and then you can rest. What do you remember before passing out? What was the dessert you had? Who gave it to you? Mrs. Pendleton?"

Sara tried to gather her scattered thoughts. "Yes…she baked an apple pie for me. I had some salad for dinner and I ate the pie and then started reading a book. I got up…" She frowned, pressing fingers to her temples. "Got dizzy. It was odd, because it felt like I was going to pass out again, like I did when I found out Axel was dead. But this was different. It was…"

"Foggy?" Harry leaned close. "As if you needed to sleep and couldn't stay awake?"

She nodded. "Exactly. I tried to find my phone, but it seemed so far away."

He swore softly. "The doc found sleeping pills in your blood. Lab confirmed the scrapings from the dessert plate contained apple pie with a high amount of sedatives. There's a warrant out now for Emma Pendleton's arrest."

If her head was foggy before, it was clear now. Sara struggled to sit up. Harry helped adjust her.

"Mrs. Pendleton? My nice neighbor lady? Impossible. She wouldn't hurt a fly…"

"No, but she sure as hell planned to hurt you." Harry's jaw clenched and he took a deep breath, his grip on her hand tightening. "She knocked you out with sleeping pills and then turned on the gas in your apartment so you'd suffocate. If you hadn't opened the living room window, you'd be…"

His voice trailed off and looked away. She understood. *You'd be dead.*

Suddenly despite the oxygen pumping into her lungs, the room seemed to compress around her and it was hard to breathe. Her blood chilled. Emma Pendleton tried to kill her.

The nice neighbor who had little money and baked pies. Sara's stomach roiled. The pie, the pie with the funny taste to it…

"It makes no sense," she rasped. "She never had a problem with me. Why?"

"We'll find out why when we get her into custody, and we *will* find her. She fled the scene when the building was evacuated and all the residents were in the streets in case your apartment blew up from the gas being on."

He glanced toward the hallway. "I've asked for an officer to remain outside your room at all times in case she returns. Vita was kind enough to stay with you until I could arrive."

Needing an anchor, Sara gripped his hand. Calm, capable Harry. He'd saved her. Amid the aching pounding in her head flashed a warning hard to comprehend…

Mrs. Pendleton tried to kill me. She hates me that much she wants me dead.

"How long do I have to stay here? When can I go home?" She feared the answer. After knowing she wasn't safe in her own apartment, Sara wasn't certain she wanted to return anytime soon.

Harry ran a finger down her chilled cheek. "They're keeping you overnight as a precaution. I promise, you're safe now. Sara, can you think of any reason why Emma Pendleton would want to hurt you?"

Air seemed to suck out of her lungs. Sara took a deep breath, glad for the fresh oxygen flowing into her body. "No. I mean, we weren't close. I did favors for her because I felt sorry for her. She had little money and offered to bake pies for me when I refused money for buying her groceries. I never took money from her. Maybe she was insulted?"

It was all too bizarre and terrifying to think someone she trusted, and helped, turned out to be that cold and calculating.

His hand felt warm against her face as he cradled her cheek. "Sweetheart, I don't know. What about friends visiting her? Relatives? She has a daughter named Amy DeLucca who lives in South Carolina. Married to a Mario DeLucca, has three children under the age of fifteen. Did Amy or her family ever visit her?"

Police must have already found out about Mrs. Pendleton's relatives and searched her apartment for evidence. Sara tried to focus. "She mentioned her daughter once, and said they were not close. She seemed sad when she talked about Amy, so I never questioned her again. I don't remember any friends visiting her, either, but it wasn't as if I spent much time with her. I bought her groceries when I could. Is this important? I never met any of her friends. Why would she want me dead?"

Sara fell back against the pillows, suddenly exhausted again. Harry cupped her cheek, his blue-green gaze filled with tender concern. "I'll find out. I promise I'll get answers."

Harry's phone dinged a text and he scrolled through

it. Rest seemed impossible, but she felt exhausted. Sara gave a longing glance at his cell phone.

"Can someone go to my apartment and bring my cell phone?" she asked.

He withdrew a phone from his jacket pocket. "Here. The crime scene techs had to go over it, but they cleared it for me to bring to you."

Shuddering, she looked at her phone, realizing her apartment, in fact, her life had become a crime scene. Her mother also lay in a hospital bed, only Regina wasn't conscious. It was too much. She fought the tears welling up.

"I need to check on Mom."

With the edge of his thumb, Harry wiped a stray tear trickling down her cheek. He handed her a box of tissues, silently took her cell phone and dialed. Despite her distress, she felt a surge of wonder. He understood. Harry knew she was too upset to call the Springfield hospital and check for herself.

By the time she restored her composure, he'd hung up. "No real change, but the charge nurse said Regina is showing promising signs of waking up. She's had more bouts of consciousness. That's a good sign, honey."

The distant look came over him again. Sara recognized it. He was deep in thought.

"Sara, you've lived in that apartment most of the year. You're from out of town… How did you find that place? Were you searching for a low-cost rental?"

She nodded, her thoughts muzzy again. Sara pressed her fingers against her pounding temple. "I wasn't sure how long I'd stay in Chicago, so I needed a place with either a month-to-month or a six-month lease term. Maybe even a sublet. Rents are so expensive. I was ready to move further away from the city when Lila told me about the apartment. She knew I was searching."

His gaze sharpened. "Lila used to live here?"

"No, she said she'd heard of this place and they offered month-to-month rentals with a low security deposit. Lowest I found. In fact, the real estate agent I worked with told me the landlord agreed to split the security deposit into five payments I could pay each month with the rent."

"Generous landlord." He frowned. "Maybe too generous."

His phone pinged again. Harry's brow furrowed as he read the text. He stood, kissed her cheek.

"I have to go, Sara. Get some rest. I'll return when I can."

Sara's eyes closed as he left the room. So tired, so very tired. Yet for a few minutes she could not sleep. The image of Emma Pendleton's careworn face kept floating before her.

The woman who wanted her dead had almost succeeded. But why did such a nice elderly neighbor wish to kill her?

SOMEONE TRIED TO kill Sara.

There had to be a nexus between Emma Pendleton and Axel Colton's murder. Regina Sandoval had been assaulted and left for dead and then Sara was targeted. The threads connecting all of these incidents seemed stronger, but he couldn't pinpoint a motive.

At his desk in the police station, Harry sifted through Colton's file. He must have missed something. Regina had not had contact with her ex-lover in years. She hid Sara's existence from him. Had Pendleton known Regina or even Colton? Nothing in Colton's background or in the intel they pulled on Pendleton indicated anything.

Detectives had already been in touch with Amy De-Lucca. The woman insisted she had not heard from her mother in more than a year, not since she and her family had moved from Chicago to South Carolina. They had a fight when Emma refused to enter an assisted-living center close to Amy's home and insisted on staying in Chicago.

Eyes weary from strain, he sat back, drumming his fingers on the desktop. The green banker's lamp on his desk provided a warm glow, but the words in the file provided no answers. Out in the squad room, the major case squad detectives worked overtime, taking leads, trying to track down Emma Pendleton. Pendleton had tried to kill someone close to Harry, and his team didn't take that lightly.

They would work tirelessly until they closed this.

A knock sounded on the open door of his office. Harry glanced up to see Sean, bleary-eyed and wearing rumpled clothing. The guy looked as tired and sleep-deprived as Harry felt. "What are you doing here? You have kids. Go home."

"Not until we find Pendleton." Sean dropped a file on his desk and then plopped into a chair. "The daughter's insisting her mother isn't a killer."

He snorted. "They all insist that, even after the relative confesses."

"It doesn't make sense. Nice old lady tries to kill the woman down the hallway, the one woman who runs errands for her and cares for her." Sean ran a hand over his face and yawned. "Can't make the connection. Even the neighbors were stunned."

"What about the landlord?"

Sean pointed to the file. "It's all there. Not much. Building's owned by a shell company. Ajax Real Estate, LLC. We have a guy researching it now, but there's no clear paper trail. Landlord is listed as an attorney. They're questioning him now, but he just collects the rent and deposits it into the holdings of Ajax Real Estate."

"Did you talk with Lila about why she recommended that apartment to Sara?"

"Briefly. She honestly doesn't remember, just heard it around that they had cheap rents. Maybe one of her clients."

Harry's tired brain pinged a sharp thought. He sat up. "Maybe we're looking in the wrong place. The rents in the building are all inexpensive…building is old, somewhat run-down. I'm going back to the hospital to check on Sara. I want to know how and why she ended up in that place. Check on Emma Pendleton's background. Go back, way back."

"Her marriage record? Already checked. Her husband, Mark, died of a stroke two years ago."

"Before that. I want birth records, school records, medical records. There's a connection here we're missing. If she skinned her knees as a kid, I want to know it. She's our prime suspect right now and until we find and question her, I need to know everything about her. I also want to know if there's a connection between this shell landlord and Pendleton. Tie that damn attorney up until he barks out how much rent Pendleton paid. Or if she was late with the rent."

Sean nodded and left. Harry's phone rang. Sara. He was relieved to hear her voice sounded stronger.

"When can they spring me, Harry? I'm bored and can't rest. They keep checking my pulse to make sure I'm alive."

Harry grinned. "By tomorrow you'll be released."

Someone rapped at his window and he glanced up. "Gotta run. If you're bored, watch the Food Network. Think of some new way I can get indigestion."

A breathy laugh and a whispered "Thank you for saving me."

Too emotional for words, he grunted a response and thumbed off his phone.

His gut kept telling him there was a connection that would tie all the threads neatly together. They just had to find it. In the meantime, Sara remained in danger. But he'd be damned if anyone tried to kill her again.

I'm not losing her, not like I lost Marie and John. Never again. Not on my watch.

Chapter Fifteen

After a restless night, Sara was ready to leave the hospital. The doctor had released her late the next morning, under strict orders not to drive for at least a full day. But instead of Vita arriving to drive her home, Harry showed up in her room.

"My personal escort?" Sara smiled up at him as she sat in the wheelchair the medical aide pulled up to the bedside.

"You're staying with me." Harry picked up the bag with her personal items. "Sorry sweetheart, you are not going back to that place. Not until Emma Pendleton is found. I brought your coat and a hat. It's cold out again. So much for our warm spell."

Her heart fluttered with excitement at the idea, though she dreaded knowing she couldn't go home. It felt horrible to think of what happened in the one place she should feel safe.

"Much as I love the idea of spending time with you, Harry, I need to get to my stuff. All my things are back in my apartment."

"I have everything you need. Toothbrush, you name it. Let's go."

He drove his department-issued sedan, moving carefully through traffic. Sara wanted to throw questions at him, but she was emotionally spent. He glanced at her as he pulled up before his apartment building.

"You okay? You're awfully quiet."

"Tired. Worn-out." She studied her hands. "Did you get any answers yet, Harry?"

"We're working around the clock. Got a lead on Emma Pendleton that Sean's checking out now. Soon as I get you settled upstairs, I have to return to the station."

His apartment was neat and tidy, with modern furnishings, and far larger than hers. The sofa was butter-soft tucked leather, and there was a glass coffee table and a wide-screen television on an entertainment center. He even had a separate dining room with an antique wood table and six chairs. In the corner of the living room, an easel held a half-finished painting of a snow-covered landscape.

"This is quite good," she told him, admiring the painting. "Pretty."

"Look at the left corner."

When she did, she saw a small splotch of red lying on the snowy field. "Is that a body?"

He grinned. "I told you my job interferes with my art. Case I solved not long ago. Good way to get it out of my system."

Harry set down her suitcase in the bedroom. "You can stay in here. Take a nap if you wish to rest." He gazed around. "I changed the sheets and there's fresh towels. If you want to shower, let me know—I don't want you to do it without me."

Images of them naked and wet sucked her breath away. "That sounds amazing. I'd love it. But don't you have to return to work?"

Sara felt her cheeks pink. Then he grinned and touched her face.

"Much as I'd love to shower with you, I meant I need to be here in case you feel dizzy again. Don't want you passing out."

A faint ping of disappointment. "Of course. I could use a hot shower."

He jerked a hand at the bathroom. "Help yourself. I'm going to make us lunch."

After she showered and dressed in the yoga pants and the oversize Chicago PD sweatshirt he'd left for her, Sara joined him in the kitchen. Harry set a plate before her.

"Homemade beef stew. Thought you'd like a hot meal."

She sat at the table, inhaling the scent. "A man who cooks and lets me use all his hot water. What more could I want?"

AFTER LUNCH, HARRY washed up and left for the station. Sara wandered around for a few minutes, but his king-size bed looked too tempting. Sara lay down on the quilt and fell fast asleep.

She woke up to the sound of the front door opening and closing. For a moment she felt disoriented. It was dark outside and she was famished. Then she inhaled and smelled Harry's cologne, distinct and spicy. She was no longer in the hospital, nor at her apartment, but his place.

Harry came into the bedroom, flipped on the light. Sara winced.

"Just woke up, huh? How did you sleep?" he asked.

"It was wonderful." Sara yawned. "Thank you. Just what I needed."

She sat up and hugged her knees. "What's new? Did they find Emma Pendleton? Please tell me they did."

Funny how she never knew she could fear an elderly woman so much. But there was little doubt the woman tried to kill her.

"She's in police custody. They're bringing her in from South Carolina." He tugged off his tie, dropping it on a nearby chair. "You're safe now, Sara."

Sara knew she should feel relieved, but felt only empty. Sad. Her elderly neighbor would spend the rest of her short life behind prison bars. Everything seemed topsy-turvy.

"Hold me," she whispered. "I feel like my world is collapsing."

Immediately she was in his arms, snuggled against him. Here she felt utterly safe. Harry was a rock, her anchor.

For a moment she rested there, and then her stomach gave a loud grumble. Harry laughed and kissed her head. "I think my lady needs food. I'm neglecting my host duties. How about some dinner after I shower and change?"

IN THE KITCHEN, she watched him bustle around in jeans and an old CPD police shirt. The delicious smells of stir-fry made her mouth water.

They ate at his dining room table. She sipped her wine as he told her how he'd found a place to live.

"After Marie and John died, I sold the house and moved here. Buddy of mine gave me a break on the rent. It's not far from the station, and there's a terrific gym for working out and an indoor pool, plus the view can't be beat."

Sara sighed and sipped the excellent vintage he'd poured. "My apartment is a box compared to your palace. But it's cheap. I never planned to live there as long as I have. I needed a place that was closer to work, and wouldn't break my budget."

After dinner, she helped him load the dishwasher. Harry wiped his hands on a towel and grabbed a roll of duct tape from a drawer. "I need to show you something."

She followed him into the bedroom, watching as he

removed a white terry-cloth bathrobe from the closet. "Sit on the bed."

Curious, she did as he requested.

He took the belt of his terry-cloth robe, set it aside. "Hold out your wrists. I'm going to tie you up."

She tilted her head. "Kinky, aren't we?"

Winking at her, he turned serious. "Later, maybe. For now, I want to show you how to get out of restraints if something ever happens to you. You need to know how to protect yourself, Sara. I don't want anything happening to you."

A little worried, she watched him tear off a piece of duct tape from the roll and hold it up.

"Duct tape is usually what many criminals use because it's easy to buy without suspicion. If you're conscious while someone is binding you, lean forward. Make fists with your hands and bring your arms together so you can break the tape easier. It's not impossible to break duct tape."

He instructed her to raise her arms over her head. "Now bring them down and make sure your elbows go all the way down."

She tried. No luck. But on the fourth try, she did it. Sara beamed. Harry gave an approving nod and gently removed the rest of the tape. Then mischief flashed in his blue-green gaze. "Shall we try tying you up with the belt now?"

She licked her lips, a different hunger rising. "I have something better in mind."

When he joined her on the bed, she wrapped her arms around him and kissed him deeply.

Sara opened her mouth beneath his, drawing him deeper into the kiss. When they parted for air, both breathing heavily, she watched his gaze darken.

"You sure about this?"

Sara kissed him again. "As long as you have protection, and I don't mean your gun, Harry, I'm absolutely sure."

It was as if she'd opened floodgates. They shed their clothing, tearing it off each other in their eagerness to get naked. Her breath caught. Harry was rock-hard all over, solid muscle over his flat abdomen, his biceps. Her breath caught again as she spied pockmarks in his shoulder and stomach. They were deeper and more puckered than the recent scar on his arm. Sara touched them.

"Bullet." He shrugged as if it were nothing, as if everyone had bullet scars. "Got careless during a pursuit."

Shivering at the thought of him lying on cold pavement, bleeding, maybe dying, she slid her arms over his chest. "Stop being careless."

Muscles jumped beneath her touch as she touched him, then he shuddered as she kissed his neck, tasting the salt of his skin.

Heat smoldered in his gaze. She wasn't innocent, but Sara knew this was different. Sex was sex. This was far deeper, and lasting. She felt it with her whole heart.

Naked, she shivered as he touched her in turn. Sara arched as Harry thumbed her cresting nipples. When he bent his head and took one into his mouth, she clung to him, everything inside her spinning with sheer desire. He swirled his tongue over the taut peak, then suckled her. She was growing hotter now, a fire stoking inside her as the sweet tension braced her body.

They fell onto the bed, as he kept kissing her breasts. She whimpered, her hips rising and falling, driven by instincts of her own.

Gathering her close, Harry kissed her deeply, his hand drifting over her belly, down farther. She made a startled sound, which he soothed with his kisses, as he slid a finger across her wet cleft.

Sara gripped his wide shoulders as he began playing with her. Slowly he began to pleasure her. It was consuming. Sara strained toward him as he teased and stroked, his hands sure and skillful. The ache between her legs intensified and she pumped her hips upward. Every stroke and whorl sucked air from her lungs until she gasped for breath, ready to burst out of her skin. Tension heightened, spiraling her upward and upward. And then the feeling between her legs exploded. Sara screamed, crying out his name as she dug her nails into his wide shoulders.

Her eyes fluttered as she fell back to the bed, spent and dazed. She watched him open the nightstand drawer, reach for a condom. Spent from orgasm, she saw the puzzled expression on his face.

"Damn. It's been a while. Not sure I remember how to put this on. Help me?"

The teasing look in his eyes made her laugh. Sara helped him roll on the condom, then they kissed once more.

Nudging his hips between her legs, he braced himself on his hands.

"Sara," he murmured, his gaze dark and burning. "You're so damn beautiful. So sexy."

Harry laced his fingers through hers. Slowly he pushed into her. He pulled back, and began to stroke inside her. His muscles contracted as he thrust, powerful shoulders flexing and back arching.

Sara drew him close as they moved together. The delicious friction was wonderful, the closeness of his body to hers, his tangy scent filling her nostrils. She pumped her hips, as he taught her the rhythm, feeling the silky slide of the hair on his legs. He began to move faster, his gaze holding hers.

Emotions crowded her chest as she gripped his hard shoulders. It felt as if he locked her spirit in his.

His thrusts became more urgent. Close, so close...she writhed and reached for it, the tension growing until she felt ready to explode.

Screaming his name, she came again, squeezing him tightly as she arched nearly off the bed. He threw his head back with a hoarse shout. Collapsing atop her, he pillowed his head next to hers.

They fell asleep in each other's arms. Twice more in the night Harry made love to her again. It wasn't sex. Sara knew it with every fiber of her being. It was deeper and richer.

She had never felt anything like this before, and knew no matter what, Harry had nestled deep into her heart and wouldn't leave.

Sara could only hope he felt the same way.

HARRY COULDN'T BELIEVE IT. Felt as if every cell in his body responded when they made love. Sex was sex, but this was something more. Lasting. Even with his wife, much as he loved her, it hadn't been this electrifying.

And that made him feel vulnerable in a way he hadn't since Marie died. Sara wasn't the one-night-stand type. She was the marrying type. But he couldn't think about that. For now, he wanted to hold her close, and watch her as dawn slowly crept over the sky.

Sara roused, her long black hair silky to his touch as he tunneled his fingers through the strands. He loved looking at her like this, languorous and sultry, a small smile playing on her mouth.

His own smile died as he remembered how he could

have lost her. Harry felt all the night's pleasure evaporate at the memory of that visceral pain. Seeing her so pale and still on the floor, his emotions raging with fear and pain…

Like seeing Marie at the medical examiner's office when the doc had lifted the sheet. For the first time, he became one of those grieving people like the ones he'd had to tell many times in his role as a homicide detective… *I'm so sorry for your loss.*

I can't put myself through that again.

Being numb and indifferent to life had pulled him through one day after another. He learned to present a facade to the world that fooled several. But with Sara, it was different. She'd peeled him back like an onion, and got to what he furiously guarded for more than two years.

His heart.

Sara raised herself up on one elbow. Harry watched her, his heart beating fast once more. She looked so sexy with her long hair curtaining her face, her big eyes studying him with such tenderness.

With a jolt he realized she was not basking in the afterglow, but had something on her mind. He steeled himself.

"Harry, there's something I need to say. Something in my heart." She bent her head and plucked at the sheet. "After losing Axel before I had the chance to get to know him, I resolved to never again waste time."

"Go on," he said, knowing what was on her mind.

"I love you, Harry. I know we haven't known each other long, but I'm pretty sure I love you."

Fire died in her eyes as he sighed. She swallowed hard.

"I guess this is a little premature." She laughed a little as if to cover her embarrassment.

He caught her arm. "No, it's not you." He cursed. "That sounds bad."

Harry sat up, took a deep breath. Damn, he hadn't

wanted to hurt her, and here he was, about to do that very thing.

"I can't say it, Sara. I don't even know if I'm capable anymore of saying it, to anyone." He looked directly at her. "I care for you, Sara, and I know you're feeling vulnerable now after what happened, but you deserve the truth."

"Harry, what are you telling me?"

His body tensed as he forced the words out. "All my love died that day with Marie and John."

She put a hand on his arm. "I understand, Harry. I do. But life goes on and there are better days ahead. You have to have hope that you can love again."

"Maybe." He shook his head. "I don't think so. Not now, and maybe not ever. You deserve the truth, Sara. You're a wonderful, caring woman. If you're expecting me to fall in love with you, it's not going to happen."

Sara clutched the sheet to her breasts. Then he watched as the light dimmed in her brilliant green eyes. He knew, and cursed what he'd said.

But she deserved the truth.

Her voice remained steady. "Have they cleared my apartment as a crime scene?"

When he nodded, she inhaled. "Good. I'm going home."

Sara slid out from between the sheets and reached for her clothing. Harry reached for her. "Sara, don't do this."

Dismay filled him when he realized tears shone in her eyes. Tears he had put there. No one else.

"Don't do what, Harry? Don't go home? Don't stop seeing you?" She laughed, but there was no humor in the sound. "It's best we end this now, before it really begins."

He rubbed a hand over his tensed jaw. "Emma Pendleton may not have worked alone. It may not be safe to return to your place."

What a stupid-ass excuse to get her to stay. Sara was smarter than that. He knew it and she knew it.

She shrugged into her shirt and then buttoned it. "You say you're a great cop, Harry. I'm sure you'll find out what you need from Mrs. Pendleton. Goodbye and thank you for everything."

"Sara, please. I don't feel right about you going back there. Wait, let me get dressed at least and I'll take you..."

"Fine."

Sara left the bedroom and went into the living room. Never had he dressed in such a hurry. He was pulling on his jeans when he heard the front door quietly click shut.

Damn it.

By the time he reached the street she was gone. Frantic, he kept calling her phone. No answer.

Half an hour later, his phone pinged with a curt text. I'm home. Safe. Good luck with the case, Harry.

Harry closed his eyes, not sure who he hated most at that moment. The dirtbag who'd wiped away all his hopes and dreams when he'd killed Marie and John.

Or himself, for letting Sara walk away.

Chapter Sixteen

Work became everything for Harry after Sara walked out on him. He focused on the case. Always the job. The job was there for him, would always be there for him as a salve for wounds that never healed.

Emma Pendleton was due to arrive this morning at the station. She had purchased a one-way bus ticket to Myrtle Beach, South Carolina. Police halted the bus before it reached its destination.

He'd wanted everything on Widow Pendleton and finally got it. Two yearbooks, one high school and one from middle school, sat on his desk, along with piles of papers.

Harry began leafing through the middle school book. On impulse, he called Sara. Still not answering his calls. He left a voice mail.

Suddenly his phone dinged, indicating a text. He glanced at it. Harry, I understand. I do. I do care about you, more than I should, so please don't call me anymore because it hurts too much. I'll find out from Sean and January what happened with the case.

He pocketed his phone, ignoring the tightness in his chest.

It was important to be thorough in an investigation. Much as he itched to interrogate Pendleton, Harry knew sometimes suspects wouldn't talk and had to be cracked.

Holding something over them, a piece of evidence that could connect them, helped to make a suspect break down.

When two uniformed officers finally brought Pendleton into an interrogation room, he closed the yearbook. Harry left his office, went to the room and stared at her through the one-way glass.

"Let's do this," he muttered to Sean.

Sean would stay with him, in case Harry lost control. Surely he wanted to throttle the woman for trying to kill Sara.

They sat at the table across from Pendleton. Harry's heart pounded and his rage simmered on low. Sean glanced at him. He nodded.

"What happened, Emma?" Sean's voice was soft and reassuring. "We found traces of sleeping pills in the remnants of the pie you baked for Sara. Why did you do it?"

The woman burst into sobs. Unsympathetic, he watched Sean slide a box of tissues over to Pendleton.

"I didn't want to," she wailed.

"Sara was your friend."

Pendleton nodded and wiped her eyes.

Enough of good cop. Harry leaned forward, locked his gaze to Pendleton's. "You wanted to kill her. Sara, the person who bought you groceries and looked after you. You tried to kill her with the same damn apples she bought you. Admit it."

"No, never, I didn't…"

"You baked the pie. We found a container of sleeping pills in the trash, Emma. Your prints were all over it. The DA is going to send you away for a long time. Forget the assisted-living center in Myrtle Beach. You'll spend the rest of your days in a cold prison cell."

"No, please. I had no choice! She made me do it!"

"Who?" Sean asked. "Who put you up to this?"

The elderly lady shook her head. "She said I didn't have to pay rent if I kept an eye on Sara. I didn't want to do it. But if I didn't, she would kick me out and I'd be on the streets. She even threatened to hurt me at one point."

"Who?" Harry practically shouted the question.

Pendleton shook her head. "She'll kill me if I tell. She has money, the means to do it. I'm just an old, penniless lady."

The rheumy blue eyes darted around the room. "I tried to protect Sara."

"Protect her?" Harry had to fist his hands beneath the table in his rage.

"The plan was for me to mix an entire bottle of sleeping pills into the pie so she could slip into Sara's apartment. I didn't know she would turn on the gas! But she mentioned something about how I should leave right after I gave Sara the pie because something bad might happen in the building. It might blow up. And then she laughed, and it was an awful laugh. Evil."

The woman took a deep breath. "I tried to warn Sara. I told her to open her windows, it was so nice out, maybe take a walk. And then, then I called 9-1-1. I got a taxi to the bus station. I'm sorry! Sara was so good to me! I didn't want to hurt her!"

Harry forced himself to calm down. Yelling would accomplish nothing. "I'm sure you didn't want to harm her. It must have been hard on you, knowing you had to do something you didn't want to do. This person sounds terrible. Was it an acquaintance?"

"We were friends once." Pendleton wrung the used tissue in her hands. "Good friends in high school. Best friends. We did everything together, shopped, dated. She once gave me a pair of her expensive nylons when I had a date and money was tight."

"A good friend who asked for a favor?" Sean asked. "Tell us about this friend."

"I hadn't seen her in a long time, and then she sent a sympathy card after my Mark died. We started exchanging letters and I told her I was down on my luck."

Now they were getting someplace.

"Who is this friend?" Harry demanded.

"I want a lawyer," the woman said in a quavering voice.

Sean exchanged glances with him. Harry rubbed a hand over his face. "All right."

Damn. She had to clam up just as they were getting someplace. Now all they could do was wait.

SARA COULDN'T BELIEVE it when Vita called her with surprising news. Her grandmother Carin wanted to meet with her.

"I hope it's okay that I gave her your number, Sara. She said she knows who you are and wants to get to know you better. She sounded pretty upset, and nice, for a change." Vita sighed. "Maybe losing Axel has made her aware of what's really important."

Telling Vita it was fine, she hung up. Sara couldn't believe it. After all these years, thinking she had no family interested in her, her grandmother had not only acknowledged her existence, but wanted to meet with her.

Carin's voice had sounded quavering with emotion when she called Sara minutes later. "I want to take you to my late son's house, my dear. Your father's house. There are a few things of his you should have."

She'd told her grandmother the doctors prohibited her from driving for another day. Carin told her she would come and drive her to Naperville.

"I want to get to know you better, Sara," Carin had said. Pacing the living room, she kept glancing out the window. A real grandmother at last! Maybe Carin wasn't the warm and fuzzy type, but they surely could find something in common. The fact Carin acknowledged her and wanted to know her better fired her with excitement and anticipation.

Her phone buzzed. Harry.

I can't do this. Not now.

Sighing, she turned down the volume on her phone, and then pocketed it in her trousers. Carin might be old-fashioned and frown upon cell phone interruptions. Sara wanted to make a good impression.

Smoothing down her cranberry sweater, she ran to the door and flung it open.

Carin Pederson was short, elegant and rail-thin, wearing a Chanel coat, leather gloves and a felt hat. She smiled at Sara. "Sara, what a pleasure to meet you."

Resisting the urge to hug her, Sara smiled back. "Welcome, Carin. Please come inside."

Her grandmother entered, but did not remove her coat. She shivered. "May I have a cup of tea. It's rather chilly in here."

"I'm sorry, I forgot my manners. I was so excited to see you. We can go into the kitchen."

Her grandmother frowned. "I'd rather take tea in the living room, thank you."

It must be an etiquette thing.

"Please, sit on the sofa. The tea will be ready soon."

She bustled around the kitchen, heating up the water on the gas stove, and set sugar and milk in a little creamer on the living room table. Not much sugar, but hopefully Carin wouldn't mind.

Sara set the teacups on the living room table. Her nose wrinkled. Her grandmother, like some elderly women, wore too much perfume. It was rich and spicy, almost like men's cologne.

Carin shivered again. "My, it's cold out."

As Sara started to sit, Carin sighed. "I hate to bother you, but could I have some more sugar, dear?"

Sara returned to the kitchen, calling over her shoulder. "You can take off your coat and gloves. I'll turn the heat up."

When she returned with the sugar packets, her grandmother smiled at her. "Thank you, my dear. When you get old, like me, you get easily chilled."

Her grandmother sipped the tea. "Delicious. Please. I hate to drink alone."

Sara took a sip of tea. It did need sugar. She added a teaspoon and sipped again. It still tasted odd…

Suddenly all her instincts surged like a red flare on a dark road. She'd tasted this aftertaste before…the apple pie.

"Excuse me. Need to use the ladies." Sara barely got the words out.

She sped to the bathroom. Inside, she fumbled for her cell phone, dialed 9-1-1. Everything started spinning. Her legs felt like cooked noodles. She slid to the floor by the bathtub.

"Nine-one-one, what's your emergency?" the dispatcher droned.

The bathroom door banged open. Instead of Carin, her uncle Erik stood at the threshold.

"Hurry." The phone tumbled from her fingers to the floor. This couldn't be happening. It was a nightmare and she'd soon wake up.

Erik crossed the room, picked it up. Carin entered, shaking her finger.

"For shame, Sara. Such bad manners, leaving me to

make a phone call." Carin pointed to the phone. "Erik, dispose of that dreadful thing. I hate those phones. So disruptive."

Too weak to fight him off, she watched, her vision growing blurry as Erik took her cell phone and pitched it into the wastebasket.

"Let's go, Mom. I'll take her," he told Carin.

"Please, don't..." Sara struggled to form the words. "Please."

As Carin turned and left the room, Erik fished the phone from the trash. He met her gaze, put a finger to his lips, then slipped the phone into his pocket. Her eyes closed.

She felt him hoist her upward and drag her out of the bathroom.

Hurry, Harry. Please hurry.

BACK IN HIS OFFICE, Harry began searching the ancient high school yearbook a detective found. He flipped through it. Class of 1957. Coiffed hair on the girls, short buzz cuts on the guys... He worked his way backward from the W's and found Emma's photo. Nothing popped out. Nothing familiar...

Then suddenly he spotted a familiar name close to Emma's. His blood froze.

"Son of a..." Harry slammed the book shut and returned to the room, rapping on the glass.

Sean came outside.

"Anything?" he asked.

"Not yet. Old lady still insists on a lawyer. We're finding her a court-appointed attorney now."

They had no choice. Had to wait. Harry put an officer in the room with Pendleton and returned to his office.

Sean followed. Harry pointed to the yearbook and the photo he'd found.

Sean's eyes widened. He swore under his breath.

He called Sara. Still not answering her phone, or not answering his calls.

Sean jerked a thumb at his office door. Harry looked up and studied the thin, young-looking attorney with a briefcase in hand. Kid couldn't have been more than twenty-five. Wet behind the ears.

"I'm Jonathan Casey, Mrs. Pendleton's court-appointed attorney."

Ignoring the outstretched hand, Harry jerked his head toward the hallway. "Let's go."

He gave the kid two minutes to consult with Pendleton and then went into the room. Sean accompanied him. This time, Sean did not smile. Neither of them did.

But they had to find the nexus to weave the final thread from Pendleton to this case.

"I've advised my client not to answer any questions," Casey squeaked.

Harry focused on Pendleton. "We know who your high school friend is. If you confess everything, we can arrange a deal with the district attorney. We'll do everything we can. You may get off with time served."

Harry gave her his most intent stare, ignoring the sputterings of the kid. He watched as Emma Pendleton's shoulders sagged and she stared at the table. He could almost feel sorry for her.

Almost.

"Tell us, Emma," he said in his softest, most persuasive voice. "Tell us about the friend who wanted you to do bad things to Sara."

The woman cracked.

"My daughter wanted to move me into a nursing home!

So she let me move into the apartment building for free. It was a tiny studio on the first floor, but I had to stay in Chicago. I'm too old to start over and my dear Mark is buried here in the city. Then she asked me to switch apartments to one on the third floor down the hall from Sara. She even paid the movers to take my furniture there. It was a one-bedroom, much bigger than the first-floor apartment, with a real kitchen, not a kitchenette. All I had to do was keep an eye on Sara, and report back to her."

"Carin Pederson." Harry sat back, satisfied. "Sara's grandmother. Why? Because she loved her granddaughter? Or wanted to hurt her?"

Pendleton shook her head. "She said something terrible had happened and it was all Sara and Regina's fault."

Harry's heart skipped a beat. "Terrible as in something terrible Carin did?"

The woman began crying again. "Last time I saw her, Carin said it was an accident. She didn't mean it. If Sara had never come to Chicago, it never would have happened."

All the threads suddenly wove together in a neat, organized tapestry showing the real picture. Pendleton's lawyer patted her shoulder.

"I have more questions," he said tightly.

Casey sniffed. "My client refuses to answer any more questions."

Oh yeah. We'll see about that. He went to Pendleton and leaned close. "Carin tried to kill her own granddaughter."

Emma blinked. "I, I don't know!"

"Tell me! Tell me unless you want to spend the rest of your days locked up in a cold jail cell!"

The woman broke down, holding up a hand as her lawyer protested. "She said she had to do it! Sara had to pay with her life. I tried to warn Sara…"

Harry forced his voice to remain level. "If she tried again, same method, where would she do it? You know this woman, Emma. You were friends. You know what kind of stockings she wears, for God's sake. Where? Her house?"

Emma wiped away a tear. "No. She said she wished she could blow up Axel's house. She hates that house in Naperville…where the accident happened. She wished she could destroy all evidence it ever existed."

His blood ran cold. Harry jerked his head at Sean and they left the room. "Ping Sara's cell phone. We have to find her. She's in danger."

He tried Sara's phone again. No answer. Suddenly his phone dinged an incoming text…from Sara. Yet it wasn't Sara texting him.

Carin has Sara. Axel's house.

Cursing a blue streak, he checked his gun, grabbed his Kevlar vest.

When he returned to the squad room, Sean was cradling the phone to his ear. "Sara's phone pinged off a tower in the vicinity of Naperville."

Axel Colton's house.

"Call Naperville, get backup at Axel Colton's house now. Tell them to approach sirens off. This may turn into a hostage situation."

His vehicle fishtailed as he sped out of the parking lot. Harry prayed he wouldn't be too late.

Sara's grandmother had her. Axel Colton's killer, who now wanted to kill her granddaughter as well.

Chapter Seventeen

Her grandmother wanted her dead. Sara blinked as she struggled to wake up. The surface beneath her was hard and cold. She touched it with her fingers. Tile. Her mouth was dry. She licked her lips, tried to fight welling panic.

Slowly her vision cleared. Sara struggled to sit up and realized her hands were tied in front. Something sticky. She tried moving her legs and they were also bound with duct tape.

Fear did little. She had to remain calm if she was going to get out of this.

Remembering what Harry taught her about being tied up, she started to test the tape. Sara tried to focus. Elegant surroundings. Luxurious…a large house. She was in a dining room, could see the kitchen from where she sat.

Smell something foul…gas.

She leaned against the wall as her grandmother entered the room. Carin sat in a chair before her, her careworn face creased into a frown. Sara steeled herself. She had to pit all her wits against this madwoman.

"Carin, why are you doing this? I never hurt you. Whatever it is, we can work it out."

Her grandmother avoided her gaze and stared at the window. "I've always hated this house. So modern, I told

Axel. He never listened to my advice. Did you know he insisted on using natural gas for cooking and heating?"

"Carin, please, you don't want to do this…"

"By the time police arrive, the house will be demolished. I failed the last time. I failed with Jackson's kidnapping. I will not fail again."

Shock filled her. "You helped kidnap Jackson? Your own great-grandson?"

Carin sniffed. "He was never in any real danger. I only wanted the thirty million, but Donald, that stupid man I hired to kidnap Jackson, bungled everything. Fortunately he will never talk. I have connections."

The woman smiled and cold dread filled Sara as she realized Carin killed Donald Palicki, her accomplice in kidnapping Jackson.

"Now you're the last mess to clean up. Did you know if natural gas ignites in an explosion, it can do all kinds of damage? It can shatter windows and blow everything apart so that by the time the fire department arrives, little will be left."

"You're my grandmother," she whispered.

Carin finally met her gaze, her face screwed up in fury. "You were a mistake, Axel's mistake, and because of you and your mother, Axel is dead. He refused to listen to me! I told him to get rid of Regina. But he insisted he had wronged her and wanted to make up for everything he had done. I begged him not to. I told him he and his brother would inherit thirty million dollars, I had arranged it. Then he realized I forged the will. It was a fake. He was going to the police about Dean's will. I grew so angry… I picked up the candlestick with both hands and swung…"

Her voice trailed off. "I didn't mean to kill him."

Sara's heart broke. Carin killed her own son. There

was no reasoning with her. The woman was insane. She had to stall for time.

"The police thought Dennis Angelo killed Axel."

Carin laughed. "Fools. Dennis was perfect. He was eager to plant the candlestick in Nash's trunk to frame Nash for Axel's death. I had to throw the police off the trail and give them a suspect. But it wasn't enough. I really wanted it all on your darling mother, that bitch. Dennis's brother, Eddie, agreed to work for me after I ran Dennis off the road. He wanted more money. Eddie is younger and more gullible. But he got greedy after he nearly broke into your apartment. He broke into another apartment and got caught. I had to get rid of him as well."

Carin smirked. "It is amazing what prisoners are willing to do for a little money, such as shank a man to death."

Her grandmother had tentacles everywhere, like an evil octopus. "You're insane."

Money can't buy you love, Sara thought wildly. Had Carin ever loved anyone? Even the son she had killed? She'd always harbored hope that her paternal grandmother would be sweet and motherly, like Mrs. Pendleton.

Even that illusion had been stripped away. Was there anyone she could trust?

Harry. He didn't love her, but he wanted to keep her safe.

Erik came into the dining room, saw her, stopped short. His nostrils flared. "Mom, what are you doing?"

"Shut up, Erik. Go start the car. I won't be long."

"Mom, you can't do this! You said you only wanted to scare Sara."

"I said go to the car. Now!"

Erik glanced at her, and turned around, heading for the door.

She was on her own. Had to keep her talking. "But

you have money, lots of money. Why couldn't you simply pay him off?"

Carin's face grew red. "Pay him off? I have no money! I needed that inheritance from my sons! Dean owed it to me after all the years I put up with him."

Her grandmother stood, a roll of duct tape in her hand. She thought fast. "Wait! Before you do this, can I at least sit in a chair? This floor is hard and cold."

Carin laughed. "It won't be for long, but I suppose." She yanked Sara up, pushed her into the dining room chair she'd vacated. She tore off a piece of duct tape and slapped it over Sara's mouth. "Enough of this chatter. Accept your fate. You'll die in a blast and this house will be destroyed, as it should be."

Her heart in her throat, Sara watched Carin walk into the adjacent kitchen, twist knobs. Remembering what Harry taught her, Sara stood. Carin went into the basement, perhaps to tinker with the gas heater. Not much time. She raised her hands above her head, brought them down hard.

Nothing, except her arms hurt. She tried again, and again. But she felt too weak from the drugs Carin put into her tea.

The tape wasn't tight around her ankles. Enough room to shuffle slowly into the kitchen. Sara tried once more and succeeded in loosening the tape around her wrists. Not torn.

Frantic, she shuffled to the knives in the stand, and managed to pull one free with her teeth. Sara stuck it between the stove and the granite counter and began sawing at the tape.

Free!

Footsteps sounded on the stairs. The gas smelled terrible, gathering in the air. Sara sawed the tape at her ankles, cutting herself, ignoring the sharp sting. She pulled free.

The element of surprise was with her. Stabbing Carin was too risky. Her gaze wildly whipped around the kitchen. There. Hanging above the island were several pots and pans. Sara grabbed a brass frying pan.

The click clack of heels sounded on the kitchen tile. Close, closer...

Now!

Sara sprang up, screaming and rushing at Carin. Her grandmother made a choking sound, her arms pinwheeling as she tried to balance herself. Carin screeched and swung at Sara.

Sara swung back, the frying pan hitting Carin squarely on the head. Her grandmother moaned and collapsed.

She ran to the stove and began turning off burners when a hand grabbed her ankle. Enraged, she kicked free and then stepped on Carin's wrist. Bones snapped and her grandmother screamed and then moaned, clutching her arm.

The front door burst open and Harry rushed into the kitchen, gun drawn, along with what seemed like dozens of armed police.

"Don't shoot," Sara yelled. "The gas is on and this whole place could explode!"

"We had the gas company shut off the line after receiving a tip." Harry gestured to Carin, who was moaning that her wrist was broken. "Restrain her and take her to the hospital."

Shaking, Sara leaned against the counter, her breath coming in short gasps. All the adrenaline faded, leaving her drained and icy. Harry crossed the room, holstering his handgun.

His eyebrows rose as he picked up her weapon of choice. "You beaned her with a frying pan?"

"She went from the frying pan into the fire," Sara said weakly, her knees suddenly turning to jelly.

He placed it on the island. "Didn't I tell you to try out cast iron for serious cooking?"

Her mouth wobbled as Harry shrugged out of his jacket and placed it gently around her shoulders. "You okay, Sara?"

The nod turned into a head shake. "I'm fine," she managed to say and then burst into tears.

Harry pulled her against him tight. He whispered into her hair, his hands rubbing her back. "Damn, I was so scared we'd be too late. I'm an ass, Sara. I'm so sorry for hurting you. I can't believe I almost lost you."

All she could do was cling to him, feeling relief it was all over.

Chapter Eighteen

Harry took her statement at the emergency room. He insisted on a doctor seeing her, which didn't take long. The cut on her ankle was superficial and she hadn't inhaled enough gas to affect her.

He escorted her to his sedan afterward, and then slid behind the wheel. Harry stared straight ahead.

"What happens to Carin now?" Sara huddled inside his jacket. It smelled like him, spicy and delicious.

"She'll be tried for murder, but the DA will probably work out something to send her to a psychiatric institution after she's released from the hospital. She's totally insane. Killing Axel sent her off the deep end." Harry glanced at her. "Erik helped her, but at the last minute had a bout of conscience. He used your phone to call 9-1-1 and told them about Carin's plan to blow up his brother's house. He's been arrested, but the DA will cut him a deal in return for his testimony against Carin."

Harry shook his head. "We can tie her to Jackson's kidnapping as well. We matched Carin's prints on the tranquilizer dart used to stun Myles Colton when he tried to pay the ransom."

It seemed too unbelievable still. Sara's stomach still roiled from everything.

Harry reached over, stroked her cheek with the back

of his hand. "It's all over now, sweetheart. You're safe. She can't hurt you now."

Numb, she nodded. "So much for having a good relationship with my grandmother."

His intense gaze searched hers. "How about focusing on a relationship already established? Your mother is awake and wants to see you."

Sara's heart beat faster. "She's okay? I need to see her."

"I'm taking you there now. I need to officially interview her, and I thought you would want to come along." Harry flipped on the lights on his sedan and the siren.

Sara blinked. "Is that permitted?"

He winked at her. "Official police business. Buckle up. I'll get us to Springfield as fast as I can."

HARRY WAS GLAD he was sitting and driving. His insides still shook at the idea of how close Sara had come to buying it. It had taken an attempted murder for him to wake the hell up and realize how much he truly cared about her.

How he'd fallen in love with a woman courageous enough to declare her love for him first.

He filled Sara in on the case as he drove to Springfield. Dean Colton had never realized the lives of his two sets of twin sons would end up entangled the way they did. Nor would the patriarch ever imagine his ex-lover, Carin, would forge a fake will to direct thirty million dollars to her illegitimate twin sons, Axel and Erik.

Erik had resented his father's lack of involvement in his life and began asking Dean for favors. Mary Martin had been one of Erik's lovers, so he asked Dean to find her a job in Colton Connections. Instead, Dean had recommended Mary Miller to Alfred's wife, Farrah, after Farrah mentioned she needed a full-time live-in domestic worker.

Seeing he had an inside person at Alfred's house, Erik

asked Mary to steal things from Alfred's house. He and Carin took glee in knowing they duped Alfred, Dean's legitimate son.

"The candlesticks and the silver platter were given to Erik and Axel by Dean, who felt guilty after Carin nagged him about wanting to give her twins personal items to remember their father by. Dean gave them a couple of heirlooms belonging to his side of the family. Erik wanted more. Axel did not. He did agree to store the candlesticks in his house, which unfortunately led to his demise. Axel had changed."

He glanced over, saw Sara stare out the window. "I suppose my uncle Erik had a change of heart when he saw his mother trying to kill me," she said.

"Not as much as Axel's change of heart." He turned on Bluetooth to stream blues music. Sara liked B.B. King. It would help to soothe her when he told her what she needed to hear next.

He made small talk about music for several minutes. When she requested a bathroom break, he pulled off I-55 at a rest stop, standing outside the women's room.

Emerging from the restroom, she frowned upon seeing him. "I don't need a bodyguard, Harry."

Here we go. Bare it all, Harry.

"Sara, you need to know something about me." Harry jammed his hands into his coat pockets. "I can be a callous SOB, even when I care. When I care about someone, I get overprotective. It doesn't mean I don't trust you. It means I don't trust myself. I know things ended badly with me, but I'd like to start over."

Sara smiled and kissed his cheek. "Can I trust you to get me a cup of coffee?"

Soon they were back in the car, but he made no attempt to pull out of the parking space. He turned on the music again.

"Sara, you need to know something and it may upset you."

She took a deep breath. "All right. Tell me."

"Six years ago your father hired a private detective to find Regina. Apparently your brother's death haunted him and he wanted to find her and apologize."

Harry's jaw clenched. "Erik told us his twin confided in him that Axel had gone to the funeral of a friend's little boy and all he could think about was the son he lost. Axel wasn't sure how to make contact with Regina again. When the detective found your mother, Axel discovered he had a daughter as well."

Blood drained from her face. "My father knew I existed?"

He gathered her trembling hands into his. "Knew you existed and not only that, wanted to keep tabs on you and your mother. He hired Dennis Angelo to get a job at Regina's office. When Dennis got fired, Erik suggested sending Eddie to do odd jobs for your mother at home."

She began to cry. "My father, the one man I always wanted to know, was spying on us. Why couldn't he have reached out instead?"

Harry gathered her into his arms and stroked her hair. "I don't know, sweetheart. Sometimes a man does things he regrets and needs time to work up the courage to make amends. Sometimes that never happens."

He handed her the box of tissues he'd brought, knowing this news would upset her. When she'd put herself to rights again, he got back on the interstate.

Sara folded and unfolded her hands. "Tell me about my mother's attacker. Was it Carin?"

"Yes. Using a fake name, Carin had called Regina's office weeks ago, pretending to be interested in insurance. They gave her Regina's cell number and Carin waited until she was alone, tracked her down to the house. Regina obviously didn't recognize her."

"Mom had recently gotten her license to sell insurance. She probably thought Carin was a potential client."

So much betrayal and so much heartache. Harry could only hope that Sara and her mother could start fresh.

And that he could be a part of Sara's life, if she wanted him.

Chapter Nineteen

All she'd wanted was a real family to call her own, relatives to celebrate holidays and birthdays with, and a support system. Instead, she'd gained a grandmother who tried to kill her and a father who knew about her, but never sought her out.

Sara tried to sort through her feelings as they entered the hospital, but all she felt was foolish. She'd easily fallen into the spider's web her grandmother wove. Even her apartment was controlled by Carin. Sara had no idea Carin owned the building. Neither did Lila, who recommended it. Erik had confessed he placed the flyer in the employee break room, advertising the low-cost rental, at his mother's behest.

Harry didn't press her to talk. His big presence was comforting as her heart pounded harder as they came closer to her mother's hospital room.

The door was open. Regina sat in a chair by the window. Joy filled Sara as she ran over to embrace her.

Thoughtful Harry hung back as if he knew they needed time.

"Mom, you're going to be okay." Sara hugged her, her eyes swollen with tears. "I thought I'd lost you."

Regina hugged her back, and then glanced up. Her beautiful face was still covered with ugly bruises, but she seemed stronger. "Detective Cartwright. Thank you for saving Sara."

He glanced at Sara. "Your daughter saved herself, Mrs. Sandoval. She's a pretty smart woman. Smart enough to outfox a coldhearted killer."

Regina sighed. "I can't believe Carin did all this."

Harry pulled up a chair, beckoned for Sara to sit while he perched on the bed's edge and reached for his notebook. "I have a few questions. First, I need to know exactly how and why Carin got into the house to attack you."

It didn't take long. Regina clarified that she'd let Carin into the house to talk to her about Larkspur Insurance. Carin was an elderly lady and Regina thought nothing of letting a stranger inside until Carin mentioned admiring the house and wanted to see the basement. Carin pushed her down the stairs.

"Then Carin stole one of the envelopes you had used in order to mail that letter to you and place suspicion on you, Regina." Harry closed his notebook. "Carin was constantly nagging the police for updates. She wanted to frame the both of you for Axel's murder."

Sara clasped her mother's hand, unsure where to begin. "Mom, Axel knew where you were. He knew about me…" Her voice broke. "Axel was the one who sent Eddie Angelo to work for you when I was in college."

Harry nodded. "Sara, I don't know if he knew you were his daughter at that time, but he wanted to make sure you and your mother lived well."

He softened his tone as he addressed Regina. "Axel regretted Wyatt's death and driving you away, Regina. He may have been an irresponsible person in the past, but he did love you. But you heard that for yourself when you went to see him in Naperville, didn't you?"

Regina wiped her streaming eyes and then dabbed at

them with a tissue Harry thoughtfully held out. "Right before he died, I met Axel at his house. He called me and told me he wanted to meet with me and promised if I didn't feel comfortable, I could cancel. I had canceled a couple of times previously and then realized for your sake, I needed to find out what he wanted. So I drove to his house…and told him all about you. He promised to make up for all the past pain he'd caused. He wanted to do the right thing. No matter what he had to do, he would do right by you to make up for lost time."

Too late. Axel wanted to know her. And he'd finally worked up the courage to meet her when he died.

Harry filled in the rest. Axel had infuriated Carin, especially when Carin discovered Axel was going to hire an attorney to legally dispute the new will Dean had left. He wanted nothing to do with Colton Connections or the thirty million dollars Carin claimed her children were due.

Regina bit her lip and stared out the hospital window. "Axel told me he was meeting with his mother later. He died later that night when Carin hit him over the head with the candlestick after they argued. I don't know how she can live with herself…to kill your own son."

Harry checked his cell phone. "I need to make a few calls. Sara, I'll be outside. Take all the time you need."

She talked with her mother for a while, telling Regina of her plans to remain in Chicago and continue working for Yates' Yards. The job offered challenges she never anticipated. Regina told her the doctor planned to release her in two days.

When she saw her mother getting tired, Sara called for a nurses' aide to help Regina back to bed. She promised to visit the next day and went into the hallway, where Harry waited.

"I want to remain here with Mom." Sara felt a flutter

of hope in her chest. "Maybe you can stay with me and we can spend the night here."

He studied her, his hands warm against her face. "We'll find you a hotel and a rental car, sweetheart. I have to return to Chicago."

Sara felt a stab of disappointment. "Of course. You have to return and wrap all this up."

"Yes, and there's something else I have to do. Something I've needed to do for a long time." He kissed her, his mouth warm and firm against hers. "I'll call you when I'm through."

AT THE POLICE STATION, the mood had shifted to relief and joy that the case had finally wrapped up. Harry was greeted with plenty of congratulations and spent time in the captain's office, going over details. When he emerged into the squad room, Sean had news to share.

He and January wanted to have a quick but large Christmas wedding to make up for their elopement earlier in the year. Harry promised to be there.

He hoped Sara would be his date. But he wouldn't ask her, not until he finally took care of personal business.

The trip to Naperville felt less bittersweet than it had previous times. Harry pulled into the long driveway of the Russo house and parked. He jingled his keys in one gloved hand and blew out a breath.

It was time. Long past time, but he was ready now.

A white-capped domestic worker answered the door when he rang the bell, and ushered him into the formal living room. She told him to have a seat and left.

How many times had he sat here before with Marie, stiff as wood, trying to make pleasantries with her father? Trying to assure him he'd take good care of his little girl.

When the Russos entered the room, Harry did not

stand. Dominic sat on the sofa across from him, glaring, while Arlene sat beside her husband. Arlene, who had lost her only child and only grandson. He focused on her face, the careworn lines carved there by time and grief. Unlike Dominic, Arlene never blamed him for the loss.

It was for Arlene he did this.

"Well, what do you want?" Dominic snapped. "You asked us to be home because you had something to say to my wife and me about Marie and John. Are you ready to admit it was your fault they died?"

Harry looked at both of them. "It was my fault, in a way. If you want to blame someone for their deaths, blame me."

A soft snort of satisfaction from his ex-father-in-law. Harry continued holding their gazes. He had to remain strong, think of how Marie would encourage him. He could almost feel her at his side, whispering it was okay.

"I can't tell you how many times I wish I had died in that car wreck and they were still alive. I didn't, and nothing I can say or do will change the past. I can only change today and hopefully, make a difference in tomorrow. As hard as their deaths were on me personally, I can't imagine losing a daughter and a grandson."

Dominic started to speak, but Arlene put a hand on his arm. "Hush, Dominic. Let Harry talk."

He gathered all his courage. "I want to apologize to both of you for their deaths, if that makes you feel better. And I want you to know, as much as I loved them, still love them, and will always love them, I'm moving ahead with my life. I've met someone special. She'll never take Marie's place, but she's a good woman and I love her."

Dominic said nothing, but tears formed in Arlene's eyes. She wiped them away. "I'm happy for you, Harry. Marie wouldn't want you to pine for the past."

She glanced at her husband. "Nor would she want us to do the same. It's time for forgiveness."

To his surprise, the old man slowly nodded. "If that's what my wife wants, then so be it. I apologize for anything I've said to you, Harry."

A tremendous burden inside him eased at last.

He took the St. Jude medal and folded it into Arlene's trembling hand. "Here. Marie would want you to have this back. It is your family heirloom."

Arlene stared at the medal and nodded. She smiled through her tears. "Thank you, Harry."

"If there's ever anything I can do for you, let me know," he told her.

"Sometime, if you can, if you have time, I'd like to talk with you about Marie and John. The memories." Arlene wiped her eyes. "It helps me."

Harry smiled gently. "I have time now. And in the future. Take all the time you need."

Chapter Twenty

It had been a beautiful Christmas Eve wedding and dozens of Coltons attended. Vita and Rick generously opened their home as January and Sean formally said their vows, the twins peacefully napping through the ceremony.

At the end, there was a brief but poignant candlelit memorial for Alfred and Ernest Colton.

After January asked for her help, Sara planned everything, turning the gardens at the Yateses' into a Christmas dream, with potted poinsettias lining walkways and Christmas trees decorated with twinkling lights. Some guests chose to stroll the walkways, admiring the effect. Rick and Vita decorated the spare greenhouse with lights and garland, setting tables and chairs there for those who wished a quiet place to talk and get away from the crowd.

All the women wore red or green or gold, with the men in black tie. Sara wore a new red Dior dress, thanks to the contractual advance her former company had given her. She'd agreed to consult for them in her spare time after the president of Caymen Reynolds personally assured her he'd fired Ernie for sexual harassment and misuse of company funds after a thorough investigation.

Sara couldn't believe how many Coltons had attended. The buffet reception was a blizzard of names and faces. She met Alfred's widow, Farrah, and many other Coltons.

So many her head spun. Damon Colton, an agent for the Drug Enforcement Agency, brought his girlfriend, Ruby. Heath Colton, president of Colton Connections, quietly thanked Sara for the memorial service honoring his father and uncle. Heath's fiancée, Kylie, admired the gardens and told Sara what a beautiful job she'd done in decorating. Myles and Lila were there as well with their significant others.

Harry had agreed to be her date. He'd given her space and time, which she appreciated, but today, she needed him at her side. He helped her navigate through the various guests, always watchful and charming. After an hour of socializing and then eating the delicious food she'd selected, he pulled her aside to a quiet area in the living room.

"Sara, we need to talk." He drew in a breath. "About us."

In his silk tuxedo, the same one he'd worn at the lounge at the Four Seasons, Harry looked resplendent and intent. She smoothed down an imaginary wrinkle in her Dior dress, her stomach tight. They hadn't discussed their relationship or a future.

"Now? Can't it wait?"

"I don't want to wait." He kissed her hand. "I'd like to start over again with you, if you want. I want to make this work. Maybe we could actually have an actual, formal date?"

Joy filled her, and anticipation. "You're not afraid of starting a relationship with me?"

His mouth quirked. "I'd say we already have a relationship. Not exactly conventional, but I'd like to try. I'm a cop, Sara. I'll always be one. I'm damn good at my job. I can't promise there won't be times when the job comes first, but you'll always come first in my heart."

A shadow crossed his face. "I'm ready to try being in

love again. I love you, Sara. I didn't realize how much until I thought I'd lose you forever to that stone-cold woman."

He glanced away. "I'll always love Marie and John. But I know Marie would want me to move on and learn to love again. If you're willing to try with me."

Emotion filled her. Sara could barely speak. She blinked hard, knowing how difficult it had been for Harry to reach this point. "Yes. I'm more than willing."

His mouth was warm and firm against hers. She kissed him hard, wishing they weren't surrounded by hundreds of people. Someone whistled and yelled, "Get a room, Harry!"

Her eyes flew open as he released her and mock scowled at Damon Colton. "Go get a room yourself, Colton."

Damon grinned and walked away with Ruby. Harry rested his forehead against Sara's. "So, want to go out with me?"

"I'd love it. But I get to pick the restaurant. No hot dogs."

"Deal. As long as we first get you a new place to live. There's an apartment opening close to mine. A little further of a drive for you, but…"

"It sounds wonderful. I can afford it now. Anything is better than staying at that building."

More people drifted into the living room. Vita headed in their direction, greeted them and then her warm smile dropped.

She lowered her voice. "May we go to the greenhouse? It's private there. I need to talk with you, Sara."

Vita glanced at Harry. "You should hear this as well, Detective."

"Please. It's Harry."

In the greenhouse where Sara once danced beneath the snowfall, Vita drew them over to a corner partly hidden by potted trees adorned with lights and a bistro table and two chairs.

"Sara, please sit."

She sat, Harry standing behind her, his presence reassuring. She wondered if after all this, Vita was going to ask her to leave. Silly idea, but perhaps the memories were too much.

Vita's mouth trembled. "I have something for you. I'm sorry I didn't give it to you sooner, but I felt it wasn't the right time. Now that all has been resolved, I realize it is the right time."

She handed her a white envelope with Sara's name on it. The handwriting was bold and masculine. Sara swallowed.

Vita nodded. "It's from Axel. The attorney handling his estate sent it right after Axel died, along with a note addressed to me with instructions to give it to you should something happen to him. I suppose I held off on giving it to you because I was afraid you'd be hurt."

Holding the letter, almost afraid to open it, she took a deep breath. "Wow. This is intense. He must have trusted you."

Vita's smile held both sadness and cynicism. "Axel feared your mother might destroy it. Or his mother would. Carin did not want him to have any kind of relationship with you. He said in his note to me I was the safest person to hang onto it if he died, until I felt the time was right. He knew I could keep a secret and keep it well."

Another revelation. "You knew I was his daughter?"

A gentle hand on her arm. "Not until after he died."

She kissed her cheek. "I'll give you some privacy."

When Vita left, Sara looked at Harry. She took a deep

breath past a throat clogged with emotion. "I can't… I can't read this. Can you read it for me? You should see it, Harry. There may be something in here that is a clue to what happened between Axel and Carin. Not that it matters now."

Concern filled his face. "You can read it, sweetheart. I'm right here."

Pulling the chair close, Harry sat next to her, his hand gripping hers as she began to read aloud.

"My dear daughter,

"I discovered your existence six years ago, but lacked the courage to tell Regina. Knowing how much Regina did not want me in your life, I decided to wait until you were older. Your mother went to extraordinary measures to hide your presence from me, and I felt I must respect her wishes. I asked my brother Erik to check up on you, and send someone to help your mother if she needed it. He sent one of his former employees, Dennis, to work for your mother's office, but Dennis got fired. So I hired Dennis's brother Eddie to try to get a job doing yard work for your mother. I even provided fake references for Eddie. Eddie reported back that Regina was well and from her talking about your college studies, you seemed happy.

"I came to Yates' Yards one morning to pick up Lila for lunch and saw you in the break room. I wanted to speak to you, I truly did, but failed to work up the courage. Perhaps later I will. You were drinking from a mug that read WORLD'S GREATEST DAD and the irony was bitter for me. I took the cup that you held and wished I could live up to that saying.

"The private detective I hired to find your mother said he could run your DNA from the mug and give me proof positive you were my daughter. I tried to work up the courage to pursue this avenue, and ended up writing you this letter instead.

"I wanted to be a good dad for you, Sara. I failed with Myles and Lila and utterly failed with poor Wyatt. How I wish I could have started over again with you when you were young! If you are reading this now it is too late for me. But I wanted to let you know I love you.

"I am proud of you, Sara. I wish nothing but the best for you and your mother.

"Love, your father, Axel Colton."

She smoothed down the paper, her heart filled with grief and yet filled also with a sense of needed closure. So much regret. Regret she'd never worked up the courage to confront Axel before he died. Regret for Axel failing to work up the courage to tell her he knew she was his daughter.

And yet in the letter, she knew what she'd always wondered. He loved her. No matter what, he knew she was his daughter, loved her and wanted to make amends.

A heavy weight lifted from her heart. Sara looked at the letter and wiped away tears.

"Bye, Dad," she whispered. "Be at peace."

Then she turned to Harry and sobbed in his arms, partly for all she had lost, but also for all she knew she had gained.

WHEN THEY RETURNED to the house, Harry knew what Sara needed. Not privacy or isolation, but family.

He fetched her a glass of champagne, told her he'd

be back soon. When he returned, several Coltons were with him.

Sara looked confused and then a smile touched her beautiful face. Harry's heart turned over at her joy as the cousins began chatting with her.

He could live with that radiant look on her expression for the rest of his life. Maybe there would be more than one wedding here at the house.

Carly Colton beamed and hugged him. "I'm so thrilled you and Sara found each other, Harry. You deserve happiness."

He kissed her cheek. "Thanks. I do."

She grinned. "Keep saying that, Harry. I have a feeling you'll be saying it soon at another wedding."

Carly took Sara's hand. "Now, what is this about you decorating and arranging this wedding?"

"There might be more weddings if we can talk Vita and Rick into it." Simone Colton sighed. "This is a beautiful venue."

Sara looked helpless. Harry laughed. "Go on. Go talk weddings and decorating with them. I'll be fine."

Harry watched Sara walk off with her cousins, who looked eager to get to know her better. Once she had no relatives. Now she had dozens, embraced by everyone eager to get to know her. He smiled. Once he never thought he could love again.

Sara Sandoval had changed everything.

Some days life was definitely worth living again. This was one of them.

* * * * *

COMING SOON!

JOIN US ON SOCIAL MEDIA!

Stay up to date with our latest releases, author
news and gossip, special offers and discounts, and
all the behind-the-scenes action
from Mills & Boon...

 millsandboon

 millsandboonuk

 millsandboon

It might just be true love...

MILLS & BOON

MODERN

Power and Passion

Prepare to be swept off your feet by sophisticated, sexy and seductive heroes, in some of the world's most glamourous and romantic locations, where power and passion collide.